The Ghost and Mrs. Miller

by

Sandra Tilley

The Ghost and Mrs. Miller

Cover Art by *Debbie Taylor*

The Wild Rose Press, Inc.
PO Box 708
Adams Basin, NY 14410-0708
Visit us at www.thewildrosepress.com

Publishing History
First Fantasy Rose Edition, 2017
Print ISBN 978-1-5092-1428-0
Digital ISBN 978-1-5092-1429-7

Published in the United States of America

Dedication

To Pat
for giving me the opportunity
to pursue my dream
and to Suzanne and Sheila
for not letting me give up

Jesse tapped my watch.

"What's your rush, Lib? I wanted to talk about Neil's office building. My real estate guy said he's been trying to get you to show him the property."

Neil's diaphanous form grew more solid, and he shook his fist in Jesse's face. "It's not for sale."

"Why are you annoyed?" *Oh, my God. I'd asked Neil a question—out loud.*

Jesse answered. "I'm not annoyed. Now my real estate guy is a little pissed because you won't return his calls."

"He's wasting his time calling. I haven't made a decision on selling Neil's building," I said.

The air crackled and swelled. A cloud of Neil hung heavy over Jesse. "Why's he so interested?"

Eli's plastic cup crunched in his hand. "Not a cool time to talk business."

"Still protecting her." Jesse leaned back and then an ah-ha look sparked a grin. "Wait a minute. Are you two together?"

Before I could answer, Neil jumped in my face. "Well? Are you together?"

"Don't be stupid," I said to Neil.

Eli smashed his coffee cup flat and shot Jesse a deadly look. "You heard the lady."

Chapter 1
Anniversary Armageddon

I'd colored inside the lines my whole life. Like any good Southern girl growing up in the Bible Belt, I knew lines, and I knew rules. And I knew what happened to girls who didn't. So I painted my canvas with broad bands of color, daring a few bold brush strokes close to the edge—close enough to smudge the lines. Close enough to discover that fate's coloring book has no lines.

The night of my nineteenth anniversary, fate sat cozied up in the passenger seat, and I turned at the lighted road marker onto Magnolia Avenue. I scoffed at the speed limit; and when my left hand went for the turn signal, I resisted the urge. I sped through the stop sign, squealing my tires into the turn. Defiance pulsed through my arms and exited the tips of my fingers clamped around the steering wheel.

The street light illuminated Neil's shiny, white BMW, precision-parked with measuring- tape accuracy between two white parallel lines. I had no doubt he'd engaged his blinker at the requisite one hundred feet. I eased my five-year-old SUV close to his back bumper. Too close. Neil would freak if he saw my unwashed family car almost kissing the bumper of his worshiped 725 Series.

I swung open the car door. One hundred percent

humidity washed my face in the sweet scent of magnolia blossoms. I breathed in the familiar smell of home and held it like a good luck charm.

High heels in place of my sensible pumps, I hopscotched around uneven segments of the sidewalk where unruly magnolia roots sprouted through the concrete. Rebelling. Testing boundaries. Breaking rules. I wanted to be a magnolia root.

Three marble steps led to the portico of the elegant nineteenth century home that had been renovated into a stylish office building. Gold letters on beveled glass announced Neil Miller, CPA. Neil's dream. As husband and wife, we'd worked as a team to put those gilded letters on this door—his door. I dreamed of a beach house and sand castles and sunsets.

I grasped the door handle. Cold steel greeted my warm palm. My heart rate ratcheted up a notch. *I could walk away.* So what if Neil had to work tonight. Business always came first. After eighteen other anniversaries, one pretty much blended into the next, and it didn't require a special celebration for him to present his usual gold envelope with a spa gift certificate tucked inside.

I straightened my spine. Plans had been implemented. I'd bribed the kids to stay with friends—even robbed the play money from their Monopoly game. I'd dressed to impress and waited. And waited. Pacing back and forth in my strappy high heels until my feet ached. I considered a glass of pinot grigio, but alcohol makes me sleepy, and I wanted to be wide awake when Neil got home. At nine thirty, I swiped on lip gloss and grabbed my car keys. We'd been idling in neutral far too long. Maybe a jump start was what we needed. *What I needed.*

So here I stood on the threshold of Neil's kingdom—alerts firing like bottle rockets. I flexed my icy fingers and then batted them against my thighs. Why did I feel so...so...exposed? I'd been here a thousand times. And I was fully dressed. A giggle erupted in a hiccup. Not like the time I surprised him at home wearing strands of Mardi Gras beads—just Mardi Gras beads. I was a purple, green, and gold goddess. Souvenirs of our trip to New Orleans. How long ago had that been? Before kids. I thrust the key into the lock and listened to the tumblers tick into place.

The single cylinder clicked and echoed off tall ceilings. The door closed behind me with a whoosh. Vintage wooden bookcases climbed the walls like ladders up to the ceiling where diffused lighting illuminated classic crown molding and cast the room in a mellow, after-hours glow. Something felt off. Instead of the natural scent of old wood and lemony furniture polish, the air smelled greasy, like French fries. I dug my thin heels into the Berber runner in the hallway. The door to Neil's office stood ajar. I stopped. A soft, feminine laugh drifted through the partially opened door.

Blood gushed like sharp blows to my temples. *Please, God, let me be wrong.*

I pushed the door. Sheri saw me first.

Neil had hired her six months ago. Single mom of two, top of her class, on a fast track to getting her CPA certification. Fast track was right. I didn't like her the first time I saw her. This time I felt pure hate.

Sheri parted her Scarlett Johansson lips and puckered. "Libby. We were just talking about you." She pressed close to Neil and smiled, engaging top and bottom teeth.

Neil whipped his head around. Our eyes met. In a nanosecond, his face morphed from surprise into shock and then froze in fear. His head wobbled atop his toothpick neck, and the whites of his eyes flashed like neon. *Oh, shit. Oh, shit. Oh, shit.*

Rage pulsed white-hot, searing the inside of my skull. My faithful partner had betrayed me, and this woman had invaded my territory and had the nerve to taunt me. Instinct screamed *attack*! And as much as I wanted to yank out every shiny auburn strand in her head, I froze.

I said nothing. I revealed nothing. It didn't matter; I'd already lost. So I did what I do best—hold in my hurt and pretend. I shot her my best sticks-and-stones glare, wishing I could materialize boulders big enough to crush her and my weaselly excuse for a husband. I propped one hand on my hip and slid the other into my pocket. "So you two were talking about me?"

Her demure smile puckered tight, like a loaded pistol aimed straight at my heart. Neil's chin drooped to his chest, and a puppy-like whelp leaked through his skinny limp lips. He turned to Sheri and scrambled to untangle himself. She held tight, and he shoved harder. His eyes darted frantically from me to the exit I barred, and his mouth opened and closed like a large-mouth bass. This was the man I'd trusted my whole life? And he'd traded me for her? Did nineteen years of working, raising kids, planning a future count for nothing?

Shock and disbelief battered mortal blows to my façade. How could I be so naïve? So stupid? Tears stung my eyes, and my vision blurred. I pictured myself melting into a puddle at their feet. No. No. No. I blinked until my eyes cleared. *This is not my fault.* I wanted to smash my fist into Neil's gaping mouth. I wanted to smear Sheri's plump lips over her high cheekbones. Dammit, I wanted to feel passionate and bold like the hussy standing before me rubbing her hands all over my cheating husband. I wanted to cry. Instead, I thrust my head back and sneered at them like they were something I'd find on the bottom of one of my students' desks. I pulled my phone from my pocket. "Say cheese," I said. Right before the flash.

I twirled around and sashayed toward the door.

"Libby! Libby! Let me explain." Neil's words bounced off my back.

I raised my middle finger in response and kept walking.

"Libby! Wait! Please! Libby! Libby!" Neil's voice cracked.

"Let her go," Sheri said.

"I can't let her go. She's my wife."

I kicked the door shut and left my footprint.

Once outside his office, my bravado dissolved into goo, and my peanut butter legs threatened to fold. I leaned forward to maintain my momentum. Escape lay at the end of the hallway. Humiliation, hurt, and heartache blocked my path. But Sheri's I-win-smile and blood-red lips swirled like a matador's cape. A wounded bull charged through the door.

I had to get away. I didn't want to share a lungful of their noxious air. I ran, careful to blend with the other night shadows. Wary toes negotiated the broken sidewalk and the renegade roots. I didn't want to be a magnolia root anymore. I wanted to be home. I wanted to be safe. I pressed my car's remote, and the lights flashed twice. I skidded into the driver's seat. Breaths came in gusts—shallow and quick. My heart clanged against my chest walls like an iron clapper. Pounding. Pounding. Pounding. I curled my shaky fingers around the hard plastic steering wheel one at a time, securing myself to a tangible object. My husband had chosen another woman to celebrate our anniversary. Tears dripped down my face, and I wiped at them with the back of my hand. *Why didn't I kick him in the balls or claw her eyes out?* Because I'm a coward.

Round, red taillights of Neil's precious car mocked me. I reached into my purse for a tissue and heard a clank. I pulled out the two miniatures of Crown Royal I'd taken to toast nineteen happy years. I considered chugging both. From the dark depths of my cavernous purse, lay the white envelope containing the anniversary card I'd bought my low-life husband. I ground my teeth and bit the inside of my cheek. *I'm not a coward.* Claw-like hands clenched the plastic package and ripped out tissue after tissue, littering the interior with white fluff. "He'll be sorry. I'll make sure."

Overhead, I switched on the interior light and dumped my purse onto the passenger seat. I swiped my runny nose and dabbed my eyes with bits of tissue. I stacked everything I could use into a pile. Nail file, hand lotion, hand sanitizer. Breath mints, antacids, and aspirin. Definitely the two bottles of booze. I opened the glove box and chucked insurance papers and napkins to the floor and found about ten packets of salt, five or six packets of ketchup, and more hand sanitizer. I scraped pieces of torn tissues into a mound and poked them into the half-full bottle of water from my cup

6

holder and crammed the other items into my pockets. Even his stupid card.

I had no idea how much time had passed—one minute, five minutes—and I didn't know when or if Neil would come running out the door. Blood drummed in my ears. I snuffed out the overhead light and sneaked in the shadows to his fuel tank and popped open the cover. I chunked the fuel cap underhanded at the trees. Using a nail file, I pushed the protective flap of his gas tank out of the way and poured in the water/tissue cocktail, crinkling the flimsy plastic bottle to get every drop. My hands shook, but I managed to empty bottles of hand sanitizer and water and booze into the gateway of the car's circulatory system. I snapped open the breath mints and orange-flavored candies flew in all directions. I squatted on the sidewalk beside the rear tire and held my breath, listening. I groped for loose mints with catchers' mitts for hands. I held the aspirin bottle close to my body and managed to keep its contents intact. Unopened salt packets and ketchup slithered down the chute. I stared at the card in my hand. Crawling on all fours to the rear of Neil's car, I rolled up the card into a cylinder and forced it into the tailpipe. I jumped to my feet and sprinted back to my car.

My hands fumbled the keys. I forced a calming breath down into my lungs and pressed the ignition. Neil's car didn't look so cocky. I gunned the accelerator and recoiled on impact. The metallic crunch tickled my insides. *Overkill? Nope. Just icing.*

Giddiness gurgled up my gullet. I backed away and then stomped the gas pedal. I pulled my phone from my pocket and took my eyes off the road long enough to scroll through my contacts and tap my best friend's number.

****

"You. Did. Not." Bluetooth technology shared Emily's horror through the car's speakers—in stereo.

My vocal chords twisted into a knot. "I took a picture of them with my phone." Sheri's haughty grin flared in my head. "She smiled like she was glad I caught her. I wanted to ram my fist into her mouth and knock out every one of her perfect white teeth. I'll send you the picture."

"What a…a…witch!"

"It's okay to say *bitch,* Em." My phone vibrated. Neil. Again. Every time his name came up on my screen, my blood pressure red-lined. I hit *decline*. Every time. "Can you believe the asshole is calling and texting me? You've got to see this picture." I did the thing I'd lectured my fifteen-year-old never to do—I texted while driving. I tapped the screen of my phone and found my camera roll. The last photo came up. Irony. Neil practically forced me to get this phone and even showed me how to use the speedy camera option. I don't know why I thought to take a picture. Maybe to make sure I really saw what I saw. Or maybe to document the exact second my life collapsed. I touched the arrowed icon and pressed *message*. My tires grated over the grooves beyond the white line on the right shoulder. I looked up and with my free hand jerked the wheel to the left—too hard. The car crossed over the reflectors down the center lane and rumbled.

"Crap. Hold on." I let off the accelerator and veered back to the right. Again the right shoulder warned me I'd gone too far. I got back to the center of

8

my lane and resumed my messaging.

"It's coming," I said. Then flashing blue lights reflected in the rear view mirror. My stomach did a nose dive to my knees. "Oh, shit."

"What's the matter?"

Nausea hit hard and headed uphill. "I'll call you back. The cops are pulling me over."

I eased to the side of the road and killed my engine. Police strobe lights buffeted my car and drowned me in a sea of blue. Ducking beneath the glow, I sent up a small prayer and reached for my purse. The handle snagged on the gear shift, and its contents dumped into the seat and onto the floor. I patted the floor and found my wallet. Using my side mirror, I focused on the man in uniform getting bluer and bluer. I exhaled a jagged breath. *Don't cry.*

The patrolman for the Birmingham Police Department directed the beam from his flashlight around the inside my car and then leaned in close. Close enough for me to see his smooth, fair skin, close enough to see that he probably didn't have to shave every day. "I need your license and registration, ma'am." His southern drawl sounded harmless, but his right hand lay poised over the gun in his holster.

I handed him my license. "I'm so sorry, officer." I reached into the glove box and remembered I'd thrown my registration and insurance cards onto the floor. "I got a little distracted and might have swerved a bit." I scrabbled around the floorboard for my papers. "Was I speeding?"

The officer trained the light on my documents. "No, you weren't speeding, but you were all over the road back there, Ms. Miller." Then he rested his hand on my lowered window and thrust his head inside my car. "Have you been drinking?"

I chewed the inside of my cheek to keep from flinging his condescending tone back into his face. I swept my bangs to the side. "I don't drink and drive." I answered in police-perfect pitch.

He pulled his head back but stayed eye-level. "Why were you weaving from one side of the road to the other?"

My mind raced through my options. I knew he couldn't fine me for catching my cheating husband, but I didn't want a ticket for texting and driving. "Well, uh…"

He straightened up, and shone his light in my face. "I need you to step out of the car, please."

We were on the main road to my community. A community where privacy was a premium. I couldn't let anyone see me stopped by the police. I brought my hand up to shield my eyes. "You said I wasn't speeding. And I told you I haven't been drinking."

He moved the light away from my face and continued. "Ma'am, are you prepared to take a breathalyzer test?"

"A breathalyzer test?" My voice rose an octave. "I haven't had a single drop of alcohol. I don't need any kind of test."

"You can take a breathalyzer test, or I can arrest you." His tone left no room for negotiation.

Ice cold fingers of panic seized my gut. "Arrest me?" My voice reached a high-pitched nasally whine. "Oh, God. Can this night get any worse?" I grabbed my stomach. "Is there a law against swerving on the road?"

"You were driving recklessly."

Reckless driving? A breathalyzer test? "I'm a teacher at Grayson Valley Middle School." *What if a parent drives by and sees me? Rumors about a teacher taking a breathalyzer test would spread faster than Ebola.*

The young policeman put his hand on the button of the radio clipped to his shirt. "Ms. Miller, please don't make me call for backup."

I gripped the window sill and my nails scraped metal. "Wait a minute. Do you know Captain Eli Anderson? He'll vouch for me."

"Of course I know Captain Anderson, but I can't disturb him at this time of night."

I angled my wrist so he could see my watch. "It's just a little after ten." I squeezed my eyes closed and fought the tears leaking out around the edges. "Officer, it's my anniversary and I caught my husband cheating. I've had a night from hell, but I promise I haven't had a single drop of alcohol. But I am guilty of texting." I looked up at him and thrust my phone into his face. "Look, Eli Anderson is first in my contacts. He's been friends with my husband and me since we were in diapers."

The young policeman raked his hand across the back of his neck. "This is highly irregular, Mrs. Miller."

"Eli will be really mad if he finds out you wouldn't let me call."

Air whistled between his lips. "He'll have my ass."

I tapped Eli's number and put my phone to my ear. My throat ached from holding back tears. He answered on the third ring. "Anderson."

When I heard his crisp, one-word answer, I sucked in and choked on my own saliva. I tried to say his name, but one cough after another closed my throat and made it impossible to speak. I shoved my phone at the young officer.

"Captain Anderson, this is Officer Sean Willis. Mrs. Miller passed me her phone."

"Her license says Elizabeth Carlisle Miller. Hold on." Officer Willis turned to me. "Are you Libby Miller?"

I nodded between coughs and tried to listen.

"She insisted on calling you and started coughing real hard and couldn't talk. So she handed it to me, sir. You see, I stopped her out here on Highway 11 because I thought she might be driving under the influence, but she refuses to take a breathalyzer test."

"Yes, sir. She's all right. Just upset." The young officer turned his back for privacy. I clapped both hands over my mouth. "She said you'd be mad if I didn't let her call. I hope I did the right thing. This is my first solo shift.

"She was weaving and crossing into the oncoming lane. She admitted to texting," he said.

"I agree, sir. It explains the erratic driving. And something else, sir. She said she caught her husband cheating. That's why I let her call you. And because she taught my sister in seventh grade."

The officer continued, "No sir, I won't mention my sister. A warning sounds perfect. Yes, sir. I'll be happy to."

The young officer approached my window and handed me the phone.

"Eli, is he taking me to jail?" My shrill words ricocheted off the windshield and slapped me in the face.

"Of course not. Officer Willis is going to follow you home to make sure you get there safe and sound. Is there anything I can do to help?"

"No…no thank you. I just want to get home." I wanted to ask him to tell his deputy not to tell his sister about me but decided to settle on just getting away.

"Lib, if you need me—"

I cut him off. "I'll be fine, Eli."

****

When my front door closed behind me, I leaned against it. Even with all the lights on, the house felt different. In less than two hours, everything had changed. Thank God the kids were away. At least I didn't have to face them tonight. But what about tomorrow?

Heels in hand, I plodded across the cool hardwood of the family room. The phone in my pocket vibrated again. Ignoring Neil's tenth text, I looked at the last photo. Tears fell, scorching my eyelashes and branding my cheeks *betrayed*. I slung the phone onto the sofa and followed a trail of Monopoly money up the stairs. I kicked and scattered the paper bills and watched them flutter to the floor. A trail of money to entice my accountant husband. I thought I was so clever.

A trace of lavender was my second reminder. The suffocating scent reeked from our bedroom where flames had drowned in hot wax. The smoky, flowery scent clung to the comforter and sheets, where more colorful phony money ridiculed me.

Phony. How appropriate.

From the medicine cabinet I removed a bottle of blue-green nighttime cold medicine—my emergency sleep aid. I gulped three deep swigs, crawled onto the bed, and hugged my knees to my chest and waited for oblivion. I'd deal with Neil tomorrow. I'd deal with life tomorrow. But, Scarlet, *what do I tell the kids tomorrow?*

Chapter 2
Day One

Door chimes drifted in and out of my consciousness, but persistent pounding penetrated the fog of my drug-aided sleep. I tossed off the comforter and sat up. I'd left the lights on, and my wrinkled blouse and cockeyed skirt reminded me why I was still dressed. I fell back on the pillow. *My life is forever changed.* The pounding continued and grew louder. Annoyance throbbed in my head, and I rubbed my temples. *How dare the cheater show up here.*

I flounced off the bed and marched down the stairs, gathering steam and ammunition. When I got through with him, he'd need to call 911. I yelled from the foyer. "What do you want? You don't live here anymore."

"Libby, it's Eli. I need you to open up. Please."

The wrong voice came from the other side of the door. A wave of adrenalin sent me from angry to high alert. I wrenched the door open. Eli and the officer who'd stopped me earlier in the evening stood on my front porch. My heart flip-flopped against my rib cage. I hugged my body. "Why are you here? What time is it?"

"It's a little after two." Eli motioned for Officer Willis to stay on the porch. "I need to talk to you. We should go inside."

Hundred watt light bulbs from the fixtures flanking

the double doors emphasized the tight, straight line of Eli's mouth. Fear clawed up my spine. My voice came out in a low-pitched gasp. "My kids?"

Eli bowed his head. "It's Neil. He's gone."

My hands bunched his shirt between my fingers. "What are you talking about? Gone where?" *Did Neil run away with that woman? Wasn't it enough to disgrace me? How could he do this to the kids?*

He lifted his head. The pain in his eyes landed a fist to my chest. I stepped back. "Neil had an accident on his way home. He hit the overpass on I459."

The gas tank! I smoothed my wrinkled blouse and poked in the shirttails. "An accident? But I left him at his office." *With Sheri*, I didn't say. I tried to lick my dry lips, but my mouth was too dry to wet my tongue. "Was there...anyone in the car with him?"

"He was alone."

Alone? Anger stung me like a hornet. Not the last time I saw him. "I guess it's a good thing he dropped off his assistant before his accident. Where is he? He'll be sick that he damaged that precious car of his."

Eli's hands fell to his sides, and his chin hit his chest.

The muscles in my knees went slack. "He's okay. Right? Where is he?"

"The car went over the overpass." Eli shook his head and tears glistened in his eyes. "No, Libby. He's not okay."

The room swirled around me and went black.

****

I opened my eyes. Eli sat on the floor beside me. "Where are Reagan and Trey?" His mouth molded his words slowly and distinctly.

16

The hardwood floor felt cool on my legs. My head rested in the palm of Eli's hand. I struggled up on my elbows. "Did I fall?"

His face moved close. "Not quite."

Why was Eli at my house? And why was he asking about my kids? *Oh, God.* My stomach twisted into itself. "Neil," I whispered.

Eli's rough hand grazed my forehead, and he swept my bangs to the side. "He died instantly."

I watched Eli's mouth move. Five syllables hovered between us. One heartbeat. Two heartbeats. Three. Blood pumped through my veins in short bursts. I sprang upright. "Oh, God. He has to be all right. He has to be all right. Oh, God. Oh, God. The gas tank!" Every heartbeat was a knife through my chest. I covered my mouth to keep from crying out.

"It was an accident not an explosion." Eli gripped my shoulders. "I'm so sorry."

I slapped at his hands. "No! You're wrong. He can't be dead. I saw him and Sheri."

He hauled me close, burying my face into his shoulder. "Libby, Libby, Libby." He gently rocked, murmuring my name like an apology.

I rolled my head side to side. "I'm so confused." I jammed my hands against his chest and pushed. "Why are *you* here? Why are you telling me this?"

"Officer Willis got the call and recognized your name and address. He called me." Neil had been Eli's best friend since before either had lost their first baby tooth. Eli's voice broke. "I identified Neil."

The walls closed in around me, and I fought to get up. "I can't breathe!" On all fours, I crawled into the dining room and cowered in a dark corner. That's when

I saw the glow. Twelve feet straight up Neil balanced on the crystal chandelier, still in his light blue button-down shirt, tucked into creased khakis. He dipped a shoulder and looked down at me.

"Eli!" I pressed my hands over my eyes.

Strong hands grabbed and lifted me up. "What is it? You're white as a sheet."

I pinched my eyes closed and levitated my hand toward the ceiling. "Do you see him?"

Eli looked up. "Is your chandelier rocking? Must be a draft."

I opened one eye and looked up. "Can anyone else see you?" I asked the vision poised above us.

The chandelier hung like a three-tiered wedding cake. Neil sat on the small lights on the top layer and leaned against the wire connecting it to the ceiling. He shrugged.

Eli put his hands on my cheeks and turned my face to meet his. "What do you see up there?"

"It's Neil."

Eli's eyes blasted open and darted behind me toward Officer Willis and at the ceiling and back at me. He lowered his head and brought us eye to eye. His grip tightened, and his voice got low and gruff. "Don't let anyone else hear you say stuff like that." His hold relaxed, and he began kneading my shoulders. "You have to keep it together."

He guided me into the family room, and I collapsed on the sofa. *It's the shock. Neil can't be there. He's dead.*

I leaned forward and crushed my head between my hands.

"Where are the kids?" Eli asked.

The kids. My throat tightened. "Trey's next door, and Reagan's staying at a friend's house."

Eli sat beside me. "I'll go with you to get the kids." Eli ran his hands over his head and propped his elbows on his knees. "If you want me to, I'll help you tell them."

The kids. Those two words, like a one-two punch right to the sternum. I swallowed the bile rising in my throat. *This can't be real. I'll wake up, and Neil will come home. Things will be back to normal.* Except catching him with Sheri. That part was real—I had a photo. W*hy did I have to pick tonight for a showdown?*

For five months, I'd tiptoed around egg shells. Ever since our night in the ER when Neil had experienced chest pains. It didn't matter that the doctor diagnosed acid reflux; Neil said he'd been given a new life. So he spent his free evenings at the gym, and I spent my evenings cooking his fat-free, gluten free, taste-free meals. He'd pulled away, and I'd gotten tired of chasing him. Or maybe I'd just gotten tired.

Eli breathed up my air. I couldn't think. And I needed to figure things out. "You need to go home." *So I can fall apart and check out the chandelier in the dining room.*

Eli stood firm. "I'm not leaving you."

The only way I could get rid of Eli was to convince him I was okay. I did some mental fine-tuning and hit the Libby-who-can-deal-with-anything switch. I had to be calm but sincere. "I know you want to help. But I've got to get my head around what's happened, and I need some space." I touched his hand. "Please."

"Why don't you go upstairs and get some rest, and I'll wake you in a few hours."

I wanted to scream *quit arguing with me and go home*. Instead, I focused on my calm Libby voice. "Please. I need to sort out some things before I tell the kids."

Eli dipped his head. After a few long seconds, he stood. "I don't want to. But I'll leave. Call me later?"

I nodded, but I knew I'd think of an excuse not to call him. I appreciated his wanting to help, but Neil waited in the dining room. Or I'd lost my mind—either way I didn't need any witnesses.

As soon as the door shut behind Eli, I ran into the dining room and looked up. No Neil. "Oh, God. I've lost my mind."

"I'm in here." Neil's quiet voice came from the kitchen.

He sat on the counter and dangled his long legs over the side. When we were kids, my dad called him a long drink of water. He'd filled out some in his thirty-seven years, but being a jogging fanatic kept him long and lean. He braced his elbows on his knees and rested his chin in his hands. I edged toward him. The man I married nineteen years ago. *He's here. There's been a mistake. He can't be dead.*

The cool light from the moon gleamed through the window over the sink. Neil sat like a still life painted in watercolors. The irises of his eyes, once warm and brown, faded to the color of desert sand. Blurred earth tones from the tile pattern on the backsplash behind him softened the angles of his face. The hint of color in his blue, button-down oxford shirt and khaki slacks blended into a wash of pastels.

I reached out my hand. "Can I touch you?"

Neil held out his hands palms up. "You can try."

I touched his hand. Only air. "Did you feel that?"

"No. Nothing."

I leaned against the counter. "Are you a ghost?"

"I don't believe in ghosts."

I pushed my hand all the way through his chest. "How do you explain this?"

"Let's say I'm a spirit."

"So what is your *spirit* doing here?"

"I don't know. The last thing I remember is hitting the overpass."

I rocked my head back and forth. "This can't be happening." I pinched my arm, hard. "Ouch. What's going on? I catch you with Sheri, and the next thing I know the police are banging on the door telling me you're dead."

"Don't act so inconvenienced." Neil squared his shoulders, and his eyes flashed a soft mocha. "Before I'm even cold, good ol' Eli comes running to your rescue."

I stepped into Neil's glow. "What are you saying, Mr. Cheater?"

Neil sat taller and peered down his narrow, transparent nose. "We're going there?"

I poked his chest but my finger stabbed air. "Oh, yes. I caught you with Sheri. And on our anniversary!" My voice reached its alto limit and scaled upward into the soprano range. "And you have the gall to accuse me of something? With Eli? Do you think I'm a complete idiot?" My pitch spiraled into a crescendo.

"That a rhetorical question?" Neil grunted.

He'd engaged his modus operandi: divert and conquer. Instead of taking the bait, I tamped down my anger and banked the fire threatening to explode. "Even dead you're a self-centered asshole."

"Don't act so innocent. Everybody knows he's had a thing for you since fifth grade. Quit complaining. I'm the one who's dead."

A controlled burn parched my throat and singed my vocal chords. I leaned close and whispered, "Then leave."

He slipped off the counter and brought his face to mine. "I don't know how."

"Well, you'd better figure something out. Or I'll tell our kids how you *really* died." Tears burned tracks down my cheeks.

Neil's form rose above my head and flickered, like a light bulb burning out. "Libby. Please…"

I wiped my eyes. "Don't you run away. Neil? Neil? Ignoring the problem won't make it go away. Not this time." I kicked the cabinet and searched the ceiling where waves of energy hovered. "Some things never change."

Chapter 3
Forty-Eight Days

Neil didn't let the fact of being a ghost deter him. Even in absentia, he attempted to rule our family. The good thing was that no one could hear or see him—except me. The bad thing was that no one could hear or see him—except me. He'd get in my face and argue his point, and my arguing back was not a problem when I was alone. But he was everywhere. I tried to play my role of the grieving wife and mother but was so pissed off at the cheating asshole that sometimes my concentration broke, and I'd end up talking to the air or making a response that had no relevance to the conversation. To save face I'd dab my eyes and play the poor-confused-widow.

Being an actress twenty-four/seven wore me down. I became a walking thunderhead. Today was no different. Although I woke up to a beautiful sunshiny day, black clouds hung over my head like conversation balloons in my son's comic books. I stomped across the pavement and stopped at the edge where grass separated my house from my best friend's. I planted my hands on my hips. "Instead of clinging to me, go work on a way to cross over, disappear, whatever."

"Stop bugging me. I'm working on it." Sunshine refracted Neil's aura, and his shimmering edges absorbed the green of the trees. "I'll stay as far away as feasibly possible."

I stood close enough to point my finger through his fluttering veneer. "Just one wavy line, and I promise you—"

Neil held up his hand. "Cut the threats. You've already tried to tell Emily, and that didn't work out so well, did it?"

I should have taken Eli's advice. He warned me not to tell people I saw ghosts. Neil's biting comment was accurate and squelched my comeback. "Don't. Push. Me." I pivoted on one foot in the slippery grass and stalked away from the source of my foul humor.

Knocking on Emily's back door never crossed my mind. I stormed in, flopped down in the nearest chair, and braced my elbows on the antique oak table. I squeezed the sides of my head until the pressure equalized.

Emily stood at the sink drying her hands while a steady stream of water flowed over bunches of broccoli and heads of creamy white cauliflower. She methodically folded her drying towel, laid it aside, and reached across the sink to shut off the faucet. "What's got you so worked up?" She picked up her iced tea and took a sip.

I unclenched my head. "Dog food."

Emily arched an eyebrow. "Dog food?"

"When I fed Sadie this morning, I realized it was her last can." I sagged back in my chair. "Emily, I've lost my mind."

Emily filled a glass with ice and poured tea up to the brim. She set it down in front of me. "Tell me what's upset you today." She turned back to her chore.

I examined the ceiling and looked around Emily's

kitchen for any sign of Neil. No shimmers. "We buy— let me rephrase, we *used* to buy dog food by the case. A Neil thing, you know? We'd go to Costco and buy two cases at a time to save money."

"We do the same thing," Emily finished wiping the counter and propped her back against the sink. "But I'm not getting the connection here."

"The last time I bought dog food was on our anniversary. And today I used the *last* can. That means Neil has been gone for two cases." I rested my head on the table.

Emily waited a few seconds. "You're going to have to help me out here."

I sat up. "Two cases. Forty-eight days. I'm counting my days in cans of dog food." My voice quavered up my throat. "Don't you see? I'm measuring my life in Alpo."

Emily picked up her glass. "You know what I think? I think you need to let the kids feed the dog."

"You know what I think? I think I need a life." I took a big swig, and ice cubes hit me in the nose. Icy tea splashed and dripped down my chin.

Emily snapped off a paper towel and handed it to me. "Neil has been gone less than two months. You have to give it more time."

There it was. The reason I came. Her smile, her soft voice, her even tempo. The yin when I was yanged out.

"I don't want to give it more time. I want to be fine now." I sounded more like a four-year-old than an almost forty-year-old.

Emily picked up the colander. "Way I see it, you've been dealing with a triple whammy. Before you even had the chance to get over catching Neil cheating, you had to bury him. And now, instead of grieving for yourself, you have to help the kids." Emily jostled the colander. Broccoli and cauliflower bounced up and down in a vegetable ballet. "It seems to me the most important thing right now is to reassure the kids. Reagan and Trey lost their dad. And they probably think if it can happen to him, it can happen to you."

"You're right. I want to grieve, but he won't let me!" Didn't matter how many times I vented to Emily, she always listened and talked me down from the ledge.

She set aside her veggie medley and stared out the window. "Explain something. Neil cheated on *you,* so why do *you* feel guilty?"

I walked to the sink and stood shoulder to shoulder with my friend. The forest grew up to her property line and spread out in hundreds of shades of green. But I didn't see the trees. I saw the panic in Neil's eyes when he realized he'd been caught. And I saw her. There was no fear or panic in Sheri's smile. Only triumph. And it spawned an emotion so foreign that it frightened me. I'd wished them both dead. But that wasn't the only thing I couldn't share with my sweet friend.

Emily pressed her shoulder closer and touched her head to mine.

Salty tears rained down my face. First I wiped them with my hands and then my sleeve. "He kept yelling my name, but I wouldn't stop." I heaved out my words with the sobs. "If I hadn't shown up at his office—"

"You might never have found out about Sheri," she said.

"But all those texts and calls." Even if I nailed my

eyes shut and plugged my ears, I could still hear the dings and see my phone screen flashing in the dark. "If I'd responded, he might still be alive." But I'd derived a sick satisfaction ignoring text after text. Hitting *decline* on his calls pumped me with righteous power.

"It's not your fault." Emily always thought the best of people. Even when they didn't deserve it.

It was my fault. I'd tampered with his gas tank. But I couldn't tell her or anyone else. Because if I caused his accident, I killed my children's father. The trees outside the window spun in circles, blurring into whipped green butter, and my knees buckled. I grasped the edge of the sink and slunk down, down, down. My knees hit the tile, and I smeared my wet cheeks down the smooth wooden cabinets.

"Oh, Libby." Small, determined hands tugged. "I won't let you do this. None of this is your fault."

I felt Neil before I heard him. "She's right. Blame me."

I looked into his eyes and wanted to stroke his sad, frail face. "You don't know." Emily helped me stand, and I turned on the faucet and flushed cool water over my eyes and cheeks. "I didn't push his car off the overpass, but I have to live with what I did."

She handed me her dish towel. "What did you do that was so terrible? I wouldn't have answered his texts or calls either."

I scraped my face with the terry cloth, grating off layers of guilty skin cells. "I rammed his car."

"Big deal. You dented his bumper," she said.

I inspected the towel, hoping I'd wiped the guilt from my face. "I hit it really hard. What if I damaged the gas tank?"

"Quit your worrying. If you'd hit his car hard enough to damage his gas tank, you'd have damaged your own car too much to drive away." On my back, Emily rubbed circles of sympathy. "Now tell me, how's counseling going?"

Weariness draped heavily around my shoulders, and I dumped myself into a chair, grateful for something solid under me. "Helping the kids a lot."

"I'm glad. What about you?" Emily hesitated, "Do you still…you know…think you see him?"

I combed the corners of her kitchen for signs of him and fought the urge to confide in my friend—again. "Do you really want to know?" Once before I'd tried to explain Neil's unusual existence to her, and she suggested I get professional help. When I shared my secret with the first counselor, he prescribed mind-numbing medication. I found another counselor who would see me and the kids, and I kept my secret to myself.

I sat down and massaged my temples. "Why can't I get Neil out of my head?"

Emily's melodious voice soothed the rough edges and worked like a magnet to defuse my negativity. "He's been a part of your life since you were kids. And best of all, you had two wonderful children together."

I folded the bright yellow placemat like an accordion. "Yeah. Childhood friends to man and wife." By the standards of an outside observer, we lived a good life. Rewarding jobs, nice home, great kids. But like everybody else, we had our troubles. I had a questionable pap smear once. Turned out to be nothing, but the wait for the biopsy results aged us both. "Things weren't great, but I wasn't prepared for any of this.

Even after Neil's episode."

"What a scare." Emily sighed. "If it had been Reggie, I'd have fallen apart."

"I did fall apart—on the inside. Seeing the kids' faces when I dialed 911 made me keep it together." I flattened out the placemat and snuffled a chuckle. "Remember the spreadsheet?"

Emily's face relaxed and she smiled. "Yep. On the fridge right next to Trey's soccer schedule."

"Always the accountant." I studied the ice in my glass. "Preemptive Strike is how he labeled the spreadsheet. Said it could have been a real heart attack, but he'd been given a second shot." In typical Neil fashion, he created a plan of action and developed a spreadsheet outlining daily exercise routines and a healthy diet. For all four of us.

"And his comments by your name." She put a hand over her mouth and struggled to keep her sniggles from sneaking out.

"He called me a slacker and wouldn't let me count wine as a fruit. It's made from grapes. Grapes are fruit."

"Uncooperative. Inflexible." Emily's shoulders started shaking. "Why didn't he use real words like pig-headed and stubborn?" Emily snorted.

She was one of those who couldn't laugh out loud without snorting. And every time she snorted, it made me laugh. So she snorted, and I laughed. We both needed the release.

I dabbed my eyes. "He thought posting the darn thing on the refrigerator would shame me into joining his fitness program."

She patted her chest and took a deep breath. "I didn't mean to make fun of the dead. I guess he wanted to share what he was doing."

"But not what he was thinking." His steady, cool façade comforted the children and helped neutralize their fear of losing him. But he kept his thoughts to himself. And I didn't try to pry anything loose.

Emily gave me a somber look. "I don't think many men share what they're thinking."

"Well, they should."

Neil's faux heart attack caused a tiny rip in the curtain of our life. A brief glimpse of our mortality had more effect than I wanted to admit. Our lives had been tangled together for so long, neither of us knew how *not* to be a pair. But things changed.

Chapter 4
Can't Sweep Away My Troubles

When life is in a complete state of flux, do something routine.

I walloped my broom against the stone patio with more force than necessary to sweep away the smattering of leaves and dirt. It had been sixty days since my *Anniversary Armageddon*—as I'd come to think of it. Admittedly most of the days had passed in a blur, with family and friends rallying around us. And then there was Neil. Still here. Still a mystery. He may have been trapped, but so was I. We both dangled in limbo. It would have been easy to succumb to a drug-induced haze, but I had to stay strong so my kids would feel safe enough to grieve.

Even our golden retriever perceived the bizarre tilt in the Miller family's universe. Sadie made an arcing circle to avoid my angry broom and then dropped all sixty-five pounds onto our welcome mat. She tucked her back legs under her haunches and stretched out her long front legs, daintily crossing one over the other. She planted her head on her paws, and her sad brown eyes followed my movements as if waiting for an explanation.

I leaned against the broom. "It's not my fault." I reached for a bright yellow tennis ball under a chair by the gas grill and pitched it out of the way. I swept under the chair, but Sadie hadn't chased the ball as I'd hoped.

"Don't look at me that way. Bad things happen." I made a quick pass with the broom and stopped. Her big droopy eyes looked up at me, and I sat down beside her. "I don't know what happened, girl. Things were going great." I stroked Sadie's head. Silver strands mixed with the honey blonde of her coat reminded me that neither one of us was getting any younger. As if on cue, we both sighed. "Okay, maybe not *great*. But no worse than most couples I know." In one long stroke, I ran my hand down her back. Sadie got up and ambled away. Even the dog knew nonsense when she heard it. "You're right. It wasn't normal." I stood and attacked the grass clippings and leaves with short, powerful strokes.

"Who are you talking to?" All six feet of long, lanky Neil stretched along the handrail from the back porch steps leading down to the stone patio. He put his hands behind his head and lay back. Empty air filled the space between him and the wood surface. He closed his eyes, and rotated his tranquil face toward the sun.

How could he lounge around like nothing happened while my nerves smarted like I'd fallen into a beehive? "I'm talking to Sadie."

I stopped sweeping and studied his ethereal form reclining only a few feet away. His serene pose piqued my wrath always lingering close to the surface. I'd caught his scrawny ass cuddling his newest office acquisition, and I wanted him apoplectic with remorse and shame. He should be on his knees begging my forgiveness, not lolling around like he belonged here. Not anymore. "We need to talk."

He closed his eyes and strung out his words slowly

and deliberately. "And what do we need to discuss this time?"

I almost gagged on his condescension. "Are you kidding me?" My voice scrambled up the scales.

Neil sat up and swung his legs over the handrail and blasted me his patent pending patronizing smile. "What now?"

I stopped mid-broom stroke and secured the broom handle in front of me. I curled my lips into a syrupy smile and let my sarcasm flow. "Hmm. Let me think. What would a faithful, loving wife want to discuss with her cheating, no good, and in your case, dead husband?"

Neil's form jerked, and he stood up ram-rod straight. Waves of alarm crossed his translucent face.

I aimed my worst teacher-look at his airy form. Fury spewed from my lips. "I want to know how long you'd been screwing her."

"Not this again?" Neil looked down at his hands. "I made a mistake."

"Made a mistake!" My voice echoed off the water lapping at the dock. I pointed the broom handle like an extension of my accusatory finger. "You didn't forget my birthday. That would be a mistake. You cheated on me!" Indignation made me ruthless. "And you cheated on your kids." I gripped the broom handle in both hands and hurled it end over end across the patio and into the weeping mulberry bush.

Neil's aura wavered and his eyes grew dark. Shades of blue and khaki strengthened and then weakened. "What do you want me to say? I'm sorry? I *am* sorry. How many times can I apologize?"

The timbre of my voice moderated slightly below

manic. "Answer my question. How long had you been screwing her?"

He fixed his eyes on the ground, his voice barely audible. "The time you caught us. First and only time."

"I don't believe you." I spit gritty words at him.

"Once. I promise." He looked up at me. "Why would I lie?"

"Why would you cheat?" I threw back at him.

"Libby, I—" Neil faded.

"What about all those nights you told me you were working?"

"We were working." He flickered. "I'm not saying we didn't…engage in a…little flirtation."

I grabbed handfuls of my hair and pulled. "What is a little flirtation? Is it like a little chicken pox? A little snake bite?" An avalanche of anger tumbled and banged into my hollow gut. I clutched my stomach. "Your little flirtation destroyed my life. Everything we worked for. Nineteen years. Wasted."

A look of disbelief lit up his milky face. "I gave you a good life."

Scalding heat flashed from my stomach to my tongue. I moved in close enough to bump into his nothingness and craned my neck to get my best angle. "You *gave* me?" I clenched my hands and pushed my knuckles into my stomach to keep from punching his stale air face. "I'm on to you. Your self-serving blame-someone-else tactics don't work anymore. I spent my best years building and struggling—every bit as hard as you did. And what'd I get? *Your* name in gold letters on beveled glass."

"Those gold letters you disdain gave you all this." He stretched his arms wide. "What more could you have wanted?"

My throat ached, and I fought back tears. "How about honesty and loyalty?" I stalked to the end of the patio and snatched the broom out of the shrubs. "Something you wouldn't know anything about." I swung around to face him. "My life could have been so different."

He flipped his hand, discarding my feelings into a wisp of air. "Like you had so many other choices."

Rage pommeled my chest like fists. Breathing ceased. I clasped the broom to my breast. "I had choices you knew nothing about." I wrung out the words with the last of my air.

He hovered in a sitting pose on the deck railing.

I massaged my chest, coaxing air into my lungs. "I could have been an accountant like Sheri. I could have been a child psychologist like I'd planned. I could have been a freaking astronaut!" Air burst into my lungs. "I could have been happy!"

His pompous glow dimmed. "Maybe you weren't the only one unhappy."

I sank into a deck chair and dropped the broom. "But I didn't cheat." I scuffed my feet over the uneven stones. Neil and I had hauled each rock from the lake and pieced our patio together like a jigsaw puzzle. We'd cemented the patio, and it would remain intact forever. But no amount of mortar could make us whole. "When did you stop loving me?"

He opened his mouth to speak and then shut it tight. He looked right and left, like he was looking to escape. Then he shifted back into Neil-mode. "Perhaps you should ask yourself that question."

I huffed out a weary breath. "What are you talking

35

about?"

"I was your high school sweetheart and husband for nineteen years. I've only been dead for two months. Why aren't you despondent with grief? Or at least sad?"

The weight of his words pressed down, pinning my eyes to the ground. I felt his eyes digging into my skull, but I couldn't lift my head to meet his accusation. I removed a flip-flop and swatted at a line of ants traveling inside the groove of grout between the stones. "The therapist says we handle grief in our own way." I turned my head to the side. "How can I be sad if you're still here?"

"I'm working on it," Neil said.

"Yet here you are." I couldn't grieve because I was so angry. And I was so angry because I couldn't grieve. I reached for the broom and stood. "You know what? Let me help. I'll Google how to get rid of unwanted cheating dead husbands."

Neil pressed his hands to his forehead. "Yes. I cheated. And for the millionth time, I'm sorry."

I wrangled the rubber thong of my flip-flop between my toes. "You're sorry you got caught."

Neil cocked his head and sniffed. "Maybe if you'd spent as much time on me as you did your precious Foundation."

I drew back the broom and considered swatting him.

Neil held out his hands and then let them fall like free weights. "That was completely uncalled for. And I apologize. I was lashing out. I'm sorry. I'm proud of the work you do to help abused kids."

"Don't use the Foundation as an excuse to cheat on

me. Or to stop loving me."

His shoulders folded, and his head dipped like a turtle retreating into its shell. "You're right. I cheated." He sighed and raised his head. Sorrow swam in his eyes. "But I never stopped loving you."

"Well, it doesn't matter anymore, does it?" I brushed by him and jogged up the steps to the back door. He followed me into the kitchen. "I don't care how you do it. Just disappear."

Trey and Marcus walked into the kitchen. "What'd you say, Mom?"

Oh, crap. I had to watch myself. Trey and Emily's son Marcus were like Siamese twins—where you found one, you found the other. I'd forgotten they'd been downstairs playing video games. I put on my game face and switched to my mom voice. "I was asking where you and Marcus go when I can't find you. It's like you disappear."

"We only got five more weeks of summer," Marcus said.

Trey grabbed two sodas from the refrigerator and opened them. "We gotta enjoy our freedom much as we can before we go back to jail."

The boys laughed all the way out the door. *Oh, to be twelve.*

Neil watched from across the room where the sun shone through the window over the kitchen sink. Traces of him glowed through the light. "Trey's more like his old self."

Neil's comment tweaked a raw nerve. He didn't belong here, butting into my domain. I hated Neil, but I loved my kids. No amount of anger could change that. So I bit my tender tongue, already scarred from earlier injuries.

Neil examined the blades of the ceiling fan and tried to move one. "Reagan's never home. You think that's wise?"

My tongue let loose. "She's fifteen. She's a cheerleader. She's a freshman in high school. Even before the accident, twenty-four hours were not enough for all her activities. So now that you're dead you've acquired some sort of fatherly insight?"

Neil drifted from the bright light of the sun to the shadows. "Did you tell the counselor? Maybe she stays busy to avoid coming home and facing things."

"You don't know what you're talking about." I blew out a loud breath. "I told you the counselor said we handle grief in our own way."

"How about you?" he asked.

I stopped and scrunched my eyes. "Where did this sudden concern for me come from?"

"What's that supposed to mean?" Neil propped his hands on his nonexistent hips.

"Just what I said. Why do you care?" I walked into the family room and fluffed the pillows on the sofa and gathered gum wrappers off the coffee table.

Neil slunk close behind me. "Where's Reagan now?"

"The cheerleaders are selling coupon books at the mall." I added a smirk. "To defray part of the expense of cheerleader camp. So butt out, Neil. I don't need your help."

Neil's profile wavered.

I picked up the throw pillow Trey had left on the floor. "Where do you go when you're not *here?*"

The lines of Neil's face came into focus. "I don't

go anywhere. I just *am*."

"'I just am.' From the man who said everything had a balance sheet, and the debits had to equal the credits? You're sounding kind of Nietzsche." I refolded a lap blanket and laid it over the arm of the recliner.

"I've had more time to reflect."

"Reflect? Pfft." I walked back into the kitchen and picked up the two twist tops Trey left on the counter and flipped them into the garbage. "Reflect on about how to leave."

His outline grayed into the stainless refrigerator. "That's all I think about."

I glared at him. "Well?"

"I'm trying."

"Have you considered the problem's this house? You grew up here. And then we moved here." Fifteen years ago when Neil's parents decided to downsize, we'd bought the house from them. We'd done major renovations, but it was still his childhood home. "Maybe you're somehow tied to this house. Why don't you Google it?"

"I've considered the house theory. Without help from Google, thank you." Neil's silvery form fluttered, and I couldn't make out his facial expression. "I did think of something and might need your help."

I wrenched the plastic garbage bag from the bin. "Believe me. I'll do whatever it takes to help you go."

Neil glided closer, and I could barely make out his presence against the beige wall. "Maybe you have to forgive me before I can leave."

I wanted to forgive him, but I had so much raw anger churning inside me. "I'll give it a shot." I mashed down the garbage and tied the red drawstrings.

"Okay. Here goes. I'm sorry, Libby. Forgive me?" He didn't sound sincere.

I wondered if I could lie. That way I'd never have to see his cheating face again and could get on with my life. "Yes. Absolutely. I forgive you." I looked him in the eye and waited a few seconds. *Big surprise.*

Chapter 5
Old Friends

Two months. Two whole months since Earth altered its axis. My axis. Obviously Neil didn't feel the world tilt because his hazy figure still hung around like a resident voyeur. Which interrupted my prospects of any kind of future until he left, so I put my weeping and wailing on hold.

School started in a week, meaning summer was over. Thank goodness. Summer had always been our favorite time. Until this one. I'd dealt with an interloper questioning my coping and parenting skills while the kids had spent their lost summer in counseling, asking questions that have no answers.

Seven days to finish my pre-school to-do list, and I'd saved the most unpleasant errands for last. Which included parking in downtown Birmingham. Parking meters lined both sides of the street like tin soldiers. The ones on my side were blockaded with orange cones—the universal symbol for aggravation.

"Why don't you park behind my office?" Neil's voice added to my frustration. Road construction and a backseat driver. Yippee.

"Don't tell me what to do." I saw Neil's shiny form from the corner of my eye. "It's too darn hot. For a quarter, I can park between your office and the Board of Education building and get both errands done." I made an illegal U-turn and pulled straight into an empty parking spot.

Neil's pallid hands gripped the dash. "Dear God!"

I pointed my finger at his face and dared him to say another word. I leapt from the car and swung the door closed. A blast of August heat smacked me in the face. I rummaged through my purse, hoping to find a stray quarter at the bottom. My hair, once styled and fluffy, fell flat against my head; and sweat rolled in a straight line down my back.

I snapped my purse shut. "Darn."

Neil's shimmering fingers made a zipping motion across his lips.

I gave him the eye. "Wise move." I dug out my keys, pressed the button, and unlocked my car. I jerked the passenger side door open and hunted through the ash tray full of coins. Pennies. Pennies. And more pennies. Balancing one foot on the pavement and my knee on the passenger seat, I wedged my head under the seat and reached back as far as my arm would stretch.

"If Granny Carlisle were alive and saw this, she'd have a stroke."

A Southern drawl in a deep, smooth baritone. A voice I knew as well as my own. My head bumped the dash as I unfolded my body. I turned and met his sparkling hazel eyes. "Hello, Eli."

He grabbed me in a bear hug. "You look great."

Neil fluttered over. "He means your derriere. Delicacy and discretion were never Eli's forte."

When my feet touched down, I rearranged my clothing and tucked my shirt back into my shorts. "What're you doing here?"

"I need to see my new accountant about some stock

stuff." A shadow crossed over his eyes and stole their sparkle. I didn't have to be a mind reader to know Eli was thinking about Neil—his former accountant. "Lost my ass on a sure thing." He took my hands and held me out at arm's length. "How've you been? I got tired of leaving messages."

His gaze cut deep, and I bled guilt. "Sorry." I'd intentionally ignored his calls. "We've had a lot going on." I played the guilt card right back at him.

Eli's shoulders drooped, and a wave of conscience swamped me. He'd been nothing but supportive, and I was being petty. But I didn't want to talk about that night. Not about what happened before and not about what happened after I'd caught Neil with Sheri. "So, if you're here, who's protecting us from crime in the streets?"

A mountain of mischief crossed his Popeye-arms and cocked his hip. "Even cops have days off."

Elias Anderson. Growing up, I expected him to be on the *other* side of the law. But here he stood, Captain Elias Anderson of the Birmingham Police Department. I think his dad gave Eli a Biblical name, hoping for a little help from above. But everybody knows what they say about preachers' kids. And Eli was the poster child.

"You headed to Neil's office?" Eli's words floated down.

"Ask Eli to go with you." Neil spoke into my ear.

I jerked toward the sound of Neil's voice. "Why?"

Eli looked at me. "Why what?"

Inwardly, I hit the re-start button. Outwardly, I fluffed my hair and covertly searched for Neil. "Since I had to come downtown anyway, I thought I'd go by Neil's office. I want to get the deed to the building and some other documents. Why...don't you come with me?"

Eli cleared his throat. "You selling the building?"

The sun blinded me. I cupped my hands over my eyes to answer him. "I haven't decided. We had life insurance on the mortgage, so it's mine, free and clear."

Towering a foot over me, I shifted so that Eli's broad shoulders blocked the sun's rays and moved right into Neil's line of sight. I looked past Eli and spoke to Neil. "I'm still considering my options. I know how much you loved that building."

Eli looked down on me from his six feet and four inches.

Neil smiled. "Yeah. My statement to the world. We'd made it."

He sounded like the old Neil. The Neil I married—not the business snob who'd obsessed over getting his name on the door of a fancy office building. His comment sent an unexpected warmth to my chest. For months I'd vacillated between betrayal and loss with no middle ground. I stretched out a long breath and stemmed the tidal wave of emotion threatening to drench me.

Eli looked confused. "I guess...I...loved it."

I couldn't let Neil distract me again. I adjusted my purse on my shoulder. "What's not to love about it?"

Eli shifted his weight. "Like they say. Location. Location. Location. Neil was a visionary."

I retrieved a large manila envelope from my bag. "I don't have to make a decision now. But I had to drop off some teacher stuff at the Board of Education, and Neil's office is on the same street. Thought I'd kill two birds—so to speak."

"That looks official." Eli craned his neck at the envelope I held.

I cleared my throat and assumed an imperial pose. "Take a good look at Jefferson County's Teacher of the Year." I patted the envelope. "This is my entry for the state competition."

"In my book, your work on the Home Safe Foundation makes you Teacher of the Universe."

"I never thought a simple in-service presentation training teachers to identify child abuse would grow into a city-wide program."

He tugged his collar away from his neck. "Okay, I can't lie. I knew you'd been nominated for Teacher of the Year. I saw you on TV."

"That makes four. I forced Reagan and Trey to watch with me when it aired."

Neil poked his head up and rested it on Eli's shoulder. "I'm insulted. I was part of the viewing audience too."

Two heads on Eli's body. A laugh tickled my throat, and I coughed into my hand.

"You can add my department. Came on at shift change, so I got to tell double the folks that I knew a celebrity," Eli said.

Neil shifted his head to Eli's other shoulder. I laughed too hard to cover it with a cough.

"Laugh all you want. You're a celebrity, and as your most loyal fan, I think you need to let me buy you a drink to celebrate." The crinkles around Eli's eyes showed how easily and often laughs played around the edges.

I glanced at my watch. "Too early for beer."

"Coffee Cup is close." He led with his head and his

body followed.

I scrambled to his side. "Do you have a quarter to put in the meter?"

Eli closed his eyes and jangled the coins in his pocket like he was drawing for the lottery. He withdrew his fist and offered an open palm containing enough change to buy the meter. "Help yourself."

I took two quarters.

Eli wiggled his fingers. "Aw, take a couple more." He flashed me a lop-sided grin. "I'm optimistic."

I picked up two more quarters. "You get the parking, and I'll get the coffees. You okay with an iced latte?"

With our iced lattes in one hand and bottled waters in the other, we zigzagged through a fog of fresh brewed aromas until we found a table near the window. Eli placed his drinks beside mine, and we sat side by side. "I know the Home Safe Foundation is important to you, but the guys on the force and I get to see the direct result of your hard work. You make a difference."

I twisted off the cap on my water and took a sip. "It all began with Tommy Thornton. Now the only bruises he and his mom carry are on the inside. But it doesn't help that it's been two years, and Mr. Thornton still hasn't gone to trial."

Eli leaned back in his chair. "Tell me about it. We arrest the scumbags, and then we have to keep seeing their rotten faces."

"How could any judge let that man roam the streets after he nearly killed his child and his wife?" My throat tightened, and I tried to swallow. I still saw Tommy Thornton's face. He was the smallest kid in my seventh grade English class and sat in the last seat of the last row. As far from me as he could get. He'd take his seat and fold his shoulders into himself, until he disappeared. I thought he tried to act invisible to avoid being picked on. It was when I moved him closer to the front that I saw the bruises. "If I'd called you sooner, the torment would have ended sooner."

"You did all you could do. Never doubt that. Because of you, they have a future." Eli nudged me with his shoulder. "I've been worried about you."

I looked at my bottle of water, wishing I could slip inside and avoid his eyes. "I should have called."

"You've been dealing with your own demons." Eli laid his hand over mine. "How are you?"

My eyes stung. *It's been bad. But I'm handling it.* "The kids are doing better. Of course they have their moments. Sometimes at dinner I see them look at the clock. Like they expect him to be coming home from work."

Moisture welled in his eyes. "It just doesn't seem possible." His burly hands pulled me in tight. "God, I miss him."

Neil had been quiet. Too quiet. Maybe Eli's serious demeanor had stunned Neil into silence. The old Eli viewed nothing sacred or out of bounds for a laugh. Prankster should have been tattooed across his butt. I liked this softer side.

I sniffed. "No crying today." I took a sip and set my bottle on the table. "Tell me what's going on in the world *out there*."

His cleared his throat and sat up. "I talked to your buddy Allison last week." He took a swig of his chilled coffee and screwed his face up like a prune. He twisted off the top of his water and chugged. "I can't believe I let you talk me into this stuff. I'm a cop. I drink coffee—not this milky crap." Then as if sharing a secret, he leaned in. "You didn't hear this from me, but Allison's going to call you about planning another reunion. She wants a *yearly* reunion."

"Leave it to Allison." We'd been friends since she transferred to our school in eighth grade. "She thinks it's her job to keep us all connected—whether we want to be or not."

"Hey, I like the idea." He bounced his eyebrows and curled his lips into a rascally grin. "That means I'll get to dance with you at least once a year." He jived his huge body side to side and sang a few bars of "She's a Brick House."

Heads turned and my face burned red-hot. "Thanks to you, Jesse, and Neil, that song makes me break out in hives."

Eli looked at his hands. "The three musketeers." It was a sad declaration.

The nickname fit the three neighborhood boys who lived the *all for one and one for all* mantra. Not a sad memory. Images of stick swords and sparring triggered a smile. "The three *evil* musketeers."

"Evil's a bit strong," Eli said.

"I can still see Neil carrying his backpack holding his black three-ring binder and Jesse's sharply creased jeans rolled up."

Eli wadded a napkin between his hands. "Don't forget Jesse's comb in the back pocket. An extension of his arm." He gave me a serious look. "But Neil's binder contained important stuff—like the building plans for our fort."

"And you were the brawn?" I was enjoying our

little stroll down memory lane. Maybe a little too much.

"You saying I didn't have brains?" Eli pressed his hand over his heart. "That cuts deep. I had brains. Just weren't engaged most of the time."

The air over Eli trembled.

I'd hoped Neil had gotten lost. Or maybe sucked into the expresso machine. I fanned him away like second-hand smoke. "Don't give me that poor-misunderstood-me look. You guys trashed our play house regularly and then cannibalized our bicycles for parts."

"We called it war games." Eli laughed. "But you and your sisters got us back. Big time."

"Yeah, well, it took years." We grew older and the prank-playing field leveled out somewhat. Tossing rolls of toilet paper into unsuspecting trees didn't take any particular skill or strength. Jesse lived on the other side of the train tracks that bordered our subdivision. But he stayed at Neil's or Eli's more than he stayed home. And they lived down the street from me. Easy targets.

"Jesse didn't want to get dirty and usually found an excuse to leave. Neil and I had to clean up all that shit."

Neil crowded over me. "You have any idea how many Saturdays you cost us?"

"If I had it to do over, I'd soak the toilet paper with water. Really give you something to complain about." I gulped. I glanced at Eli to see if he noticed I was talking to an absent entity.

Eli's thick fingers smeared the condensation rolling down his glass. "Yeah. All those years ago and here we sit." He raised his glass and added, "Here's to my buddy, Neil: the man who got the prize. I miss him every day."

I gave Neil a smirk. "Bet you feel bad now."

Eli lowered his cup. "Huh?"

Uggg. I had to keep Neil out of my head. "I meant I'll bet you feel bad for not treating me like a prize."

"Are you kidding? You're the only girl we took to our clubhouse. We voted you the fourth musketeer. Our d'Artagnan."

Their infamous clubhouse. Good memories. "That was before high school. Before you and Jesse got too *cool* for me."

Eli's lips curved up in the right places, but his dimples were a no-show. "Don't compare me to Jesse."

"He's your best friend. That speaks volumes."

"*Was* my best friend. You know that changed after what he did. He's the one—"

"Don't go there, Eli." My voice held a warning.

Neil snuggled in close. "Yes, let's go there."

Eli exhaled through gritted teeth. "Why can't we even talk about it?" He rubbed his hand through the thin layer of hair. "Hell, I've tried to explain for nearly twenty years, and you shut me down every time."

"The whole episode was a mistake. Period." I kept my face in neutral.

"Did you tell Neil about that night?"

Neil shimmered. "Tell me what?"

I squared my shoulders. "There was nothing to tell."

Eli leaned in. His breath grazed my cheek. "No one knows about us?"

I shifted in my chair to put a few inches of safety between us and stared straight ahead—and right into Neil's eyes. "There was no us." Frost crystals formed on my words.

Mental parrying between the two men wore me down. Eli wanted to dig up the past I'd buried deep—from myself and especially Neil. I didn't want to open old wounds, and I didn't want to explain anything to Neil. I stood and the chair squawked backward. "I need to go."

Eli's smile failed. "I thought you wanted me to go with you to Neil's office, and what about turning in your form to the Board of Education?"

I unhooked my purse from the chair and searched for an excuse. "I just remembered I promised to take Trey and Marcus to get school supplies." No eye contact. I stuffed my napkin into my cup and grabbed my debris. Hoping for a fast and furious getaway.

Eli followed me outside and tugged at my arm. "Whoa, girl. Afraid somebody's going to buy all the paper and pencils before you get there?"

I scanned the streets for traffic. "The boys will be waiting."

Eli stepped in front of me and squashed me in a baby-bear hug.

I squirmed out of his hold. "Gotta go, big guy." I dashed between two parked cars.

A horn blasted my eardrums, and Neil shouted, "Stop!" My body jerked backward to a dead halt. Strong fingers gripped the waistband of my shorts.

I tried to break free, but Eli's hand held tight—his face as white as Neil's. "They have laws against jaywalking."

"Damn it, Libby!" Neil glowed stronger and fear registered in his pasty brown eyes. "You could have been killed."

I could have been killed. My insides collapsed like

a bridge of dominoes. Eli and Neil stared at me big-eyed and wide-mouthed. The consequences could have been bad. No the consequences could have been devastating. What would my kids do if something happened to me? I wanted to fall apart. I wanted to cry and kick and scream. But not here. Not now. I wriggled free of Eli's grasp and faced both of them. "You giving me a ticket for jaywalking?"

Eli's hands shook as he straightened my shirt. "You scared the hell out of me."

I knocked his hand away. "Is that a *no* on the ticket?"

Eli gave me an anemic grin. "I figure I owe you for all those years of harassment. Call it even?"

I looked both ways and hoped I could fake it long enough to get to my car. I jogged across the street and yelled over my shoulder, "Champ, you're not even close!"

My remote chirped, and I slid into the driver's seat.

Neil sat solemnly, eyes straight ahead. "I tried to grab you."

I clutched the steering wheel and short breaths wheezed in and out. "I can't let things distract me."

"Like me?" Neil lowered his head.

I rested my forehead on the steering wheel and turned the key in the ignition. The vent blasted cold air in my face. "You, especially." I shifted into reverse. "You need to go."

Neil settled back into the leather upholstery. "As soon as you tell me about you and Eli."

Chapter 6
A Time for Tears

Two days before Christmas. Half-a-year milestone since Anniversary Armageddon. The kids didn't talk much about the obvious—the first Christmas without their dad. They were still catching their breath from hurdling past their first Halloween and their first Thanksgiving without him. Though out of character for Mr. Starched Shirt and Creased Khakis, Neil loved Halloween. He dressed like a vampire or zombie—makeup and all—to divvy out candy. This year, Trey manned the treats bucket, dressing in a light blue button-down shirt and khakis. At Thanksgiving dinner, no one mentioned the obvious when Neil's mom set an empty plate and flatware at his place at the table. Neil took one look and flitted to the den to watch football.

Now Christmas. My heart ached for my children. A few teary moments had troubled our Christmas rituals, but we'd decorated the tree and draped garland on the stairs. I wasn't brave enough to face climbing a ladder to string outside lights.

Being privy to Neil's persistent presence was a double-edged sword. Seeing and talking to him every day reminded me of his infidelity. But it also reminded me of the loss to our family. But because I saw and talked to him every day, I couldn't grieve over his demise. He didn't belong anymore. And as long as he loitered, I remained a tire spinning in sand—getting nowhere. There were days when being trapped in limbo-land with no-good Neil and forever being on guard around him threatened to unravel my mental framework. Add to that the normal wear and tear of the holidays and staying cheerful for the kids. My mental framework was one thread-pull away from a tangled ball of wool. Even though the kids probably thought about their dad every day, they accepted the sad fact he was gone. The only fact I accepted was that Neil was keeping me from getting better.

My decision to fight the manic hordes of shoppers at the mall two days before Christmas was idiotic. But I needed a gift for a Christmas party. I'd accepted the invitation, hoping for a needed diversion. Neil's folks lived near the mall, and I'd dropped off the kids to wrap gifts and to stay the night. I wished I could have dropped Neil off, too.

I checked the price sticker on the bottom of a black lacquered jewelry box at Pier One, and a pair of hands covered my eyes. "Guess who?"

The muscles in my neck stiffened and then relaxed. The familiar voice made me grin. I put down the box and reached for the hands on my eyes. "Superman?"

"You peeked." Eli spun me around and licked his lips before he pressed a chaste kiss to my ear.

I fidgeted with my clothes. Maybe he did have X-ray vision.

Eli pointed a sausage-sized digit at my nose. "You're not ready for Santa?"

I blocked his finger. "Santa's done. I need something for a party tonight. You like this?"

Eli waved his hand dismissively. "Sure. What

time's your party?"

"Seven thirty."

"It's only six now. How about a cup of coffee?" He tapped my nose. "But none of that latte crap."

I wanted to forget our last meeting. Eli had opened our past like a can of tuna, leaving a lingering smell and Neil's hungry curiosity.

Eli and I sat across from each other with our coffees and a mountain of nostalgia between us. Eli was divorced. Jesse was divorced. Neil was dead. Fate had made me a widow, but who's to say if Neil had survived, that we wouldn't be a divorce statistic like the other musketeers? Growing up, divorce was unheard of in our neighborhood. Parents took the *till death do us part* of their marriage vows seriously. Even Jesse's parents—the perfect example of *for better or worse.*

I sipped my coffee and gave Eli a once-over. Time had been a fickle friend. From the neck down, the former star linebacker still sported a body of tempered steel. However, the thick brown locks that spiked out in all directions when he removed his football helmet were gone. Skin showed through his precisely combed hair.

From our table we watched a constant stream of people flow by, commenting on mothers with weary faces parading tired, whiny kids dressed in their stiff, new Christmas outfits up to Santa's throne. I recalled similar journeys to get the essential keepsake to be displayed on the mantel. Most of the shoppers hustled by us, shoulders hunched, eyes strained forward. Men sat around us and played games on their smart phones. For them, tomorrow was their big shopping day. But the couples caught my attention. They were everywhere. Holding hands. Smiling at each other. A pang of envy hit me. *Last Christmas I had a husband.*

Who was I kidding? Last Christmas Neil spent his usual eighty hours working. At least I thought he spent his time working. I was half a couple then. Just like now.

Eli's voice broke into my mini pity-party. "So, you got big plans for Christmas?"

I shrugged. "Oh, you know. The kids open their gifts, and we do the family thing." No need to share my worries about how the kids would handle their first Christmas without their dad. Or how I wished we could skip this Christmas and pick it up next year when the wounds were less raw. Nor did I care to add that Neil's parents would show up at lunch and sing their praises to Saint Neil. After the accident, they'd raised Neil to sainthood status. *He was no saint.* Sometimes I wanted to lash out and scream the truth about Neil's affair. But I knew I never would.

"How about you and your son?" I asked to be polite.

"I won't get to see Lee until Christmas night. We'll have dinner at my folks' and open presents." Eli scraped his cup around the table following it with his eyes. "It sucks, actually. I'd rather be with my kid on Christmas morning." His voice sounded dull and flat. "But it wasn't in the custody agreement." He looked up, crimped his lips into a tight smile, not hiding the pain in his eyes.

I patted his hand. "Remember when you found out you guys were having a boy?"

"Yep. Neil went with me to buy Lee's first football." He placed his other hand on top of mine. A hand sandwich.

I wanted to tell him that the holidays kicked everything out of whack. That he'd see Lee and that Lee still had his father. Eli withdrew his hands and stared over my head. His jaw tensed, and his eyes went black.

Someone tugged my hair, and a too-friendly man's voice said, "Ho, ho, ho."

Hazard warnings came too late. "Hello, Jesse." The other musketeer had arrived.

"Merry Christmas, gorgeous." Jesse bent down and pecked my cheek.

I brushed off his kiss. "Eli, look who's here."

Jesse King. Childhood friend, neighbor, nemesis. Our relationship was shallow at best and adversarial at worst. There were no boundaries he was afraid to cross, and he had a way of making me feel like he was the spider and I was the fly. His campaign of intimidation started in junior high when he auctioned off a pair of my underwear. In high school, he didn't miss a chance to remind me that I didn't make cheerleader. Seeing him made me want to duck. Because with him, you never knew what was coming. Few saw the real Jesse. The Jesse who could smile in your face while he shoved the knife deeper into your back. But then few had known him from the beginning—like I did. Like Eli did.

Eli accepted Jesse's outstretched hand. "It's been a while, dude," Jesse said.

Eli's obligatory shake was abrupt. "Yeah, we missed you at the funeral."

Jesse placed his hand on Eli's shoulder. "Hey, man, glad you were there." Jesse turned to me. "You know I'd have been there if I could."

My obligatory response matched Eli's. A slight nod. His absence at the funeral didn't surprise me since he wasn't the main attraction. I focused on the clock over Jesse's shoulder and wished I could wiggle my nose and make the hands move.

Jesse grabbed a chair from another table and placed it between Eli and me. He rotated his head from me to Eli and back again. "Man, it's good to see you guys."

Years ago, for the sake of his friendship with Neil, Jesse and I slid into an un-negotiated truce. Jesse, who at one time ranked right at the top of Eli's list, now didn't even make his top one hundred. But Jesse didn't care—never had. He crossed a black shiny loafer over the knee of his perfectly creased jeans. His hair, still thick and dark, curled at the collar of his red and white plaid shirt. Always in style. Jesse sprawled in his chair like it had been custom made for his body. Jesse was still the best looking of the three musketeers. Shamelessly his dark eyes read me like a menu.

Eli pushed his empty cup to the center of the table. "You shopping?"

Jesse shifted his gaze to Eli. "Yeah. Picking up something for Ryan. You think my ten-year-old is too young for a pellet air rifle? I'm sure his mom won't be happy. But hell, I like pissing off my ex-wife."

"Why?" Eli flattened his hands on the table.

"Why what?" Jesse asked.

Eli sat back in his chair. "Why do you want to piss her off?"

A look of incredulity crossed Jesse's face. "Because she's my ex, man. She got what she wanted." Jesse thumped his chest.

"Why put your kid in the middle?" Eli propped his

arms on the table. "It's Christmas."

Jesse stared out into the crowd. "When I was a kid, I hated Christmas."

I knew why Jesse hated Christmas. Holidays meant his dad drank even more than usual, and that meant his mom took more abuse than usual. And I imagined Jesse did, too.

Eli leaned closer to him. "You're the dad now. It's up to you to make Ryan's Christmas special."

Memories weighed me down, sinking my mood lower and lower. Our threesome reminded me of its missing member—Neil. The four of us had shared so much. Jesse and Eli bantered back and forth like nothing had changed. Didn't they understand? Nothing could ever be the same. They could finish their coffee and walk away. Go back to their normal lives. But when I walked out of here, I'd be thrown back into a hurricane of emotions and changes over which I'd lost control. I needed to get away. *Take a deep breath. Smile.* "Oh, my goodness. Look at the time."

Wavy lines quivered behind Jesse. I wondered when Neil would show up. Our foursome.

Jesse tapped my watch. "What's your rush, Lib? I wanted to talk about Neil's office building. My real estate guy said he's been trying to get you to show him the property."

Neil's diaphanous form grew more solid, and he shook his fist in Jesse's face. "It's not for sale."

"Why are you annoyed?" *Oh, my God. I'd asked Neil a question—out loud.*

Jesse answered. "I'm not annoyed. Now my real estate guy is a little pissed because you won't return his calls."

"He's wasting his time calling. I haven't made a decision on selling Neil's building," I said.

The air crackled and swelled. A cloud of Neil hung heavy over Jesse. "Why's he so interested?"

Eli's plastic cup crunched in his hand. "Not a cool time to talk business."

"Still protecting her." Jesse leaned back and then an ah-ha look sparked a grin. "Wait a minute. Are you two together?"

Before I could answer, Neil jumped in my face. "Well? Are you together?"

"Don't be stupid," I said to Neil.

Eli smashed his coffee cup flat and shot Jesse a deadly look. "You heard the lady."

Jesse was being Jesse—making trouble. I answered Neil, but my response hit a nerve with Eli. They were too close and pressing in. I wanted to run away from the memories. From the three musketeers. From everything. The air felt thick and clogged my windpipe. I pulled my shirt from my neck and rested my hand at my throat. My pulse beat out an SOS. I pressed my fingers to stop the dots and dashes and warned my feet to stay put.

"Uh-oh." Neil said.

If I thought things couldn't get worse, I was wrong. A woman I hated worse than rattlesnakes walked by wearing a white blouse a size too small tucked into a black skirt a foot too short. Flanked by two little boys, her hands held fast. She walked past and long red curls bounced on her shoulders. Breathing ceased. Blackness pinched my vision to a pinpoint.

Neil swooped in front of me and hovered on his knees. "Please, please, please don't say anything."

I pressed my chest, forcing air up through my trachea and breathed in. I uncrossed my legs and wound them around the chair legs to hold me down. All of my anger and rage streamed at the woman who'd ruined my life, and if looks were lethal...But then the smaller of the two boys started crying and pulling away from the line to see Santa. She bent down, dried his cheeks, and hugged him.

"Maybe I should introduce her." I said.

Eli and Jesse gave me confused looks. "Huh?"

I couldn't look away from the Santa display. The other little boy helped his mom console his little brother. "See that redhead in line with the two little boys?"

"She's hot," Jesse inspected her from top to bottom. "You know her?"

I wanted to scream and throw my coffee cup at her, but she wasn't a monster. She was a mom. A single mom. Like me. "How about you, Eli?"

Eli raised his hands in front of him. "No thanks. I've got socks older than she is."

Jesse laughed out loud and whacked Eli on the back. "What happened to you? Man, I remember when we'd be all over that."

"Some of us grow up." Eli shrugged off Jesse's hand. "Anyway, I've found that those with great packaging are just great packaging. How old is she? Thirty?"

"Twenty-eight," Neil said.

My nerves drummed inside. "Neil said she's twenty-eight."

Eli and Jesse both turned to me. "How would Neil know how old she is?"

Neil lunged in front of me. "Please, don't make a scene."

"She was Neil's assistant." I turned away from Neil. "They were working late the night he had the accident."

Eli reached for my hand. When he did, he knocked my cup over. Lukewarm coffee flowed over the table and down into Jesse's lap.

Jesse jumped up, knocking his chair over backward. His hands frantically scrubbed at the small wet spot on his jeans. "Shit, man!"

Jesse's distraction interrupted the bomb ticking in my head. I tried to find Sheri in Santa's line, and she and her boys had disappeared. Could the disturbance have caused her to see me, or did her little boy talk her into escaping a trip to Santa's lap? It didn't matter. "Guys, this has been fun, but I don't want to be late."

Jesse ran his hand up my arm and gripped my shoulder. "Let me buy you dinner sometime. One old friend to another. We can talk about old times."

"Sure," I said as I pulled out of his grasp. "I'll call you." *When hell freezes over.*

Eli stood and held out his arms. "It was great seeing you."

I reached up and planned a quick hug and a fast retreat. But he held me close and whispered. "Call me anytime. I'll be there."

The space behind my eyes throbbed, and I fidgeted with my purse strap and bit my lips to stop their quivering. "I'll see you soon. We have a reunion meeting at Allison's."

I slung my purse over my shoulder and picked up my shopping bag. "I hope you guys have a great

Christmas. Be sure to tell your families hello."

I wove in and out of the crowds of people, dodging tables and strollers. Neil, my shadow, stayed on my tail. I ran out the exit and through the parking lot. In the safety of the car, I rested my head against the cool glass of the window, and tears dripped down my face. Forget the party. I'd lost the urge to be around people. In the passenger seat, Neil's aura sputtered on and off like a light bulb with a damaged filament. I wiped my eyes and breathed a sigh. Neil remained uncharacteristically quiet. My weak moment passed, and with every mile of the twenty-minute ride home, my resentment festered.

I hit the garage remote. "Christmas Eve eve and I'm glued to you." The garage door made a muffled sound as it closed behind me. "Dammit! This is your fault!" I slammed the car door and stretched my arms to the ceiling. "Well?" I searched for any sign of him.

Neil flashed on and off like someone flipping a light switch. "Can't...hear...you." He made static noises. "You're...breaking...up." More static noises. "Brea...king...up."

What a night. My husband's mistress walked within ten feet of me. Close enough to see the absence of a panty line. My cheating husband's a ghost buzzing in and out like a firefly, and he's making static noises to avoid an argument. No one would believe this. I don't believe this. The intro to *The Twilight Zone* should be cuing. I covered my eyes, but I could still see Neil flashing. On off, on off, on off. My lips twitched. I tried not to. But I smiled.

"Hey, I saw you smile!" Neil flashed brighter as he jumped up and down.

"It was a weak moment. I'm going upstairs." I

paused on the steps. "Sometimes you're easier to deal with as a ghost."

We climbed the stairs together, and I watched the man beside me. Though not striking, Neil was a nice-looking man. And thanks to years of running, his lean six-foot frame hadn't changed much over the years. When the gray filtered into his brown hair, I thought he looked like he matched his fancy office building.

"Any way you can change that light blue shirt? It makes you look washed out."

Neil snorted. "Really, Libby? I'm a ghost and you want me to worry about a shirt?"

"I thought you said you didn't believe in ghosts." Our banter was too easy. Too personal.

"I've changed my mind. When are the kids getting home?"

"I'll pick them up tomorrow." I pitched my purse onto the island in the kitchen and headed for the den. "You want to explain why you don't want to sell your office to Jesse?" I talked to Neil like he was still a part of the family unit. I worried that this was my new normal.

He kept pace with me. "The guy's a dick."

"I agree." *It had always been my opinion.* "You didn't always feel that way. What changed?"

"It's complicated." The old Neil-tone kicked in, triggering the play button to mental media archived in my brain.

"Because I'm too stupid." Bitterness glazed my tongue with acid.

"See what you do? You jump to conclusions. I never said you were stupid."

"Then explain." I sat on the sofa, crossed my legs,

and waited.

Neil faded and disappeared into his camouflage. "I don't want Jesse King in my office." I couldn't see Neil, but his voice came loud and clear.

I lay back and gazed up at the ceiling. "Well, I don't want you in my house."

Chapter 7
The Gang's all Here

Seven months and still counting.

I packed sorrow in with the Christmas decorations and stacked the plastic bins in the attic. The universe breathed a sigh of relief. We'd survived.

January meant the start of a new year. New opportunities. A new life? Not as long as Neil hung around. It's not like I could change the locks. My life was a circus, and I was the ringmaster. My kids occupied center stage, and my students got the second tier. Neil dominated the fringes where I conned my anger into hiding.

It wasn't until the associate pastor at my church made a statement that gave me hope. In his New Year's sermon, he said that if we always did what we'd always done, we'd always get what we'd always gotten. He looked right at me. I'm sure of it. I didn't know the phrase was famous until Emily told me that Henry Ford had said it, too. All I knew was it was perfect, and my pastor was a genius.

If I wanted change, I had to do something different. I called my friend Allison and accepted her invitation to work on the class reunion committee. Its members were the bedrock of my life. We'd grown up in the same neighborhood and traveled through the educational system like a school of piranha—some of us hungry for knowledge while a few others only hungry for mischief. Either way, our tattered teachers facilitated our communal departure. Yep, these were my people. They would require nothing of me, and if things got too messy or I decided that different was too scary, I could always play the grieving widow card.

However, on the night of the reunion meeting, my confidence went AWOL. In all my bluster, I'd forgotten about Neil. My skin itched like I was being attacked by herds of mosquitoes, and red claw marks streaked my arms. I had to stay clearheaded and be on guard. Neil would come. These were his people too. If I didn't stay focused and slipped... The last thing I needed was word to get out that poor Libby Miller had cracked.

Allison breezed through my door first. "Libby! Thank you so much for letting us meet here on such short notice. Gosh, your hair looks good? Fresh highlights?"

Petite, blonde Allison Webster Downs entered a room and generated instant energy. Bouncing curls framed sky-blue eyes always on the lookout for a challenge. "I can't believe the dishwasher flooded my kitchen. You should see the mess. The water got under the floor and made the wood buckle in ripples like this." Allison made wavy motions with her hands. "They're tearing out my floor even as we speak." She smiled big, showing lots of perfect teeth. Allison was more than beautiful. She was one of those girls my grandmother described as pretty on the inside and outside.

"I can't believe you left Jackson with that mess." I led her through the foyer and rocketed past the dining room and the infamous chandelier.

She waved away my concerns. "I dealt with it all day. He can handle the second shift."

We'd been friends since eighth grade when Allison and her family moved to our school from Pensacola, Florida. Being a Navy brat, she'd been to Japan and Germany and England. Places I'd only read about. Our PE teacher Mrs. Rowland asked me to buddy up and show her around, and it was the best match ever. She joined everything. No club was too large or too small. Her picture appeared in the yearbook nineteen times her senior year—a school record. As assistant editor of *The Rendezvous*, I can confirm the fact. She'd pulled off our ten-year reunion, and in true Allison fashion, she'd rounded up our regular cast of characters for our twentieth one.

She took both of my hands and the easy familiarity in her face took me back to eighth grade. "Are you doing okay? How about Reagan and Trey?"

I tried my standard spiel: "Things are getting better every day. It just takes time."

She tilted her head and squeezed my hands. "It's me you're talking to."

I squeezed back. "He was sleeping with his employee."

"I can't believe you told her." From the dining room, Neil's voice resonated.

Allison's blue eyes outgrew her face. "Shut up! The redhead?"

Neil streamed into the family room. "Why don't you post it on Facebook!"

I concentrated on Allison and pretended I didn't hear him. "Oh, yes. Neil told me he hired a single mom with a great resume. I met her once, and her assets were obvious. Twenty-eight, perky boobs, tight little tush."

Allison swept her hair back, and her face shifted from shock and awe to disgust. "But we still have to do some sort of memorial at the reunion."

"Put a footnote in the program," I said.

Neil's khakis and button-down shirt followed us. "You're vindictive enough to do it."

I flipped my hair and gave Neil a sugary smile.

"Now, Lib, he might have been a scumbag husband, but he was our classmate. How'd you find out he was cheating?"

"I caught him on our anniversary."

Allison's mouth formed the words, but made no sound. "Oh. My. Gosh."

I patted her arm. "I'm doing okay. It's just that it feels like I'll never get rid of him." I looked toward the ceiling.

"I'd be so mad at him for cheating, I don't know how I'd get over him dying. Who all knows about this?"

"Emily, my neighbor. You remember her." I didn't tell Allison that Eli knew or anything about his role in the whole debacle. "Then there's Sheri."

Allison plunked her hands on her hips. "You're nicer than I am. I'd be screaming it from the rooftops."

"You wouldn't hurt your kids," I said. "Reagan and Trey are having a hard enough time."

Her expression went from haughty to heart-felt in less than a second. "Bless their hearts. Is there anything I can do?"

"Financially, Neil planned for everything. The house is paid for, and the kids' college funds are intact. And I have my job. We're good."

"I've always loved this house. It's so open and airy. I guess it's all the windows. When we were kids, I couldn't wait for Neil's birthday parties. We played chase in the back yard and ran right to the lake."

"Bet you didn't come into the house. None of us did," I said.

"That's for sure." Allison chuckled. "At one of Neil's parties, maybe fourth grade, I was dying to go to the restroom. I banged on the door, but Mrs. Miller wouldn't let me in. She told me to pee in the lake. I told her I couldn't, and she told me to squeeze my knees together. So I ran down the street to your house. Your mom got so mad at Mrs. Miller."

"She and my mom clashed over other things too." I shrugged. "I married her only child."

"Your mom was fiery when it came to her girls. Remember when our gym teacher called you a smart-ass?"

I laughed. "She was a first year teacher, and I was a smart-ass. Mom didn't make a big deal out of it. The teacher apologized, and I got grounded. But I learned a valuable lesson that benefited me in my profession. Don't ever call a kid a smart-ass—even when they are."

"I have such fond memories of your folks. It's hard to believe they've been gone so long." Allison sighed.

A tinge of sadness pricked the place in my heart that never heals. Dad went first, but Mom followed a year later. "Mom passed when I was pregnant with Reagan. So neither of my parents saw their grandkids. But grandkids changed Neil's mom. You should see what she lets the kids get away with. Especially now that Neil's gone." She missed out on so much, but she had time to catch up. Unlike her son. She locked us out of her house, but Neil locked his family out of his life. It was more important to Neil to own a prestigious business and enjoy the perks that came along with it. Including a shapely redhead.

"You have way better taste than Mrs. Miller." Allison ran her hand along the back of the sofa. "I've always liked this house, but I think I like it even better without Neil."

"I heard that." Neil gyrated around Allison.

"I so agree," I said.

Allison's shoulders shuddered and she rubbed her arms. "Ewww. I just had a creepy crawly feeling all over." She looked around. "Maybe I shouldn't speak ill of the dead."

The doorbell rang, and we both jumped. We twittered nervously and ran to the foyer, Allison sticking close.

"Hello, ladies." Our class president Buddy Bolinger sauntered in.

Buddy and I had been friends since kindergarten. He and Allison became friends when she was elected vice president of the senior class. As his second in command, she made sure Buddy's administration ran like clockwork. Thus giving Buddy the time to fulfill his campaign slogan; *Buddy Bolinger: Everybody's Buddy.* After Neil's accident, he called almost every week trying to perk me up. In his easy, down-home accent, Buddy delivered his home-style anecdotes about his wife's fruitless attempts at dieting and his colorful in-laws. I never dreaded his calls.

"You girls look mighty pretty." Words rolled off his tongue like cold molasses.

"Talk about a schmoozer," Neil said. "And the

hair."

I squinted my eyes into what I hoped was a menacing slit and mouthed, "Stop."

Buddy still parted his hair, more gray now than dirty blonde, on the right side with his signature swooping bangs. He hugged Allison and then me. "How's my girl doing?"

I gave him a brotherly smack on the cheek. "Don't worry about me."

"Lorraine's the worry wart. She told me to ask you to bring the kids over. I couldn't believe how much they've grown. That Trey is the spitting image of you. And Reagan…" Buddy's voice caught.

I knew what Buddy thought. *Reagan was the spitting image of her dad.* I gave his arm a little hug. "I know."

The sunlight through the tall windows glistened through Neil as he flitted near the ceiling. I kept him in my peripheral vision.

"Her highness is here." Neil called from the window overlooking the front porch.

I knew who he meant. Charlotte Crocker-Crane added a serious element to our meetings. When she married, no one was surprised at her insisting on hyphenated maiden-married names. Success was in her blood. She'd gone from president of the student government in high school, to the Law Review at Samford University, to a respected corporate Birmingham attorney. With the grace of a gazelle, her tall, svelte frame glided into the foyer. Shiny, brown hair fell straight down her back. Mrs. Crocker-Crane was a chic chick.

Charlotte's aloof façade masked her reserved,

brainy nature, and many shared Neil's assessment of her until they got to know her. Instead of a posse of friends, she chose a *band of sisters*. And only we few knew that being childless wasn't her first choice. And even fewer knew how much she enjoyed slot machines and tequila shots. Charlotte wasn't arrogant—just several thoughts ahead of most of us. I held her shoulders and touched my cheek to hers so not to wrinkle her starched, white blouse tucked neatly into her creased black slacks.

She smiled and pulled me into a hug. "Surviving?"

"Always," I gestured toward the family room. "Allison and Buddy are here."

Neil materialized beside me. "Enough with the ice queen. Romeo's here."

I didn't wait for Eli to ring the bell. I opened the door and walked to the porch. Eli unfolded his tall, solid frame from his bright yellow Hummer. Tiny butterflies congregated around my belly button. I couldn't hide the smile that tickled my lips. The perfect vehicle for a guy we called *Tank* in high school. A short-sleeved forest green polo shirt stretched so tight across his chest I could read the trademark without my glasses, and his khaki cargo pants had never felt the heat of an iron.

Neil skidded through the door to the front porch. "What the—"

At Christmas, Eli had about ten hairs on top. Today his head was as slick as an onion. The new look fit him. Larger than life and nothing cautious or half involved with Eli. He looked good. And so did the perfectly trimmed goatee on his handsome face. In typical Eli style, he skipped the three steps up to the porch and

73

Sandra Tilley

bounded straight through Neil.

"I like the clean, shiny look," I said.

He grabbed me in a bear hug and hefted me up to his eye level. "You always look good."

I couldn't maintain his hazel-eyed stare. "You're squishing me." And the butterflies in my belly.

Eli set me down. He winked as he ran his hand over his slick head. "Smooth, huh."

"The new Eli." I hung back and observed him as he greeted the others.

Neil circled Eli and landed next to me. "The new Mr. Clean, if you ask me."

I turned my back to Neil and tried to stay centered and not let him draw me in. One misstep with Neil, and my friends might think I was eccentric. Or worse.

Eli shook hands with Buddy and slapped him on the back. He grabbed Allison and gave her a loud, sloppy kiss. When he came to Charlotte, he hugged her chastely. Even Tank could be intimidated by Charlotte.

Neil wedged himself between Allison and me. She whispered behind her hand, "Eli looks good, doesn't he?"

Neil yelled at Allison. "Are you serious? I've seen more hair on a bar of soap!"

I smirked at Neil. "Still looks like one of the Three Musketeers." I led the group through the house to the backyard where we'd all spent lots of summer days. When we bought the house, the old dock was rotten. I suggested building a double-decker boathouse, and Neil loved the idea. Expansive windows offered a panoramic view of the lake. The perfect setting for our meeting. And the weather cooperated. The mercury topped at a balmy sixty-six degrees, warming our winter day.

74

I walked between Allison and Buddy. Neil hugged the periphery, and like a chameleon, absorbed his surroundings, turning the brown of the dead, leafless trees and then bright blue and white against the winter sky dimpled with white fluffy clouds. I stumbled and stepped on Buddy's foot. "Oops. Sorry."

Buddy thrust out his hand and steadied me. "Easy."

"Buddy, how's Lorraine?" Allison asked.

He wagged his head from side to side, without disturbing a single hair on his head. "When she heard about the reunion, she decided to lose ten pounds. My poor Lorraine," he said, "even if she lost twenty pounds, she'd still have a big ol' butt. She gets it from her momma."

Neil interrupted with his commentary. "Buddy's appraisal is completely accurate."

"That's not fair." I said to Neil.

Buddy stopped. *Darn it, Neil.* I took Buddy's arm and pulled him along. "It's not fair to compare Lorraine to her mom."

Buddy picked up where he'd left off. "Now if she took after her daddy, she'd be tall and slim like her brother. Of course she'd chew tobacco and be able to spit in your eye from across the room, too." We were all laughing when Eli and Charlotte caught up.

Eli looped arms with Allison and me. "Buddy, are you entertaining the girls?"

Charlotte fell in step beside Buddy. "Lorraine's a lovely person."

"She's beautiful through and through. Even with her big backside." Buddy grinned and kept walking.

Neil wafted over Buddy. "Can't change genetics."

Charlotte flaunted a foil-covered plate under

Buddy's nose. "Libby made chicken fingers for appetizers."

Buddy slowed to a stop and lifted the foil. He inhaled deeply. "At our house, fried chicken is only a fond memory."

Eli chuckled and tightened his elbows, drawing Allison and me to his side.

Neil hovered over the group. "Charlotte could use a few of those chicken fingers. Can you believe how skinny she is? I like a woman with a little meat on her bones."

I sneered at Neil. "It's not the bones you want." *Triple darn.* Allison and Eli stared at me. Blood drained to my toes. "I like chicken fingers because they have no bones in them."

Allison gave me an odd look. "Well, Buddy, tonight you can eat your fill. And maybe sneak some home for the boys," she said.

"I wish I could. But Lorraine might smell chicken on my breath." Buddy's deadpan delivery hit the marrow of our funny bones.

Eli bent over and laughed out loud, providing me the perfect opportunity to unhitch my arms.

Neil bounded through the air. "Buddy's so witty. Ha. Ha. Ha."

I stuck my tongue out at Neil. Thank goodness no one could hear Neil but me. "Buddy, you're a riot," I said.

The five of us laughed through the backyard right up to the water's edge. A mile and a half of paved road wound around Mountain Woods Lake where twenty houses claimed watery backyards, and their boat docks dotted the shoreline.

The undeveloped property was the well-traveled woods of our youth. Honeysuckle Ridge was our boundary line and ran along the tops of small hills on the north side of the lake. From up there we could make out most of the curvy road around the lake and our western boundary, the railroad tracks.

Over the years, owners formed an association and developed the lake into a sub-division. Despite a modernized electronic entrance gate, the lake and surrounding area remained unchanged, and now my kids travelled our well-worn trails.

"Man. How cool is this?" Eli stepped on the dock and examined the wooden structure above his head. "If we'd had this baby growing up, we wouldn't have thrown bed sheets over swing sets to camp out." Eli's wide smile stretched his goatee into a wide V.

"Welcome to my double-decker boathouse, complete with running water and air conditioning." When Neil and I bought his family home, remodeling started here. "The design's mine, and I helped Neil drive every nail and paint every square inch." I patted the support pillar of my sanctuary. "My addition to our little community."

"We had some good times in this neighborhood." Eli closed his eyes and breathed in. "I can almost smell the honeysuckle." His shoulders slumped, and he rubbed his hand across the back of his neck. "If Neil were here, things would be perfect."

"We all miss him," Charlotte said.

"I feel like I should see him riding out of those woods on that red bike of his." Buddy said.

I didn't respond. I didn't know if things would be perfect if Neil were here.

Eli yanked a lock of my hair. "Hey, Libby, remember Honeysuckle Ridge? We'd fly over that ridge and hold our breath till we hit bottom…" Eli's voice drifted off. I didn't see a nearly forty-year-old police captain destined for the chief's job. I saw the face of a ten-year-old with the breeze in his face and the sky in his eyes. The boy who gave me my first box of Valentine candy.

Charlotte crossed her arms and stifled a grin. "Eli, does this little trip through our childhood have a point?"

"I think he crashed on his head a few too many times," Allison said.

"You girls are picking on Eli," Buddy drawled.

Neil joined in, "By all means, pick away."

"My point, counselor," Eli began, "is that the trees and fences were overgrown in honeysuckle vines, and when it bloomed, we'd pull out the middle thing—"

"The pistil," I said.

Allison arched her eyebrows.

"I taught one semester of science," I explained. "Dissecting comes in the second semester, and I refused to touch frog guts. That's why I teach English."

Oblivious to our interruption, Eli continued. "We'd lick the drop of honey off the end of it. Didn't y'all do that?"

"I didn't." Charlotte answered and turned to Allison.

"Sounds gross," Allison said.

Buddy patted Eli on the back. "The girls are just messing with you. We all played in those woods, and the honeysuckle grew like kudzu. All of us sipped the nectar of the vine."

Eli looked at me. "Remember what we called it,

Libby?"

"Honeysuckle wine." How could I forget?

Neil flashed bright. "Uh-oh. Brace yourself."

Sadie, our golden retriever, zigzagged across the backyard. The neighbors' new puppy—a yorkie named Maddy—yapped close to her back paws. Trey and Marcus ran all out to catch up.

"Mom!" Trey shouted over the puppy's shrill barking. "Stop Maddy!"

"Grab her leash," Marcus yelled.

Neil hovered on the dock. Sadie passed me and ran to Neil and cowered beside him. "Can she see you?" I shouted over the yapping and reached for Sadie's collar. I hoped the others didn't hear me.

"You think it's possible?" Neil asked.

Sadie plopped down at Neil's feet. Maddy's leash caught on the chaise lounge, and the chaise made a scraping sound as the puppy launched at me, bringing the chaise with her and hitting Sadie's left flank. Splash. Sadie jumped in.

"What the hell?" Neil charged Maddy.

As if the switch had been turned off, the barking stopped. "Get this dog," Neil cried. Maddy looked up at Neil, tucked her tail, and began a backward retreat.

Marcus and Trey bounded onto the boat dock.

"Get out of the way, boys!" I leapt over a chaise lounge to stop Maddy's back-side plunge. My right foot landed solidly on the wooden deck, but my left foot teetered on the edge. I thrashed my arms, and my body bucked and reared, trying to restore my balance. The eyes of the reunion committee fixed their laser gazes on me, holding me aloft like an aerialist on a high wire. As if in slow motion, Allison clasped her hands over her mouth, and Charlotte plunked her hands over her ears, and Buddy laid his hands over his eyes. I wondered if they knew how silly they looked. Like three monkeys.

Splash.

Eli kicked off his shoes. "Hold on, Libby!"

I lay on my back in the cold water waving my hands in the air. "No! Eli. Don't!"

Too late. When he engaged all those muscles, inertia took over.

Eli jumped in.

Roars of laughter came from the shore.

Eli stood in thigh-deep water. I secured Maddy in my arms and started laughing. My shoulders jiggled, and I reached for Eli's arm to get on my feet.

"Damn, this water's freezing." Eli slipped his arms under my knees and plucked me out of the water. One arm secured Maddy, but my other arm shot around his neck, and he shifted my body closer. Maddy lurched from my grasp and jumped to the dock. I trailed my hand down Eli's chest, leaving wet, muddy fingerprints. A giant spasm rippled over him, and he cinched me tighter. His mouth crinkled into a mischievous grin. "Cold?"

I shivered. The cold burned my cheeks—and warmed other places chilled far too long.

Chapter 8
Tree House

Our first reunion committee meeting ended with a polar dip. Eli and I stood on the shore dripping and waved goodbye.

"That went well," Eli said.

I was too frozen to laugh. "I'll go get us some dry clothes and a towel." Neil had tons of running clothes that still hung in his closet. It would be interesting to see how Eli filled them out.

"I have my workout bag in the car. I'll change down here in the guest bath. Then we'll have those chicken fingers. Swimming makes me hungry."

I pulled my wet hair into a ponytail, washed my face, and threw on some sweats. I hurried down the stairs, stopped at the landing, and scanned the family room. Eli sat on the edge of Neil's chair. His body pitched forward. Behind Eli, Neil sat on the back of his chair and propped his feet on Eli's shoulders.

Neil measured Eli's neck with his hands. "Can you believe this guy's neck size? Probably bigger than his IQ. You have to admit it was pretty stupid of him to jump into three feet of water to save you."

I tightened my ponytail. "Jealous?" Oops. I rolled my lips inside and clamped down.

Eli looked confused. "Huh?"

"I'm jealous that you can change so fast." I walked

through Neil. "Lucky you had your workout clothes in your car." I focused on Eli's white t-shirt, reading BPD in dark blue letters across his chest. My eyes flowed to the narrow waistband of his navy sweats. I swallowed, but my mouth was too dry to cooperate.

"Lucky is jumping instead of diving into three feet of water." Eli breathed in and his chest expanded.

My eyes snapped back to Eli's face. A crimson flush crept up my neck to my cheeks.

"You should blush." Neil flicked away.

"Good riddance." I sucked in my breath. "I mean what a way to end the reunion meeting." I fled to the kitchen, looking for something to do with my hands. I swept invisible crumbs into the sink.

"I'm starved. Let's take these chicken fingers and eat them in the boathouse. Got beer?"

I'd stocked the fridge at the boathouse with beer and soft drinks. Allison thought to bring the chicken back into the kitchen. "We can snack while we go through the folders Allison left us. Don't want to waste food. Not with Buddy and his boys starving."

"I'll bring these." Eli snatched the plate from the counter and walked beside me through the backyard. The foil crinkled as he worked his fingers underneath and snagged a chicken finger. "I can't help it. I'm a growing boy." He ate the whole thing in one bite.

My eyes skimmed the area for wavy lines or a fuzzy silhouette. So far so good. When we got to the dock, I led the way up the stairs of the boathouse. "I love this view."

"I'm liking this one myself." His words smacked between chews.

"Don't you know you're not supposed to talk with

your mouth full?" I grabbed the plate and walked inside.

The air around us stirred, and Neil appeared at the window. I wanted to throw something at him.

"I didn't know how much I missed this place." Eli stood in front of the full length window and gazed out over the water. "Your old house is around the bend in the lake." He pressed his face to the glass. "If I could see past that outcropping of rock, I could see the railroad tracks."

He didn't notice me. The lake held him hostage. I know because it did the same to me, and I'd awakened to it every day. "This is my safe place. My tree house."

Eli inspected the floor and ran his hands over the walls. "You guys built this?"

Neil floated on the other side of the glass, and the setting sun shone through him. "We were happy then." Neil winced, and I realized I'd said it aloud. I bit my lip and told myself he deserved it and shuffled Allison's color-coded folders on the glass-topped coffee table. "Want to eat first or go through these folders, Mr. Entertainment Chairman?"

Eli waggled a chicken finger. "I have food. A beer would be nice."

I tossed Eli a paper towel, squeezed a sliver of lime into a Corona for him, and popped open a Diet Coke for me.

He grabbed a napkin and scrubbed his mouth and fingers. "Come sit down," he patted the sofa, "I want to hear how you've been doing."

The dreaded question. It was usually punctuated with sad eyes and a long face. I applied my rote recanting response: "I'm doing fine. Kids are doing fine. Everything's fine."

"When I saw you at Christmas, you weren't in much of a talking mood either."

Guilt stabbed me in the side. Eli wasn't asking because it was the thing to do. He cared. And he didn't deserve my pissy attitude. I sat beside him, facing forward to avoid eye contact, and held out his beer. "I'm sorry." I meant it.

He took his beer and set it on the coffee table, and then pried my fingers from my Diet Coke can and set it next to his Corona. He steadied his hands on my shoulders and brought his face within inches of mine. His eyes shifted into neutral, like he was giving me permission to open up.

He gave me a gentle shake. "Lib, it's your old bud from forever, and I asked because I want to know how you're *really* doing."

I looked into his waiting eyes. He tightened his grip and rested his forehead against mine. His hands slid down and rested on my upper arms.

I breathed a long sigh. "You knew about Neil's affair, didn't you?"

"Here we go again." Neil's annoyed voice floated down from somewhere above us. "Don't you get tired of playing the poor-me card?"

I wanted to stick out my tongue or acknowledge Neil but swallowed my response.

Eli's hands went slack, and he raised his head. Both anger and pain passed over his face. "I felt so guilty. I wanted to cry, and I wanted to kick his ass. At the same time."

Neil wrangled his way between us, and I moved away from Eli. "Tell me about you and Lindsey."

Eli ran his hands over his bald head and reached for his beer. "We're cordial to each other. Can't say I don't feel guilty about the divorce—for Lee's sake." He leaned back on the sofa. "I hate shuttling him back and forth. Joint custody they call it."

Lindsey and I were never close, but I knew something was up at the last reunion. The only thing that got any attention from her was her cell phone. "Lindsey seemed distant at our last reunion."

"Things weren't good. But I didn't help matters that night dancing with you."

In an exaggerated motion, I placed my finger at my temple. "Oh, let me guess. I wonder which song we were dancing to…"

Eli began singing, *"She's a brick house—"*

I put my hand over his mouth. "Enough. Please." His soft lips, warm breath. Then Eli poked out his tongue, and I jerked my hand away like I'd been stung.

I scoured my hand on my jeans, and Eli threw his head back and laughed.

I reached for my diet soda and sat back. Did I really just put my fingers on Eli's lips? *Take a deep breath.* "First reunion, Jesse was between bimbos and came by himself. He, Neil, and Jack Daniels spent the evening crawling down memory lane. Then when Jesse and I danced to 'Unchained Melody,' Neil got furious. I had no idea it was *our* song."

Eli crossed his legs and propped his ankle on his knee. He fidgeted with the laces of his sneakers. "Speaking of our friend Jesse, have you heard from him since Christmas?"

"No. Why would I?"

Eli sighed. "He called me last week and asked if

you'd started going out."

I didn't like the sound of this. If Jesse had a question about me, he should ask me. "And he asked you?"

Eli looked down at his hands resting in his lap. "Maybe since he saw us together at the mall, he might have thought you and I were…" Eli's voice faded as if he couldn't finish the thought. "Just wanted to give you a heads up in case he calls and asks you out." Then he rubbed his hands over his head again. "I must be allergic to something up here. My head keeps itching."

Neil swung by. "Interesting development."

I waved Neil away. "I'm allergic to you."

Eli's face had what-the-heck-are-you-talking-about written all over it. I gulped and then began scratching my head. "I meant to say maybe we're allergic to each other." I smoothed my hair. "If Jesse King asks me out, he's wasting his time. I've done my time with the three musketeers."

Eli pushed a strand from my face. "Just giving you a heads-up."

His hand tingled down my face. "Don't worry about me, big guy. The three musketeers did one thing right. They made my sisters and me tough as titanium."

"Speaking of your sisters. One was always banging on the piano, and the other one walked around with a crown on her head."

"It was a tiara. Joy loved beauty pageants," I said.

"Is she still blonde?" He had a smile in his voice. "And what about Carol? She and Anthony still together?"

"Yep. They stay busy with their law practices." I laughed. "And Joy has two daughters. All three are blonde. Through and through."

"Your family seemed pretty normal, but your grandmother gave me the heebie-jeebies." He shuddered and the boathouse trembled.

I gave him an incredulous look. "You were scared of my ninety-pound granny?"

"When she pointed those crooked fingers, it looked like she was putting a spell on me."

"You idiot. She had arthritis. She couldn't help it if her hands were crooked."

"She didn't like me."

"She liked you better than Jesse."

"That's not saying much. But she spoiled you rotten."

Neil flickered into view and perched on top of the red and green folders spread across the coffee table. "You can say that again."

I squinted my eyes into my mean-teacher look. "I was not spoiled. Remember I was the middle child between Attila the Hun and Barbie. If Granny hadn't lived at our house, I would have been invisible."

Eli petted my head like I was an Irish setter and ran his hand down to my neck. He gathered his lips into a poor-pitiful-me pout. "Middle Child Syndrome. Poor baby."

I jabbed his unprotected ribs with my elbow. "When you're the middle kid, people underestimate you and leave you alone."

"I've never underestimated you." His deep, silky tone joined the symphony of night sounds skipping over the lake.

He settled in beside me, and we sat in an easy silence. Neil pounced from the coffee table to Eli's head and tap danced. My neck snapped tight. "Crap."

Neil flaunted his license to annoy. His look of pure contentment made me want to rip the Cheshire grin off his face.

Eli palmed his head. "What is it?"

I glanced up. "Thought I saw a bug."

"Something touched my head. Wasn't a spider, was it?" Eli stood up and flailed his arms, searching the air for spider webs. "I hate spiders." He scrubbed his shiny scalp. "I really hate spiders."

"Sit down, Eli. I'm sure it's nothing." I stared at Neil wishing he were a spider so I could squash him.

Eli brushed his hand over his head and sat on the edge of the sofa, his eyes scanning the ceiling like a search beam. "Got a flashlight?"

"It's okay, Eli. I didn't see a spider."

"Don't care what you say. I felt something." Eli rubbed his head with both hands.

Neil cackled overhead. "I'd forgotten Mr. Courageous is afraid of spiders."

I remembered our pranking the great prankster and almost laughed with Neil. Halloween of eighth grade. The Three Musketeers planned a campout in Neil's back yard. Neil distracted Eli, and I hid plastic spiders and spider webs in Eli's sleeping bag.

I ran my hand over Eli's slick dome, and I puckered up. "Afraid of a little spider?"

Eli ducked his head and chuckled. He tilted his head sideways. "Not a little one."

Laughter spurted out. I covered my mouth and kept laughing. I fell back and bounced my head on the sofa cushion. "Thanks, I needed that."

"Glad I could help." Eli clamped his hand on my

knee. "Now I need something."

I looked at Eli's hand. *How long had it been since any man, other than Neil, had touched my knee or any other part of my body?*

"Hope he doesn't need a loan." Neil's voice disrupted my thoughts.

I rolled my eyes at Neil's stupid comment. "Really?"

Eli laid his hand over mine. "Yes, really. I need to apologize. Neil's scare last year." He took in a breath and let it out slowly. "I should've been there for him."

I flicked his guilt away with a twist of my wrist. "It was nothing."

"He was lucky," Eli said.

I slumped into the soft cushions. "It scared the crap out of us." The specter of our mortality haunted us until Neil got the all-clear, "I think it changed us. You know, thinking about what could have happened. I guess fear can do that to you." I'd hoped we'd move closer together. That didn't happen.

Eli leaned back into the sofa. In the dim light, his shoulders drooped like they carried a hefty load. "I know things have been bad. You think you've made it through the worst part?"

A sharp pain reminded me that I couldn't bury my fear deep enough. "The worst part is worrying that something will happen to me, and my kids will have no one."

Neil hovered in a corner. Silent.

Eli wrapped his arm around me and pulled me close. "As long as there's life in me, they'll have someone."

His declaration was sincere and selfless. Raw

89

emotion burned my eyelids. Eli had been our friend a long time. He'd been my friend longer. Rays of moonlight sparkled over the lake. Like bookends, we sat, shoulder to shoulder.

"Do you believe in ghosts?" It popped out before I thought about what I was saying.

Neil's voice intruded on my thoughts. "I know where you're going with this. Not a good idea."

Eli took a moment before he answered. "I believe in an afterlife. But angels flying around interfering in our lives? No. Why are you asking me this?" Eli cut his eyes at me. "Have you seen anything unusual?"

"Pfft. Don't be silly." I wagged my hand in his face. I shelved my thoughts of sharing Neil's condition. "It's stupid. But Reagan got her learner's permit yesterday. She got all teary because her dad didn't know."

Neil sat on the coffee table. "What'd you tell her?"

I looked away from Neil and spoke to Eli. "I told her that her dad knew and was really proud of her."

Eli nodded. "That's a great answer."

Neil butted in. "Is she okay? Trey get upset too?"

"We're going to hit bumps in the road," I said, looking at Neil. "But we're going to make it."

"You're an amazing woman," Eli said.

Neil bowed his head.

Eli bumped my shoulder. "Why'd you pick Neil?" The lilt in his voice was so kid-like. Took me back to catching lightning bugs and drinking from hose pipes. "I don't get it." Eli swung his head my way. "I always figured it would be Jesse. Good-looking guy, needed saving and all."

"It's not like I drew straws." At one time or

another, I'd loved all three of the musketeers. "You and Jesse were stars on the football field. Neil was an asterisk. Made him humble."

Neil hovered at eye-level and thrust his ghostly face into my line of vision. "I don't like being called an asterisk."

"You're right," Eli said. Jesse and I hogged the limelight, but Neil was always there for us. He didn't let all that fan shit go to his head."

A self-righteous glow emanated from Neil. "Unlike the other two who shall remain nameless."

I addressed Neil's wavy form. "Believe me, he loved basking in your limelight."

"I still don't like being called an asterisk." Neil pouted.

Eli took a sip of his beer and set it back on the table. "You didn't answer my question. Why Neil?"

I thought for a second. "Valentine's Day in fifth grade."

Eli bobbed his head up and down. "We were in Mrs. Franklin's room."

"We cut hearts from red doilies and glued them on white paper bags and taped the bags to our desks," I said. "Neil's valentine wasn't in the bag, it was on top of a red, heart-shaped box. I was the only girl in class who got a box of candy. Neil risked all your jibes and ridicule. For me." I tapped my chest.

Eli's head fell back, and his rich baritone laughter rattled the windows. Wave after wave of laughter rolled over him.

"What's so funny?" I shoved him. "Are you making fun?"

Eli struggled to get his hee-haws under control.

"Was anything missing from your heart-shaped box?"

I crossed my arms and gave him my best teacher look. "Actually, several pieces of candy."

"The ones with nuts in them?"

"How do you know that?"

"The box of candy was from me."

I swatted his arm. "Bull."

Eli crossed his heart. "Swear."

"Why didn't you tell me?"

"Neil asked me not to."

"Well, hasn't this been a night of revelations?" I leaned back on the sofa.

Eli swallowed and inclined his head. "There's something else I need to tell you. But, sitting here and talking and laughing has been so pleasant. I hate to bring you down. Charlotte reminded me tonight that if I didn't tell you, someone else would."

Dread shimmied up my spine. What now?

"Tom Thornton committed suicide last night. He tried to break into the house where Tommy and his mom were staying, and she called the police. Tommy and she are fine." Eli stroked my leg.

I released the breath I'd been holding. "How sad. But I'm so glad Tom didn't hurt them again."

"He still hurt them. Tom shot himself in their front yard."

A cocktail of misery and relief circulated through my veins. "Oh, dear God. Did Tommy see?"

"Gratefully, no. But Mrs. Thornton did." He took my hand. "If you hadn't gotten them away from him, this could have ended so much worse."

"I could be going to three funerals instead of one."

Chapter 9
Red, Red Wine

I snuggled into my chair and scrolled down my list of emails, hoping to see one from Eli. Like I had every day for the last three weeks. The dog disaster and chilly dip into the lake hadn't doused the attraction. And it wasn't the heat from the laptop balancing on my legs keeping me warm. I'd had my doubts about helping with the class reunion. But even with the melee in the back yard, the committee meeting made me realize what I'd missed in the last months. Friends. Old friends. Real friends.

Neil's khaki-clad presence brushed by me like a whisper. "You busy?"

Heat rushed to my cheeks. Quickly I changed screens. "Stop reading over my shoulder."

The muted colors of Neil's blue shirt and khakis came into view. He sighed. "I miss email, Facebook, Twitter, Google."

I closed my computer. "Wonder if those voice-activation programs work for a ghost's voice? Of course it would be a tragedy if you got lost in the Ethernet." Something to hope for.

The phone rang.

"Uh, oh. Trouble next door," Neil said.

"You clairvoyant now?" I picked up the receiver and checked the caller ID. "Hello?"

"Libby, this is Reggie."

"Hi, Reggie. I didn't recognize your number. What's up?"

"Get over to my house. Now."

The hairs on my arm jumped to attention. "What's happened?"

"I left her a note. She's going to need you, Libby."

"What kind of note?" Dial tone. "Reggie? Reggie? Reggie?"

I darted out the back door with Neil on my heels. "What's going on? How'd you know?" The cold pavement startled my bare feet. Tiny pebbles dug into sensitive soles, and I staccato-stepped across the driveway. "Ouch. Ouch. Ouch."

He cruised along beside me. "You should have worn shoes."

"You should have swept the driveway. Wait. You can't sweep. You're a ghost." I sped up in spite of the pain.

"You don't have to be so touchy. I merely made an observation." Neil sped up, too.

Outrunning a ghost? What was I thinking? I stopped at the manicured lawn between our driveways. "How'd you know something was wrong at Emily's?"

"Sometimes I have flashes."

"I squiggled my feet in the grass oasis. Flashes? So why'd Reggie call me?"

"That info was not in the flash." Neil drifted ahead.

I passed Neil and barged through Emily's back door. She lay sprawled over her island clutching a paper towel. Groceries and plastic bags scattered on the floor. Fresh flowers lay on the counter.

"Reggie's gone." Emily's tears fell onto the

granite. "He left a note."

I placed my hand on her back. "What kind of note?"

Without moving her body, Emily handed me the crumpled paper towel she'd been holding.

"He wrote on a paper towel?" I smoothed out the wrinkles and read silently.

I'm sorry to run out like this, but I had to get away to figure things out. You deserve better.

Love,

Reggie

Neil hovered over my shoulder. "Don't you find it a bit unorthodox that he signed a Dear Jane letter, *Love, Reggie?* He's running from something."

"So what do you think his note means?" Blood drained from my face like a gas tank falling from half full to flat empty. I felt dizzy.

Emily stared at me like I had daisies growing out of my head. "It means just what it says. He left me."

"Let's think about this." I guided Emily into a chair. She needed a shot of sugar. "I'll get us some iced tea."

Emily rested her head on her forearms on the wooden table, and I set her glass out of elbow reach. "Have a sip of this."

"No, thanks." Her gentle voice, barely audible, showed her good manners, even in the face of adversity.

I grabbed cans of corn, peas, and water chestnuts and opened Emily's pantry door. Like theatre seats, all the cans stood in ascending order according to food groups, size, and color. All labels clearly visible. I thought of my own pantry, piled the cans in, and closed the door.

I heard a low whistle and turned to see Neil sitting on the island, swinging his legs. "Somebody should take lessons on organization." I angled my head toward the door and mouthed, "Go."

Emily lifted her head. "Today is February twenty-eighth."

February twenty-eighth…February twenty-eighth. My thoughts raced through data. *What was the significance of February twenty-eighth?* My eyes opened wide and froze. "Today's your anniversary." And I'd forgotten. *What kind of best friend was I? And what kind of sick asshole would dump his wife on their anniversary?* The same kind of asshole who would get caught cheating on his anniversary.

Another anniversary Armageddon. Dammit. I slapped the table with both hands. Up popped her head. I leaned in. "You want to go to the bank and clean out all your accounts?"

"I don't know what to do." Emily butted her head on the table.

I touched Emily's arm, and she lifted her head.

"I thought we were happy." Her red-rimmed eyes mirrored the defeat in her voice.

When I caught Neil, I adopted the idea of being blindsided; but I was not being honest. I saw signs. I just chose to ignore them. "He hasn't been acting any differently?"

Emily massaged her forehead with the heel of her hand. "That's what's so confusing."

I shoved Emily's glass within her grasp and took a sip from my own, looking over the rim. "No phone calls or late nights at work?"

Emily stopped rubbing her head. "You don't think?" Emily extended her hands in front of her face to physically ward off my insinuations. "Stop right there. I'd know if he were cheating on me."

I set my glass down hard. "I thought I'd know, too." And if I'd been paying attention, I might have.

"He cleaned out the attic and the basement. How alarmed should I have been?" Emily's comment reeked of sarcasm. She ran her hands over her face. "I'm sorry. I didn't mean to sound so hateful."

I gave her a curt head-bob. "I like it. Sounds kind of feisty."

Emily took a long sip. "He's been spending a lot of time on the computer. Oh, and last week he went off on Andrea when she told him she needed the deposit for cheerleading camp."

"Has he been to the doctor lately?" I dumped my ice down the drain.

"What're you suggesting?" Emily's knuckles went to her lips.

"Nothing. I promise." A serious diagnosis would explain his bizarre behavior.

Fear filled Emily's eyes. "What if he has cancer or a brain tumor?"

I put my glass into the dishwasher. "I don't think it's anything…physical."

"You think he's having some sort of mid-life crisis?" Emily pushed away from the table and trudged to the sink.

Neil wavered into view. "It's definitely some sort of crisis."

I turned away from Emily and made eye contact with Neil. If looks could exterminate pesky ghosts, Neil would have vaporized.

Emily bowed her head and clung to the edge of the sink. "What do I tell the kids?"

"You have two days. They won't be home until Sunday. Let's face telling the kids when the time comes. For now, wine—and lots of it."

Neil propped his hands on his airy hips. "What will that solve?"

Sheesh. How dense can he be? "You got a better idea?" I shouted at Neil. I cupped both hands over my big fat mouth to keep Emily from hearing my brain screaming *crap! Crap! Crap!*

Emily sank into a chair. She looked at me with dry, tired eyes. "No. I have no ideas."

I ran home to get shoes and two bottles of wine. As I placed the pinot noir for Emily and pinot grigio for me into a bag, I gave Neil a warning. "You don't belong, so do whatever you do to stay out of our way."

"You'll regret this tomorrow," Neil said.

"That's not your problem. You heard what I said." I ran out the back door and across the driveway.

Emily and I hunkered down in her family room with our liquid hors d'oeuvres, entrée, and dessert.

Neil slunk in and sat on the sofa between Emily and me. "This behavior is counterproductive. All you'll accomplish is a hangover."

I thrust my glass into Neil's face. "To a good night's sleep." We clinked our glasses on the end of his nose.

"I'm out of here," Neil said.

I tipped my glass to him. "Good."

Emily chugged the contents of her glass. "Yep. It's good."

Neil stopped at the door. "You'll regret this."

I gave Neil a look to get the heck out.

Emily refilled her glass and then motioned to mine. "Bottoms up."

"I'm savoring mine." I sipped the crisp, fruity elixir.

"Not tonight. Drink up." Emily held the bottle aloft, waiting to refill my glass.

Sacrificing the delicate flavor of my smooth, pinot grigio, I emptied my glass.

Emily poured me another generous serving and set the bottle on the coffee table. She cocked her head to the side, her eyes hazy and slack. "I have one question." She waggled one finger. "Why'd the jerk pick our anniversary to leave me?"

"Hmmm. Good question." Synapses flashed in brilliant philosophical bursts. May have been the wine on an empty stomach. "How do any of us choose when we make life-changing decisions? Did Reggie specifically choose his anniversary to dump you and the kids? Did Neil choose our anniversary to die? And is an anniversary different than a simple Tuesday or Thursday?" Amazed by the heightened clarity of my brain functions, pure knowledge flowed through my lips. "Is there ever a *good* time to maim and kill?"

Emily tapped the side of her wine glass with her French-manicured nail tips. "What about Christmas? He could have put the note in my stocking." Her slurred voice the antithesis of the sharp click, click, of her nails.

Whether her words were sarcastic or alcohol induced, I followed suit. "And you know, since he's so into using paper towel stationery, at Christmas, they make paper towels with little Santa Clauses along the edges."

"That would have been more imaginative than using a plain white select-a-size." Emily turned her glass upside down and shook it over her tongue, and then she put the glass to her eye and squinted into the crystal goblet. Emily let out a deep sigh and stared down into her empty glass. "You know, maybe an anniversary is as good as any time to break a heart."

"I don't think it requires any special day to break a heart. Neil broke mine long before I caught him."

She set down her glass. "Neil's been gone eight months. You're okay. Right?" Alcohol had rounded the edges of Emily's words, but the hope in them was unmistakable.

I threw hope right back at her. "Absolutely." Maybe I was getting better, or maybe I was lying. My fickle heart wouldn't make up its mind.

Emily sighed and lay down on the sofa, pulling the blanket over her head. I scrunched up my legs to fit on the short side of her sectional sofa. It was in the quiet times like these, waiting for sleep, words played over and over and over like a soundtrack caught in an endless loop. *Whatever happened to happily ever after?*

****

I woke up to a demolition derby inside my skull. Too bad the magic of wine is only temporary.

I kneaded my temples. "How's your head?"

"Doesn't hurt as much as my heart." Emily sat up and clutched her blanket with both hands. "I don't think I can survive this."

I stretched my neck to work out the couch-kinks. "Believe me. You'll survive."

Emily lowered her head and tugged the blanket tighter under her chin. "He could have prepared me. Left some breadcrumbs. Something."

"There are always signs. Is his computer password protected? We could go through his files and look for clues."

"His password is always the same." Emily stared at her wedding band. "Clues?"

"You ignored my advice, and now on top of Emily's troubles, she has a hangover." Neil's voice preceded his faded khakis.

Emily looked past me, focusing on nothing I could see. "What do I do now?" There was no question mark in her words. They weren't meant for me. But I knew those words all too well.

Emily's resignation mushroomed, choking us in a cloud of despair. I gripped her hand, and her eyes overflowed. I had to save her from drowning. Through my alcohol-headache haze, I flipped my emotional lever from pity party to evasive action. Rather than face the reality of the moment, I engaged emotional dodgeball. "We can cut Reggie's face out of your family pictures." I gave Neil a sticky smile. "Wish I had."

Emily's eyes came into focus. "I can't do that."

"What about drawing donkey ears on a few snapshots?"

"This is beneath you, Libby," Neil said.

Emily twisted the gold band on her left hand. "I know you're trying to help." Dark, oily clumps of hair strayed across her face and emphasized the dark circles under her eyes. From head to toe, Emily's petite five-foot frame screamed surrender.

"Where's my cocky drinking partner from last night?" I touched my toes to stretch my back. Big mistake. Blood rammed the top of my head like an eighteen-wheeler. I grabbed the sofa and waited for the pain to pass.

Emily curled into a fetal position and pulled the blanket over her head.

I couldn't sit idly and watch her suffer. I needed to come up with a diversion. Where was the mental clarity I possessed last night? I paced behind the sofa, squeezing my temples, hoping for relief and insight.

I climbed over the sofa and pulled away her blanket. "What about tossing his clothes in the yard? A therapist would call it a catharsis."

"It would be like I'm cleaning him out of my life." Despair drifted on a sea of sadness in her eyes, and Emily was treading water. "I don't want to clean him out of my life."

I wished I could clean Neil out of my life by tossing his clothes. "It's your call. But I need coffee." I pulled her upright, linked her arm in mine, and led her to the kitchen. Emily picked up her phone and stopped short.

She seized my arm. "Reggie called. I didn't hear the phone ring, did you?"

We sat down and listened to the voice of the man who had left her only twenty-four hours earlier.

"Emily, it's me. I know you probably don't want to talk to me, and I don't blame you. I don't know why I called. I guess I wanted to make sure you're okay. I, um...I can pick up the kids at the church tomorrow. And don't worry about the lawn. I'll take care of it next week. If you don't want to be there, I understand. I guess you can go to Libby's. I didn't fix the shower drain in the guest bathroom. Sorry. Emily, if you need anything, anything at all, call me at my parents'. I—I guess I'll hang up now."

Emily's small frame shrank smaller and smaller as Reggie's tortured voice rambled on and on, like he was reaching through the wire to cling to her as long as possible. There was more to his leaving. The defeat and agony in his voice made me feel sorry for the bum.

Deep creases formed between Emily's soft brown eyes, but she wouldn't take her eyes off her phone.

I got up and went to the sink where she'd left the flowers she'd bought at the grocery store. From the drawer, I took scissors, cut the green rubber band holding the bunch together, and began snipping the ends. Reggie was Emily's green rubber band. She loved and grieved with such passion it made me question the quality of my beliefs about Neil and about myself. It's just that after being married so long, jobs and kids had diluted our passion to the long-term-married level. It didn't mean I didn't love Neil. I'd loved him as long as I could remember. Until the night I caught him with Sheri. The flowers trembled in my hands. He cheated on me. And he died. I should have been sadder. I should have been destroyed. Like Emily.

I opened the cabinet under the sink and took out a vase. "You need to pull yourself together before the kids get home." I turned on the tap and filled the crystal container.

Emily stood. "What time is it?"

I placed the flowers into the vase. "It's close to noon. Why don't you soak in a hot tub?"

Emily placed her palms flat on the table and pulled

herself up to a crouch. "How do you do it? Stay strong for your kids day after day?"

I checked out the ceiling. No Neil. "Being pissed off all the time helps." I yanked the flowers out of the vase and dumped the whole bouquet into the trash. "My cheating husband died and left me to raise the kids." I dried my hands on Reggie's Dear Jill letter. "All my kids have is me, so falling apart is not an option. I fight like heck to keep the negative stuff compartmentalized. But the bottom line is I don't have a choice. And now, neither do you." I grabbed both of her shoulders and made her stand up straight. "You get up in the morning, and you push through the haze—for your kids." I tugged at the stringy mess she'd shoved behind her ears. "First thing you need to do is wash your hair and put on make-up. Then you smile. You smile when you make the kids pancakes, you smile when you carpool, you smile at the cashiers at the grocery store. You act as if everything is okay. Because sometimes that's all you can do is act."

Feral fear shone in Emily's eyes. "I can't do this. I'm not strong like you."

I pulled her into a hug. "Focus on the big picture. If you show your kids hopelessness, it'll spread faster than a bad cold. If you need to fall apart, do it with me. But act positive with the kids. One day at a time. One foot in front of the other. Who knows? If you act as if everything is okay long enough, maybe everything will be."

"I'll try. I really will." Emily pulled away, fidgeted with her hair, and attempted a smile. "Think I'll start with a shower."

Reggie had reduced Emily to a mumbling mess.

Men. Dammit. I wanted to kick a man. Any man. I gritted my teeth and stalked home. My soul sensor detected Neil following behind me. "What could make Reggie walk out on his family?"

Chapter 10
Time to Purge

I left Emily's house, and barbs of sunlight stabbed my brain. Neil kept close on my heels soaking in the sun. "Tried to warn you."

I used my hand as a visor and headed home. "You think there's a woman involved?"

"He never seemed like the type."

"Neither did you." I held my head, trying to keep the pain inside.

Neil followed me upstairs to our room. "Their problem is their business. You don't need to get involved."

"So now you're telling me what I need?" I opened the door to his double-decker walk-in closet. Cobwebs radiated from the corners and met in the middle. I fanned them out of my way. Since the accident, his closet had felt off-limits. Boxes and boxes of shoes were stacked on the shelf. "How many pairs of shoes does a man need?"

Neil sat protectively on the top of his stack of shoe boxes. "Don't give me grief about shoes. It takes two closets for yours."

"Women are supposed to have lots of shoes." I thumbed through racks of pants on hangers. "And how many freaking pairs of khaki slacks do you have? Look at this. One, two, three…" I counted. "You have twelve pairs of khakis."

I grabbed all twelve pairs—hangers and all.

"What are you doing?" Neil dove at my head.

"Watch me." I walked through the bedroom and juggled hangers to free a hand to open the glass doors that led onto the balcony."

Neil tried to block my path. "Libby, take a deep breath. This is not like you."

I pushed through him and chunked the whole load over the wooden rails. I'd been acting as if everything was going to be fine for the last eight months. I needed a jump-start to hurry it along. Hangers and slacks clattered to the ground. Yes! Double fist pump.

Neil's aura vibrated, moving the air around him. His skin tone glowed normal and his irises grew a deep brown. "You've lost your mind!"

Fist pump forgotten. "You're not transparent...you're...almost solid. Real." Possibility spiked my heart rate. Then I remembered. Neil was gone. "But you're not real." Sadness bound my heart in its cold hands. I stumbled backward until the mattress touched the backs of my legs and collapsed.

Tears streamed. Silently at first and then the skies opened. I covered my face with my hands and wailed. "Dammit...Neil." I strained to get words out between sobs. "Emily's...so hurt. She can...barely think...or even carry on...a conversation...Sadness is choking the life out of her." Waves of sobs battered my body.

Neil sat on the bed beside me. "Emily's reacting normally. But why are you so distraught?"

"It's me." I hiccupped, "If it's so normal, why wasn't I devastated?" I hiccupped again. "I want what Emily has. Pain from loving not hating."

Neil slumped. "I don't know what to say."

I rubbed my face with my shirt. "You can start by explaining why you chose that redheaded bimbo over me."

Neil ran his hand across the back of his neck. "I didn't choose her over you. And she's not a bimbo."

"How dare you defend that home-wrecker!" The muscles in my body coiled tight, ready to strike.

"Do we have to talk about this?"

"Yes. We. Do. And no disappearing. I want to know how you could throw me away for a midlife fling."

"It just happened." Neil faded to his new normal pastel self.

Heat burned my cheeks. "It just happened? A zit just happens. A toothache just happens."

"I did it. I'm guilty. Isn't that enough?"

"What would a twenty-eight-year-old want with a forty-year-old married man with two kids and a mortgage?"

"I'm only thirty-seven."

"Oh, please." I walked to the window.

"It was lightning." His words were lyrical and intimate.

I swung around to face him. "What was lightning?"

"Her touch," Neil whispered.

I hugged my chest and fought to breathe. "In nineteen years, I never felt lightning."

"I know." Neil raised his head. "Please let this go."

Nausea hit me. "I have to know if you loved her."

"It had nothing to do with love." Neil's eyes pleaded with me as they dulled to gray. "Libby, you were my first love and my only love."

I banged my palms against my head. "Then why?"

"I was weak. I was stupid. She was available." Neil faced me. "You're the only one I'll ever love. Always."

I shoved through his chest. "There is no more *always* for us." I went back into his closet and loaded my arms with suits, shirts, work-out clothes, anything I could grab.

Neil followed me into his closet. "I'm so sorry. I wish I could fix things."

"I asked for the truth." I carried my mountain of designer apparel through the glass doors. "If you want to fix things, leave." They still smelled like my summer rain fabric softener. Muscles in my throat constricted and sparked a burning sensation behind my eyes. I marched to the railing and tossed over my load.

"Mom! What are you doing?" Reagan's voice pinged my radar.

I looked over the railing. *Oh, crap.* I felt light-headed and clutched the rail. Reagan and Trey stared up at me, backpacks in hand, standing in a sea of Neil's clothes strewn haphazardly among purple and white pansies.

Neil crossed his arms and gave me a satisfied grin. "Let's see you dodge this."

I put on my game face. "What are you guys doing home early?"

"Wait'll you hear, Mom. The youth minister broke his leg," Trey said.

"You guys are just in time to help me clean out your dad's closet." I gestured to them with both hands to come on up.

I heard the kids' footsteps charging up the stairs. I compressed about twenty hangers of Neil's shirts and wrestled them off the metal rod.

Trey charged into the closet. "What are you doing with Dad's stuff?" The panic in his voice warned me to dial down my enthusiasm.

"Mom, what are you doing?" Reagan's voice sounded too calm and too controlled.

I held the shirts over my head, trying to muffle my voice. "Cleaning out your dad's closet."

"Why today?" Reagan asked.

I maneuvered past them. "The homeless men's mission needs these."

Trey pressed close to the wall to let me pass. "You sound funny."

Reagan stood in my path. "Have you been crying?"

My camouflage didn't hide my nasally twang. "The people at the homeless shelter called, and they have people in desperate need."

Reagan took a step toward me. "Why are you throwing them in the yard?"

"Yeah, Mom. It looks weird," Trey said, taking a stance beside his sister.

Neil floated between Trey and Reagan, and attempted to put his arms around their shoulders. "How do you respond to that?"

I lowered the mound of shirts and beamed my supermom smile. "It's like this. We can pile these clothes in bags up here and have to carry the heavy bags down, or we can toss the clothes over and stuff the bags down there. Sounds logical to me."

I hustled by them, and they followed me out to the deck. I stopped by the railing.

"It kinda makes sense," Trey said to Reagan.

I balanced my load on the wooden rail. "Want to

help?"

Reagan slouched into a chair. "I can't do this. It's like we're throwing him away."

"It makes me too sad." Trey's voice wavered.

I laid the pile of shirts on a deck chair. "Come with me." I led them back into Neil's closet.

I stretched my arms to encompass the enormity of Neil's closet. "Look at all these great clothes. There are homeless men who have to wear the same dirty, stinky, worn-out clothes every day. Think how good they'd feel in this soft, warm shirt." I rubbed the sleeve of a perfectly pressed white shirt. "And many don't even own a winter coat."

I sat down cross-legged under the newly vacated space, my back against the wall. Trey sat on one side and Reagan on the other. I took their hands. "It makes me sad, too." Neil sat on the shelf with his shoes, and I looked at him as I spoke. "Your dad doesn't need these anymore. We're getting rid of his things, not him."

I heard Trey sniff, and he turned his head and swiped at his eyes.

I gathered our hands into a cluster. My children. My strength. "Your dad's not in these clothes. He's inside you, and he always will be."

Reagan let the tears roll down her cheeks. "Sometimes I forget and think 'I'll ask Dad when he gets home.'"

Trey sniffed again and wiped his eyes and nose on his sleeve.

"He's gonna miss everything. Me getting my license, senior prom, graduation." Tears puddled in her eyes. "Who's going to walk me down the aisle when I get married?"

"I will," Trey said.

The sincerity in my sweet son's voice fractured the hard coating I'd built around my heart, and when his sister wrapped one arm around me and the other around her brother and squeezed—my fortress cracked into smithereens.

Reagan touched Trey's arm. "I want you and Mom to walk me down the aisle."

The three of us sat in silence. Instead of feeling cramped or confined, sitting in Neil's closet felt like being hugged.

Reagan broke the spell. "Dad would want us to care for the homeless."

"Before you give everything away, can I have something of Dad's?" Trey asked.

"Of course, sweetie." I pulled him close. "I think you both should choose something."

"I want the Alabama hoodie he bought when we went to the Alabama-Auburn game." Trey blurted out his choice as if afraid someone would call it first.

I nudged my daughter. "Reagan?"

Reagan laid her head on my shoulder. "I don't want any of his clothes."

"Make sure Trey gets my grandfather's pocket watch, and Reagan gets my grandmother's sapphire ring."

"Great choices." Uh, oh. The kids looked at me.

"What's so great about a hoodie?" Reagan asked.

"I must have been thinking out loud. Your dad wants, I mean wanted you to have his grandmother's sapphire ring."

"What about me?" Trey asked.

I patted his hand. "He wanted you to have his

grandfather's pocket watch."

Trey's body wagged like a pup catching a sniff of bacon. "Can I have it now? Where is it?"

I smoothed his hair to the side. "I have the ring and the watch in my jewelry box. But we have to clean up in here first."

Trey scrambled to his feet. "Come on, Reagan. Mom can chunk the stuff over, and we'll bag it."

Neil braced his arms on the doorjamb. "If you think getting rid of me will be as easy as getting rid of my possessions, think again."

Chapter 11
Once Upon a Time

At the end of Emily's driveway, I sat and tied my shoes. My cleaning marathon hadn't purged my demons. My attempt at renewal had left me empty. I tightened the laces to a fraction below tourniquet tight. I needed to get out of the house, away from the mountain of black plastic bags plump and still waiting for the Goodwill truck. Emily suggested we resume our daily walk around the lake. Routine would be welcome.

"Can we call a truce?" The sunlight shone through my crisply-dressed, dead husband.

Great. Ruin the moment. I closed my eyes and did neck stretches. "You need some sort of alert mechanism to let me know when you're coming to annoy me."

"We need to find a way to peacefully coexist until I figure out how to…to…fix things. I promise to stay out of your way, and I won't butt in unless you ask." Neil sounded contrite.

"I'll think about it. Now go away."

"Who are you talking to?" Emily asked.

My eyes flew open mid-stretch. I didn't hear her walk up. "Just thinking out loud. You ready?" I stood and dusted off my rear.

It was good to see Emily putting some effort into getting back into our normal routine. Only two weeks ago Reggie left his infamous note. I knew the wound was still fresh, but I wanted her to take charge. Grow a backbone. Emily wanted to mope around and wait for Reggie to come to his senses.

I took off, walking more briskly than our usual snail's pace.

Emily caught up and matched me step for step. "Something bothering you?"

I slowed my pace. "The male species."

"That include your dearly departed husband?" Emily and I fell into a regular rhythm. "I didn't understand how you could hate Neil…until…."

"Until Reggie left you." I wanted to do an eye roll, but refrained. "Another thing I find helpful is hate. I find hate to be liberating."

"Liberating? You don't look free to me." Emily swung her arms in time with her feet.

I pumped my arms to match her cadence. "I'm not sitting home waiting for my husband to decide if he wants me."

"Let's not go there. Our situations are totally different. I promised to give him some time." Her tone let me know I was crossing over into her business.

But I couldn't stop myself. "What if a year from now he's still asking for more time?"

Emily held up a hand and slowed to a walk. "Ignoring your sticks and stones. I love Reggie. And I want him, and I want love. It's what we all want."

I matched her gait and scanned my surroundings for shimmers of creased khakis. "I want passion. I want heat. I want sex." We'd stopped walking, and I looked at Emily. "Remember the early days when Reggie's touch set you on fire? Well, I want to throw gasoline on that bonfire."

"I get it! I get it!" Emily fanned her face. "Whew."

"Neil found it with Sheri. It's my turn." Jealousy scored my heart with a rusty hacksaw.

"I get it. You want passion. But you know what makes passion burn like a bonfire? Love. When you find love again, you'll find passion."

I resumed walking. What if I never found love again? Would I be doomed to live without passion? "Tell you what. Until love finds me, I'll keep hating."

Emily stayed even with me, focusing forward. "Are you familiar with Elizabeth Kubler-Ross's stages of grief?"

"I studied it in psychology class. Why?" I asked.

"I think we're both going through the stages of her grief cycle."

I set my tone range to minimal sarcasm. "Reggie's not dead."

Emily puffed out a sigh. "The end of a marriage is like a death."

Our shoes tapped against the planks of the wooden bridge, and I stopped. "Death of a marriage?" I hadn't thought of it that way. "Maybe you have a point."

Emily took a few steps and paused. "If Reggie were dead, I wouldn't be expecting to see him, and it would be easier to accept that he's gone." Emily paled and slapped her hand over her mouth. "That sounded terrible. I don't want Reggie to die! I'm just saying that his desertion is painful because I still see him."

She couldn't fathom a life without Reggie because he's still alive, and I couldn't heal because Neil won't move on. "So if we find someone to whack Reggie, your problems will be solved?"

"Do you always have to make light of my

problems?" She sped up. "I thought you were my best friend."

I jogged to catch up. "Sorry. I was being insensitive." I wasn't sorry. Instead of clinging to hope and rationalizing her behavior as stages of grief, I thought she should make an appointment with an attorney.

She swished her hand like shooing a stubborn fly. "Why do I bother explaining anything you?"

"Dammit, Emily. I hate Neil for what he did, but I hate Reggie for what he keeps doing."

Emily waggled two fingers. "Stage two is anger. That's where you're stuck." She flipped her head and took off.

Neil floated into view beside me. "I agree with Emily. You have anger issues."

"I have anger issues?" I yelled at Neil. "And whose fault is that?"

My caustic comment was meant for Neil, not her. A look of bewilderment froze on Emily's face. "I'm not saying you don't have a right to blame Neil. I'm saying you're stuck."

"Isn't denial the next stage?" Neil asked.

I glared at him. "What about denial?"

Emily answered, "You skipped right past that one."

"I'm not stuck anywhere. I like stage two. Being angry is energizing." I turned away from Neil and caught up with Emily. "Stage three is bargaining," I said, "and I'll make you a bargain. Join me in my self-improvement plan, and we'll work on toning and tightening up. Make some wardrobe changes, and maybe even try a new hairstyle. And then if you still want Reggie, I'll shut up."

"We're looking for two different things. You want to be bold and daring because you think you've missed out on something. I just want Reggie."

"I want a man to make me feel desirable again. Is that asking too much?"

Emily shook her head. "Maybe that's the path for you. But I'm not ready to start on a new future. I haven't given up on the old one."

"I think you're in denial, Emily. Maybe doing something, *anything*, will help you get out of your rut. Or maybe it'll spark Reggie into action." I needed a partner to implement my self-improvement plan, and Emily needed a Vulcan mind-meld, but a diversion would have to do.

Our walk ended where it began—at the end of Emily's driveway.

"Maybe exercise will help. But I won't bash Reggie." Emily opened her mailbox and took out a pile of catalogs and envelopes.

I sat on the grassy apron beside the road. "Okay. I'm going to work out a full plan for us to get in shape and get out there."

"You can get out there all you want. I'm just along for the ride." Emily stood by my mailbox. "You realize that you're sitting on the side of the road, right?"

"I just want to rest a minute. Besides, I own this." I pulled my knees to my chest and patted the ground beside me.

Emily smiled and sat.

A low rumble reached my ears and vibrated all the way down to my bottom planted on the ground.

Emily cocked her head to the side.

"Sounds like a sick muffler." I scrambled up to get

a better view of the curve. "Or a Sherman tank."

Emily joined me. "Sounds like we need to call the EPA to me."

Neil came into sight. "A 1980's Pontiac Bonneville like your Uncle Rollyn's."

A dirt-colored vehicle long as a city block slowly rounded the curve. When the young driver saw us, he tugged his baseball cap lower and hit the gas. Rusty polka dots etched into the chrome of the once shiny bumper were half hidden by black, oily smoke billowing in its wake.

Emily held her nose. "Phew. I hope those fumes aren't toxic. Have you ever seen that car before?"

"Not in several decades." I'm no alarmist, but the guy and his car creeped me out. "Am I imagining things or did he hide his face when he passed us?"

"I couldn't see very clearly through the exhaust cloud." Emily rifled through her mail. "I'm sure he's working for someone around the lake or else he couldn't have gotten through the gate."

"Maybe we should call someone," I said.

Emily started up her driveway. "You going to call Dell?" She giggled.

The president of our Property Owners' Association Dell Farmer—whose parents had a twisted sense of humor—didn't inherit their wit. He took his job seriously. One time a neighbor reported littering, and Dell called the police and asked them to send the CSI Unit to analyze the litter and find its owner. Dell couldn't understand why they hung up on him. "Calling Dell would be my last option."

Emily shuffled through her mail as she walked. "I think I'll go check on the kids."

"I'm going around back and sit on the pier for a little while. Want to join me?"

"I'll join you," Neil said.

"Don't bother," I answered Neil with a ventriloquist smile and waved at Emily.

She called across the pavement. "I'll make sure things are okay over here and see you in five minutes."

I glared at Neil. "Don't you need to go look for the Golden Gates?"

"It's *Pearly* gates. And I think I'll hang out here and learn about this new plan of yours."

****

Neil stood by the water's edge. "I've always loved this place."

Though transparent, I could make out Neil's uniform: light blue shirt, khakis, and brown shoes. Or maybe my mind had programmed the image into my memory.

"What about that not butting in plan you mentioned?" I asked.

"I never regretted buying this place from my folks." Neil ignored my comment. "Only twenty minutes from downtown with all the amenities of the country. And the new security gate is an added bonus."

The security gate sequestered the twenty houses around the fifty-acre lake and was designed to limit access to non-residents. Like the man in the old brown car. How'd he get in? And why? "We wouldn't have liked the gate when we were kids."

Neil chuckled. "Emily's here."

Her footsteps sounded hollow on the wooden dock.

Emily sat next to me and propped her feet up on the chaise. "All the kids are at my house."

"They'll be fine for an hour." I leaned back. "I love it when there's no wind, and the lake is smooth like that. Reflections are so clear it makes it hard to tell what's real and what's not."

"Lucky you. You grew up here," Emily said.

"Pre-clothes dryer days weren't so picturesque. Think clotheslines running across these backyards like power lines. Then imagine flapping sheets and stiff blue jeans."

"We had clothes lines in our backyards, too. But in Iowa, if we hung clothes out in winter, they'd be lost in the snow until spring," Emily said.

"Guess Alabama seemed like a foreign country. Especially the language."

"Kids are kids," she said. "We spent our days outside, and just like you our curfew came with the fireflies." Emily chuckled behind her hand. "The language. Even after two decades, I still can't call a garden hose a hose pipe."

I kicked her chair. "Makes me sad that the kids won't get to experience the freedom we did. Times are different."

"I'd never consider leaving my doors unlocked like we did as kids," she said.

I shook off the reminder of the old car we saw today. "When you were a kid, did you camp out in your backyard?"

"We never made it through the night." Emily laughed and the tight lines in her face disappeared.

"We'd throw sheets or a bed spread over our swing set and make a tent." I giggled. "My two sisters and I tried, but Neil, Eli, and Jesse would sneak over and throw rocks at us or make noises to scare us."

Emily lay back and closed her eyes. "Times have changed."

I rubbed my hands over my face. "Yep. Back then husbands and wives stayed together and worked through the good and bad and even the dull and boring."

"Once upon a time…when the good guys always won, and everybody lived happily ever after." Emily's voice wilted on the happily ever after.

"Why are you letting Reggie decide your happily ever after?" I banged my hands on the arm rests. "It's time to shake things up."

Emily gave me a cautious look. "How much shaking up are we talking about?"

"Well, I've been thinking. If I want passion, romance, and desire, I guess I need a date."

"A date? I wouldn't know how to start, if I wanted to. And I don't want to."

"I found tons of books on dating. And the magazines. You won't believe."

Emily snorted. "How different could it be?"

"Get ready for shock and awe." I pulled a magazine and several books from a plastic bag I'd stashed under my chaise lounge. "Let me show you what I found at the book store."

Emily leaned in and question marks filled her eyes. "You actually found instruction books on dating?"

"I could have spent a whole paycheck in that one section. Look at this one. "How to Get a Date if You're Courting Forty.'" I found comfort in the sheer number of books on dating.

"Let me guess. It's a new genre: *Sex and Seniors*."

"Sarcasm doesn't become you, Emily. I'm the

smart-ass." I laid the books aside and reached down. "Peruse this." I tossed her a magazine.

I watched Emily read the teasers on the cover and flip through the pages. When she opened to the page I had marked with a yellow sticky note, her mouth opened, and the whites of her eyes were as glossy as the pages she read.

"Did you read this? Can you believe they're teaching you how to, to, *you know*. And with diagrams of where to put your mouth. Is this pornography?"

I leaned back in my chair and crossed my arms firmly across my chest. "I told you we were out of touch. But I have a plan."

I lowered my voice in case my husband's ghostly ears were listening. "If I can get a date, I will likely, well hopefully, have sex. But I can't let any man see me naked until I lose some weight." I looked down and sucked in my stomach. "And get a tan."

"Whatever you say." Emily turned the page and continued reading.

"I say let's kick it into high gear. Tomorrow we start jogging around the lake, rain or shine." A plan of action. "No more wussing out because it's too hot or too cold. And I don't want to hear, 'I'm too tired.'"

"Uh huh, sure…" Emily looked up. "Can I take this home?"

Chapter 12
Sweet Embrace

We met at our usual spot—Emily's driveway. For five minutes, I stretched and jogged in place feeling strong and confident in my baby blue jogging suit with matching shoes. Emily sauntered up in paint-splattered yoga pants, t-shirt, and her once white Keds.

Emily did a weak side stretch. "Whoa. I haven't seen that jogging outfit since you took it out of the box."

Neil bought it for Christmas several years ago. I'd never worn it because it was too *matched*—too serious for a casual walk around the lake. "It's a *jogging* suit, Emily. We're going *jogging*? Aren't those the shoes you wear to work in the yard? Do they have an arch support?" My sarcasm fell on deaf ears. Emily's enthusiasm from our last meeting forgotten.

She hitched up her pants. "I couldn't get off the phone with my sister-in-law and didn't have time to find my running shoes or dig out an accessorized ensemble. Won't matter, you'll be eating my dust." Emily dropped to a three-point stance and took off down the driveway.

My baby blue running shoes slapped the pavement. "Dusting off your old track skills?"

Emily caught my arm. "Think we're supposed to pace ourselves. At this rate we'll blow out before we get to the bridge."

A burning stitch stabbed my side. I clutched my hand to my body, dragged my left foot, and hobbled. Five minutes into my first jog and the left side of my body was paralyzed with pain, and I couldn't take in enough air to satisfy my lungs. Emily thought I was kidding. The tears convinced her.

I bent over double. "I need to sit down."

We staggered to the rest area. "I guess it's true what they say about spring chickens."

I was too winded to reply orally and raised my middle finger.

"Now, now. Merely an observation," Emily said. We dumped our aching bodies on a bench under a cluster of bare crepe myrtle bushes. Winter had stripped them clean, but spring would restart the cycle.

The pain in my side diminished enough to form words. "I think we need to modify our benchmarks. Losing weight might be too hard. Maybe I'll just keep my clothes on."

Emily removed a shoe and shook out a small stone. "Or turn off the lights."

****

Adjustment is part of smart planning. Jogging campaign abandoned. Walking would have to suffice. For immediate gratification, we got a haircut and highlights and then bought two boxes of tooth-whitening strips.

I threw the bag into the back seat, and an idea hit me. "When was the last time you went to Victoria's Secret?"

"You mean this decade?" Emily wasn't being sarcastic.

I turned the key in the ignition. "To enter the dating scene, sexy underwear is a must."

"If *you're* entering the dating scene," Emily corrected.

"I haven't had x-rated undergarments since my lingerie shower. Want to go see how much things have changed in the last twenty years?"

"We had a couples' shower, and the theme was *outdoor entertaining*. Reggie loved it." Emily clicked her seat belt.

"At least barbeque accessories aren't embarrassing. At my shower, my mom almost fainted. Heck, I almost fainted." I merged into traffic. "It's a shame to be this close and not at least check it out."

"I'd love to check out their things, and who'll know?" Emily giggled. "Did you wear that stuff?"

"Every last thing. Even the edible panties," I said.

She fanned her cheeks. "You're kidding, right?"

"What do you think?" I changed lanes and slowed to a crawl behind a line of cars.

Emily took a lipstick from her purse, lowered the visor, and painted her lips. "You were wild and crazy."

At one time Neil and I were both a little wild and crazy. "Guess we got lulled into ordinary." I turned into a parking spot.

We strutted through the mall with a single-minded quest. We smelled our destination before we saw it. A heavenly scent of femininity lured us across the threshold into that magic realm known as Victoria's Secret. A sales clerk younger than the bra I wore greeted us. "How may I help you ladies today?"

Her dazzling smile sidetracked me. "Your teeth are so white. Do you bleach?"

Emily elbowed me. "You can't ask her that."

"Oh, I don't mind." The young sales associate displayed her sparkling white orthodontic marvel. "I've been using tooth whitening strips for about a week, and you're the first person to notice."

I gave an unbleached smile to our new young friend. "Actually, we bought whitening strips, too. Today in fact."

Emily interrupted our tooth conversation and cut to the chase. "Great teeth, but we need your help.... uh...." Emily didn't have her glasses on, so she practically put her face on the young girl's chest to read her name tag. "Uh....Tiffany."

"That's why I'm here," Tiffany said. "Would you like to start at the top and work your way down, or vice versa?"

"Let's start at the top," I said.

Tiffany's eyes twinkled and her smile dazzled. I had to turn away. "Let me show you our Secret Embrace Bra. It's our best seller."

According to Tiffany, the combination of underwires and padding would transform our breasts from mediocre to magical. And for panties, thongs were the only way to go. So we grabbed bras and matching thongs of every color. Arms loaded with our treasures, we followed Tiffany to adjoining fitting rooms—all the way in the back. Tiffany was a sweetheart, but we sent her away. We didn't want our young, nubile friend in the dressing room for our transformation from ordinary moms to love goddesses.

I tried on my Secret Embrace bra first. My breasts stuck out so far I couldn't see my feet. That hadn't happened since my second pregnancy. But they definitely looked perky. Very perky. "I wonder if boobs can be too perky," I mused aloud.

"Not in my book." Neil sashayed around my fitting room.

I stomped my foot. "Get away!" I hissed the words between my teeth.

"Aw, come on, Libby. This is the most entertainment I've had since…well…since…a while."

I wagged my finger in his face and whispered. "If you want a truce, you'll leave right now. And I'd better not see a single fluttery line."

"I can provide a second opinion." His pleading came through his colorless face.

"You," I aimed my index finger at his face, "out!"

His form fizzled like a dying sparkler. I checked my dressing room and poked my head out the door to make sure I didn't see any telltale signs of Neil. I hitched up my self-confidence before dropping my pants and trying on the matching black thong.

"Libby, come quick!" The alarm in Emily's voice sent me to high alert, and I ran into her dressing room. "Can you believe these?" Her eyes glistened as she gently caressed her new bosoms. "I have cleavage." Emily's modest breasts rose high and firm in her Secret Embrace bra.

"Ooooo, nice. You need one in every color." I spoke in a hushed tone. Tiffany was right. Magic.

Emily turned sideways to admire her boobs in profile. Then she shifted her curiosity to my bra and then to my thong and started laughing.

I sucked in my gut. "I don't think I look bad."

"No, Libby, the bra looks great." Emily tried to explain but snorted and pointed at my thong. "The crotch is on the side!"

"I thought they felt funny." I looked down at Emily's thong. Laughter spewed out, and I sank to the floor and put my hand over my mouth. I tried to breathe but I was sucking laughs down my throat. I pointed at her undies.

Emily snorted and plunged down beside me. "I have mine on wrong, too!"

We sat in the floor with our perky boobs and cackled. "I'll have to hide all my new undies," Emily said. "If my daughter sees these, she'll tell my mother."

I strained to get to my feet. "You're forty years old, for goodness sake."

Emily stood and re-aligned her thong. "You talk big, but you'll be hiding yours, too."

I snuck back into my dressing room. "Let's get out of here. I…uh…I need to stop at the hardware store for a furnace filter."

Our little field trip brought out the old Emily, and we brainstormed places to hide our new underwear. Everything was cool until I turned into Home Depot's parking lot.

"Stop!" Emily screamed.

I slammed on the brakes. "What is it?"

Emily's face was void of color. "Don't ask. Just get out of here fast."

And then I saw him. Reggie was helping a lady put something into her car. I hit the accelerator and the car lurched forward. The tires squealed out of the parking lot.

Emily's face was the color of Neil's. "Put your head between your knees and breathe."

Her hand trembled as she took a notebook from her

purse. "Don't worry about me. I'm fine." She scribbled on the page.

"Reggie was putting that woman's purchases into her car." Neil said.

"Why would he do that?" I asked.

"If I didn't know better, I'd think Reggie worked there," he said.

"That's impossible," I answered.

Emily stared at me. "Who are you talking to?"

"Shit! I can't take this anymore." I saw a children's park about fifty yards ahead, and swerved into the parking lot stopping beside a picnic table. No kids or parents in sight. "Get out of the car." I left the door open and stormed over to the picnic table.

Emily followed me like a man on death row.

"Hurry up." I said, pointing at the bench. "Sit." I propped my hands on my hips. "Dammit, I'm tired of this. Emily, Neil's a ghost and he's standing beside you."

She whirled her head from side to side so fast her eyes jiggled.

I held my hands up to calm her. "Before you freak out, let me explain. I tried to tell you before, but you thought I was crazy." I pressed my hands down on her shoulders until she sat on the picnic bench. "Look at me. Do I look crazy? Have I done anything to make you think I'm a crazy mother, a crazy teacher, or a crazy person?"

Emily kept her eyes riveted to mine, gingerly nodding her head at appropriate times.

I sat beside her and bumped her shoulder. "I need you to believe me."

She gave me a weak smile. "I want to believe you.

I do. It's just…so…" She swallowed. "Does he look and sound the same? Any…" she tapped her back, "wings?"

"Oh, please. He's no angel. And yes, he looks the same. Same khakis and same blue shirt. Just transparent."

Emily did a one hundred and eighty degree sweep. "So is he…dead?"

I puffed out a long sigh. "Of course he's dead. But for some reason he's stuck here. Stuck to me."

Emily looked skeptical. "Libby, you're my best friend, and I trust you. But can you understand why it's a little hard to believe Neil's a ghost?"

I massaged my neck. What could I do to convince her? I looked at Neil. "Help me."

Emily put her hand on my arm. "How can I help?"

"Not to you. To him!" I directed her attention at the picnic table where Neil sat on a pillow of air.

"What do you want me to do?" Neil asked. "She's not going to believe you."

I got up and paced in front of him. "Tell me something only she knows."

Neil crossed his arms over his chest. "I'm not doing this."

I stopped in front of him and aimed my finger at his nose. "I swear if you don't help me, I'll dump your ashes into the toilet and flush."

Neil rose and filled the space in front of me. "Don't threaten me. You promised—"

I leaned in close. Close enough to touch nose to nose. "Yeah, well, you promised to be faithful till death do us part. It's called payback."

Neil inspected his cuticles. "Emily wrote the

131

woman's tag number in her notebook."

I blurted out. "Neil said you wrote that woman's tag number in your notebook."

Emily didn't look convinced. "You could be guessing."

"Tell her the tag number is 1A54231," Neil said.

"Neil said the number is 1A54231."

Emily dug the notebook out of her purse. She looked down and flipped through several pages. She gasped and looked at me. "How'd he know that?"

I rubbed her arm. "He watched you write it."

Emily's eyes burst open, and her hands smacked her cheeks. "That explains things. Your odd comments and some of the harsh things you've said that hurt my feelings. I thought it was the anger thing." She searched the area around her. "Can anyone else see him?"

She believed me. She. Believed. Me. The kink in my neck relaxed, and my entire body unwound. I had an ally. "Just me."

Emily hugged me. "I'm sorry I didn't believe you." She pushed me away and felt the air. "Is he close?"

I pulled her arms down. "You can't feel him."

Neil laughed. "Your disclosure is quite the show."

"I'm not going for funny," I said.

Emily looked at me. "Did I say something funny?"

I huffed. "Not you, Neil. He thinks this whole thing is a joke."

Emily grabbed my hands. "Ask him if he knows when Reggie's coming home."

I squeezed the bridge of my nose. "He's a ghost. Not a fortune teller."

"So he can't fly,"—Emily flailed her hands and arms in squiggly motions—"or whatever he does, over my house?"

"No, Emily. He's attached to me."

Neil coughed. "That's not actually correct."

"What are you saying?" A funky feeling prickled my skin.

Emily stayed at my side. "Are you talking to me or Neil?"

"I'm talking to him." I trained my glare at my dead husband. "Explain."

"I've been exploring boundaries. And I'm not attached to you per se," he said.

"So what are you attached to *per se*?" I couldn't resist a little sarcasm.

Emily shook my arm. "What's he saying? Does he know anything about Reggie?"

I raised my hand to shush Emily, and turned to Neil.

"I went to Emily's house the day Reggie left and watched him write the note. And I've been able to move freely as far as Jesse's old street."

Resentment welled-up in my throat, and I wanted to gag. "Why are you just now telling me this? And why in the heck did you come with us today?"

Emily shook harder. "Tell me what's going on."

"Hold on, Emily," I said. "I'm waiting for an answer."

"I get bored. And I heard you were going to Victoria's Secret." Neil smiled.

I pranced away from Neil. "According to Neil, he's not attached to me. In fact, he didn't have to come with us today, but he's a peeping pervert."

Emily's face froze. "He saw us in our underwear?"

"Not you. Me," I said.

Neil fiddled with a pine twig hanging over the picnic table.

"The important thing is you're not a permanent appendage." I rolled my head in a circle to the right and then left. "What are your departure plans?"

Chapter 13
A Snake in the Grass

March. Nine months since my world spiraled out of control. And the spiraling didn't stop with me. Next door, Reggie had turned their world upside down as well.

If there were a Best Friend of the Year award, Emily's mantel would collapse under the weight of her monster-sized trophy. She'd rallied past her mental turmoil and encouraged my notions to re-enter the social world and even indulged me with a shopping jaunt. I had new underwear and a new dress. My next step would be a date. I put it on hold to volunteer my house for the reunion meetings. My motives weren't altruistic. I didn't like being away from my kids too long at a time, and having the meetings at my house meant I could keep them close while my former classmates and I planned a reunion.

Fifteen minutes into our March meeting, and Eli was the only member missing. Allison flitted around passing out updated lists and new color-coded folders when my double-decker boathouse rocked. It rocked again. She stopped mid-sentence and held up a hand. "Feels like Eli's here."

Heavy feet pounded up the wooden stairs, vibrating the floor. Four pairs of eyes watched the door.

Eli walked in, a tight smile stretched across his

lips. He stepped to the side and gestured to the door. "Look what the cat dragged in."

Playfully shoving Eli aside, Jesse King skidded in and struck a pose—the King was in the building. Lean and well-made and not a single gray hair. Despite physical abuse from opposing teams, our invincible quarterback Jesse King flashed his stunning white teeth still perfectly aligned.

Eli crossed his arms and backed up to the door jamb. I observed from the background while the remainder of the committee orbited Jesse. His beloved phrase came to mind: *It's great to be the King.*

Maintaining his post by the door, Eli looked like a thunderstorm gathering strength.

Jesse hugged and high-fived. Buddy sat on the sofa beside Charlotte and scooted over to make room for him.

But Jesse didn't sit. He headed my way, black eyes pinning me in place. My stomach muscles twitched, tied into knots, and then threw a back tuck. I held my breath and accepted a quick smooch, and displayed the mandatory smile. I turned to help Allison, and Jesse grabbed me and tugged. I tumbled, flapping my arms and struggling to keep my feet flat. I landed square on Jesse's lap, and we both fell into the oversized chair by the bar. Everyone laughed. Except Eli. Except me. A déjà vu moment. I wanted to deck him. But didn't dare. No one upstaged Jesse. I squirmed to get away, but his grip tightened and held me hostage.

"Hey, guys, remember when I auctioned off Libby's panties?" He rasped my cheek with his GQ approved day's growth and fake-whispered for all to hear. "I'll bet you don't wear the white cotton ones with days of the week on them anymore."

Even twenty years later, my cheeks burned. Pied Piper Jesse King stood in the midst of his sixth grade groupies and dangled my panties overhead. The panties he'd stolen while a guest at my twelfth birthday party. The birthday party my parents made me invite him to. He kept them barely out of my reach until Eli stepped in, snatched the panties from Jesse, and threw them to me. And then dragged me out of the fray—and out of Jesse's reach.

I powered my way from Jesse's lap, getting in a few sharp elbows in the process, and mentally strung together a list of appropriate obscenities. And then Neil crowded into my face. "Do not give him the satisfaction of getting under your skin."

"What do you know about it?" Anger vaporized into awkwardness. I'd let my guard down in front of witnesses and conversed with my dead husband.

"I grew up with him. Remember?" Neil corkscrewed through the ceiling.

"Lib, I'd put money on it." Jesse rocked back and grinned.

I wanted to kick him in the groin for stirring up these memories, but I was too glad he'd made a smooth transition from my comment to Neil. "They weren't even my panties. You stole them out of Carol Ann's drawer," I lied.

Everyone laughed—except Jesse. Except Eli who hadn't left his post.

Charlotte spoke in a well-modulated, lawyer tone. "Jesse, that story was hilarious for about five seconds— in sixth grade."

"Speaking of panties. What's got yours in a wad? It

was a great prank." Jesse looked around for support. Buddy and Allison shuffled through their folders, and Charlotte pasted on an I-am-so-over-this-nonsense look.

I walked to the bar and reached for a Diet Coke.

Jesse ignored Charlotte and charged on. "Eli offered me twenty bucks. But I held out for more."

In unison, all heads rotated to Eli. "You're still an asshole, Jesse." He smiled, but his stormy eyes held no mirth.

Jesse's smile lingered on his lips, but the creases between his eyes cratered. "I don't take kindly to insults, bro. Even from you. Besides, criticism coming from the master prankster himself sounds two-faced to me."

"I never pranked anyone to humiliate them." Eli's lips locked tight.

Jesse's mouth twitched into a forced smile. "Bet the coach didn't think that when you talked the football team into carrying his car onto the football field."

The air pressed down so heavy with testosterone it made my head ache. I didn't want old arguments hashed out here. Especially not because of me. Eli shifted his stance and slid his left hand deep into his pocket—his face a mask of control. I quivered. No wonder he was a good cop.

Buddy coughed into his hand. "That was our senior year when we won the state championship by you throwing that Hail Mary to Eli."

The vein in Jesse's temple relaxed, and he leaned forward and squared his elbows on his knees. "Coach Beck said to throw it as hard as I could at the biggest target."

Buddy nodded. "Eli always was the biggest kid on

the field."

Eli uncrossed his arms and leveled his gaze at Jesse. "We barely beat them. Even with their second-string quarterback."

Jesse ignored Eli. "We won. That's what counts."

Buddy walked to the window. He rubbed his jaw and stared up at the ceiling. "Seems like some kind of controversy kept their first string quarterback from playing."

"Yeah," Eli said. "An anonymous call alerted local authorities who found a nickel bag of pot in the quarterback's trunk." Eli leveled his gaze at Jesse. "Even after all that, he got a full scholarship to Ole Miss."

"Jesse, you remember that?" Buddy asked.

Before Jesse could answer, Trey wrenched the door open so hard it slammed against the outside wall. "Mom, I saw a snake by the back porch."

I jumped straight up. "A snake! A snake! I'll get a hoe!" I scurried toward the door.

Eli held up one giant paw, and I slammed to a halt. Keeping his eyes focused on me, he bent to Trey's level and put his hand on his shoulder. "I'll bet it's a huge snake with long fangs." Eli crooked two fingers and made a hissing sound.

"You think your silliness makes me feel better?" If Eli didn't find the snake, I'd be a nervous wreck every time I walked out my back door.

Eli followed Trey outside to search for the reptile.

The group bounded out the door, down the stairs, out into the backyard, and joined the search. Allison sidled up close and whispered, "Am I'm crazy, or is Jesse hitting on you?"

139

I listened to Allison with one ear and scanned the ground. "Pfft. Jesse's being Jesse."

"I don't know. Think the King's looking for someone to play in the castle." Allison stared down and scrunched closer to me.

"I'd like to confirm Allison's observation." Charlotte's willowy figure soundlessly slipped in between us. "Evidenced by his assuming a sixth grade persona."

Neil swooped in. "The guy's a nuisance to society."

I shooed Neil away like a gnawing gnat. "You worry too much." I didn't care about Jesse, the human reptile, when a real one was on the loose in my backyard.

Allison hugged me and gave Charlotte air kisses. "A snake in the grass is better than Jesse in your house." She ran to her car and called out to the group. "Good snake hunting. See you guys next month."

Charlotte waved at Allison. "She afraid she'll be late to the dojo?"

"Her Sensei won't let her break any bricks." I laughed. "She loves that martial arts stuff."

"She's been at it a long time. She should have stayed. She could have karate chopped the snake," Charlotte said.

"Not karate. Jujitsu," I said, checking for movement in the grass.

Charlotte hugged me and whispered into my ear. "At least Eli's still looking out for you." She glided away without giving me a chance to respond.

The others followed Allison and Charlotte's lead, and I waved goodbye to the last two pairs of taillights and joined Trey and Eli sitting side by side on the back steps.

"If you remember your science, Trey, reptiles are cold-blooded animals. So the cold weather makes them sluggish and they move...like...this." Eli drew out his Southern drawl, dragging every word like they, too, were cold blooded.

Trey giggled.

"Since the weather's still cool, even your mom could outrun one. Now in about a month, she might have something to worry about." They both laughed.

"Real funny, guys." I moved toward the boathouse to empty the trash can, and when I returned with the trash, I found both my kids in the garage with Eli—the biggest kid. They'd gathered in a circle and joined heads over a large cardboard box.

I dropped the bag into the plastic garbage bin. "You guys having a party without me?"

"Mom!" Trey sprinted to me and pumped my arm up and down, almost wrenching it out of its socket. "Mr. Anderson's going to put up my basketball goal."

It had been in its box since the Christmas before Neil exited our dimension. The six months prior to his passing, Neil hadn't found the time to install it. I gave Trey a serious look. "I hope you didn't ask Eli to put up your goal. We don't want to impose."

Eli folded the top flap over the box. "I offered."

"See, Mom, see, see, see." Boing. Boing. Boing. Trey bounced like a human Slinky. "I didn't ask. I just showed him the box."

"We asked Eli to stay for pizza. I ordered it already," Reagan piped in.

Eli tilted his head to the side and gave me a

lopsided grin. "I don't want to impose."

I pressed the top of Trey's head to tamp down his excitement. "I'll get the table ready, and you guys have thirty minutes to work on homework while we wait for delivery."

I opened the cabinet and took down four plates. Four. Like it used to be. I sloughed off the clingy melancholy and grabbed placemats and napkins and arranged them on the table.

Eli washed his hands and ripped off two paper towels. "What can I do to help?"

"Fix us something to drink." I opened the cupboard to show him and turned around. He collided into me and pinned me against the counter.

"Oops. Sorry." He reached into the cabinet, trapping my face against his chest. I tried to inhale, but my windpipe had shriveled shut. My palms met soft yellow fabric over molded granite as hard as the counter digging in my back.

He took two glasses in each hand and walked to the fridge. "Iced tea in here?"

I tucked my hair behind my ears and rested against the cabinet a minute to recover. "In the door." I sounded like Minnie Mouse. How could I get so flummoxed by an accidental brush against a man's body? Because it felt so…good. And it had been so…long.

"Nice." His voice derailed my train of thought.

Yes. His body was very nice.

Eli set the filled glasses on the table. "The place looks really nice. It looks like you."

I blinked. "You think so?"

Eli gestured with his arms. "Looks nothing like it

did when we were kids. Everything was white. The walls, the carpet, even that fancy white and gold furniture you couldn't sit on. Not that we got the chance to sit. Mrs. Miller usually locked us outside."

The doorbell rang, and a hungry herd stampeded down the stairs. Eli met Reagan and Trey in the foyer and swapped the pizza guy two twenties for two pies. He said since he got his favorite, it was only fair he paid.

Dinner was a brief frantic event. Trey grabbed four slices and headed to the den. First one to the remote. Reagan took one slice, and eyed another.

Eli flicked the box at Reagan. "Aww, go ahead. Guys like girls with a little meat on their bones."

Reagan giggled and wound the stringy mozzarella around her finger and slid two more cheesy slices onto her paper plate. "You won't think I'm rude if I go watch TV with Trey?"

I shooed her away. I'd gotten too lenient on the food rules. Neil would have insisted on real plates and real napkins. Speaking of Neil; I looked around for telltale signs. How could I have actually forgotten about him? Eli and I cleaned up, but I kept one eye on the ceiling. I crossed my fingers that my luck held out.

When the kids headed upstairs for showers and homework, Eli reached for his color-coded folders. "I was just wondering. Should I go check for snakes? I'd hate for you to walk into your boathouse and find a vicious viper." He made his snake fangs again.

I pushed a chair under the table. "I'm on to you, buddy. You just want to see if there are any Coronas left."

"Busted." He held the patio door open. When I

stepped on the grass, Eli yelled, "Snake!"

"Ahhhhhh!" My scream skipped across the lake.

Eli scooped me up into his arms and ran. I wrapped my arms around his neck. His powerful arms drew me in closer, and I knew nothing short of an atomic bomb could harm me. Eli nuzzled his face next to mine, and his chuckle spilled over into a loud raucous laugh.

I rolled my head to the side and studied his profile. "You're lying, aren't you?"

"Gotcha!"

I loosened my grip around his neck. "Put me down, you big bully."

Eli placed me on the dock. "Safe and sound."

"That was not funny. You could have given me a heart attack." I twirled around and jogged up the stairs.

Moonlight glowed through the windows, providing enough light to find the bar. I reached to turn on the lights, and Eli's hand covered mine. His splayed fingers flattened my hand against the light switch. "Don't. Let's sit here and listen to the quiet."

Ker-thump. Thump. Thump. Ker-thump. Thump. Thump. My pulse pounded beneath his hand. "Um…sure…I like quiet."

He reached for the window and lifted. Cool air sifted through. In the distance, a beaver's tail slapped the water.

"It's been so long since I've enjoyed this view. The last time I was here, you had no boathouse at all. Just the same old dock we used as kids." Eli exhaled a long slow breath.

I sat on the far end of the sofa and tucked my legs under me. "Replacing the dock was one thing Neil took my advice on."

Eli opened the bar refrigerator and grabbed a beer. "You came up with the idea of a double decker boat dock? I'm impressed."

"I'm smarter than I look, big guy." I puffed out my chest.

"So did Jesse ask you out?" He sounded like he was interrogating a third grader.

"Aren't you nosy? Why don't you ask him? You brought him."

He sat beside me. "I didn't bring him. He followed me."

"You think I should go out with him?"

"You want to go out with him?"

"We're both single, and he's charming," I gauged Eli's reaction.

He leapt up and paced the length of the boathouse. "Charming? What the hell does that mean? It's Jesse, for God's sake." He stopped, his body outlined by the moonlight behind him. I couldn't read his face. He flopped down on the sofa beside me. "I may be wrong, but he seems like the same old Jesse to me." He tipped his beer and drank.

I gave him a playful shove. "I can take care of myself, Eli. I'm a big girl."

He rubbed his back. "My back will never be the same."

I slugged him on the arm. It had the effect of a fly hitting concrete.

"So when do you want me to put up Trey's basketball goal?"

"That's right, change the subject," I said.

"I'm not changing the subject. You're going to do what you want to do. Just watch your back."

"You don't have to warn me." I took his beer from his hand and sipped.

Eli gave me a sad smile. "We both know Jesse King."

I held out his beer. "Why'd you stand up for me tonight? You shouldn't have called him an asshole."

"Jesse's a sociopath like his old man. That whole panty deal and the stunt he pulled at homecoming. I still want to punch him." Eli snatched the bottle and slugged it back. "Let's talk about the basketball goal."

"Nice transition, big guy. You mellowing in your golden years?" I took his empty bottle and added it to the recycling bag under the cabinet.

"First day, I'll pour the cement. We'll wait a couple of days for it to season before we put up the goal." The Jesse King dialogue terminated.

"Sounds like a lot of work. Sure you want to do this?" I cleaned the counter and put the limes back into the bar fridge.

"Hardest part is digging the hole. Mind if I bring Lee?"

Having the kids around would make things less complicated. "Absolutely. He and Trey can shovel. When do you want to start?"

"Tomorrow okay with you?" From the set of his face, I expected him to thrust out his hand to seal the deal.

"How considerate of Eli to assist his best friend's grieving widow." Neil's voice invaded the moonlit ambience.

My luck had run out.

Chapter 14
Double Trouble

On Monday afternoon, I turned into my driveway and reached to hit the garage remote. My finger froze. A pickax hung in mid-air and then crashed to the earth. Up it went again and Eli's biceps tortured the short sleeves of his white t-shirt. My breath followed the downward plunge into the hard ground.

"Quit gawking and push the button." Neil's haughty voice jarred me from my reverie.

My finger connected and the door creaked and clacked upward along its metal tracks. I looked in the rear-view mirror at Neil's shadowy form sitting beside Trey. "When did you get here?" I asked Neil. Too late I remembered the kids in the car.

Reagan rotated her head and gave me one of her fine-tuned adolescent looks. "You know they can't hear you."

Trey unfastened his seat belt and leaned between the front seats. "He brought his son to help put in the basketball goal."

Eli raised the pickax for another strike, and I drove into the garage. "Just thinking out loud, guys. Hop out. Let's see if we can do anything to help." I glanced into the rear-view mirror with the intention of giving Neil a warning look. He was gone.

Eli tossed the ax aside and slung his worn work

gloves into the dirt. "Lee, say hello to Ms. Miller."

Lee grinned and revealed a wide gap in his smile. "It's nice to see you again. My dad says I know you."

He was almost as tall as Trey but stocky where Trey was slim. Both towheads. I reached for him and pulled him into a hug. "None of that Ms. Miller stuff. I'm Libby." I brushed his blond hair out of his eyes. "I'm not surprised you don't remember me. But I've known you a long time. In fact, I was at the hospital the night you were born."

"You know my mom?" Lee turned to his dad. "You didn't tell me that."

I reached for Trey's arm. "Lee, this is my son Trey and his sister Reagan."

"Mom, can me and Lee go to the bridge to look for turtles?" Trey made puppy dog eyes. "Please."

"May Lee and I go look for turtles." An English teacher always.

Trey looked skyward, stretching his neck. "Mom," he whined.

I wagged my finger at Trey.

Eli leaned on the shovel. "I need you guys to help me. How about we finish up here, and then we'll all go look for turtles?"

"We can help? Really?" Trey asked.

Eli held the shovel out to Trey. "It's your goal. I think you should dig the hole."

Trey shot me a look that screamed, "Help!" I knew what he was thinking. No one had shown him how to use a shovel. "Just dig right in." I made a digging motion.

Trey accepted the shovel from Eli. Holding it like a giant toothbrush, he plowed the shovel into the hole and raked out a thimble full of red dirt. "Man, this is harder than it looks."

Eli must have sensed Trey's distress. "Gather round, boys. You too, Reagan." Eli winked at her. "You never know when you might need to use a shovel to hit a guy upside the head."

Reagan pointed to her feet. "I'll watch from here. Don't want dirt on my new boots."

Eli snapped his fingers. "Focus, boys. The first thing you do is plant the sharp end where you want to dig. Then you smack your foot down, not too hard, on the head of the shovel like this. And then you wiggle the shovel back and forth to get a big scoop." Eli lifted a shovel full of dirt and tossed it to the side. "Got it? Now who wants to go first?"

Eli kept out of the way and supervised from the sidelines while the boys took turns. Dirt flew in all directions, and more laughter than dirt got shoveled.

Neil materialized and hovered over the boys. "Not impressive. Anybody can dig a hole. Why isn't Eli at work playing detective rather than digging in the dirt?"

"You jealous?" I looked at Eli to see if he noticed my comment.

Eli propped his arm on my shoulder. "Not me. I'm always happy to let someone else do the work."

I waved away dust clouds. "Hope you guys like pot roast. Crock pot's been simmering all day."

Lee left the dirt storm and joined Eli and me. "Yes, ma'am." He smiled proudly, displaying his missing incisor. "Pot roast is my favorite. My grandmom makes it every time we visit. Can we have mashed potatoes, too? Oops. I'm not supposed to ask to stay for dinner. Dad said if you asked first, it was okay. He said it's rude to—" Eli smacked his hand over Lee's mouth.

Eli's face turned beet red. "He doesn't know when to stop talking."

I laughed and swept red dirt from Lee's shirt. "Lee, we'll definitely have mashed potatoes. You like corn, too?"

Blue sparkles twinkled in Lee's eyes, and he held his dad's hand away from his mouth, "Wow. All my favorites." And then he put his dad's hand back in place.

Eli removed his hand from Lee's mouth and wiped it on his jeans. "He's a little excitable."

I stooped to Lee's eye level. "They're Trey's favorite too. But we have to have something green. Will you eat green beans?"

Eli gave Lee a little shove and swatted his rear. "We'll eat whatever you put in front of us. And since Lee got us a dinner invitation, I say let's get this done. I'm so hungry I might start gnawing on this shovel."

****

Like a caravan, Eli and the kids cleared the table, bringing loads of dishes and food and placemats to the sink. I closed the dishwasher. The dishes could wait. "You guys up for a walk around the lake?"

I didn't have to ask twice. Even Reagan, on one of her rare nights at home, graced us with her presence. Outside, the boys ran ahead to the wooden bridge to look for turtles on the causeway.

Strolling along, we enjoyed the last remnants of sunset and watched the streetlights sputter on intermittently around the lake.

Reagan walked between Eli and me. "Mom said they called you Tank in high school."

"I was bigger back then," Eli said.

"Bigger than now? How's that possible?" In place of her teenage angst, Reagan's inflection expressed pure awe.

"Don't be rude," I said.

Eli waved off my rebuke. "Back then, Reagan, my job was to play football. I took my coaches seriously and got obsessed with strength training."

"So how long have you been divorced?" Reagan's voice sounded casual, like she was asking Eli what brand of shampoo he used.

My daughter's poor manners stunned me. "Reagan Elizabeth, that question is totally inappropriate."

Eli held his hand up. "She's just curious, Lib." He turned to Reagan. "Three years ago when Lee was seven."

"Is three years long enough to get through that whole divorce, grief process thing?" Reagan said.

I wished I had gone with the boys to look for turtles. No, I wished I was a turtle and could retract into my shell. "Reagan, where is this coming from?"

Reagan picked up a dead leaf from the ground and crinkled it in her hand, letting the brown bits fall through her fingers. "Mom, you and Emily sit downstairs and talk about the stages of grief. She still in denial?"

My feet ground to a dead halt. Breaking News flashed like a running banner inside my head. Emily and I had been exposed. Eli coughed into his hand to cover his snickering. Waves of shock and embarrassment rolled over me. "You—you—you've been eavesdropping!"

"Mom, really. We live in the same house. I don't

have to eavesdrop to hear stuff."

How much had she heard? I almost swallowed my tongue trying to get the words out. "Reagan, you need to leave the adult things to adults."

As if dealing with a hormonal fifteen-year-old wasn't enough, Neil's essence swaggered into view. "Touché."

"You're both making me crazy." I grabbed Eli's arm and pulled him into motion. "Teenagers." I snuck a look back. Reagan headed back home with Neil trailing close behind her. I exhaled short puffs and picked up the pace.

We rounded the curve to my house, and the turtle hunters sat on each side of the mailbox, empty handed. They jumped up and ran to meet us.

Trey took one hand and Lee the other, their bodies vibrated with excitement. "Mom, may Lee and I get some flashlights and go to the train tracks?"

They were so eager to go exploring away from the adults. I hated to be the bad guy. "It's too dark, boys."

Disappointment stole the energy from Trey's blue eyes. "Aww, Mom. You treat me like I'm two."

Neil floated into our small group. "You're being overprotective."

Anger flashed like hot grease doused with water. How dare he try to tell me how to raise my children. It was his fault that I had to be the bad guy all the time. "I am not overprotective." I lashed out at Neil. But the boys and Eli swung their heads my way. I smoothed my shirt and lowered my voice. "When Lee and Eli come back to finish the basketball goal, I promise we'll go to the train tracks."

Eli put a hand on each boy's shoulder. "Trey, I

can't tell you how many quarters your dad and I put on those rails."

Trey's face perked up. "Yeah?"

Eli hunkered down to their level and pulled the boys close. "I don't know if I should tell you this, with your mom so close and all, but when your dad and I were about your age, we'd sneak into your grandmother's purse and borrow quarters to put on the train tracks."

"And when you went back to get them, they were smashed flat as a pancake." Trey slapped his palms together.

Lee turned to his dad. "I got a bunch of quarters. When're we coming back?"

Eli nudged both boys. "Ask Libby nicely if Wednesday is okay."

"Can they come back Wednesday? Please. Please." Trey begged.

I couldn't help but chuckle. He sounded like he was two. "Sounds good to me."

Lee and Trey high-fived. "Come on, Lee, I'll show you my smushed coin collection."

"The cement should be hard by Wednesday. But don't cook dinner. I'll take us out or something. I don't want you going to any trouble for us."

"It's no trouble. We have to eat anyway, and we like having company. Spaghetti acceptable?"

Eli rubbed his flat belly. "That's my favorite."

It was a school night. Reagan and Trey said their goodbyes and headed upstairs to do homework. I walked Lee and Eli to the Hummer and waved. A blood-curdling scream shattered the dark. Air froze in my lungs.

Reagan broke through the front door and screamed again. Bright dots swam before my eyes, blinding me. My brain said duck and cover, but my heart kicked into panicked-mom mode. When I reached her, Eli was at my side.

I clenched Reagan's shoulders. "What is it?" Frantically I spun her left and right, searching for open wounds or dripping blood.

Eli put a calming hand on my shoulder and turned to Reagan. "What's the matter, sweetheart?"

Her words came between sniffs and blubs. "I dropped…my…earring down…the…drain."

My bones turned soft as warm butter and threatened an internal collapse. Visions of Reagan's imminent demise or Trey lying somewhere bloody and injured poofed into thin air. *An earring down the drain, puh-lease.* "We'll get you another earring, Reagan." Behind her back, I gave Eli an eye roll nod.

The diva of the Miller clan continued to wail. "Jacob gave them to me today. I *have* to wear them to school tomorrow." She buried her head in her hands.

"Pull your hair to the side and wear one." I felt no sympathy, and my tone showed it.

The crying stopped instantly. She peeped through her fingers and slid them down her face. "Mom," She spoke slowly, articulating each word, "you don't understand. Jacob gave them to me."

Eli looked at me. "Do you have a wrench?"

"I'm sure there's one in the tool box. Why?" I said. And then I turned my attention to Reagan, "Who's Jacob?"

Eli draped his arm around Reagan's shoulder. "We're going to rescue your earring."

Lee followed us inside and met Trey in the kitchen. Trey whispered to Lee, "She's a drama queen."

My sentiments exactly, but I kept my request free of sarcasm. "Will you boys get the tool box out of the garage, please?"

In Reagan's bathroom, Eli cleared out a place to work under her vanity and handed me towels, toothpaste, and feminine products. I secured the pile. "You don't have to do this. I can call a plumber tomorrow."

Eli slid the tool box closer to the cabinet and sat cross-legged. "We'll have this done in no time. That way we'll all get a good night's sleep." He plundered through the toolbox and came up with an orange and black screwdriver I'd bought for Neil's stocking last Christmas. He pushed the button, and the air whirred with power. "I'm impressed. Not only do you have an electric screwdriver, it's fully charged." Eli removed the screws holding the hinges on the cabinet door.

"It's a Neil thing," I said. "He had to have the best of everything—even tools. And they had to be in working order. So, when I use them, I re-charge them. Old habits, I guess."

Lee plopped down on the floor, and Trey put the top down on the commode and sat. Both bent forward, mesmerized by the hum of the electric screwdriver Eli wielded.

I turned to Reagan. "Who's Jacob?"

Reagan's red, weepy eyes looked past me, and she squatted down beside Eli. "Do you think you can find it?"

The high-pitched whine petered out, and Eli clanked the screwdriver shaft against the U-shaped pipe. "I'm hoping it got stuck right here. And if it did, I can take this section out and get your earring." He gave her a big smile, and she smiled back.

I was being ignored, and I didn't like it. I cleared my throat for a more provoked-parent inquiry. "Who's Jacob?"

Reagan looked at me like I'd stepped off a space ship. "Mom, he's the boy who gave me the earrings."

I pressed my hands over my cheeks and pulled down, stretching my lower eyelids toward my chin. The same act my daughter had used on me five minutes earlier. Eli looked at me and then turned on the electric screwdriver. The whirr failed to camouflage his laughter, and he ducked inside the cabinet. I took a deep breath and tried again. "Reagan, I get it. Jacob gave you the earrings. But who is he? Is he your boyfriend? What happened to Matt?"

Trey elbowed Lee. "Matt's cool."

Reagan sighed loudly, resigned to deliver an explanation to someone too stupid to grasp the obvious. "Matt and I broke up last week. Jacob's in my algebra class. And he and I are going out."

Eli cleared his throat, disrupting our mother/daughter moment and handed out the screwdriver. "Libby, take this. The rest I hope I can do by hand, but it might get messy. I need some towels you don't mind getting dirty."

I wanted to know more about what happened to Matt and who this Jacob person was but ran to the laundry room to get some old, ragged towels. When I got back to Reagan's bathroom, it looked like the vanity was eating Eli, saving his lower torso for last.

"Get ready, Libby. I am going to hand you the

pipe. Don't do anything with it until I can get myself out from under here."

Both boys ran to look at the pipe.

He handed me the nasty-looking pipe filled with slimy water and hair and mystery clumps I didn't want to identify. "Oh, yuck!" I turned my head to avoid the smell. But something even more unpleasant caught my eye. Neil lay stretched across the shower curtain rod. I stumbled.

Eli's long arms caught me and the pipe. "Whoa, Libby. You okay?"

I looked back to yell at Neil, but he was gone. Good riddance. But I knew not for long.

Eli carefully tapped the gunk out of the pipe into the other sink. He fished through the slippery mess and pulled out a little piece of metal. Without flinching, he scooped up the rest of the gunk and flushed it down the toilet. Sporting a broad smile, he rinsed the earring and smiled at Reagan. "Here you go, kiddo. One peace symbol earring. I'd soak it in alcohol before I put it in my ear."

Reagan grabbed Eli and hugged him. "You're the best, Tank."

I felt Neil before I saw him. "You're the best, Tank." Neil mocked Reagan in a sing-song voice.

I steeled myself, expecting Neil to initiate an all-out assault. Instead, his pale form fizzled and then faded to nothing—except his haunting voice. "My best friend is hijacking my family."

Tears throbbed behind my eyes. *Don't you dare feel sorry for the cheater.* Neil had his chance. He could have taught his son how to fix a pipe or been his daughter's hero. But he chose his dream of gilded letters on beveled glass at 511 Magnolia Avenue. Reagan poured alcohol into a soap dish, and I heard the clink of her earring. Neil flickered over her and stroked her hair. I pressed my fists to my eyes. Even my icy heart thawed at the sight of a father loving his daughter.

"Here, boys, help me put this back on." Eli's muffled command from the cabinet snapped me and the boys to attention. Eli extracted his upper torso and wedged the boys into the opening. Beside the cabinet, he balanced on one knee. He ducked his head and angled it inside to supervise each boy's turn of the wrench to tighten the pipe.

I felt sad and tired and wished Neil would go away. For good.

Eli replaced the cabinet doors, and the boys stood like little soldiers and waited for instructions. Eli leaned his hip on the cabinet and dried his hands. "Good job, boys. I hope you learned something here tonight. Because one of these days you'll have daughters of your own, and you might need to rescue an earring."

Trey waggled his head. "No way I'm having kids," Trey said.

"'Specially no girls," Lee added.

Eli struggled to keep a serious look on his face. "We'll see about that. How about taking the tool box to the garage?"

Trey and Lee grabbed the handle and hoisted the tool box through the doorway. "Is it always this much fun at your house?" Lee asked.

"Didn't use to be," Trey answered.

My heart hurt like I'd been stabbed with a butter knife. I pressed my hands to my chest. Neil and I'd clung to status quo. For the kids? For us? Maybe we chose the easy path because we were cowards.

"They're great kids," Eli said.

I massaged my chest and exhaled. "We're both lucky."

Eli gathered up the dirty towels. "It's time for me to head home, unless you have any more chores." The wrinkles around his eyes told me he was kidding.

I smiled back. "You trying to make me feel bad?"

"Just giving you a hard time. The whole evening was fun. Really."

When we got to the door, Eli hugged me warmly and whispered in my ear. "Your daughter is almost as beautiful as you."

His lips touched my cheek and electricity zinged all the way to my toes. It felt good. Really good. I caressed my cheek.

Reagan's sharp voice broke the connection. "Mom, get the phone."

I waited until Eli's red taillights disappeared from view.

Reagan shouted again. Louder. "Mom! Phone!"

"Okay. Okay." I didn't want to talk. I wanted to think about why I wanted Eli to turn his car around. But I picked up the phone. "Hello."

"Hi, Lib. It's Jesse. Got a minute?"

Jesse King? My brain snapped into alert status. "Sure, what's up?"

His practiced laugh came through the receiver. "You sure you want to know?"

I released an audible breath. "You called to have phone sex like a sixteen-year-old?"

"Not a bad idea."

I kneaded my forehead. "Jesse, what do you

want?"

"You."

I waited, but he said nothing.

"Libby, I want you."

"Jesse, let me be blunt. Why the sudden interest?"

"You're a beautiful, single woman. I like beautiful, single women."

Jesse King thought I was beautiful? I stared down at the phone. He'd surprised the words out of me.

"Tonight I felt all your curves, and it only made me want more."

I found my voice. "You're recording this, right? It's some sort of prank you and Eli dreamed up."

"Funny you should mention Eli. He wasn't happy to see me. But you're not seeing anyone, and you're fair game, right?"

"Fair game? Should I be worried about you stalking me with a big gun?"

"I got a big gun all right, but you don't need to be worried."

"Down, boy. Getting deep in here."

"Go out with me, Libby. I promise it'll be a night you won't forget."

We tried that once, I didn't say. "I wasn't your kind of girl in high school."

"We're not in high school, and I'm not giving up. I'll keep calling until I wear you down."

"Good night, Jesse." I hung up the phone.

We were both single and both looking for love—or a reasonable facsimile. Just like in high school. But all those years ago, Jesse King had shaken my world and hurled me onto another path.

Chapter 15
Funky Valentine

Two days ago when I drove up my driveway, my eyes feasted on male testosterone in a t-shirt. Today, Eli's schoolbus-yellow Hummer sat in my driveway. Led Zeppelin plinked the notes of "Stairway to Heaven" down my spine.

Almost before the wheels stopped rolling, Trey sprinted from the car. Reagan ran close behind. I knew Eli and Lee were out back. The lake draws people like a magnet. I strolled around the house and stopped to watch. And silence Led Zeppelin.

Legs stiff and arms outstretched, Frankenstein Eli stalked toward Reagan, Lee, and Trey. Reagan and Lee scooted out of range of Franken-Eli's long arms, leaving Trey an easy victim. The monster snatched Trey into a neck hold. Eli polished the top of Trey's head, creating friction and enough static electricity to stand Trey's hair on end. Eli's mellow throaty laughter resonated across the water blending with the high frequency shrieks of Trey's changing twelve-year-old voice. Eli turned and Reagan squealed when he grabbed her in a bear hug. Lee squirmed into the middle of the melee, his boyish giggles joining the happy barks of our golden retriever. A symphony of joy. Eli spread his arms wide and encircled them all and looked in my direction, waving me over with his head. Hot tears blurred my vision.

The backyard was alive with happiness, and I had an invitation.

Neil brushed against me. "Hurry. You don't want to miss this Kodak moment."

Not even Neil's snooty tone tarnished my shiny pleasure. "Don't worry, Neil. I won't." I adjusted my sunglasses and jogged over to join the group on the dock. "Been waiting long?"

Eli pointed to a stack of flat river rocks. "Just long enough to gather these and throw a few. Been teaching Lee how to skip stones over the water."

"My dad showed me how." Trey bent down and shifted through the pile of smooth stones. "He said the trick was finding the magic ones."

"You remembered." Neil knelt beside Trey and reached out to touch his son's face. Neil's lips curled into a smile.

"Watch this." Trey slung the flat rock with a side-arm motion, and it danced across the water.

"I counted five skips," Lee said. "Dad, that's more than you."

Trey's smile split his face in two. "Eli, you probably just need more practice. But I can give you some pointers if you want me to."

Pride flooded my chest. Trey's offer was genuine and filled with humility. I mentally patted myself on the back and smiled at Neil. The afternoon sun reflected a sparkling honeyed hue in his ghostly brown eyes. Neil said nothing and drifted toward the house. I cleared my throat and faced Eli. "I meant to tell you there's an extra house key under the flower pot on the patio."

Eli cocked his hip and nodded toward the patio.

"Ma'am, as an officer of the law, I'm here to tell you that's the first place a burglar looks. Tonight we find a new hiding place. But right now, I need these boys to help me put up the basketball goal."

We lived in a gated community. Security had never been an issue, and I blew off Eli's official police assessment. "What's it going to take to get this project finished?"

"This is the easy part. All we do now is assemble the pole. The boys'll be shooting hoops in thirty minutes." Eli turned to Trey and Lee and clapped his hands. "Hop to it, boys." Eli's voice cracked like a whip, and the boys ran.

"Then I'll go and start the spaghetti if you don't need me."

Eli placed his hands on my shoulders and winked. "I'll always need you."

I opened my mouth but no words came out. I searched for a come-back, but the blood pounded too loud to think. He walked away whistling, and I stumbled over my thoughts into the kitchen.

I stirred onions and fresh garlic into the sizzling ground sirloin. Questions, like the steam rising from the skillet, swirled round and round and then vanished into the stainless steel range hood. *What did Eli mean—he'd always need me? I'm sure he didn't mean anything. But why would he say something like that? Pfft. He's just being nice to the Widow Miller.* I added my secret ingredient—two jars of Prego spaghetti sauce. Since Eli loved mushrooms, I sliced fresh, baby portabellas and put them aside to add in the last few minutes. *Needing something is different from wanting something. We need air. We need food. And sex. Where did that come from?* With the lid in one hand, I leaned over the red, bubbly sauce and dipped my wooden spoon. I blew on the spoonful of tomatoey goodness and tasted. I sprinkled oregano and a little basil. And re-dipped the spoon.

Cool fingertips grazed my neck. I jumped, sending the wooden spoon flying. It thumped off the backsplash, leaving a saucy, red mess.

"Oops. Sorry. I don't remember you being so jumpy." He pushed my hair to the side and leaned over my shoulder. "How about a taste?" His strong fingers worked my shoulders and my muscles bunched tighter.

"I guess I'm a little nervous. Spaghetti being your favorite and all." Darn it. I wasn't jumpy until I had to worry about a ghost sneaking around and spying on my every move. I leapt out of his reach, grabbed a dish cloth, and began scrubbing the red trail on the stove and counter and up the wall.

"If it tastes as good as it smells, you've knocked it out of the park. Now how about that taste?" He leaned against the stove and opened his mouth.

I scooped up a sample. I gently blew on the wooden spoonful of sauce, and his eyes connected with mine. I touched the red sauce to my lips to make sure it wasn't too hot. Slowly I eased the spoon to his mouth. He opened his lips, and I slid the spoon inside. When his mouth closed around the spoon, a heat as spicy as the crushed red pepper I'd added settled in my stomach and then sank lower…

A shadow skimmed over the top of my head and my hair sprang straight up. "Get a bib before you drool all over each other," Neil said.

I jumped and lurched backward, yanking the spoon

from Eli's mouth.

He ran the back of his hand across his lips. "You trying to pull out my teeth?"

"Sorry." I looked for Neil.

"I almost forgot why I came in here. But Reagan turned us down, and we need another player."

"You've found your girl." *Did I really say that?* I put the top on the bubbling brew and followed Eli to the driveway. I cast a look back for signs of Neil. Why did I feel so guilty? Eli and I were only friends.

Outside, the boys were already sweaty and red-faced. "Whose team am I on?" The boys poked each other and pointed at Eli.

I swaggered around the boys. "What are you laughing at? I can play basketball."

"You go, girl," Eli said, giving me a high five. "Show 'em what you got." He bounced the ball to me.

I dribbled around the driveway court untouched, thanks to my full-bodied partner, and bounced the ball a couple of times before my big shot—granny-style. Nothing but net. "Swoosh!" I flapped my arms and strutted under the net.

Reagan stepped in front of me and broke up my courtside dance. "Phone. And, Mom, the funky chicken is so not cool."

I rolled my eyes at her—for a change. "You guys go ahead without me. Let me get the phone."

When Reagan handed me the phone, she mouthed, "It's a man."

I strode past her, leaving a warning glare in my wake. "This is Libby." My voice rushed out.

"Hey. You're breathing hard. Must be thinking about me," Jesse said.

165

"I was playing basketball with my son. This not a good time." Talking to Jesse with Eli in my driveway felt wrong. And then there was the problem of Reagan around the corner listening.

"No problem. I was just checking to see if you'd changed your mind yet. You will go out with me. It's only a matter of time."

"Why are you doing this?" I asked.

"I don't know. Karma?" Jesse said.

"The only karma we share is bad karma." I listened for signs of Eli.

"Maybe I'm trying to make amends—like in those twelve step programs."

I gripped the receiver. "Really? What addiction are you trying to work through?"

"Does being an asshole count?"

My hand relaxed, and a giggle escaped. "What step are you on?" Why am I participating in this inane conversation? I need to get off the phone. Jesse's not charming; he's Jesse, for goodness sake. And Eli is waiting outside. A nice person who really is charming.

"Whichever one gets you to go out with me," Jesse said.

"I'm hanging up now. Goodbye." I hung up the phone and stifled a smile. All it takes is one, and Jesse's under your skin like a rash.

"Who's Jesse?" Reagan asked.

"An old friend." An old friend on the phone and another old friend outside. I'm not playing with fire— I'm juggling torches.

The kitchen door opened and Eli limped in. "Those boys were running me ragged. I came in to see if I could cook the spaghetti."

I took down plates. "Sure. There's the pot. Do you put oil in the water?"

"Yep, olive oil and a little salt." Eli poured a hefty amount of oil into the water, set the pot on the range, and adjusted the flame.

I took silverware from the drawer and lots of napkins.

Eli uncorked a bottle of pinot noir and set it aside. Then gave me one of his crooked smiles. "Do you know how to test the spaghetti to see if it's done?"

"What do you mean?" I knew that look. I'd been on the receiving end of Eli Anderson's shenanigans too many times not to recognize the wheels of mischief turning.

He crossed his arms and leaned against the stove. "How can you tell if spaghetti's done?"

His question had the feel of a talk show host reading from a script. "Is this a trick question?"

"Absolutely not." He reached for the bottle of wine.

"I cook it about ten minutes, like the package suggests, and then cut it with a fork to test desired doneness. Is there something wrong with that?"

"That's one way." He poured two glasses of wine.

I stole peeks at him while I tore chunks of lettuce and filled a big wooden bowl. He used spaghetti noodles like drum brushes playing the side of the pot. I studied his profile. I didn't realize I was staring until he turned and caught me. I fumbled the bag of baby carrots, sending orange rockets all over the counter. He sneaked one and popped it into his mouth. I corralled the carrots into a pile and reached for my glass.

He held the package of spaghetti like a maestro.

"Water's almost ready."

I tipped my glass and observed him over the rim. He merged into the routine around here way too easily.

When the timer beeped, Eli called into the den where Reagan sat in front of the TV. "Reagan, go and get the boys, and tell them I said to wash up."

He answered my questioning look. "Trust me."

"Here they are," Reagan said. "With clean hands even."

He arranged us into a semi-circle around the stove, and then Eli transformed into a ringmaster. "Let me have your eyes here, please. Tonight I'm going to demonstrate how to test spaghetti to make sure it's cooked properly." Eli fixed a serious look on his face. With one hand on his hip, he bowed to their level and spoke to each child. "Never try this without adult permission."

Reagan did a half eye roll, and I covered my mouth to hide my chuckle. She cut him a break. Not me. I get the full business.

Carefully he scooped out a long, thin noodle. He held it aloft, inspecting it thoughtfully. Then he whipped it over his head like a lasso. Splat. The noodle clung to the wall.

"Yep, it's done." Eli peeled off the noodle, plopped the end into his mouth, and slurped it down.

Lee cackled. Reagan and Trey waited for my reaction.

Neil's pale form glimmered overhead. "Surely you're not buying into this nonsense."

I admit under ordinary circumstances I'd be screaming like a banshee about sticky noodles on my walls and nasty germs. But these were extraordinary circumstances, and I was becoming an extraordinary woman. And it was big fun.

"We can take Eli at his word, or we can test for ourselves."

The kids laughed and yelled and jockeyed for position closest to the stove and held out their hands. I took the pasta server from Eli and passed out noodles. Even Reagan joined in the fun. Slurps and laughter blended with other kitchen smells. It felt like family.

The noodles were a big hit—even piled high and covered in sauce. Dinner ended too soon, and I reluctantly started clearing the table.

Eli took me by the shoulders and directed me back to my chair. "Sit, madam, and we'll serve dessert." He held the chair for me. "Reagan, please flip on the coffee and get the dessert plates. Guys, go to my car and bring in the cooler. Carefully."

Lee bumped Trey. "Told you we had a surprise."

Eli cleared the table, and the kids scattered, set on their instructions. I breathed in the aroma of fresh coffee.

"Okay, Mom, close your eyes. And no peeking," Reagan said.

Lee joined in. "We'll tell you when you can look."

Behind me, in the midst of the clatter of cups and plates and the squeak of styrofoam, the kids whispered and giggled.

"You better not peek." Trey tapped the table. "Now open your mouth and see if you can tell what kind of dessert."

I opened my mouth, and squinted. I didn't mean to cheat. Eli slipped in a forkful of the surprise dessert. "It's tiramisu. My favorite! And this is heavenly." I opened my eyes, and four warm bodies hovered over me. Five including Neil.

Fork poised, Trey asked, "Can we eat ours now?"

They dug in, and Trey and Lee would have licked their plates if I hadn't been watching.

Eli clapped his hands together. "Okay, kids, it's a school night. Let's get this kitchen cleaned up."

"Why don't you and Mom take a walk around the lake, and the boys and I will clean up," Reagan said, stacking Lee's plate on top of Trey's.

"Are you crazy?" Trey began. Then he winced and changed his tune to a gritted-teeth tempo. "Sure, Mom, we'll help."

"I'll help too." Lee's tongue claimed the last smear of creamy delight at the corner of his mouth.

Reagan ushered us outside. "Take your time. You know you want to walk off all those calories. We've got this covered."

We walked down the driveway. "What's up with them?"

Eli tucked my arm through his. "For someone so smart, you can be kind of dense. It must be a *Joy* thing."

When Eli invoked my ditzy blonde sister Joy, I realized I'd been a bit thick. The kids were playing matchmaker. I looked at Eli suspiciously.

He held out both hands. "Cleaning up was all Reagan's idea." Success punctuated his sentence.

Remembering Trey's initial reluctance to help clean up brought a chuckle. "Reagan should have let Trey in on her plans before she kicked him."

I took a stutter step to get back in sync with Eli's languid stride. "That was really nice."

He looked sideways at me. "Why do you sound so surprised?"

"You're not the boy I knew in high school."

"I think I got smarter as my hair got thinner." Eli stroked his bald head. "Are you the same girl I knew in high school?"

I thought for a moment. "In some ways. Seeing Jesse last week dredged up some painful reminders of my forgettable high school years."

Eli shook his head. "You might have been untouchable, but never forgettable."

I kicked a small rock. "I wasn't popular like some girls."

"Granted, you weren't as popular as Debbie Weaver who flashed her tits more often than she brushed her teeth. But you had Neil. You were automatically off-limits. Back then you were smart and nice. At eighteen, I didn't want smart and nice. I wanted what all eighteen-year-old boys want." Eli picked up a dead branch and lobbed it into the dense undergrowth. "I don't dwell on our high school years. I'm glad they're over. I don't want anyone to judge my whole life by four years of high school. People change. I've changed."

"In a good way." I bumped him with my shoulder as we moseyed along the dimly lit road. "Did you really have a crush on me in fifth grade?"

He poked his hands into his pockets. "It started way before that."

"And now he's trying to pick up where he left off," Neil said, drifting between us and the water.

Why couldn't he stay away? Things were going so well. But Neil didn't want things to go well. "And you

171

can't do a thing about it," I said to Neil.

Eli picked up a rock and threw it. "I know. Sometimes we want what we can't have." His voice came out flat and distant.

The moon reflected on the water, shimmering through Neil. "You can't let him steal my family."

I bared my teeth at Neil. "Don't put this on me. You threw me away." I hurled my caustic comment at Neil, but Eli caught its impact.

Eli slowed, and exhaled a long breath. "Do you believe in second chances?"

Second chances. The thought zipped through my head, but before the words reached my mouth, Neil nose-dived in front of me.

"He doesn't get a do-over. He can't have you or my kids." Neil's angry words rang in my ears but made no sound across the water. Agitation brightened his aura. "Ask him what he buried in the grave with Skipper."

I nibbled my pinkie nail and glared at Neil. Why'd he bring up Skipper? The mutt made the rounds at all of our back doors, begging for a handout. Even though Jesse fed him first so he'd get to claim him, he was the neighborhood dog. We loved that ugly, scruffy brown dog. The night he died we'd been out playing with him until a summer shower caught us and ran us to our separate houses. Our parents said the wet roads caused the accident, but we knew better. Neil mentioning Skipper was odd. He had another motive.

Neil pressed closer. "Go on. Ask him what he buried with Skipper."

"What did you bury in the grave with Skipper?" My words were sing-song light and cool.

Eli stopped dead still. "Why would you ask that question?" His voice sounded stiff.

A strong reaction for a dog he buried nearly three decades ago.

"Just curious," I said. We all knew what happened to Eli's dog. What our parents didn't say. But driving was only one of the things Jesse's dad did when he was drunk.

Evidently Neil, Eli, and probably Jesse had a secret. Neil was pissed off at Eli and wanted to torture him by threatening to share it with me. I'd played into Neil's plan.

Eli resumed walking. "It's curious to me that you'd even think about a dog that died so long ago."

Neil plunged at Eli. "It was a Valentine, and he wrote something on the back. Ask him what?"

Intrigue niggled at my nerves. I jogged to catch up. "Eli, do you trust me?"

"What kind of question is that?" His look was rank with suspicion.

"I'm going to tell you something strange—more than strange. Unbelievable. I need to know if you trust me enough to believe me."

Neil crowded between us. "I know what you're doing, Libby. Don't."

I brushed Neil away. "You started this."

Eli stopped. "I started what?"

"Not you. I was talking to Neil," I said.

"First it's Skipper and now Neil. None of this conversation makes sense. What in hell's going on?"

"Neil's a ghost. I tried to tell you the night of the accident when I saw him in the dining room hanging from the chandelier. I thought if anyone believed me, it had to be you. I guess I was wrong."

Eli's face went from wary to red alert. Muscles in his jaw twitched, but he managed a controlled smile. He extended his hand. "Now, Libby, I believe *you* believe Neil is still here."

Fury bubbled up into my throat. I slapped his hand away. "Don't patronize me. I'm not some jumper you're trying to talk down from a ledge. Think about it. I had no idea about Skipper. You're right, I haven't thought about him in thirty years. Neil told me to ask you."

Eli put on his cop face. "He's here?"

I searched for hints of Neil who had chosen to evaporate. "I can't see him right now. But I feel him."

Eli scrubbed his hands over his face and finished with a quick swipe over his slick head. "Try to understand how difficult this is. I'm a police officer. I base my life and job on facts and clues."

"Where's your faith in me?" I wanted to jump up and down like a kid.

"Lib, you're freaking me out."

I stomped up to Eli and whacked my hands on his chest. "You want facts? I'll give you facts. Fact number one: I had no idea you buried a Valentine in Skipper's grave. I wasn't there. Neil told me to ask you. Fact number two: Neil said before you buried the Valentine, you wrote something on the back. Fact number three: You thought your secret was safe—until Neil opened his big mouth. Now I have two questions for you. Why did you bury a Valentine in the grave with Skipper, and what did you write on the back of it?" Eli's heart thumped faster and faster beneath my hands.

Eli covered my hands with his. "Ask Neil."

My fingers memorized the rhythm of Eli's heartbeat. "Neil, what did Eli write on the back of the Valentine?"

Silence. "Dammit! Where are you? If you don't answer me, so help me, I'll tell the kids—"

"Aren't you tired of that empty threat?" Neil asked.

I spoke to the air but kept my eyes locked on Eli's.

"It's not an empty threat. Give me an excuse to tell them what a low-down, no-good husband you were."

Eli stood motionless, barely breathing. But his heart raced.

"You won't tell them anything." The air stirred, but I saw no shimmer or shadow. "Now I regret letting my temper reveal our pact at Skipper's funeral. Me and my big mouth."

"Well, it's too late for that. Why'd you want to hurt Eli?"

Eli moved into my line of vision. "Who hurt me?"

I held up my hand.

A cool breeze brushed my face. "I still think he's trying to steal my family."

"You didn't want me." The words blistered my tongue.

"The Valentine was from you. Eli put a Valentine from you in Skipper's grave. That's all I'll share. No more threats. I'm done." Neil blended into the shadows of the night.

My mind repeated Neil's words over and over. I understood Neil's concern and even his vengeful trick, but I wanted to know what was so important about a Valentine buried in the grave with the dog. I crossed my arms over my chest. "Neil said it was a Valentine from me, but he refuses to tell me what you wrote on

175

it."

A low whistle passed between Eli's teeth. "Holy shit." The whites of Eli's eyes glowed fluorescent.

"Now you believe me?"

Eli ran his hand across the back of his neck. "Holy shit."

Neil's little mystery was wearing thin. "Tell me. What did you write on the back?"

The roar of a rotten muffler drowned out his answer, and then a car appeared, taking the curve too fast—right toward us.

My feet stuck to the ground like Velcro. Eli picked me up and dove into the shrubbery. He'd saved me, but not my innocent mailbox. Pieces of dented metal and splinters of wood lay scattered on the road and in the grass.

Eli snapped to his feet. Hunched and wary, his elbows jutted out from his body, his fists clenched and ready to attack. He watched the car speed away, and turned to me, his eyes dark in the ambient light. "You okay? Got a partial on his tag."

I beat my hands against my backside and legs brushing off chips of pine bark from the flower bed. "The maniac could have hit us!" My burst of energy fizzed at the sight of my mailbox. "That could have been us."

"Did you recognize the car or the driver? Have there been other disturbances?" Still in his policeman role, Eli fired questions at me.

The red flag had broken off the smashed mailbox and lay at my feet. I soccer-kicked it across the road. "He was flying around that curve. What if the kids had been with us? He could have—"

Eli retrieved his phone from his pocket and tapped the screen. "Have you ever seen this car or the driver before?"

"It's the same rusty rattletrap Emily and I saw when we were walking around the lake a few days ago. What are you tapping into your phone?"

"The partial tag number. I don't want to forget it. I'll plug it into the database later. Now tell me about the last time you saw him." He held the phone poised and ready.

"Emily and I had just finished our walk and were standing right here when we heard his loud muffler. He was creeping by until he saw us. Then he hit the gas and hid his face."

Eli dusted off his slacks. "Did you report it?"

"He's just a kid," I said.

Neil slid into view. "Tell him you've been too busy dodging Cupid's arrows."

Eli's head swiveled back and forth. "Is he here?"

Hairs on my arms swayed in the breeze, prickling my skin. "Why do you ask?"

He rubbed the back of his neck. "It feels like a herd of ants are stampeding up my neck."

I scrubbed my arms together. "You didn't hear him, did you?"

Neil flashed an evil smile. "Let's try it again." Neil sidled close to Eli and ran his hand over Eli's bald head.

"Shit." Eli ducked and covered his head with his arm. "Now they're charging across the top of my head."

"Cut it out, Neil," I said.

He grabbed my hand and tugged. "Let's go." His body shuddered. "We can finish this *inside*."

I pulled back. "Are you going to tell me what you

177

wrote on the Valentine?"

"Nope. It's between Neil and me."

Chapter 16
Who Are You Going to Call?

Coffee cup in hand, I walked out front and waved one last goodbye to Emily's gray mini-van loaded with kids, bags, and dogs. Her parents lived on a farm north of Birmingham, and in less than an hour our kids would be riding horses, feeding cows, and chasing chickens. Emily planned to drop off the kids and head to the outlet mall before coming home. I opted for my own plan to spend the next twenty-four hours catching up on projects and putting the latest series of events into some sort of perspective.

For the first time since Neil's awful departure, I felt good. The kind of good that seeing the scale five pounds down brings. The kind of good that engenders hope. Knowing that Emily and Eli believed me about Neil lightened the weight of my secret and made me feel less alone.

Neil and Eli's secret intrigued me, and I planned on getting the complete story. And today, not even the crazy driver with the rusty muffler could dampen my spirit. I sucked in a kid-free breath and held it, filling my lungs with sweet, spring air. Though officially still a few weeks away, a layer of yellow pine pollen dusted the boat dock; and tiny buds pushed through the bark on the branches promising a new beginning. A thrill of independence and possibilities tingled every pore.

Nervous energy hummed through my body. I was too torqued to spend the day painting my nails or cleaning out closets. I wanted a big job. A physical job. Being a single mother of two and the master of my universe, I didn't have far to look. I needed to re-stain the boat dock, but that meant going to the store to buy stain. Same thing with mulching the flower beds. I didn't want to spend my energy pushing a shopping cart down the aisle at the nursery. I could power-wash the eaves. The temperature at its current fifty-five degrees meant a chilly back spray. I looked up. Leaves and pine straw jutted out of the gutters. Neil cleaned out the gutters. How hard could it be?

I donned jeans and one of Neil's long-sleeved running shirts and bounded down the stairs to the basement and into the garage. Mr. Neat and Organized had hung the metal telescopic ladder on two red hooks on the wall where his car used to park. I lifted one end of the ladder, and the other end fell off its hook, sending ten feet of aluminum crashing to the cement floor. I shook off the ringing in my ears and found a pair of Neil's work gloves. They hung loose on my hands but were better than nothing. I reached through the top rung and shouldered the ladder like a single strap on a back pack. And pulled. And pulled. The screeching of metal scraping cement made my teeth ache. And I pulled some more, dragging the ladder to the front yard.

The house was built to fit the topography, and the land flowed in a natural slope from the street to the waterline. The back and sides were two stories tall, but the roofline in front stood only about fifteen feet above the ground. However, the gutter over the front porch was only about ten feet high. That's where Neil always propped the ladder. Like I'd seen him do, I wrangled the ladder back and forth and then kicked the base into place. Up I climbed, one rung at a time.

I gripped the gutters with my left hand and threw my right leg over and scooted out onto the roof and sat up. Confidence pumped though my veins. The sharp angle pitched me forward, but I compensated by planting my feet in front of me. It didn't look far to the ground. I inched my way to one of the dormers and hauled myself up. From my vantage point in front, I was unable to see the lake or my family home, only hills and trees. But I knew Eli's childhood home lay around the curve, and beyond the railroad tracks was where Jesse grew up. "Woo hoo!" I shouted and pumped my fist into the air. I was queen of my universe.

There were no gutters on the vaulted areas. Only across the front and back. My job looked easy. I sat down, and using my butt as an anchor extended my legs for support and crab-crawled close to the edge. So far so good. I leaned over and the stench hit me first. I turned my head and held my breath to keep from gagging and raked out black, gooey globs. One arm's reach and one breath at a time. Below me in a straight line along the ground, a trail of dark leaf debris verified my progress. I pushed up my sleeves. Crawling on this black roof in July would be torture. I finished my run across the front, and then it hit me.

To get to the gutters on the other side, I'd have to climb over the ridge. *Maybe this wasn't a great idea.* No one knew I was up here, and I had no clue when Emily would get back. *There's no cowardice in knowing one's limitations.* Limitations? Climbing over a slippery mountain of asphalt shingles and risk breaking my neck wasn't knowing my limitations. It was lunacy. I came, and I conquered. The front gutters at least. There was no dishonor in defeat. Time to tackle another chore.

I crab-scooted closer to the ladder. Climbing up was fun, but getting down was another story. How was I supposed to get both feet on the ladder? I visualized rolling to the side and slinging a leg out backward to find the rung. What do I hold on to?

I took a deep breath and then twisted my body until I was on all fours. I heard the low grumbling sound of a rusted-out muffler. I turned to look. My weight shifted, and I started sliding. I belly flopped to the roof, and stretched out my gloved hands to slow my slide, burrowing in the rubber tips of my tennis shoes like toe stops on roller skates—and kept sliding. Wildly, I pumped my legs searching for the gutter. My shoe caught the lip of the trough, and I wedged my left foot into the trench. I swallowed to get my heart back in place. Grit filled my mouth, and I spit. I tasted asphalt.

My heart pounded against the slippery shingles. *I'm on my own. I can do this.* With my right foot, I tapped behind me, searching for the ladder's rails or rungs. My shoe hit the right rail at an angle, and the metal ladder squealed against the metal gutters. Again I heard the recognizable roar of the outdated and aged land cruiser.

Anger neutralized my fear, and I raised my head. "What do you want?" I had to get down and confront the trespasser. I kicked my foot backward to find the rung, and the ladder careened right and kept going, leaving my foot suspended in mid-air. My foot floundered at first, and then jammed into the gutter.

I lay face down until the tremors subsided. Slowly I pushed my body more solidly onto the roof and then rolled onto my back. I closed my eyes to block the sun, and air slowly filled my collapsed lungs. I sat up and scrunched backward to get high enough to hail a passing neighbor. My right pocket vibrated. I braced myself on my left elbow and wrenched my phone out of my pocket. It skidded through the fingers of my giant rawhide gloves.

I lunged for it, and my butt skidded over the shingles. My elbow dug into the gritty roof and slowed my descent until I jammed both feet into the gutter. I watched my phone slip down the roof and bounce into the trench. Without the clog of leaves, the phone slid easily toward the downspout. I couldn't see the phone, and I couldn't lean over without sliding.

Neil hovered over the down spout. "Hope your phone doesn't ring. One vibration, and swoosh, down the spout."

"I so appreciate your encouraging observation. Dammit, aren't things bad enough?" I displayed an angry wrist-to-elbow scrape. "I've skinned my arms and eaten asphalt, and now I've dropped my phone. If I try to get it, I might slide off the roof and break my neck. Thanks for showing up to mock me." I blew on the ravaged skin and tenderly brushed away grains of asphalt from the abrasion on my arm.

Neil locked his fists on his waist and cocked his head into what I'd come to call his disgusted ghost pose. "What are you doing up here?"

"Sunbathing. Thought I'd kill two birds with one

stone. You know, catch a few rays, clean out the gutters." I was so glad he'd shown up—though I'd never tell him. My confidence came surging back.

"Sarcasm is not very flattering." Neil sat on the edge and dangled his legs over the side. "Looks like it's time for plan B."

"Really, Neil? Plan B? I don't have a freaking Plan B. I didn't expect to knock the ladder over and get marooned on the roof." I stroked my chest and breathed in through my nose. *Calm down. Get your phone. Call for help.* I balanced on my hands and baby-crab-walked closer to the downspout. Maybe I'd think of something when I got there.

Neil perched over the downspout. "Hope it's not set on vibrate. That would be disastrous."

"You're always so positive." I inched closer. "Do you see anything I could hold on to or tie off to?"

Neil glided up the incline. "Only a plumbing vent pipe. But it's too far away."

I ventured a look over the side. Without the ladder, it looked really far. I couldn't jump. Maybe I could hold on to the gutters and let myself drop. If I didn't break my neck first.

"Don't even think about it," Neil said.

"How do you know what I'm thinking?"

Neil poised on the vent pipe. "Your grandmother's garage. You and Eli jumped off and ridiculed Jesse and me until we jumped."

"Jumping's out of the question. But what are my options? I can sit here until Emily gets home or possibly flag down a neighbor. But if I can get my phone…"

"Do you think you can reach over that far without

losing your balance?"

I pulled my shirt over my head. The cool air whipped through my sports bra. "If I toss my shirt over the hole, I won't have to worry about my phone shimmying down the spout. I'll slither over to the edge and pretend it's leaf gunk and scoop it out."

Neil's form glistened in the sun. "It might work."

"Wish you were solid. I could use a hand." I tossed the gloves aside and wrapped my shirt around my neck. Planting my rubber soles into the gutters, I lay back. I shifted my feet along the gutters and skidded my back over the uneven tiles. I can't see the phone."

Neil hunkered down. "Just a little more. Little more. Little more. Stop."

Feet braced on the gutter, I eased up to a sitting position. I wadded up my shirt and drew back to throw.

"Easy, Lib, or you'll knock your phone down the drain."

I changed my pitching form to underhand and flipped the shirt. Too hard. The sleeve unrolled and snagged the phone, jarring it into motion. The shirt skimmed the gutter and toppled over the edge. In slow motion the phone moved toward the gaping hole of the downspout. I held my breath. Any abrupt movement could send me over with my shirt. So I watched and waited for the clink-clank of my phone tumbling down the chasm.

Neil thrust out his hand, and the phone stopped sliding.

I almost lost my balance. "How'd you do that?"

Using his index finger, he pushed the phone inches from my feet. "Got lucky, I guess."

"That wasn't luck. You've been experimenting!" I

wanted to pursue my observation, but I also wanted to get off the roof. "Don't think we won't discuss this later." I leaned over and grasped my phone and clutched it to my chest. It vibrated against my skin and rang. I looked at the screen and then at Neil. "It's Jesse." I knew how the settlers felt when the cavalry arrived. I tapped *accept* and yelled. "Come help me! I'm stranded on my roof and need a ladder."

"On your roof?" Laughter played in Jesse's voice.

Jesse didn't understand the seriousness of my predicament. "Let me start again. I climbed on my roof to clean out the gutters and accidentally knocked my ladder over. Now I can't get down. Can you please come help me?"

"This is my lucky day. I'll be there in five."

Neil floated into view, anger a dark shadow over his face. "You called Jesse King?"

"I didn't call him. He called me."

"Why would he call you?" Neil sat beside me.

I thought about what to tell him.

Neil dropped his hand into his lap. "It's your business, but I don't trust him."

"He said I'm a beautiful, single woman."

"And you believed him." Neil's lip lifted at the corner.

Anger flashed. "You're right. How could I be stupid enough to think a man could find me beautiful?"

Neil's eyes grew round. "Wait. I didn't mean it like that. Of course you're beautiful. I just know the kind of woman Jesse's attracted to."

"Go away, Neil."

"Okay. I'll go. But are you going to let him see you like that?" He gestured his hands over his chest.

"It's a sports bra. It covers more than a bathing suit top."

An engine droned up my driveway, and a car door slammed. Jesse stood in my front yard. "You're what I'd call a damsel in distress."

"Quite coincidental for Jesse to be so close by, don't you think?" Neil asked.

I bit down on the inside of my cheek. "I just want to get down from here."

"One ladder coming right up." Jesse's head peeked up above the roof line. "Man, what a view. Not that I'm questioning my good fortune, but why was your shirt on the ground?" He held out my shirt, but his eyes settled on my chest. "I can't believe I'm encouraging you to put clothes *on*."

I slipped the shirt over my head and rammed my arms through the sleeves.

Jesse vaulted up to the roof and put his hand to his forehead to block the sun. "It really is quite a view from here. Our old house is that way. I hated it when they fenced the lake."

"First one was a split-rail fence, and we crawled right through." I didn't want a trek along memory lane. I wanted down.

The hand at his side clenched into a fist. "We all know who they wanted to keep out."

Why did he have to bring this up now? I spent most of my childhood not thinking about Mr. King. "It wasn't you."

Jesse gave me a wry smile. "My old man was a piece of work."

We lived too close not to hear the yelling or see the results a bottle of booze had on Jesse's dad. I had always wondered why Mrs. King didn't take Jesse and run away. Now I understood how hard it is for a mother to survive alone. Besides, it was the Deep South thirty years ago. Some people took the "For better or worse clause" to mean just that. But when Jesse grew up and filled out, things got better for Jesse and his mom but worse for Mr. King. Jesse was a toned athlete and a head taller than his dad and no longer a defenseless child.

Jesse's thoughts followed his gaze toward his old home and spilled over his lips. "My dad started a trash business." His mouth curved into a dead smile. "A garbage man. Quite fitting actually. Do you know how embarrassing it was to tell people my dad was a garbage man?"

"Your dad's work had nothing to do with the problems at home. Besides, he built his business into a successful company." And every week Mr. King bought a full-page ad in the football program featuring his son and his scoring record. "Your dad's business didn't deter your groupies."

Jesse's head snapped back in my direction. "Well, this son of a garbage man has big plans. I'm going to a recycling conference in Montreal. Come with me? I double-dog dare you."

He couldn't be serious. I hadn't even agreed to go out to dinner, much less out of the country. "The altitude's getting to you. I can't go to Montreal."

Jesse grinned. "I could leave you up here until you say yes."

I leaned back on my hands. "I still don't understand why you're interested in me. Why now?"

"I told you I like beautiful women. And I like to

date beautiful women and show them beautiful things."

A bad taste rose in my throat. "I didn't feel too beautiful when you stood me up for the homecoming dance."

The crease deepened between Jesse's eyes, and his voice came out low and sad. "I wish I could get a do-over for that night. Things might have turned out so different for me. I'm sorry, Lib. Really."

I propped my hands on my knees. "Yeah, well, words are cheap."

"Let's get you down from here." Jesse extended his leg over the rails and stepped down onto the ladder. "I want you to back over here on your knees and let me guide your foot. When you feel the metal step, ease your other foot back. I'll hold you."

My heart pounded. "I can't. I'm afraid."

"I won't let you fall. I promise." His smooth easy tone quieted the drumming in my chest. "Now ease over here. That's it. Jesse slid my foot toward the ladder. "Perfect. One rung at a time. I've got you." Jesse's voice cooed and soothed my liquid limbs, and we descended.

When my feet touched down, I wanted to kiss the earth. Fear and strain from the ordeal seeped out of me. My rescuer—the source of so much adolescent angst, was my hero. Tears stirred behind my eyes, and I tried to walk away to get my emotions under control. I was embarrassed enough without the waterworks.

Jesse caught up and draped his arm around my shoulders. "Wait up, hotshot."

I twisted out of his arm and pressed my hands to my eyes. *Please be the old Jesse.* If he acted all warm and fuzzy, the dam would burst.

Then he turned me into him and took my hands in his. "What were you trying to prove up on that roof? That you're still bold and daring?"

I concentrated my energy on holding back the tears. In hindsight, climbing up there without backup might not have been my smartest move. But I didn't have to answer to Jesse, Eli, Neil, or anyone else. My body tensed, and my voice came out harsher than I intended. "It's my damn roof. And I don't need to climb up on a roof to prove I'm bold and daring—I teach seventh graders."

He laughed. "Miss Independent. I always liked that about you." Jesse's soft hand caressed my face. A lone tear strayed down my cheek. Then another tear. And another. I couldn't stop the deluge. I covered my face.

Jesse pulled my hands away. "You're okay now." His cheek brushed mine, and his breath warmed my skin. He put a hand behind my neck and an arm around my waist and pulled his body against mine. His lips skimmed my eyes. My cheeks. And then found my mouth. Hot and wet, his tongue parted my lips, and his urgency exploded. I stopped for a breath, and he pulled me back into the maelstrom.

Until Emily's horn blasted me back to reality.

Chapter 17
What Just Happened Here?

"What were you thinking?" Emily's question reverberated across the lake and inside my head.

Lately the normal speed for our daily walk around the lake was somewhere between saunter and stroll. Today Emily's pace matched her level of exasperation, and I ran to keep up. "Obviously I wasn't thinking! I don't know why I kissed Jesse King!" My cheeks flared in shame. I'd fallen prey to the wiles of Jesse King. Again. Being stood up for the homecoming dance twenty years ago couldn't compete with his soft lips and warm hands. I took a few quick breaths to get my breathing under control. "Slow down. I can't run and talk."

"I thought you and Eli were getting close. But I drive by and see you lip-locked to a guy with a full head of hair! Obviously not Eli."

"It was a reflex. He helped me down from the roof and caught me at a weak moment. Or maybe I wanted to see if I remembered how to kiss."

Our shoes clapped in time as we made our way around the lake. "In your front yard in broad daylight!" Emily stopped. "Well? Is it like riding a bicycle?"

Neil's essence spiraled upward. I cringed. His haughty voice echoed in my ear. "Looks like Mr. Quarterback can still field a pass."

"Whatever. It just happened." I turned to Emily. "My shadow's here."

She searched the air for signs of Neil, and caught the toe of her shoe on the pavement and lunged forward. "I wish I could see him. Does he look the same?"

"Exactly the same. Blue shirt and khaki pants even. He's not up there. He's right behind us," I said, and picked up our pace.

"So he doesn't look like a ghost?" Emily asked.

I threw her an irritated look. "I don't know what a ghost looks like. Neil's the only one I've ever seen."

"Is he…like…transparent?" Emily asked.

"Sometimes he's more transparent than others. I think it depends on how strong he feels and reacts to things. But usually, he's more faded than transparent."

"And…Is he like the ghosts in cartoons?"

I laughed. "Yep. A cartoon describes him perfectly."

Neil coasted beside me. "You guys are hilarious. Tell Emily her hair looks nice."

I knew there was something different about Emily, but I'd been concentrating on Jesse's hot lips. "Neil said your hair looks good. You get a haircut?"

Emily smoothed her hair. "Neil noticed?" She looked up and shouted, "Thanks, Neil."

"Don't encourage him."

We ended our walk at our usual spot. Emily's mailbox.

She pulled the door open and reached inside.

Neil hovered over my shoulder. "Ask Emily if she has anything she wants to tell you."

I followed her lead and withdrew a stack of mail

from my new box, thanks to Eli. As I flipped through several white envelopes I casually asked, "Neil said there might be something you want to tell me."

She stopped sorting her mail, and lowered her voice to a whisper. "How does he know?"

I crammed my mail under my arm. "What does he know?"

"Reggie called last week to see if he had any mail," Emily said.

"So you talked to him last week?"

"Sunday night. And the next night, and the next. We've talked every night."

"And?" I knew there was more.

Emily scuffed her feet in the grass. "He's coming over tonight."

"I'm not believing this. What in the hell does he want?"

Emily squared her shoulders. "I didn't tell you because I knew you'd freak out—exactly like you're doing."

"Excuse me? This is the man who left a note on a paper towel telling his loving wife of twenty years he needed space?" My words hung like icicles.

"Reggie's dealing with some complex issues, Libby. And he's sorry." Emily looked away. "Don't be mad. You've known all along that I still love him."

"So you'll take him back, just like that?" I snapped my fingers.

Emily closed her eyes. "I want my family back."

When I saw the moisture well up in her eyes, I didn't push any farther. I was her friend, and I would stand by her. No matter how much I disagreed with her. "Look, I love you, and I want you to be happy. If taking

Reggie back gets your family together, I'm all for it. One favor, though. Don't rush this. Maybe get some counseling first?"

"Try to be happy for me." Emily pleaded.

I hugged my friend, and the dam broke. I cried for Emily. And I cried for me.

I flicked the tears from my cheeks and wiped my eyes, "Hey, maybe you'll be the first to test out our sexy new undies."

Tears sparkled in her eyes. "I'll let you know if they work."

I put a good face on for Emily, but her news gnawed at me. On Sunday morning, Reggie's car was still parked in their driveway. It was all I needed to know. Sometimes I envied her and Reggie. Like a jigsaw puzzle, she could put the pieces together and get her family back. They *could* be whole again. But even if God gave me a do-over, I wouldn't. That simple admission opened my cage door and set me free.

****

I expected to see Eli and Jesse at our class reunion meeting, and I couldn't wait. Eli showed me what it felt like to be cherished, and Jess made me feel desired. Then the old Libby kicked in, worrying about how I was supposed to act around Jesse after I'd kissed him? And if Eli could tell. Anxiety ate at my concentration while Able Allison gave her reports, handed out assignments, and hurried out the door before we finished our appetizers. Buddy refused a doggy bag and followed Allison. Charlotte had a deposition out of town, and Jesse was a no-show. Eli and I waved goodbye. "No catastrophes tonight?" he asked.

I punched his granite bicep. "It's still early."

"Any word from Jesse?"

Before I could answer, my daughter yelled from the front porch. "Mom, you out here?"

"Coming." I angled my head toward the house. "You feeling brave tonight?"

Eli winked at me and beat me to the front porch. He engulfed Reagan in a big hug. "What's shaking, kiddo? Still wearing your Jacob earrings or have you traded them for a new boyfriend?"

Reagan flipped her hair back. "Still wearing them." Reagan took his hand and led him into the house. "Can I ask you a question?"

Eli looked at me as if asking permission.

I shrugged. "By all means. I'm having a glass of wine. You?" I walked to the refrigerator, and Reagan hauled Eli into the den.

"Mom doesn't think I'm old enough to go out. How old were you when you started dating?"

I heard Eli sputtering and stammering trying to get the words out. "Reagan, I'm not a good one to ask. And you know it's different for boys."

"How's it different for boys?"

Panic crept over his face. "Can you help me here, Libby? Where's that wine?"

I handed Eli a glass of wine, and I sat on the arm of the sofa beside him. "I think you're doing great. I'd like to know how it's different for boys, too." I raised my glass to him.

Beads of sweat glistened on Eli's smooth head. He took a big gulp. "Boys don't care about soft things. They like sports. Football and baseball and basketball. Any sport. And another thing, boys use bad language. But girls are soft and squishy." His eyes darted from

Reagan to me and back to Reagan. "And in your case, really pretty—like your mom."

Reagan donned a sympathetic face and patted Eli's arm. "You don't know much about girls, do you?"

A burgundy blush traveled up Eli's neck and over his face to his smooth bald head. "Maybe you and your mom can give me some pointers before Lee gets old enough to notice girls."

Trey bounded down the stairs and went for the remote. "Girls, yuck. Mom, can Eli stay for dinner?"

I turned to Eli. "Pizza again. You interested?"

"I never turn down food." Eli wrestled Trey onto the sofa and stole the remote. He clicked the off button. "Let's eat."

A comfortable group sat around the kitchen table. Reagan finished chewing and directed her attention to Eli. "Did Mom tell you about her excitement today?"

Eli's smile dimmed. "What happened?"

Trey jumped in. "Let me tell. It was so cool. We were in Emily's driveway unloading Marcus and Andrea's stuff, and we heard this car coming around the lake making a loud *vroom-broom-vroom-broom*. Mom got this wild look on her face and yelled *sh*—I can't repeat what she said, or I'll get in trouble—"

Reagan interrupted Trey. "Yeah, right. You've said it a hundred times."

"Have not," Trey said.

"Liar," Reagan argued back.

"Enough." I said.

Eli's eyes bounced from Reagan to Trey and back to me. "What are you guys talking about?"

I blew out a breath. "I said *shit*. I'm not proud of it, but I said it."

Eli laid his pizza on the paper plate. "Why did you say…the *S* word?"

Trey broke in. "That's not the best part. She grabbed a brick out of the flower bed and threw it through the old brown car's back windshield. A perfect bull's eye. You should have heard the crash. And glass went everywhere. He laid rubber getting away. Want to go see the tire marks?"

Eli's eyes narrowed and his nostrils flared. "Did you call the police?"

I laid my napkin on the table. "The president of the homeowners' association said there was nothing the police could do. We live on private property, and the driver hasn't done anything but drive around the lake. If we knew his identity, we might press charges for trespassing." I neglected to mention that the association president said the man could file charges against me for lobbing a brick through his window.

Eli wiped his mouth and threw his napkin onto his plate. "Did you tell the homeowners' association president about the mailbox?"

"He said things like that happen all the time. Nothing to worry about."

Eli wouldn't let it go. "So, people come barreling around the lake and blast your mailbox into scrap metal all the time?"

I didn't want to be interrogated anymore "Let's deal with it later. Hey, did you guys know that Eli played at Alabama?"

Trey gasped. "No way!"

"Long time ago," Eli shifted back in his chair, not satisfied with my putting him off.

I dabbed my lips with my napkin. "He played for

Bear Bryant."

"Lib, Bear Bryant was long gone before I got there," Eli said.

Reagan leaned toward Eli. "Are you like…famous?"

"Not as famous as your mom." Eli gave her and Trey a big smile.

Trey aimed his thumb in my direction. "You talking about our mom?"

"Did you see her on TV?" Eli asked.

"She was on one time. Bet you played on TV a bunch of times," Trey said.

"It was kind of cool seeing Mom on TV." Reagan folded her pizza lengthwise. "And it was cool when several of my teachers mentioned it."

Trey stuffed a giant bite into his mouth. "None of my friends saw it."

Reagan banged her hand on the table. "Gross. Mom, say something."

I picked up my plate. "Son, don't put so much into your mouth. And swallow before you start talking."

Trey made a big deal about chewing and held his hand up as his pause button. "Okay, okay. Mom's famous. Eli, can we go throw the football?"

Trey yapped at Eli's heels like a feisty puppy. I turned on the flood lights, and Reagan and I grabbed another slice of pizza. We sat on the patio munching and listening to Eli answer Trey's questions about sacks, draws, reversals. Reagan tossed her crust to Sadie, who swallowed it whole and wagged her tail for mine.

Reagan wiped her hands on her jeans. "Can I try?"

Eli smiled and tossed the football underhanded—

right into Reagan's arms.

Reagan chunked the ball to Eli, but Trey scooted in front of him and caught the wobbly pass. "You throw like a girl," Trey said.

Reagan examined her nails. "Think I'll quit while I'm ahead. Mom, I'm going upstairs. Night, Eli."

"Hold on to those earrings." Eli called to Reagan, and then he pointed the football toward the water. "Go long, Trey." Eli's voice boomed, and Trey ran.

Trey ran, staying within the boundary marked by the flood lights. "Got it!" He clutched the football close to his body like Eli had shown him and ran to the patio. "Thanks, Eli. Me and Dad threw the ball some. But he said all he ever did was ride the pine in high school. I guess my dad wasn't too good."

Eli sat on the steps, and Trey plopped down beside him. Eli took the football from Trey and rubbed his thumb over the lacing. "Your dad was a good ball player. Believe me. I was there. He could run and zigzag with the best of us. The problem was your dad had his heart set on playing quarterback. And there was nobody better than Jesse King. If I could have gotten that into your dad's head, he'd have been an awesome running back."

"But you guys were still friends, right?" Trey asked.

"The best," Eli said.

"Will you tell me some stories about my dad?"

"I've got tons of them, and I promise I'll fill your ears full. But it's late, and you need to hit the showers."

Trey opened the door to enter but turned like he forgot something. "Can we do this next Sunday night? And you bring Lee?"

Eli looked my way. "Hate to wear out my welcome."

I brushed off the seat of my jeans. "Fine by me. Say goodnight."

"Night, Tank." Trey extended his hand.

Eli shook Trey's hand like it was the most normal thing to do. "Next time we'll work on that spiral."

"Thank you, pretty lady, for another great evening." Eli hugged me tight, lifting me up high enough for my shoes to fall off.

I walked him to his car barefooted. When I came into the kitchen, I swung a shoe in each hand. Reagan waited, leaning against the counter. I dropped my shoes and slipped my feet into them. And then I rolled my lips inward and saved my silly grin for later.

"Are you guys dating?" she asked.

I loaded glasses into the dishwasher. "We're good friends. Have been since before we could walk." Delight, as startling as a sneaked kiss, stilled my hands. "Eli was my first friend."

"Nope. Can't see you and Eli crawling around slobbering all over everything." Reagan grabbed an apple from the bowl and buffed it on her shirt. "Do you *want* to date him?"

"Never thought about it," I lied.

"Do you want to kiss him?"

I gave her a warning look. "You're crossing the line."

"That's how I can tell if I like a guy," she said.

"Reagan Elizabeth! Who've you been kissing? Jacob?"

Reagan bit into her apple and walked toward the stairs. "You're crossing that line, Mom."

200

"Parents don't have lines," I yelled at her back. "If we did, I'd be jumping up and down on those lines. With both feet!"

The doorbell ended my tirade. Through the thick beveled glass, I recognized the towering form and opened the door. "Forget something?"

"I left my red folder in the boathouse. Allison gave me a homework assignment, and I don't want to get on her bad side."

"Follow me, big guy. I'd hate for you to incur Allison's wrath. I'll let you help me close up and turn off the lights."

As we walked through the damp grass to the boathouse, Eli trailed his fingers up and down the narrow valley of my spine. "I haven't felt Neil all night."

I stopped abruptly. It was the first time Eli mentioned Neil. I chuckled nervously. "I thought I just imagined telling you. I haven't seen him either. He comes and goes. He seems to be staying away for longer periods. But I don't dare hope."

Eli held the door open for me.

A cold breeze blew through the open window, and I reached to close it.

"Leave it open." Before I could turn, Eli closed his mammoth arms around me and clasped his hands at my waist, locking me in place.

"I generate a lot of body heat." Eli spread his hands over my stomach and drew me into him.

My heart flapped inside my chest like a hooked fish on the boat dock. Warm, calloused hands slid slowly up my arms and stopped when they found my shoulders. I wanted those rough hands on my skin.

Touching me. Holding me. His grip tightened, and he rotated my body. Our eyes came together. And my heart stopped.

Reflected in the dark pools of his eyes was a longing and knowing that pierced far deeper than my present or past. Like a corkscrew, his laser-sharp look drilled past my defenses, all the way to my core. And exposed me. Libby Miller. A woman terrified of facing the world as a single mother, yet hell bent on being independent. A woman who ached to be loved.

His look left no doubt. He wanted me.

As gentle as a breath of air, his mouth touched mine. His lips, so soft and moist. I wanted to taste them. Tentatively I slipped my tongue between his lips. Minty. I should have known. Our tongues danced delicately at first, tasting and testing. He snaked his arms around me and drew me into the safe harbor of his embrace. He sucked in my air and then covered my mouth with his, dipping his tongue into an abyss of longing and desire. I clung to his shirt and accepted his love like a transfusion.

His tongue tripped over my teeth and licked my lips. "You taste just like I remember."

Chapter 18
Glass Slipper

I'd kissed two men within twenty-four hours. And they weren't cousinly-kisses either.

"Ms. Miller?" The tinny voice of the office intercom scattered my thoughts and my riveting lesson on direct objects.

Classroom noise ceased. All eyes turned to me.

"Yes?" I spoke to the metal box on the wall whose voice belonged to Gloria Mitchell, school secretary and good friend.

"We have a delivery for you in the office. Do you want to send someone to get it, or do you want to pick up these gorgeous roses during your planning time?"

Flowers? For me? Before I could answer, one of my girls yelled out. "What color are they?"

"Shh, Melissa." I gave her the teacher-eye. "I'll stop by after class."

"Aww." A chorus of feminine voices objected in perfect harmony. "Ms. Miller, we want to see them."

I checked the clock on the wall. Only five minutes of class left. "Okay. Melissa and Victoria, go to the office and get the flowers."

The girls paraded into the classroom holding aloft a tall vase of red roses like the Olympic Torch. Although the bell saved me from answering any personal questions from my students, I wasn't so lucky with

Leah and Angie, my young colleagues down the hall. They elbowed their way into my classroom against the flow of seventh graders exiting.

"Move over, guys. Coming through!" Angie Simmons, seventh grade teacher, cheerleader sponsor, and human megaphone burst through the door and buried her nose in the bouquet. "Oh, my gosh! We heard about your delivery." Angie, the extrovert, never learned to use her inside voice. This trait served her well on the cheerleading squad in high school and college, but local libraries posted her name on the banned list.

Leah Drauch, the third member of our teaching triangle, propped her hip on the edge of my desk. Leah took a more measured approach, which is why she taught seventh grade math instead of Angie. Best friends since birth, cheerleading was the glue that bound. "Okay, you had a reunion meeting at your house last night, so these have to be from one of the high school reunion guys."

I shrugged my shoulders. "The girls brought them in right before the bell. I don't know who they're from."

Angie plucked the small white envelope from the bouquet and waved it in the air. "One way to find out."

I held out my hand. "The envelope, please." The rectangular piece of card stock held their eyes captive. "And the winner is…"

I put the card back into the envelope and stuck it into the flowers.

"No fair." Angie's full bottom lip rolled out in a pout.

"You want us to guess?" Leah asked.

I couldn't hold the words in any longer, and they burst from my mouth like champagne uncorked. "Eli. The flowers are from Eli."

"The bald dude?" Angie asked.

"The bald cop dude," Leah added. "So what are you going to do?"

I pulled a long-stemmed rose from the vase and rubbed the red, velvety petals against my cheek. "Send a thank-you note."

"If somebody sent me roses, the last thing I'd be thinking about would be a thank-you note." Angie sat in one of the student desks. "Hey, Leah, you send Dirk a thank-you note when he sends you flowers?"

Leah sat in my chair and rotated the vase. "It's only one time. Two Valentines ago. Should I have sent him a thank-you note for my engagement ring he hid inside?"

Angie smacked her hand on her forehead. "Maybe that's why he's never sent you any more."

"Okay, make fun of the old teacher. Just remember I'm still your mentor and write your final reviews." I waved the card under Angie's nose. "If it makes you feel better, I'll let you read what he wrote on the card."

Angie snatched the card, and Leah leaned over her shoulder. They both looked puzzled. "What does he mean help him with his homework?"

"Allison assigned him to find a band for the reunion, and he wants me to go with him Friday night." I took my purse from the bottom drawer.

Angie's eyes grew wider than her smile. "So he's like asking you out?"

"A *real* date?" Leah's bottom skid off my desk. "You ready?"

"Ready or not." I attempted a confident smile, but a

seed of terror had already taken root.

****

Finally, Friday. Neil had been uncharacteristically quiet, but I wasn't complaining.

At precisely seven p.m., doorbell chimes tolled.

For the hundredth time, I smoothed my dress and checked my reflection in the hall mirror. The deep "V" of my chic little black dress, enhanced by my Secret Embrace bra, created the perfect valley for the single strand of pearls. Was I exposing too much?

I held my breath, sucked in my stomach, and opened the door. Eli started to speak but closed his mouth. Slowly his eyes traveled in mechanical precision from top to bottom, scanning me like a bar code.

A digital tingle marked his path.

A soft whistle escaped his lips. "I think I'm at the wrong house."

I twirled around. "You like my new dress? Emily talked me into buying it. She said it was a good investment."

"I don't know about the investment aspect, but it sure shows off your assets." And then with a sweeping bow he announced, "Lovely lady, your carriage awaits."

"You make me feel like Cinderella." I shut the door.

Eli waited at the bottom of the steps. "Well, Cinderella, does that sexy dress fall off of you at midnight?"

I walked past him. "You make me crazy."

"Hey, I'm a sensitive kind a guy. I believe in fairy tales." Eli's innocent voice made me smile. "Maybe I need to set my watch."

I pushed him off the sidewalk. "You promised me dinner, and I'm starving." No man had looked at me the way he did. Ever. Food was not on my mind.

Downtown, he parked under a brightly lighted sign, announcing, "Paisano's. Only Italian food in town." Aromas of fresh bread and garlic lured us inside. Grainy, black and white photographs depicting dirty-faced factory workers, horseless buggies, and railroad cars lined the walls and chronicled steel production and Birmingham's transformation into the Magic City.

Like other patrons crowded into the small, cozy room, we faced each other across a small round table covered with a red and white checkered tablecloth, complete with a candle burning in a wine bottle with wax dripping down the sides. A young girl filled our water glasses and deposited a basket of rolls and a glass bowl of butter.

Eli scooped out a roll and split it in two. "You have to try this garlic butter." He scraped his knife over the yellow mound and heaped the butter over each side. He took a man-sized bite out of one half and held out the rest for me. I leaned in and bit.

"How do you like it?" The candlelight danced in his hazel eyes.

"Delicious. But I'm going to need a whole roll of breath mints after I eat every one of those."

"Neat place, huh?" Eli offered the basket. "They'll bring more."

I chuckled. "A little different from meals at my house."

"What do you mean? No throwing? No hitting? No yelling? This is a nice change, but I like the chaos of the kids."

His words felt genuine and warm like the atmosphere. I liked this man. In fact, I'd liked this man before he grew into a man.

****

The night was cool, but warmed considerably when Eli slipped my hand into his. "Ready for your surprise?"

"There's more?"

"That was just dinner. A man's gotta eat. Now comes the surprise."

"Do I have to close my eyes?"

"No. Then I'd have to carry you."

"You saying I'm fat?"

"You did eat three rolls."

I hit him with my purse.

We stopped at double doors. Poised overhead was a clear plexiglass slipper as tall as I was. "The Glass Slipper?"

He opened the door and "Honky-Tonk Women" blasted out onto the sidewalk. He locked my hand in his and led the way. My pupils adjusted to the subdued lighting, and I casually took in my surroundings, glancing at the band onstage. My head swiveled in a bobble-head move, and my mouth fell open. On stage were our high school classmates Jimmy Evans and Mike Arnold and their band The Outsiders. I bobbled back at Eli, and he grinned—dimples fully engaged.

"I told you it was a surprise," he bellowed over the music.

The song ended, and Jimmy Evans grabbed the microphone from the stand and kicked the cord out of his way. "Good evening, ladies and gentlemen. Y'all turn your attention to the table on my far left." He pointed the microphone in our direction.

Mike leaned into the microphone and said, "The table with the tall, bald guy and the good-looking blonde."

Jimmy elbowed Mike out of the way and spoke into the microphone. "Mike and I went to high school with those two. Hi, Libby." Jimmy's voice boomed over the crowd and Mike waved wildly in the background.

Mike shoved Jimmy aside and took the microphone. "Libby, what are you doing with that big ugly dude? Hey, Tank, here's your request."

Twinkle Toes Tank hauled me to the dance floor singing "She's a Brick House." As per my usual reaction, I covered my eyes and let him lead me to the dancefloor and endured.

****

The trip home we bantered high school recollections like a friendly game of catch. Home came too soon, and when we drove through the gate, the full moon reflecting on the lake filled the car with silvery moonlight. In the driveway, he killed the engine and unbuckled his seat belt. He reached over to remove mine, and his fingers brushed against my breasts. "Do you remember the first time I kissed you?"

His contact scorched my skin. My hand went to my chest. He's asking about kissing. Is he going to kiss me? Wish I had a breath mint. "Technically, it was on the playground in first grade."

"Okay. The first time I kissed you on the mouth."

He's going to make me play twenty questions first. Sheesh. Do it! "That's easy. We were at Linda Gore's birthday party in seventh grade playing spin the bottle."

"I cheated."

I grabbed a handful of his shirt and pulled his face close to mine. "So did I."

His lips lingered a millimeter away. One heartbeat. Two. Then he crushed them to mine. They. Fit. Perfectly. I parted my lips, and a faint rumble came from his throat.

His tongue licked and teased, and I locked my arms around his neck and returned each thrust and parry. I pulled away and blew a warm breath over his moist lips. Then he took a second helping and kissed my lips, my chin, my neck.

"Oh, God." Eli's voice was husky. "If I'm dreaming, don't wake me."

I loosened my arms and caressed his face. And with the delicacy of a surgeon, his thumb stroked my lower lip. My breath stopped. His fingers trickled down to bare skin. My chest rose to welcome his hands.

"I've wanted you for so long." The darkness hid his face, but his words tinged my skin with pure desire.

I wanted to feel his hands on my body, his lips on my skin. "Let's go inside."

No words were spoken on the sixty-second walk to the front door. When we reached the door, he grabbed my shoulders and looked down at me. My own need and lust reflected in his eyes.

He pushed my back against the door and pressed the length of his body to mine. Energy ran the length of his body and awakened every cell it touched. I wanted to go inside and drown in his touch. Reaching behind me, I pressed down on the lever to open the door. Locked. I tried it again. And again. And again.

"Where's your key?"

My stomach roiled. I remembered where my keys were. "In my car. Where I always leave them."

I walked to the garage door and yanked the handle. Locked. Frustration rose like acid reflux. My own stupid mistake was ruining my chance to know what it felt like to be wild and reckless. Under the flower pot at the back door, my last hope. I ran as fast as my sexy sandals let me. I knocked the flower pot over. No key. I pinched my eyes closed. Eli had told me to find a better hiding place, but I hadn't gotten around to it. I tried the door anyway. Locked.

Misery and disappointment rode my shoulders, and my feet plowed through the damp lawn. "My keys are in my car. My car is in the garage. And all of the doors are locked."

"What about your hidden key?"

I shrank lower. "I meant to find a new hiding place. It's on the windowsill in the kitchen."

"You're saying we can't get in?"

"We can break a window." In my current state of mind, dynamite sounded like a good idea.

He smiled. "No, we'll think of something. What about a neighbor?"

Emily! Hope exploded. New life jump-started my legs into motion, and my heels were light again and already clicking toward her driveway. "Emily has one. I'll run next door to get it." I tossed my hair and controlled my gait like it was a walk around the lake.

"Want me to go with you?"

I grabbed my phone from my purse. "I'll only be a minute."

Emily's cool, moist lawn chilled my toes. I was on

a mission. It was nearly eleven, and I didn't see any lights on. I tapped her contact.

"Libby, why are you calling so late? Is everything okay?"

"I'm locked out, and I'm on your front porch."

The front porch light came on, and the door creaked open. "How did you get locked out? And wow, you look amazing."

Emily stepped back and ogled my new black dress, letting her eyes travel all the way down to my strappy little toeless shoes. "Where've you been? Maybe the better question is who've you been with?" Grabbing her robe tightly around her neck, she leaned out the door and looked toward my house.

"I don't have time to explain. Eli's waiting on my front porch. I need my spare key."

"Eli. Huh? Waiting on your front porch?" Emily tightened her belt.

"Yes, Eli. I can tell you all about it tomorrow, but tonight I need my key." I strained to remain patient.

Emily opened a drawer in the foyer table. "Why didn't you tell me you had a date?"

Because you've been up Reggie's butt. "You've had a lot to digest." Checking my sarcasm, I adjusted my pearls and put a smile in my voice. "Emily, give me my key, please."

Emily placed her hands on her hips and eyed me suspiciously. "Do you have on the black thong?"

I held out my hand and struggled to keep my voice even. "*Please* give me my key. Now." Breaking a window or kicking down the door or smacking Emily sounded better and better.

Emily dangled the key. "You're going to do it,

aren't you? Don't you remember what the books said? Never on the first date!" Emily yell-whispered, and her words fizzed between her lips.

I gritted my teeth. "Emily, I don't care what the books say. You can preach to me tomorrow about right and wrong. But tonight I feel like a desirable woman."

I grabbed the key and ran across Emily's lawn. I crossed my fingers that he hadn't gotten cold feet. But when he saw me, his lips curled into a grin.

I turned the key, and the lock rewarded me with a solid click. My neurons ignited, sending signals to my synapses vacillating between anticipation and terror. I pushed the door open.

Moonlight streamed from the sky lights. I searched the room for traces of Neil. *Please not tonight.* I walked to the small table and bent to turn on the light.

Eli closed the door and walked up behind me. "Don't." He wrapped his arms around me and planted feathery kisses on my neck and shoulders. He unclasped my pearls and laid them on the narrow table. I leaned back against him. His hands wandered, leaving a fiery trail.

This is what I've been missing. "Let's go upstairs."

"You sure?" His voice was tight.

I kicked off my shoes and gripped his hand and tugged. He followed along, hopping on one foot, taking off his shoes and socks. Halfway up the stairs, he stopped and cupped the back of my neck in both hands. "This is a big move. I don't want to push you to do anything you're not ready for."

In one smooth, deliberate motion, I slipped my dress off my shoulders and let it fall to the floor. I felt powerful. I felt beautiful. I felt free.

His hands tightened. "Oh, God. Lead the way."

I led him down the hall to my room. *I want this. No. I need this.* From the pit of my stomach to the tips of my freshly manicured nails, electricity hummed.

We stopped at the foot of my king-sized bed. "Libby." Two simple syllables. Bold arms pulled me close. Close enough to feel how much he wanted me. Close enough to feel the flame burning below. He lowered his head and covered my lips with his. My tongue raced to sip and taste and touch, afraid it would end. His fingers flicked behind my back, and my bra fell loose. "I want to be inside you. Now."

He lifted me onto the bed and white spots muddled his face. I closed my eyes and took two shallow breaths.

"Open your eyes." His belt clinked when his pants hit the floor. "I want you to know who's making love to you."

Passion whirled through my body like a red storm, and I arched to receive him. All of him.

A loud crack ripped the air. Then the sound of wood splitting. And then came the thud—we hit the floor.

Chapter 19
Night Shadows

I opened one eye. Like mighty Atlas, Eli knelt, arms outstretched, holding the king-sized mahogany headboard. His hazel eyes flashed a medley of shock, embarrassment, and determination. "You okay?"

Shimmers of Neil hovered on the motionless blades of the ceiling fan. "Glad we increased our liability insurance." Neil's sarcastic voice rained down on me.

I wanted to turn on the ceiling fan and sling Neil's inert form against the wall. "Shut up, Neil." I scooted down the medium-firm incline, grabbing a pillow on my way. At the bottom I stood, covering myself with a king-sized pillow.

Eli balanced on his knees. "I knew he'd show up." He removed one hand. Nothing happened. He removed his other hand. Headboard stayed in place.

I aimed my voice upward. "Great timing."

A tiny smile peeked around Eli's lips, and he shook his head. "If I didn't know Neil was a ghost, I'd suspect him of sabotage."

Eli stood, and it was obvious the mood had passed. My cheeks flushed red hot, and I backed up toward the bathroom.

"Toss him his boxers for God's sake," Neil said.

I picked up Eli's boxers and offered them to him, wishing I could stretch the nylon and cotton blend over my burning face.

Eli pulled on his boxers. "You know what they say about three being a crowd? In Neil's case, three's an army. An army of fire ants."

An airy shape in light blue and khaki floated beside me. "Can't you find someplace to go? Someplace other than here?"

"I hope you're talking to Neil," Eli said.

"Sorry, Eli," I called through the bathroom door.

"When my head started stinging, I knew." Eli squatted and assessed the damage. "Looks like the headboard came loose from the rail. I need to replace the screws so you can sleep in your bed tonight," Eli said.

"I'll get the tool box. And Neil, you get lost."

Within fifteen minutes—bed was repaired. Belt buckled. Shirt buttoned. Tool box shut. I nestled my cheek against Eli's chest and listened to his heart. He enveloped me in his arms. "Tell me you don't believe in omens," I said.

Eli hooted and my faced bounced off his chest. "No, but I didn't use to believe in ghosts either." He kissed me on the forehead. "May have to wear a helmet, but I'm not giving up."

We stopped in the den, and he thrust his feet into his shoes and stuffed his socks into his pockets. Seeing our trail of clothes made me feel cheated. We'd come so close. It must have registered with Eli, too. He pulled me close and kissed me. This time, the only lump I felt was a sock in his pocket.

He drove away, and I stood there in my sweats. Barefoot and alone. I hugged myself against the cool of the evening and watched his taillights disappear into the night.

A faint glow in Emily's backyard got my attention. I looked again, and a person was smoking a cigarette on Emily's patio. Not Emily. She would rather eat dirt than smoke a cigarette. The moonlight outlined a man's silhouette. The half-hidden face of the man in the old car flashed across the movie screen in my head. My breath came in spurts. My brain screamed, "Call 911!" I searched for a stick or a rock or a rocket launcher.

I pounded my pockets. No phone. The cold pavement burned my feet. How do I get back inside without the intruder seeing me? I stooped and tip-toed over the driveway, eyes trained on the invader. Tiny rocks cut my bare feet. I breathed through my nose to keep from yelling out. I scraped the dirt and pebbles from my feet and glanced back to make sure he was still on Emily's patio. There he stood, calmly puffing smoke at regular intervals. *A burglar taking a smoke break before breaking and entering?*

I stepped and tripped over something metal. My hands groped in front of me for something to break my fall. On the way down, my bony shin hit the handle bars, and I jammed my fingers into the spokes of Trey's bicycle tires. Pain registered in triplets. "Shit! Shit! Shit!"

I untangled my hands and sat back, holding my leg. *If I survive this, I'm going to ground that boy until he's thirty.* I twisted my head toward Emily's back yard. The intruder was gone.

"Libby? Are you okay?"

"Reggie, you scared the crap out of me. I thought you were an intruder. Did Emily tell you about the creepy guy in the old car?"

"Couldn't sleep and didn't want to wake Emily, so I snuck outside. If she'd told me about some creepy guy, I'd have been more alarmed when I heard the crash."

"You almost gave me a heart attack. What are you doing here?"

"I thought you knew."

I threw him a look that should have turned him to stone, but the darkness saved him.

Reggie folded his wiry frame, sat cross-legged, and spun a tire. "Emily told me I had to explain things to you, but I hadn't planned on doing it in the middle of the night." He looked at me. "What are you doing out here?"

I sat flat and stretched my legs out in front. "Watching Prince Charming drive away."

"Emily told me you had a date. How'd it go?"

"Well, Reggie, the fact that he drove away should give you a hint."

He leaned back and supported himself on his hands. "We're concerned that you're rushing things."

Reggie's comment sent the needle on my sarcasm meter into the red zone. "Coming from someone who wrote a farewell note on a paper towel, I can see how you'd be an authority."

He dusted his hands on his pants. "You're right. I don't have the right to meddle in your life. I'm sorry."

His words, sincere and humble, tempered my tone. "I'm a little on edge. My plans didn't work out as planned."

"This dating thing…You're over Neil?" He crossed his hands on his knees.

"What choice do I have? He's gone." I rubbed the

golf-ball sized knot on my shin.

"How do you get through the grieving?"

"That's Emily's area of expertise," I said.

Reggie's body slumped. "I deserved that."

"You're lucky to get another chance." I stretched my back and moved my toes hoping I could walk.

Reggie unfolded his legs and stood. "I plan on spending the rest of my life making it up to her."

My shin ached and my backside was numb. I gratefully accepted his hand up.

"When did you start smoking?"

"It's a disgusting habit, I know. I started back up again about six months ago—right after I lost my job. Emily hates it, and I promised I'd quit soon."

I flexed my leg. "Emily didn't tell me you lost your job."

"She didn't know until last week."

"Why would you keep it from her?" Was he keeping anything else from her?

A humorless laugh drifted my way. "Ever heard of downsizing? I understand it up close and personal."

"But your bills? How'd you pay them without a job? And how'd you keep it from Emily?" Since Neil's physical departure from our lives, I knew on a monthly basis how expensive living was. With nothing coming in, they had to be living in the red.

"First I maxed out the credit cards. Then used up the equity in the house to pay the credit cards. Borrowed money from my parents. I thought about cashing in my 401K. The only reason I didn't was because of the penalties and the time involved."

If a loving husband would keep something from his wife, what about a cheating husband? Could Neil be hiding something from me? Could that be why he's stuck here? "I guess I don't understand why you didn't tell Emily."

"Ego. Kept thinking I could fix it. But things piled up higher and higher. Finding a job hasn't been easy." Reggie blew out a long, slow breath. "I thought many of the jobs out there were *beneath* me. Suffice it to say, this has been a humbling experience."

"But the paper towel thing?"

Reggie took a moment before he answered. "I know I hurt Emily. And I won't make excuses for what I did. But in my feeble mind, there were lots of reasons."

"So, you're saying that on that fateful Saturday morning you just snapped?" Recalling that morning made my voice sharp and raw.

"I deserve all the barbs you throw at me. But that morning Emily woke up so happy—our anniversary. She kept asking me what I wanted to do to celebrate. Worst of all, she tried to guess what I had gotten her. I hadn't gotten her anything. I couldn't. I had no job, no savings, no hope. Or so I thought. And I bolted. I thought it would be better if I left—forever."

Even though I wanted to kick him in the balls for all the suffering he put Emily through, the fresh pain in his voice wore down my resentment. "What changed your mind?"

"Actually, it was Neil."

My mind raced. Could Neil communicate with Reggie? "What are you saying? How could he change your mind?"

"He died. No more chances to make things right. It told me not to piss away my only one. So I faced the truth and took a job at our local Home Depot."

I smirked in the dark. "I can't see you mixing paint."

Reggie squared his body and faced me. "Let me make this perfectly clear. If mixing paint or picking up trash on the side of the road were the only jobs I could get, I'd do it. Or whatever it took to keep my family together."

I erased the smirk off my face. "I guess we're all looking for second chances."

"I don't deserve it, but I won't waste this opportunity. I'm working at Home Depot in the accounting department—on the bottom rung of the ladder." Even though the darkness prevented me from seeing his smile, I heard it in his voice. "But they promised at my ninety-day job review to evaluate my performance and see what's available. I'm hopeful. Finally."

Tears came to my eyes, and I fought to keep them out of my voice. "I'm hopeful for you, too. And for Emily." And I was. But I was jealous, too.

"Thanks. That means a lot coming from you. I should have trusted Emily. She's tougher than she looks." Then in a quiet voice he added, "Without her, I'm lost."

I sniffed and wiped my eyes.

Reggie reached out and touched my shoulder. "I'm sorry about your date."

"Yeah, well, like they say, shit happens." I tried for bravado.

"If he's smart, he'll be back."

Chapter 20
Choosing Sides

I'd come so close. A couple glasses of wine and I'd dropped my inhibitions—like my research suggested. But the researchers didn't know about the Bible-Belt Doctrine. He'd seen me naked, and I didn't have a ring. I was a slut.

Would I be able to look Eli in the eye? I worried so much about seeing him at the reunion committee meeting, I'd forgotten that I had to face Jesse too. Jesse hugged me a second longer than the others but made no mention of the kiss we'd shared. I'd bitten my fingernails to the quick waiting for Eli to arrive, and he'd been late. Maybe intentionally. Maybe he didn't want to face me. When Eli finally showed up, Allison was grilling committee members on their progress. He nodded to the group and slid into the nearest seat—farthest away from me. He'd laughed off our encounter, but he wasn't laughing now. Wide shoulders blocked the waning light filtering through the open door of the boathouse. And if his face were the weather forecast, we'd be running for cover. The meeting continued and we exchanged a handful of words and made even fewer eye contacts. My self-worth plummeted.

The meeting wound down and Eli manned his post at the door, shoulders back and hands clasped in front of him. He stepped to the side and cleared a route.

"Jesse, a word? Outside." Eli's generic smile didn't hide the nuance of someone accustomed to having their orders followed.

Eli blocked the only way out. The muscle in Jesse's lower jaw clenched, and then his lips warped into a one-sided grin. "Lead the way, dude." Jesse ground out the word *dude* and made the hairs on my arm bristle.

I flitted around the room, piling trash on a tray but keeping the two men in my peripheral vision. Oblivious to the tension buzzing between Eli and Jesse, Allison scooped up papers and began filing them into folders. Buddy and Charlotte, heads bent over the checkbook, looked up briefly and went back to number crunching.

Jesse followed Eli out the door. I followed quietly, hugging the handrail, keeping out of sight.

"Man, you're going all policeman over nothing. Libby's fine," Jesse said.

I stooped to peer around the wooden rail.

Eli crammed his six feet four inch hulk into Jesse's space. "I ran his plates. Benjamin Purvis." Eli's oversized fingers folded a piece of paper in half and fourths and in eighths. "He works for you."

Neil's khakis swished into view. "I told you I didn't trust Jesse. He's—"

I put my finger to my lips.

Jesse turned his back to Eli and looked toward the lake. "A lot of people work for me."

"This employee's trespassing on private property. Libby's private property."

Jesse swung around and propped his hands on his waist. "Maybe he was checking out the lake or looking for odd jobs. What he does on his free time is not my business."

"He almost ran us down." Eli thrust his face within inches of Jesse's. "If the kids had been with us, we might not have been so lucky." Eli articulated his words through clenched teeth.

Our kids could have been—I couldn't even *think* the word. A shudder racked my body, clanking the glasses on the tray I carried. *And the creep works for Jesse?*

Jesse and Eli jerked their heads in my direction.

I banged the tray on the bottom step. "Don't you think I should be part of this conversation?"

Eli spoke first. "I was trying to find out what Jesse knows about the guy in the old car you saw. The one that almost killed us."

Jesse rubbed his palms on his jeans. "Eli accused me of hiring one of my employees to stalk you."

"Funny you should use the word *stalk*. All I said was the guy works for you and has been trespassing." Eli clamped his mouth into a tight grin.

"You insinuated it." Jesse leaned back and propped the sole of his shoe against the support beam. He aimed his words at me. "Benny's just a kid. I told him about growing up around here and the lake. I'm sure he was just being curious."

Eli planted his feet. "That story might fly one time. But he's been *curious* two more times." He looked at me. "Two more times that I know about."

Jesse stood up straight and spat. "This conversation is feeling more and more like an interrogation."

Eli took a step toward Jesse. "Call it whatever the hell you want. I think you're hiding something."

Jesse stepped back and held out his arms. "I'm an

open book."

"Since you're being so open, satisfy my curiosity. How'd you know Libby got stuck on her roof?" Eli asked.

Jesse smiled and stared at me. "So she told you about my rescue?"

"Being in her neighborhood is quite a coincidence. And then calling at just the right time—another coincidence? I don't believe in coincidences."

Jesse re-crossed his arms. "Tread lightly, friend."

Eli mirrored Jesse's move and crossed his arms. "Then answer one question. How'd you know Libby got stranded on her roof if you didn't have your stalker inform you?"

I stepped between both men. "Let's take a breath."

Neil circled overhead. "This showdown has been a long time coming."

First I turned to Jesse. "Do you trust this employee of yours?"

"Absolutely," Jesse said.

I turned to Eli. "Is it possible that the man came to explore the lake?"

"And is it possible that not knowing the road, he took the turn too fast?" Jesse moved next to me. "And is it also possible that it was simply an accident, and you were in the wrong place at the wrong time?"

Eli's eyes held mine, and his feeble attempt at a smile sent a pang of guilt deep into the folds of my heart. "Anything's possible. Once."

"Y'all down here?" Allison asked, bouncing down the steps.

"I was just leaving." Eli touched his forehead in salute and headed to his Hummer.

All eyes turned to me. I wanted to run after Eli. Instead, I pressed a smile to my lips. "He has to pick up Lee," I lied.

"So we're good here?" Allison raised her eyebrows.

I shrugged. Not the time or place to share what had transpired. "See you guys next month."

Jesse picked up the tray and headed toward the house. I walked the others to their cars. After everyone had left, I found Jesse waiting for me on my front steps.

"Interesting night," he said.

Neil swooped into view. "I'll say."

I turned my back to Neil and concentrated on Jesse. "Yes. The reunion is coming together well."

Neil buzzed my head. "Ol' Jesse's up to something."

Jesse leaned against the front door jam. "Not the meeting. Eli. He acts like he owns you."

Jesse's comment gouged a bruised nerve. I whipped my head around and glared. After being dependent for twenty years, independence hadn't come cheap. I refused to let Jesse, or anyone else, dismiss it. "No one owns me." My words came out rock-hard.

Jesse stroked my back. "Don't get your fur up."

I pulled away. "You weren't there when your employee's car came at us. I still get the shakes when I think what might have happened if the kids had been with us."

Jesse wrapped an arm around my shoulder and squeezed. "I'm not making light of what happened. But I think you got it exactly right. He was checking out the lake. Eli's over-protective, and he overreacted."

A pang of betrayal stung. "He's a cop. That's what

he does. He protects."

Jesse let go. "Seems more like control to me. Don't get me wrong. Eli's a great guy, but he likes to control the situation—and people. You saw how pissed he got. Stalked off like a kid who didn't get his way."

Neil hovered over Jesse. "You're not falling for this are you?"

"You're being too hard on Eli," I said.

Jesse twisted around to look at me. "You didn't tell him I kissed you, did you?"

"You kissed Jesse King!" Neil lunged at my face. "Have you lost your freaking mind?"

Heat rose from my neck to my cheeks.

"Didn't think so." Jesse grinned and bumped my shoulder with his. "I like it being our little secret. But you still owe me a dinner out."

I gave him a half smile. "Tonight?" It was Sunday night. A school night. I couldn't go out to dinner.

"I'm free," Jesse said.

Eli typically stayed for dinner after reunion meetings, and tonight, instead of our usual pizza, I'd made spaghetti again—Eli's favorite. But he'd opted out. "I have spaghetti sauce simmering on the stove."

Jesse winked. "I love spaghetti."

I lifted the lid and stirred. Jesse looked over my shoulder. "Smells like you've been cooking all day."

"What a brown-noser." Neil drifted over the island.

I shot Neil a hard look. "Spaghetti's an easy dinner. You put it on and let it cook." I didn't tell Jesse the secret to my sauce was a jar of Prego.

Trey walked into the kitchen. "Mr. King—"

Jesse held up a hand. "Whoa, dude. My dad was Mr. King. Call me Jesse."

"Jesse, do you know how to tell if spaghetti's done?" Trey gave me a sideways glance.

Jesse's brow wrinkled. "Is this a joke or something?"

Trey looked into the boiling pot. "No, sir."

"I suppose you cook it for the time specified on the package," Jesse said.

"That's how most folks do it. But around here, we throw it against the wall." Trey bumped his fists together.

"I saw that in a movie." Jesse said. He snapped his fingers. "*The Big Chill*. Remember? A bunch of old college friends get together for their friend's funeral. Isn't that movie a little mature for Trey?"

I stirred the long, swirling stands in boiling water. "He hasn't seen the movie. Someone showed him how to test spaghetti that way, and he thought it was cool."

"Why would anyone want to throw spaghetti against the wall? I thought it was just for the movie," Jesse said.

A sigh escaped my lips. "Pasta's almost ready. You can open the wine."

At dinner, it was obvious early on that Jesse's knack lay with interacting with adults—not kids.

Trey placed his arm on the table. "Jesse, you like football?"

Jesse grinned, exposing perfect teeth in a practiced smile. "I went to Auburn, Trey. Being obsessed with football is a prerequisite."

Trey was sneaking a noodle to Sadie when confusion brought his stealth to a sudden stop. He tilted his head. "What's a pr-eq-is-it?"

"Prerequisite," I repeated. "It's like a requirement

for something. Jesse's saying that liking football is a requirement if you go to Auburn. But I'd add it's a requirement for any Alabama college."

Jesse turned to Reagan. "You a football fan, too?"

She folded her napkin. "If Auburn's winning."

"Smart girl," Jesse grinned.

"Dumb girl," Trey said. "Alabama is the greatest team of all time."

"Trey, be respectful. Football would be awfully boring if everyone rooted for the same team," I said.

Neil lowered his translucent form into the empty chair beside me and rested his head in his hands. "Isn't this cozy?"

I scooted my chair closer to Jesse and smirked at Neil.

Trey continued his line of questioning. "Did you play at Auburn?"

"No, but I went to all of the home games and most of the away ones."

"Mom's friend Eli played at Alabama." Trey announced matter-of-factly.

Jesse's smile flattened. "I know Eli."

"He comes over all the time. He brings his son Lee, and we play football in the back yard." Trey slurped a noodle.

"Would you like to toss the football around after dinner?" Jesse asked.

"No, thanks. I have homework," Trey stuffed a forkful into his mouth.

Neil shot out of his chair. "Way to go, Trey," Neil high-fived the air. "They say kids are true judges of character."

I'd never seen Trey refuse an opportunity to play

football. He was blowing Jesse off. "If you're finished, take your plate and go get started on your homework."

Reagan stopped beside my chair. She gave me a peck on the cheek and turned her attention to Jesse.

"I love your car. It's so cool the way a Corvette hugs the pavement. Does it handle as cool as it looks?" Reagan asked.

Jesse's ears spiked up like a happy terrier, and he rattled on about cylinders and horsepower and torque ratio while she smiled and nodded. Putty in her hands.

"I don't know about torque ratio or what a horse has to do with a car," Reagan said. "But I know style. And who doesn't love convertibles?" Reagan reeled him in like a tuna. "Did Mom tell you that I have my learner's permit? My friends say it's easier to learn to drive a high-performance sports car."

Neil yelled into Reagan's face. "Don't even think about getting into a car with Jesse King."

Jesse's face turned ashen.

I looked at Neil. "What are you so worried about?'

Oh, crap. I'd been ignoring Neil so well. I patted my chest and smiled. "What I meant, Jesse, is you don't need to worry. Your car is safe. She's only allowed to ride with me. In my car. And now she needs to do homework." I dismissed her with a hollow glance and smiled at Jesse. "Would you like some dessert?"

Reagan's phone trilled a text message notification. Without a backward look, her dueling thumbs led her up the stairs.

Jesse poured the wine while I cleared the table. "Having dinner as a family. Makes me miss seeing my kid. But seeing him means seeing his mother."

"Nothing or nobody would keep me from seeing

my kids." I piled the plates on the counter.

He handed me a refilled glass. "She wanted out. And I gave her what she wanted."

I took my glass. "Ryan needs you."

"He's got his mom. And I have my freedom." Jesse took a long drink.

"Spoken like his old man," Neil said. "Remember the saying about the apple? They didn't need to even shake the tree in Jesse's case."

"Jesse, a boy needs his dad." I looked at Neil. The impact of my words stunned me. The pain on Neil's face made me clutch my glass, splashing pinot noir on my hands and the floor.

"Let's not talk about my kid. Let's talk about freedom. I'm still waiting for your answer on Montreal." He replenished my glass.

I wiped up my spill. "I can't go to Montreal."

"Give me one good reason."

"I can give you two: Trey and Reagan."

"Sometimes you have to be impulsive and grab a handful of life while you can." Jesse emptied the bottle of wine into our glasses. "Let's finish our wine in that boathouse of yours. Maybe I can convince you." He led the way, dangling my glass in front of me like the proverbial carrot.

"You're on your own, Lib." Neil dissipated leaving a trail of disgust.

Reflections off the water lighted our way through the damp grass to the boathouse.

Jesse stopped at the dock and set both of our glasses on the stairs.

Uh-oh. Even in the dark, I knew what was coming. I scrubbed my clammy palms on my jeans.

He cradled my face in his hands. Soft hands. Not like Eli's. I drew in a breath. No. No. No. I refuse to think of Eli. He couldn't even look at me tonight. And then he got mad and left. Jesse's here.

Jesse coiled my hair around his hands. With the skill of a marksman, he tilted my head back and targeted my waiting mouth.

"Mom!" Reagan shouted from the patio.

Chapter 21
Pleading the Fifth

Saved by a yell. Reagan's call came a millisecond before Jesse King's lips touched mine. I had wanted Jesse King to kiss me. I needed an intervention.

"What in heaven's name has come over you!" Emily put the Diet Coke back into the fridge and brought out an opened bottle of white wine. "I think all this talk about passion has fried your brain."

I crossed my arms on her kitchen table and crashed my head down. "If the bed hadn't fallen, Eli and I would have finished what we started. And tonight I almost kissed Jesse. For the second time." I braced my head with my hands. "Am I a slut?"

Emily clonked two glasses down and poured a healthy serving into each. "I'm pleading the fifth."

I looked around the room and up at the ceiling. "Neil's not here. Where's Reggie?"

"Working late." Emily leaned her hip against the table and smiled. "Want to tell me what happened?"

I pushed my glass to the center of the table. "Eli stormed off because he thinks I took Jesse's side. Jesse weaseled a dinner invitation and suggested we finish our wine in the boathouse. I'm not stupid. I knew what he was doing. And if Reagan hadn't yelled, well…"

She set down her drink and devoted her every cell to the question on her face. "So are you glad Reagan

233

interrupted?"

I couldn't stand up to the honesty of her look and put my head back down on the table. "I don't know."

She folded in the tag at the back of my shirt. "Where does that leave Eli?"

I rolled my head sideways to look at her. "I don't know that either."

Emily sat across from me. "I guess it depends on what you want. Love or sex."

I reached for my wine. "Why do I have to choose one or the other?"

"Don't ask me. I've been married forever. Maybe that's a question for your young friends. Isn't Leah's bachelorette party on Wednesday night?"

I sat up and fiddled with the placemat. "I have to go, but I can't walk in by myself. Go with me?"

"Not a chance."

"Someday you're going to want me to go somewhere with you, and I'll tell you 'not a chance.'" I didn't care that I was whining.

"Can't guilt me into going. I'll go with you to the wedding, but I have no desire to go to Logan's Bar and hang out with those cute, toned, twenty-something teachers. Besides, the kids will be at my house."

"Maybe I can get another girl from school to ride with me." I twirled the glass in my hand.

Emily looked down her nose at me. "You can get butt naked and almost have sex, but you're afraid to walk into a bar?"

"I didn't say I was afraid." Actually I was terrified. "It's just that I have to walk in alone and people will stare."

"Yeah. Stares are deadly." She fanned the space

between us, blowing off my concerns. "You're an adult. Act like one."

****

All the way to Logan's, I repeated Emily's words like a mantra. You're an adult. You're an adult. You're an adult. And it's only a bar. It's only a bar. It's only a bar.

I parked and walked to the entrance. Nothing scary so far. I squared my shoulders, elevated my chin, and yanked the door handle. Nothing. I yanked again and the glass clattered. On the other side of the transparent panes, heads turned in choreographed precision firing deadly stares. One man pointed to the door. The sign said *PUSH*.

Strike one.

I wanted to run, but I had witnesses. I held my breath and pushed. A tsunami of sound washed over me.

To my right, people gathered in clusters along the wooden railing of the bar that ran the length of the room. All chairs were occupied, and the leftovers crammed into the spaces in between. On my left, people scurried like ants to and from the dance floor where a motley group of guitars and horns and drums blasted out oldies but goodies from speakers the size of compact cars. Straight ahead an innocuous black sign below the lighted green exit sign sent a surge of relief. RESTROOMS. I released my locked jaw muscles. A neutral zone where I could re-group or hide. I set my course and plunged through the partiers. My single-minded mission: get to the door marked Ladies.

A dark hulk stepped into my path. My eyes trailed up his black leather jacket and stopped just south of his

BPD ball cap. Eli Anderson. My Eli Anderson.

My feet stopped. My heart stopped. But not the waitress behind me balancing a large round tray loaded with drinks. An avalanche of icy cocktails tumbled over my shoulder and zoomed down my chest like skiers on a ski jump.

A collective gasp sucked the air from the room. My feet froze to the spot—like the frozen pina coladas on my chest. Eli scooped his finger into the icy mound on my cleavage. "Tasty. I don't usually like fruity drinks."

I opened my mouth but no words came out. The waitress muscled past him and wiped feverishly at my blouse.

Eli took her cloth and plopped it onto the pile of glasses at my feet and circled his arm firmly around my waist. "You can clean up at my house."

It wasn't a suggestion.

"Libby!" Angie's high-pitched voice out-staged the band. She and Leah and the other bachelorettes crowded around a table strewn with ribbons and wrapping paper and lots of empty glasses. Angie diverted their interest to my direction.

I waggled my fingers goodbye. Angie's eyes popped open, and she mouthed, "Eli?"

I nodded.

Leah lifted her gaudy white veil, smiled, and gave me two thumbs up.

Eli's firm hold jerked me through the door, leaving rational thought behind. He stopped beside a motorcycle loaded with enough shiny chrome to see my sticky reflection. He turned his ball cap backward and swung a long blue-jeaned leg over his bike. "You riding with me?"

"Don't see an extra helmet."

He offered his. "You can wear mine."

"Tempting, but I'll follow you." Neil and I had only been once, but I remembered the way.

"Stay close." He plunked the helmet over his head and fired up his engine. The throaty roar of his well-tuned Harley Davidson followed me to my car. If I followed him home, we'd finish what we'd started at my house. Totally inappropriate behavior—for the old me. Was I ready to leap into this brave new role? Was I ready to leap into Eli's bed? I'm a grown-up. Time I acted like one.

He pulled beside me and throttled up. My heart revved up, too. He motioned for me to follow, and my internal RPM's hit the red zone. I grabbed wipes from the glove box and dabbed sticky traces of cream of coconut, careful to keep the lone red taillight of Eli's Harley in my sights. Also in my sights were Eli's broad shoulders, strong arms, massive hands—all naked. All touching me. Unless Neil shows up. Then all bets are off. I shivered inside my wet, one hundred percent silk blouse.

Six minutes and we passed through the brick pillars announcing another Birmingham well-maintained planned community. Two turns and we coasted into his driveway and stopped. Front porch lights shone like runway beacons, showing me the way. *The way to what?* The voice in my head asked. I didn't answer. Because I didn't know, and I didn't care. I just wanted to feel. And my opportunity looked mighty appealing.

Still straddling his bike, he removed his helmet and hat and placed them at his feet. I glided within reach, and he pushed my back against the handle bars and wedged his leg between mine. Lightning arced between us. My breath caught, and I dug my nails into his thigh. A sliver of conscience broke through a passion-induced paralysis. Soon it would be too late to change course. I looked at my car, and then I looked back at him.

He gave me a one-sided grin. "You can second-guess yourself to death." He twirled his fingers through my hair. "I've waited twenty years for a Mulligan."

"A Mulligan?" I thought that was a golf term, and I didn't play golf.

"A second chance. I've waited twenty years for this one." He cupped my head and pulled me into his waiting lips, and a minty tongue nudged my lips apart.

The Fourth of July exploded in my head. He may have said let's go inside, or he could have said the world's on fire and we need to evacuate. Didn't matter. My lips followed his lead.

I closed the front door and checked the ceiling and chandelier. *Please stay away.*

The click of a lamp flooded the foyer in light. Eli swung toward me and positioned his hands on the door, bracketing my head. He smelled like outdoors. I took in his scent and exhaled slowly through my mouth, hoping to quiet the hammering in my ears. He bent and licked my chest all the way from the deep V of my blouse to the hollow at the base of my throat. "You've given me a whole new perspective on fruity drinks."

I patted my thumping, slippery chest. "I need a shower."

Eli gave me a mock serious look. "You'll need someone to wash your back."

The cartilage in my knees crumbled like day-old pound cake. "You might have to carry me."

"My pleasure, ma'am." He lunged.

I dodged his long arms. "I'm kidding. I'm kidding."

"I'd better show you." He led the way to a bathroom the size of a gymnasium. Masculine. Uncluttered. Numbered prints of famous golf courses graced the beige walls. Towel racks made of golf clubs held thick, white towels.

I wiped dust from a putter. "I forgot you're a golfer."

"Yep. Thanks to the University of Alabama Chapter of Phi Mu."

I kicked off my shoes and loosened my shirt. "You shouldn't have been playing football with girls."

"It was a charity powderpuff football game. Who thought a bunch of sorority girls could be so tough?" Eli held his hands palm up as if sanctioning the stupidity of his youth.

"That particular bunch of girls brought your football career to a screeching halt," I said.

Eli sighed. "Yeah. A torn ACL will do that to you."

"Did it make you bitter? Losing your dream like that?" After Eli went off to college, he became more of Neil's friend than mine. Neil and I were married, and it was better than way. I studied the man who never told our secret.

"Bitter, no. Disappointed, yes. You know what they say about one door closing? Well, when my dream door closed, I looked for another door. Law enforcement felt like a pretty good fit." Eli crossed his arms.

I unbuttoned my blouse. "No regrets?"

"Not when it comes to career choices." His eyes

followed my hands.

"Other choices?" I worked at another button. Then another.

"Uh, choices? I can't think of anything but what's under that blouse."

I had a decision to make. Bold and daring or same old me? I unzipped my skirt, and it fell to the floor. I shrugged my arms out of my soiled blouse and pressed the front release of my black bra. It's now or never. Now is here, and never is not an option. Shaking thumbs hooked the elastic of my matching thong and let it fall. I stepped out of my panties, opened the shower door, and glanced over my shoulder. "You like it hot?" I didn't recognize my voice. Smooth. Sultry. Sexy.

Blood zigzagged through my body. He couldn't reject me. Could he? Confidence began a slow seep. I couldn't handle his rejection again.

He tugged his shirt over his head. Fabric ripped and buttons pinged off the ceiling. He unbuckled his belt and hopped on one foot and then the other to remove his black, leather riding boots. Socks flew. Jeans and boxers and belt clanked on the tile floor. The full Monte. My mouth went dry.

He licked his lips like it was Thanksgiving, and I was the main course, well-basted and ready to slice. One giant step and he crossed the threshold. Blood roared like a waterfall within the confines of the travertine walls. Mist hung in the air and clung to the glass door. Legs apart and arms outstretched, he adjusted the two shower heads and ducked under the twin streams.

In my thirty-seven years, I'd only had sex with two men. Eli was the first. He rejected me, and I'd married

Neil—who betrayed me. I pressed my forehead between Eli's shoulder blades, and a dull ache throbbed in my core and settled deep. I pressed the length of my body to his.

Eli groaned. "You're killing me." He propped his hands against the wall of the shower.

I grasped the blue bar and rubbed spring-scented soap over his powerful shoulders and made foamy trails up and down his muscled back to his narrow waist. I soaped my hands and replaced the bar. Using both hands I massaged his fine, firm butt.

He turned and positioned me between the stereo shower heads. "Your turn."

He rolled the bar of soap over and over and over between his palms, creating a frothy pale blue lather.

His rough palms started at my collarbone and scrubbed over my breasts and down. Anchoring his thumbs at my belly button, his hands circled my waist and he pushed my back against the cool tile and buried his face between my breasts. I kneaded the muscles across his back. Water streamed from dueling shower heads, channeling a river between his mouth and my breasts. Soapy, calloused hands exfoliated my skin and my psyche like erotic loofas. I closed my eyes and shape-shifted into pure pleasure.

"Oh, Lib." He kissed my neck, my chin, my cheek. Urgent kisses made their way to my lips. "I love you."

I placed a finger on his lips. "Shhh."

The soap hit the floor, and caution swirled down the drain.

Pleasure, passion, promise filled the steamy mist. No longer children with nothing to lose. Now we were adults with everything to lose. I didn't care.

Chapter 22
Those Three Little Words

Eli shut off the water, and the silence thundered in my ears. He hugged me and kissed the top of my head.

Realization washed over me like a rash, and I broke out in guilt. I buried my face in his chest. Oh, my God. *We had sex.* "I can't believe we…did it."

"Oh, no, you don't." Eli held me at arm's length and looked down at me. "You're not doing that guilt thing."

I inhaled steamy, sex-laced air. The old Libby would wallow in guilt until it soaked her into a soggy lump of shame. "You're right."

He put his index finger under my chin and tilted my head up. He gave me a sweet kiss. "I love you. I've always loved you."

I covered my ears. I wasn't ready to hear those words. "Don't say that. We need to go slow."

He held my hands away from my ears. "You call what we did *slow*? Must be losing my touch."

I stepped out of the shower, retrieved a towel from the nine iron, and draped it around me. It wasn't like I jumped into bed, or in this case the shower, with a stranger. I cinched my towel a little tighter and tucked it around my breasts. "You know what I mean."

"I love you, and I'm not taking it back."

I threw him a towel. "I'm not ready to hear those

words." I fingercombed my hair. "You have a hair dryer?"

Eli snugged his towel around his waist and hopped up on the counter. He pointed his foot. "Bottom drawer."

I stooped and took out a travel-size hair dryer.

He corralled me in his knees. He took the dryer from my hands, tossed it onto the counter, and anchored my shoulders between his hands. "I never told anybody what happened that night. But I never forgot."

"Do we have to talk about this now?" I didn't want to talk about it now or ever. I placed my hands on his knees. "I never told either, and as long as I never say it out loud, it didn't happen."

"Would it have changed things?"

Hazel eyes bore into mine. We'd been friends as long as I could remember, and I'd always known Eli wanted to be more. And our senior year, after he'd rescued me from an awkward situation with Jesse, it happened. At my house, you didn't have sex until you got a wedding ring. I'd broken the rules, but I rationalized that if neither one of us ever told, it didn't count. Even though it was more than sex to me, being tied down at eighteen was not an option for Eli. So he moved on, and I ran to safe, dependable Neil.

I returned his gaze. I knew what Eli was asking. "If you hadn't rejected me in high school, would I have still chosen Neil? It doesn't matter."

"Neil never suspected?"

"Nope. Like I said, I didn't acknowledge it, so it didn't happen." I hoped my lie sounded convincing. If Neil suspected, he never let on. When the fault line in our marriage cracked, I kept my mouth shut. And let the rift grew farther and farther apart.

"We did what everybody else was doing."

I fluffed my hair, letting it air dry. "You grew up in the South. You know how things work."

"Instead of giving me a chance, you opted for Neil." He jutted his jaw at me and bit down.

I moved in closer. "He wanted more than a one-night stand."

Eli swallowed. "And I've paid for that decision a million times and then some."

"Eli Anderson—big man on campus. Football scholarship to the University of Alabama. Girls, girls, and more girls. I think you got everything you wanted."

"Except you." His voice was barely audible.

"You had me. But I got in the way of your big plans."

Eli eased off the counter. "I kept you at arm's length because you weren't like the other girls. But that night in my car…" He tucked his towel tighter. "I was jealous that you told Jesse you'd go to homecoming with him. And when he stood you up, I wanted to bash his face in for hurting you. But I was glad because I don't know what I'd have done if he'd laid a hand on you."

I cinched my towel. "We were eighteen. Blame it on hormones. I was pissed at Jesse for humiliating me." Not only had Jesse stood me up, but he sashayed past me with the class slut. "You did what you do. Take care of people." I still remembered the weight of his arm around my shoulder and his breath on my cheek as we strolled to his car.

His hands skimmed up and down my arms, tickling my skin. "I tried to take you home that night. But my libido turned down the road to the railroad tracks. Touching you and kissing you felt like the natural thing to do."

I stepped to the side and unplugged the hairdryer to break our connection. I was desperately close to succumbing to his two strong arms and delicious lips. "I should have stopped at the kissing part. But like you said, it felt like the natural thing to do." I wound the cord around and around the handle.

He cocked his head. "A two-minute performance seemed natural to you?"

My ears burned red hot. "You made up a lot of time tonight."

"I wish I'd been ready back then." He'd closed the gap and his finger skimmed my collarbone. "I'm ready now. Stay tonight and I'll show you how ready."

I ran my hands through my wet hair. I didn't want to go. "I'm not ready for an overnighter. Yet."

He walked into his Eli-size walk-in closet. A hanger twanged against the metal rod, and he came out with a light blue button down shirt. "Put this on."

I clamped my hands to my towel. "Close your eyes."

"Yeah, like that's gonna happen." He held the shirt for me.

I dropped the towel and slipped my arms into a tent, with sleeves. "Now this is a sexy look."

"Better than driving home in a sticky blouse." Eli dropped his towel and poked his feet and legs into his jeans—sans underwear. His unbuttoned jeans hung dangerously low. "Wish I could change your mind. Think of it as a night without Neil."

I eyed the ceiling. "Speaking of Neil, how's your

245

head?"

He gave me a weird look. "Huh?"

I scrubbed my head with exaggerated scratching motions. "No tingly scalp? From you know who?"

Eli's lips split into a grin. "You weren't worried about my scalp a few minutes ago."

Flashbacks to rushing water and cool travertine tile made my cheeks burn. I lifted up my limp hair and fanned my neck. "I thought I saw something move. I'm sure it was just cobwebs."

He guided his hands down to my bottom and palmed each cheek like a basketball. "I'm declaring this a Neil-free zone."

Luminous air swished between Eli and me.

"Shit!" Eli jumped back and began slapping his bald head.

Double shit.

My goodbye to Eli was quick and sweet with no promises. I jumped in the car and drove too fast. "Stay out of my life!"

Silence.

"I'm really mad this time."

More silence.

I slammed my fist against the steering wheel. "Dammit, Neil. I know you're here."

He refused my bait the whole ride home, and the quiet made me edgy. When I walked in the door, Neil sat on the edge of the sofa, bending almost in half to reach my laptop on the coffee table. His butt and legs touched only air, but his translucent hand manipulated the touchpad. I threw my purse on a chair and kicked off my shoes. "You don't fool me."

He stayed focused on the computer screen.

"Making a fashion statement?"

"None of your business."

"Only one person I know who wears a shirt that big. How's Eli?"

"We know you spied on us." I rubbernecked over his shoulder. "You updating your status on Facebook? Hopefully to *gone*?"

"I've gotten much better at directing my energy, don't you think? Check this out. I'm sending you a text."

My phone dinged. I didn't care if he sent me a text. I wanted to know what he saw and heard at Eli's tonight. I grabbed a bottle of water from the fridge.

"Watch this." Neil used both hands and closed the laptop. "And I can open it, too."

"Please tell me you're doing research on finding that white light or whatever gets you out of this dimension."

Neil shut the laptop. "Want to tell me about tonight?"

"Nope."

Neil swelled his thin form into an unintimidating bulk of air. "That's all you're going to say?"

"Yep." I chugged my bottle of water, turned my back, and headed upstairs.

He stopped midway up the staircase and confronted me. "Is Jesse next?"

I stepped through him, and a sliver of cold passed through me. I quivered. From the chill of the truth.

"You're not playing with fire. You're juggling nuclear bombs." His voice creaked.

"I don't have to answer to you, or to anyone." Neil had no right to question or to judge me or my motives.

"This is my life. Butt out."

"Your first consideration should be the children."

Anger blurred my vision and unleashed a fury that had been tethered by a thread. "Were the children your first consideration when you were screwing Sheri?"

Neil's blue shirt and khakis pulsed bright and then back to muted tones. "I deserved that."

"Where did you think it would lead, Neil? Did you have a plan? Divorce me and marry her? Raise her two young boys?" I whipped around to face him. "You had no time for your own kids, or for me. But you had time for her."

His eyes flashed dark brown. "Stop."

"I'm just getting started. Chew on this. If you'd spent half the effort working on our marriage as you did boinking Sheri, you'd still be here—in real life—not a shadow meddling in my business. Leave me alone." I tramped up the stairs.

He stayed with me. "When did you become a bitch?"

"When you became a bastard." I stopped two steps shy of the top and rotated my upper body to glare at him. "Get away from us. Haven't you caused enough pain? I can't start a life with you hanging around." I struck his chest with both hands and hit dead air. My momentum carried me forward. Silent screams seared the linings of my throat. I was going down.

Then I wasn't falling. Solid hands steadied me, and my feet touched wood. I grasped the railing and clung tight. I stared at Neil. "How'd you do that?"

He paled before me. "I don't know."

Chapter 23
Showdown

I seemed to be fragmenting in all directions. I'd found passion with Eli and yet enjoyed Jesse's phone calls. Sometimes I acted almost forgiving to Neil but then would turn hostile. Somehow in the melee, life went on. Even yearly mammograms. But I couldn't get past Neil's saving me from a nasty fall.

Right on time for our appointment, Emily walked through the back door, opened the fridge, and took a Diet Coke. "Want one?"

"I've had my quota."

Emily twisted off the cap and took a sip. "You look a little green. Feeling okay? I'm all about canceling this thing."

My hands started shaking. Before I finished telling Emily the story of my near crash down the stairs the night before, her hands shook too.

She lowered herself slowly onto a bar stool at the island. "How's that even possible?"

I picked up my purse and held it to my body. "I don't know how he did it, but he caught me."

"He may have saved your life." Emily closed her eyes. "I don't want to think about what might have happened."

"Me either, so let's drop it. You ready?" I dangled my purse in the crook of my elbow.

"As I'll ever be."

"Getting older really stinks sometimes. Our first mammogram. I hate them already."

"What do you hate, Mom?" Trey and Marcus breezed through the kitchen and Trey headed straight for the refrigerator. "You hungry, Marcus?"

"Emily and I will be back in a couple of hours. You and Marcus hang out here or next door until we get back."

"Where you going?" Trey jammed his head inside the refrigerator.

"Emily and I have a medical thing."

Trey popped out of the refrigerator. "You sick?"

I ruffled his hair. "I'm fine, sweetie. Just our mammograms."

Trey dodged out of my reach and stroked his hair back into place. "Oh, that pink ribbon thing."

Marcus sidled up next to Trey. "Our teacher Mrs. Flowers is running in some kind of race, and the other teachers are sponsoring her."

"It's called Relay for Life, and I'm one of her sponsors," I said.

"If I had to run a relay, I'd want Eli on my team. Mom, tell Marcus what you used to call him."

I let out a breath. "You tell him. We're leaving."

"He won't believe me. He doesn't believe Eli played at Alabama either."

Marcus nudged Trey. "I was kidding. Can I come over and see him sometime?"

"Can he, Mom? Maybe he'll throw the football with us."

Marcus whispered in Trey's ear.

Trey looked up at me with the innocence only a

twelve-year-old can pull off. "Mom, are you going to marry Eli?"

My purse hit the floor first and then my chin. Emily pivoted in my direction.

Trey and Marcus waited for a reply. I picked up my bag and anchored it on my shoulder. "Of course not, Trey. He hasn't asked me." I took Emily's arm. "Come on. You're driving." I marched out the kitchen door onto the patio and exhaled.

Neil waited outside. "What if he asks?"

"Not open for discussion," I said.

"I didn't say anything," Emily said. "Oh. I get it." She looked around and raised her hand in a generic wave.

Neil bounced up and down. "Let me show Emily I can send a text."

"She doesn't care if you can send her a text," I said.

"He can send texts? Really?" Emily took out her phone.

I strode ahead. "Don't encourage him."

Emily drove in relative silence on our twenty-minute drive to the women's health center and then took two turns around the parking lot before finding the closest parking spot.

I beat her out of the car. "I guess we'll have to do this every couple of years."

Emily pressed her key fob and locked the car. "Twenty-four months of dread."

"A little pain for a lot of assurance," I said.

"At least you have boobs to smash," Emily said. "The technician will have to stretch the skin all the way from my scalp to get enough to put under the machine."

"Let's get this over with." We walked through the pneumatic doors and checked in. The nurse called for me first.

I held the machine like a dance partner while the technician's cold hands placed my breast in the vise and tightened it.

"I see on your form you're a teacher." The technician was my age, and had an easy manner. "Hold your breath. Okay, let's get the other side."

One, two, and I was done and sitting in the dressing room, clasping the gown closed and waiting for the okay to get dressed. I thumbed through a Southern Living looking for a recipe that my kids would eat.

"Ms. Miller? Ms. Miller?" I'd zoned out. "We need to redo the right side." The technician smiled.

"Is there a problem?" I was nervous the first time, but this time my feet left tracks of cold terror.

"You might have moved just a touch and blurred a small part. It's only one side. I'll have you out of here in five minutes." She busied herself with getting me set up. Plates slid into place and she manipulated the machine, intent on the settings. "This will only take a second."

"You sure everything's okay?" I asked.

"I think so. You could have budged a centimeter and didn't realize it." The tech clicked and clacked machine parts. "What do you teach?" Her voice was pleasant and upbeat.

The clinic gown fell off my shoulder. "Seventh grade English. Do you have to re-do a lot of these?"

"My goodness. I have a seventh grader. She's twelve going on twenty. And don't worry about this.

The first time can be tricky."

The pancake press flattened out my breast. "Dr. Byram will get my results, right?"

"That's something else we have in common. Ruth Byram's my GYN, too."

"I taught both her boys."

"Is that right? She's an incredible doctor." The tech adjusted the machine and patted my shoulder. And don't you worry about this."

"I'm so traumatized I might need retail therapy." A nervous chuckle sneaked out.

She went to her position, shielded from radiation. "Hold your breath."

The re-do took a few extra minutes, and I knew Emily would be dressed and waiting. I power walked to the dressing area, and she stood beside my locker, phone in hand.

Emily looked up. "Hey, what took you so long?"

I opened my locker and removed my purse and clothes. "The tech said I moved or something and had to re-do the right side."

"Oh, great. Twice the torture," she rolled her eyes.

"So much for a smooth first time." I closed the curtain on the dressing room.

She draped the curtain to the side. "You're not worried are you?"

Of course I'm worried. "She said there was a blur. Probably because I moved." I slipped on my flats and walked past her. "My coupons for the outlet mall expire today."

"What are you buying?" Emily clopped beside me.

I flapped my coupons. "I don't know yet. Can't waste thirty percent off."

"Judging from your activities of late, I assume we'll be stopping by the lingerie store."

"Crossed my mind," I said, "but I don't want to entertain Neil."

"Is he here?" Emily did her usual frantic search, like she could actually see anything. Then her hand went to her mouth. "Our mammograms!"

"Relax. He's not here. When do we get the results on our mammograms?"

"Today's Tuesday. The receptionist said she'd mail our results to us and Dr. Ruth. So Friday or Monday?" Emily stepped through the automatic doors. "I'm sure the blur was nothing."

****

Neil met me in the garage. "Kids are helping Reggie cut down a dead tree."

I lifted my sunglasses. "Trey and Marcus, you mean? I can see the boys helping Reggie. But Reagan and Andrea?"

"The girls are the videographers."

I plunked my sunglasses down and opened the trunk. "Something to post on Instagram. That I can believe."

He looked into the trunk and shook his head. "You had to buy something because you had a thirty percent coupon. That seem logical to you?"

"Perfectly. And how did you know I had a coupon?" I gingerly removed my purchase from the trunk. "It's a sundial. Cool, huh?"

"I know you're nervous."

He *was* there. I lost my grip and a corner of the sundial hit the floor. "Why would a sundial make me nervous?"

"The mammogram." His voice sounded too sympathetic.

I gripped the wooden rectangle in both hands. "I don't know what you're talking about." I hefted my treasure to my thigh and shut the trunk. I walked out of the garage. I didn't need his prying today, and I certainly didn't want to discuss my mammogram. "I think I'll hang this on the patio. Perfect for our southern exposure."

"It really is akin to medieval torture." Neil straggled behind. "Don't be concerned about having to do the right breast twice. You shifted, and I thought you'd seen me."

I propped the sundial against the wall. "This is one of those times when you've trampled your boundaries. You're sticking your nose where it doesn't belong."

He viewed the sundial from all angles. "I'm trying to prevent you from fixating on the improbable negative outcome."

I wanted to put my fingers in my ears and shout la-la-la-la-la. "I'm not fixating. I'm being realistic. There's something wrong."

Neil moved in closer. "I told you I saw you move."

"Well, you're not a doctor, are you? And it's not your breast in question." I went into the garage for a hammer and nails. I refused to be bullied into telling him I was terrified of what the mammogram might mean.

"No need to obsess over this. You can call your doctor tomorrow." He used his professional, detached tone. Like he was telling a pensive client not to worry that he'd jumped to a higher tax bracket. I didn't need his professional cool.

My head pounded, and I wanted to scream, *I can't wait till tomorrow!* I gave him a faux smile. "Thanks for your concern."

"I am concerned. About you jumping to conclusions." Neil droned in my ear like a pesky fly. "One, two, three, jump! It's what you do best."

"Shut up!" I swatted. A pointless endeavor.

He pressed his nose into my space. "You think it's cancer."

My breath caught. He'd said the word. Out loud.

"And you're worried that if something happens to you, the kids will be alone." His voice softened.

"What if it is—?" I couldn't say the word.

He interrupted. "It's not cancer. But if it were, you'd do whatever you had to."

"What would our kids do without either of us?" I tried to swallow, but my throat was too dry.

"Legally, your sisters or my parents would get custody." His calm even tone didn't have the desired effect.

"Grandparents or aunts raising our children?" My voice ascended the scales to soprano range.

He smacked his hand on the table top.

The thwack echoed off the water and made me jump.

He got into my face. "You're sealing the deal before you know the facts. Listen to me. I was there. I saw you move."

My strength ebbed away. "I'm afraid."

He sat on the rock patio and a wasp winged through him. "There was a time when we communicated. Good or bad. "

"And we'd worry together." I sat beside him.

"What happened to us?"

He sighed and lay back. "My complete lapse of sanity?"

I lay back on the warm flat rocks. "You hurt me."

"Wish I could hurt for you." His wish was a harsh whisper.

"I want to forgive you. I keep thinking if I can forgive you, I can be me again."

He sat up and looked down at me. "We drifted apart because I wanted more. More money. More prestige. And even that wasn't enough."

I sat up and hugged my knees to my chest. "You can't take all the blame. You know how I am. I threw myself into the Foundation and took time away from you and the kids."

Neil looked off into the darkness. "I feel like an idiot saying this, but I was jealous of your foundation."

I sat upright. "How in the world could you be jealous of my helping battered women and abused children?"

"I wasn't jealous of what you did. Just you." An effortless move and he was squatting in front of me. "I calculated my time-table and set my course to establish my place in the business world and my impact on the community. You start a foundation and become a super star. I've never been interviewed on TV or invited to join the school board. See how petty I was?" He slumped into a sitting position. "How can you forgive that?"

We sat side by side. "I wish I'd involved you in the foundation."

"That's my fault, too. I was resentful. It's not an excuse, but I think growing up in Eli's and Jesse's shadows made me want to prove I could be somebody. Instead, I worked my way up to a self-serving, petty nobody."

"Don't be so hard on yourself." I couldn't believe those words came from my mouth. But the man sitting beside me was the old Neil. It was nice seeing him again. "You accomplished great things. Not only in your professional life. Look at our kids."

His eyes glistened in his airy sockets.

I swayed and bumped his see-through shoulder. "And you tell me not to be negative?"

"I'm proud of you, you know." His mouth torqued into a lopsided grin. The grin his son shares. The grin that pokes my heart every time he uses it. "Nothing halfway with you. When you're onboard, you're all in. That's who you are. I don't worry about our kids."

His affirmation smoothed the rough edges of my anxiety. I sniffed. "Wish you could hold me."

Neil wrapped warm arms around me and hugged. I lost it. Tears cascaded down my cheeks, dropping onto a solid Neil. "I loved you, and I've missed knowing you loved me."

"I've never loved anyone but you." His voice soothed the aching I couldn't reach.

I folded into his well-worn embrace. "I'm glad you were my husband and the father of my children."

He squeezed tighter. "I'm so sorry. About so many things."

"I'm sorry, too." I clung to him. The man I'd spent my life with. The man I'd trusted. The man I'd loved. "I've been hiding something from you for a long time."

"You and Eli." His voice wasn't a question.

My heart ached in my chest. "When did you find

out?"

I looked up, and he kissed my forehead. "Just now. It's all over your face."

"Oh, God. I'm so sorry. It was before us, and I never told anyone. My parents would have been so disappointed."

"Shhhh. Don't. I wouldn't change a thing about my life with you." He touched his forehead to mine.

The ache in my chest turned into stabbing pain, and I couldn't take a breath. I pressed his hand to my heart. "There's…something else."

Neil's eyes searched my face. "Are you all right? What is it?"

I forced air into my lungs so I could spit out the bitter-tasting words. "I did something to your car. I'm afraid I caused your accident."

"Rear-ending my car didn't cause my accident." He rubbed my back and his words skated between chuckles.

I hid my face in his smooth, light-starched Oxford cloth shirt. "I wish I'd stopped at ramming the bumper. But I…I poisoned your gas tank." I tunneled my head deeper. "I dug through the glove box and my purse and stuffed or poured everything I could find into your gas tank."

His body tensed, and his arms tightened around me as my muscles drew up tight, and I shut one eye. It took a lot for Neil to lose his temper, but I'd gone too far. I'd ended his world.

He pulled away from me and sat there. Head down and shoulders shaking. He planted his palms down on the stones and straightened his arms. Blasts of laughter sputtered from his lips.

I gaped at him. "How can you laugh?"

He reached for me, and his arms encircled me. "Had a visual of you stuffing salt packets down my gas tank."

His hug relieved the guilt I'd been afraid to share. "I've been sick with guilt worrying that I caused your accident."

He touched his head to mine. "Don't give it another thought."

I broke contact to see his face. "I Googled it. Said contaminants in the tank could make the engine quit."

"The accident had nothing to do with internal combustion. I dropped my phone between the seats and tried to get it." A sad smile crossed his lips. "Everything was my fault." He wound a lock of my hair around his finger. "Wish I could get a Mulligan."

"Eli said the same thing." Neil's energy sapped, he faded from solid to opaque to transparent until I was left holding evening air. "Why do you hate Eli and Jesse?"

"I don't hate Eli." His voice sounded hollow.

I shuffled my feet from smooth stone to gritty grout. "Then why do you hate Jesse?"

Neil moved in front of me and sat cross-legged. "I need to tell you something that I've never shared with anyone. Ever."

My derriere ached from the flagstone surface, and I moved to a chair. "Does this have anything to do with the summer before sixth grade? And you bugging me to ask Eli what he buried in Skipper's grave?"

His demeanor was solemn. "It has everything to do with burying Skipper."

I tucked one leg under and let one dangle. "The

grown-ups told us Mr. King's car skidded on wet roads. We knew he was drunk."

"We made a plan. Meet in Jesse's backyard at midnight and bring one treasure to bury with Skipper. I brought a perfect attendance certificate, and—"

I giggled. "I'm sorry. I couldn't help it. You got perfect attendance every year."

"Even back then I was practical. Now let me get back to my story. Eli brought the Valentine you gave him in fifth grade."

I waved my hands. "Hold it, hold it, hold it. Why my Valentine?"

He positioned himself on the dry bird bath. "He said since you chose me, he wanted to bury it. I know it sounds juvenile. We were eleven."

I bounced my foot and my flip-flop fell off. "That's the Valentine's Day you switched Valentines, and took credit for the box of candy Eli'd brought me."

"Yes, fifth grade was the year I became a lawless felon. May I continue?" He adjusted his position and cleared his throat. "When Eli and I got to Jesse's, he'd already dug the grave. It was only a few feet deep, and we could see the striped towel he'd wrapped around Skipper. I officiated, regaling his attributes and recapping Skipper's short life with us and then folded my certificate and laid it on top of the beach towel. Eli tossed in the Valentine. When Jesse's turn came, he stood there a few seconds and then spit into the grave. He said he wished they were burying his dad instead of Skipper. Eli and I stood there with our mouths hanging open. Jesse told us that his dad bragged about running over 'that damn dog.' And when Jesse's mom tried to silence Mr. King, he punched her in the face. Jesse said he ran to his mom, and his dad knocked him to the floor."

I ran my foot over the warm stones. "Poor Jesse. Poor Mrs. King."

Neil paced over the flagstones. "We knew it wasn't the first time, but it was difficult to hear it come from his own mouth. Eli got angry and told Jesse if his dad ever hit him or his mom again, he'd help Jesse beat him up. Of course I had to volunteer, too. Eli retrieved the Valentine and wrote one word on the back: vengeance. Jesse insisted we all sign it and threw it back into the grave. Then we spit on our hands and shook."

I bounded from the chair. "Oh. My. God. In seventh grade Mr. King went into the hospital. Said he fell off a ladder."

"It was us." Neil flopped down beside me. "Jesse called. His dad had beaten up his mom. We got there, and his dad was passed out drunk in the den. Jesse went berserk. He yelled curse words and kicked and hit his dad. Eli and I didn't know what to do. Jesse hit his dad's arm with a baseball bat, and we heard a crack. That's when Eli and I jumped in to pull him off. I can still see Jesse standing there. He looked like some kind of monster, breathing hard and clenching and unclenching his fists. He said it was our turn. We'd shaken on it. I got nauseous. We didn't want to touch Mr. King. We were afraid Jesse had killed him. Jesse jumped at us, screaming, 'You can't back down! We shook on it! We shook on it!' Jesse shoved me at Mr. King, so I kind of kicked him, and then Eli gave him a limp kick. Mrs. King hobbled into the den, and both her eyes were black. She looked down at her husband and then at us. Libby, there was no emotion on her face. Her eyes were empty sockets. She turned and walked back to her room. Never told on us." Neil's head sank between his shoulders. His form barely visible.

I resettled in my chair. "It was bad that he made you participate, but I still don't get why you hate Jesse."

"None of us disclosed a single fact relating to the incident. But a little over a year ago Jesse came to me and wanted go public with our secret. Said Eli had everyone fooled as being some great cop. I think Jesse was jealous that Eli had gotten a commendation from the mayor. Anyway, I listened to his devious dribble and got angrier and angrier. When I refused to back him up, he tried to blackmail me. He said he'd let everyone know that Jesse and I'd assaulted a defenseless drunk. And once word got out, Eli would no longer be praised as the defender of the weak, and I'd be scraping my name off my office door."

I stomped my foot. "Why in the world would he be so vengeful?"

He pointed his index finger in my direction. "He's like his old man. But instead of slinging fists, he's slinging accusations."

My toe traced the mortar holding the stones in place. "But that's all they are. Accusations."

He frowned. "Doesn't matter. Damage would be done. How many exonerations do you think make the front page?"

My cell phone rang. I took it from my pocket and the blood drained from my face.

Neil arched his eyebrows.

"It's Ruth Byram," I said.

Neil touched my arm. "It's okay."

I rolled my shoulders and punched the green accept button. "Hello, Dr. Ruth."

"Hi, Libby. Sorry to bother you this late after your grueling day at the Women's Center."

Ruth calling me at home? My heart thumped an extra beat. She'd been my doctor for ten years—since her boys were in my English class. But this was a first. "What a nice surprise. I hope." My laugh sounded nervous, even to me.

"The X-ray technician called me today about your mammogram."

My fist tightened around the phone. "Is it bad?"

"That's why I'm calling. It's not bad. It's good. The tech said you were apprehensive, and that I should call to confirm what she told you."

I liberated the breath I'd been holding hostage. "That was so nice of her. To be honest, I was a fruitcake. I can't thank you enough for calling and easing my mind."

"Lord knows you eased my mind enough with Chuck and Rob."

"They were two of my favorites. Still are. Tell them hello from me. And Ruth, thanks again. Really. Feel like I should send the technician a thank you note."

Ruth chuckled. "I'll tell the boys I talked to you and see you soon."

Every bone in my body sighed with relief.

Neil lay back, propping on an elbow. "Don't get too cozy. What do we do about Jesse?"

Chapter 24
Blindsided

I was relieved. Wrung out. Overwhelmed. The worry over my mammogram paled in comparison to the guilt I'd hoarded about Eli or my feeling responsible for Neil's accident. But Neil freed me. Now, like a bird whose cage was finally opened, I could fly. Yet, it felt like there was a stipulation: help Neil stop Jesse's scorched earth attack to discredit Eli. I didn't know how to handle a blackmailer, and I'd actually seen a softer, kinder side of Jesse King. I was so tired of juggling emotions. My gut reaction—slam the cage door shut. However, if our cease-fire held, it meant one less worry. For the short term, I chose to wait and see.

The kids had planned game night prior to Eli's and my crossing the friends-with-benefits threshold. I didn't know what to expect when I saw him. Would I be embarrassed? Would he be embarrassed? Not the old Eli. The old Eli only dated the easy chicks and changed partners like politicians changed their minds. Maybe the freedom to experience passion without strings was what I wanted. If I could look Eli in the face, that would be the test.

My body zinged with nervous energy, I swept the front porch, pulled weeds around the shrubs, and plucked dead blooms from pots of flowers on the steps. I was bending over, watering my flowers when Eli's bright yellow Hummer flashed in my periphery. The yellow stimulus made my nerves all flinch at once. The can crashed and a geyser of water spurted straight up, splashing me from my shirt down to my flip-flops.

Eli watched from the sidewalk, arms loaded with bags, as water rolled over each step in turn and down to his size fifteen boat shoes. "Should I have added paper towels to my list?"

No kiss. No hug. Just a lame joke. "Just save the steaks," I said, dabbing at the wet streaks on my shirt. Past insecurities murmured inside my head. *He's a player and you're a plaything. Not so bold and daring now, huh?*

Eli moved with comfortable efficiency, fired up the grill, and made outside preparations. After a quick wardrobe change, I worked inside baking potatoes, tossing the salad, and obsessing over my behavior. I'd wanted to be gutsy. Did I overdo it? Did he think I was risqué or just plain risky? Knee-deep in my negative thoughts, a strong arm slipped around my waist and I jumped. "You sneaked up on me!" He planted a kiss on my neck, and I fumbled the cookie sheet full of foil-wrapped potatoes. I bent to pick up silvery spuds from the floor.

Eli squatted to help and juggled hot potatoes. "You've been avoiding me." Eli tossed two hot potatoes onto the cookie sheet. "Nice gloves. They come in my size?"

My oven-mitted hands caressed his face. Eli leaned down and kissed me on the nose and then the lips. "You okay, gorgeous?"

His words and warm smile melted the knots in my shoulders. I kissed him back. "I am now."

The kids wolfed down dinner to get to the game part of Game Night. Eli helped clear the table and stack dishes. On one pass to the kitchen, I glanced into the den. The game board had been decked out with money, tokens, and orange get out of jail free cards.

Trey and Lee were whispering, and I overheard Trey say, "You ask." Then I heard Lee say, "No, you ask." I motioned for Eli and heard Reagan get involved. I pretended to wipe the counter and listened more intently. Okay, I was eavesdropping.

Reagan tapped five hundred dollar bills against her chin. "Eli's his dad. It would be better if he asked."

Eli silently moved his lips. "What?"

I pulled him to the refrigerator and whispered. "I think they're cooking up something in there. Why don't you use your detective skills and find out what they're planning?"

We walked in, and Eli plopped down between Reagan and Trey. "What's up, guys?"

Trey prompted Lee.

Lee looked at Trey and then took a deep breath. "Dad, you want to marry Libby?" He asked with the simplicity of a ten-year-old.

Eli's face turned a shade darker than blood, and he looked at me for help.

"She said you haven't asked her." Trey looked pleased with himself for placing blame where blame was due.

I stood there speechless and paralyzed. Eli fared no better. His jaw wobbled side to side, looking from one kid to the other.

"If you don't ask her, she might marry that Jesse guy Trey told me about," Lee said.

"He asked her to go to Toronto," Reagan added smugly.

I finally found my voice. "Hold it, guys. Eli and I are very good friends. We haven't even thought of marriage."

"I have." Eli sounded like a little boy who'd been chosen last for kickball.

I stared into his expectant face. "Eli, I, I..." I stammered, not knowing what to say. My mind churned. "This is not up for group discussion."

Eli bounded up. "Why don't you guys play while the grown-ups talk?" Eli reached for my hand and led me outside. He smiled and buffed the top of his head. "Talk about getting blindsided. Did you see this coming?"

I could barely breathe, and my voice came out in a whisper. "No." I didn't return his smile. "*Have* you thought of marrying again?"

"Of marrying *you*. Since I was five years old." Eli took a breath. "I hadn't planned on bringing this up so soon. But it sounds like I have some formidable competition."

"Eli, we can't let our kids badger us into making a bad decision."

Eli looked shaken by my words. "Do you think marrying me would be a bad decision?"

"I don't mean it that way. I'm not prepared for any of this. I had no idea you'd been thinking about, about, *this*." I sputtered and flapped my hands.

"I can't compete with Jesse." Eli sandwiched my hands between his. "But I love being a dad. The practices, the games, broken arms, broken hearts, you know, real life stuff." Eli's eyes brightened as he talked.

"I love being a husband. I love family. With family, even when things are bad, they're good."

I'd worried about his being too aloof, and now his seriousness was scaring me to death. He'd backed me into a corner, and I couldn't take a deep breath. "Sounds like you've put some thought into this."

"Accepting the fact that you chose Neil was hard. I moved on. But now I have a second chance."

"How do you know you want me? What if you marry me and decide that I'm just like all the other girls you've used and discarded?"

He locked his hands on his hips. "You can't be serious."

"You rejected me before."

"For God's sake, we were eighteen. Let it go."

"Someone told me we drag our past around forever." The stars twinkled overhead, and I wished I were with them. Anywhere but here.

"For most of us, the past is part of growing up. Granted, most of us want to forget it, but it is what it is—past."

I searched for the three stars in the belt of Orion. "Let's not make this bigger than it is. We had sex."

"You don't believe that." Eli's mouth stretched into a rare frown. "It was more than sex for me. Was I wrong to think that you felt something too?"

"Remember the first time? I thought you felt something then, too. But I was wrong."

"Libby, I was eighteen. You know what I wanted. But even through the haze of hormones, I loved you. I just couldn't see myself married at eighteen."

Memories of that night still poked the soft spots. I stretched my neck taut and jutted out my chin. "Well,

I'm thirty-seven, and I don't know what I want."

Eli cupped the back of my head and massaged. "Loving you feels right."

I rubbed my hands down my face. "I don't know what feels right. I know I love being with you. It feels so, so *comfortable*."

Eli stepped back, and his fake laugh sliced through my heart. "But you've had comfortable, right?"

"The kids and I love being around you. We're always wondering what you'll do next. But—"

"Wait." With his hand he turned my face toward his. "Elizabeth Carlisle Miller, I love you. I've loved you my whole life. I feel like I've come full circle and found what was always there but was always missing."

Tears flared behind my eyes, and I struggled to keep them from falling. "Eli, you've been a part of my life as long as Neil and Jesse."

"Don't put two strikes against me before you give me a chance." He took my hands in his. "I don't have a head full of hair or the GQ wardrobe like Jesse, and I don't care which color wine goes with what. I'm just me, and I know what I want. I want to love you and make you laugh until we're old and gray."

"I don't want to think about getting married. My whole life has been controlled by men. For the first eighteen years, it was my dad and then Neil. I've been on my own for less than a year, and for the first time, I'm in control of my life."

"I didn't mean to overwhelm you or intrude on your newfound independence. But I'm crazy jealous of Jesse. I know him, Libby. He'll risk everything to get what he wants. And he prides himself on leaving a trail of destruction."

"It's not fair. You're making me choose." Tears rolled down my cheeks.

Tenderly, Eli wiped a tear. "Libby, I can't handle the idea of you making love to someone else. Of loving someone else. So, yes, I guess I am making you choose." He pressed his face to mine, warming my ear with his breath. "You can't choose who you love, but you can choose who you spend the rest of your life with. Or without." He squeezed my hands and let go. Eli walked away.

My heart hammered in my chest. He didn't stop. He didn't turn around. My throat clogged. *I do care about you.* But I couldn't say the words.

He kept walking. I stood there—my feet frozen on the stepping stones still warm from the day's sunlight.

Neil crept within my line of vision. His stance sturdy and authoritative. "Can't say I'm surprised."

I threw up my hand like a stop sign, and looked through Neil and watched Eli walk away. A steel band wrapped around my chest. It tightened with each step, over the stepping stones and past long, thin stalks of pink amaryllises reaching out to him. Three strides across the rock patio and he disappeared through the back door.

I closed my eyes and willed air into my lungs. Eli wouldn't upset the kids. He'd smile, ruffle Trey's hair, and tweak Reagan's nose. And then he and Lee would walk out my front door. I'd be on my own. Why wasn't I high-fiving my newfound independence?

"What'd he expect? An instant 'I do?'" Neil settled beside me. "I guess it's true that fools rush in."

I sought the serenity of the water glistening in the moonlight. "Don't. Please." But Neil had a point. Eli

271

had no business pushing. He might be ready to get married, but I was still dealing with a dead husband. Not to mention, I was just getting used to my freedom. I'd been grounded my whole life. Now I wanted to fly. Or at least flap my wings.

The deep rumble of Eli's Hummer rattled inside my head like loose window panes. The vibration grew weaker and weaker until the droning died, leaving a sad echo inside my hollow shell. I felt like a kid whose security blanket had been stripped away. My feelings for Eli were complicated. He was dependable. He was familiar. He was Eli—superhero. Our lives, our memories, our past intertwined in tangled knots. Cutting Eli out of my life felt like an amputated limb. Gone, but leaving behind a ghostly ache.

I couldn't face my kids yet. I needed the peace of my refuge. I climbed the stairs, closed the door to the boathouse, and pressed my back against the warm oak. Calls of night birds echoed soulfully over the black, glassy surface. Not a wisp of wind rustled the leaves or cleared the fog in my brain.

"The kids sure like Eli." Neil's dislocated voice wafted down from the ceiling.

I jolted backward and banged my head on the door. "Stop sneaking up on me."

Neil glared. "What am I supposed to do, wear a bell around my neck?"

I rubbed the back of my head. "You're supposed to go away."

"Let's not get into that again. You have bigger problems. The kids are going to give you a hard time for dumping Mr. Football and the great earring retriever."

I sighed. Eli's presence filled our house like the aroma of homemade bread, welcoming and hearty. "Yeah. He fit right in." The easy way he'd drape his muscled arm on my shoulder felt so…comfortable. But like he said, I'd had comfortable.

Neil sailed to the bar and reclined. "He fit in a little too well, don't you think?"

Anger spewed up and out. "What about our heart-to-heart four days ago?" I flung open the window. "I thought you were going to have my back?"

Neil gave me his hurt look. "I'm trying to be supportive."

"If you want to be supportive and helpful, maybe it's time to go find that highway to Heaven. Unless you're worried that the road leads elsewhere."

"It's not like there's an interstate with road signs. And I'm not worried." He whisked off into the dark.

Chapter 25
I'm the Boss of Me

The kids and I trudged through the week, artfully dodging the Eli issue. Reagan and Trey sported long faces, and loud sighs resonated around the dinner table. I answered their questions as truthfully as I knew how. I didn't know what I wanted or where I was headed. All I knew was that I had to live my life.

I'd moped and isolated myself through the week, but on Saturday morning I pulled my hair back into a ponytail and put on my grubbiest clothes. I needed a distraction. A project. Nothing better than hard work and sweat to get me out of my funk. A little spring cleaning.

I gathered up scouring products and my trusty vacuum cleaner and hauled them to the boathouse. Inserted ear buds and cranked up the volume on my phone to one click below permanent hearing loss, and let Credence Clearwater Revival exclaim "Joy to the World." I cleaned windows, walls, baseboards, even the ceiling. I tackled the vacuuming with the fervor of a woman possessed, wrenching my arm out of its socket with each swipe. I caught a movement and dropped the handle and pulled the plug. "Jesse! What are you doing here?"

"Didn't Reagan tell you I called?" His voice roared over the music. "She told me to come over."

I stuffed loose strands of hair back into the ponytail holder. "I'm a mess. I wasn't expecting anyone."

Jesse pointed to his ear.

I jerked at my ear buds. "I'm so embarrassed." I realigned my rag-bag ensemble.

"Sorry to catch you off guard." He smiled. "Okay, I'm not sorry. Maybe I planned a sneak attack. But I had a little help. I figured it was the only way to get you to accept my invitation to Toronto."

This was Reagan's play, and she was in big trouble. "I can't just take off and go to Toronto."

Jesse sat on the sofa. "Is it the stigma of my business?"

"No, no, no. Of course it's not your business." *It's because you're a blackmailer, and Neil wants me to stay away from you until he figures out how to stop you.*

"When my dad owned Waste Services, it was a garbage company. But that was my dad. Ten years ago, I took over, and we became Complete Waste Services. A state-of-the-art waste management that includes recycling as well as handling toxic contaminants. This conference in Toronto highlights recycling electronic devices and hazardous waste." Jesse sounded like a commercial.

I glanced around for backup, but Neil was nowhere in sight. "You don't have to sell me. I'm proud of what you've accomplished."

He flopped back against the sofa, and his face went from hopeful to defensive. "Yeah. Who would have thought the son of a garbage man—"

I gripped his muscled forearm and remembered Neil's warning and let go. "Stop it, Jesse. You're not your father."

He dropped his chin to his chest. "His legacy haunts me." He rubbed his hands over his face, and he was back. "Let's talk about something fun." He slapped a manila folder on the coffee table. "This'll tempt you. Look at the places I printed on our itinerary. I even printed the average temperatures for both daytime and evening so you'd know what to pack."

I opened a folder filled with glossy photos of Montreal. "Sound pretty sure of yourself."

Jesse planted both hands on the coffee table. "Let's just say that I usually get what I want."

I closed the folder. "And what do you want?"

Jesse trained his eyes on mine. I didn't flinch.

He leaned back and rested his hands in his lap. "Can't I show a beautiful woman how much I like her?"

I knew what he wanted. "You want sex."

"I admit I want you."

"And you get what you want." It wasn't a question.

Jesse leaned forward and looped a strand of my hair around his finger. "Is that a bad thing?"

"It's not a bad thing. It's just not enough," I said.

"Let me guess. If you have sex, you want a ring and the license framed on the wall?"

I tapped my finger against my chin. "It doesn't have to be framed."

Jesse released my curl and walked to the window. The breeze fingered his dark hair. "Those are ideas our parents had. Besides, we've both done the marriage thing. Look what it got us. It left you with two kids to raise and me with alimony and child-support."

A low growl originated in my stomach and heaved upward, clawing its way up my throat. "Yes, I have two kids to raise." My vocal chords launched the words at his back like a sling shot. "And I'm damn lucky." I bounced up and snatched his arm, forcing him to face me. "Alimony? Child support? Is that how you value your son?"

"I don't see him much. I work a lot, and his mother makes it…difficult. Except when she needs something." His voice dropped to an ominous rumbling.

I shoved him. "And whose fault is that? I heard you say you like to piss her off. Who does that sound like?" I bored a hole in his chest with my index finger. "Let me tell you something. Nothing and nobody could keep me from my children."

Faster than an eyeblink, Jesse yanked me close. "I'm a selfish man. So save me."

Sunlight cast a mini shadow in the cleft of his chin. He tightened his grip. Too close. I placed my hands on his chest and pushed. "I'm not ready for Toronto."

He exhaled a cinnamon-coated sigh. "Can I change your mind?"

I pushed harder. "Nope."

Jesse eased his clutch. "What about dinner?"

"Dinner?"

"Tonight?'

I flipped my ponytail. "Can I go like this?"

"You can go naked as long as you're ready by seven."

****

The doorbell rang and no butterflies. Only lead BB's in the pit of my stomach. I'd been unable to work up much enthusiasm for my date with Jesse. Neil dedicated his phantom force to finding counter blackmail data strong enough to thwart Jesse's character assassination plans. And since he couldn't deliver the punch, that job fell to me. I felt like Benedict Arnold.

I opened the door, and there were no compliments. No bear hug. Only a peck on the cheek. Jesse caught his reflection in the foyer mirror and fine-tuned his collar.

I claimed my purse from the table and avoided looking at my reflection. "Still not telling me where we're going?"

"You'll know soon enough." Jesse flicked the hem of my dress. "I was hoping you'd take me up on the naked thing."

A vision flashed—me opening the door stark naked and Eli being on the other side. Sadness slowly orbited my heart.

Neil sat cross-legged on the dining room table. "Never observed the King in action from this perspective. The word *insipid* comes to mind."

I checked my purse for my keys. "Just Jesse being Jesse."

Jesse escorted me to his black Corvette, where prominently displayed on the front was a tag that declared, "It's great to be the King."

My level of expectation sank a notch, and I bumped up the volume on the cockpit sound system.

The turn signal flashed green on a NASA-approved GPS. "Almost there." Camouflaged in the foliage, a weathered sign announced Red Mountain Inn. Jesse leaned into the turn and accelerated.

Birmingham's premier restaurant sat high atop its namesake Red Mountain, named for the vein of iron ore crisscrossing its face. Jesse's late-model sports car soared up the incline, hugging the turns and twists of the narrow two-lane road. He zoomed beneath the canopy of ancient magnolia trees. At the summit, the trees opened and asphalt gave way to cobblestones. The tires thumped around the circular drive and stopped at the ivy-wreathed façade of roughhewn rock and weathered planks. The tuxedoed doorman smiled from his post beside the double-arched doors.

Jesse lobbed his keys to the parking valet, "Take care of my baby." He sprinted to my side of the car and opened the door, extending his hand. He withdrew me from the car like a treasured prize and pressed his lips to my hand. "Let the magic begin."

The man was smooth.

"I might vomit," Neil squawked in my ear.

I flicked my earlobe. "So now you're reading my mind?"

Jesse dropped my hand. "What?"

Neil kissed the backs of his hands, making loud, slurpy smacks, and mocked Jesse in a crooning falsetto. "Let the magic begin."

I tucked my arm in Jesse's. "You read my mind. This place is magical."

Our table, snuggled against the giant wall of glass, gave the sensation of sitting on top of the world. Below us, the lights of Birmingham twinkled. I sipped my wine slowly. Very slowly. This was Jesse. Couldn't let my guard down. There was not an altruistic bone in his body, of that I was sure. He wanted something. And from the flicker in his eyes and the set of his mouth, that something was me.

Jesse raised his glass. "To the loveliest woman here." His voice sounded warm and intimate.

I shooed away the butterflies dancing up my spine, and we touched glasses.

Neil spoke into my ear. "Don't let him deceive you with compliments. And wine. Remember homecoming."

"I remember homecoming—" I set down my glass and smiled, cursing Neil silently.

"Huh?" Jesse sounded confused. "Homecoming? Like in high school?"

I stalled for time to think of a cover-up comeback. I brushed non-existent crumbs from a pristine napkin while my brain whirled like a cotton candy machine. I applied a smile. "You know…I mean…It's just…I guess I'm a little confused by all your attention lately. Over the years our relationship has been, to put it nicely, a bit combative."

"I'd categorize it as playful conflict."

My bullshit meter locked in a holding pattern. "The time you stood me up at homecoming didn't feel very playful." I thought I was beyond the injury of that night. "Everyone knew we had a date, and then you took Debbie Weaver to the dance. You made it painfully clear that you weren't interested in me then, so why now?"

Jesse put his glass down and turned it one complete rotation. He took his napkin from his lap, folded it neatly, and laid it on the table. "I made a mistake."

I tossed my napkin on top of his. "You hurt my feelings."

"A lot of things happened our senior year."

Neil broke in. "Watch him. He's playing you."

Neil was right. But I hoped he wasn't going to remind me that his mom died that year. I didn't want to feel sorry for him. I swirled the wine in my glass and snubbed his droopy-eyed, poor-pitiful-me look he'd honed to a fine art. "Why'd you ask me to the homecoming dance?"

Jesse held up two fingers. "Two reasons. Neil and Eli."

Arms crossed and face tight, Neil perched on the tip of the candle flame. "I want to see how Jesse spins this."

I wanted to tell Neil to shut up, but stopped myself in time. Jesse's absurd answer landed somewhere between annoyance and disgust. "What in heaven's name did Eli and Neil have to do with you asking me out?"

"You and Neil broke up. And I asked you out before Eli did." Jesse raised his arms with palms out flat like an attorney presenting the perfect explanation in a final closing argument.

"We had a date. And after the game I waited outside the gym for you. You came out with Debbie Weaver." My voice got stronger as I got angrier. Heads turned in our direction.

"Let him have it, Libby." Neil's fragile form bounced up and down.

Jesse leaned forward, tilted his head to the side, and gave me a sexy, half-smile. "Lib, you know what Debbie Weaver was famous for. And if I told you half of what that girl promised me, I'd need a fire extinguisher for your blushing cheeks."

"You're worried about embarrassing me now? Your concern is about twenty years late." I sipped my wine to drown my thoughts of that night. Jesse didn't have the nerve to look my way. But Debbie did. She cuddled her legendary breasts against Jesse's arm and whispered into his ear. And then she laughed. A sexy, low-pitched womanly laugh. I remember the pain—as sharp and swift as a laser. I begged my feet to move, but then, a strong arm slipped around my shoulder, and Eli ushered me out of the gymnasium.

"Twenty years ago, and it still pisses me off." I slammed my glass down. Dark red droplets spattered the white tablecloth and spread into a Rorschach inkblot. "You humiliated me."

"You didn't look too humiliated to me. Not with Eli all over you."

"Stop right there," I said.

Neil hopped from one foot to the other in the aisle. "Knock out in round one."

Jesse wiggled his eyebrows. "Where did this spitfire come from? I like it."

I stretched across the table. "You stood me up. No apology. No explanation. No nothing. I'm not the little girl Eli rescued that night."

Jesse's face went from smug to contrite as effortlessly as his Corvette went from zero to sixty. "I was an asshole. But I was eighteen." He reached for my hand and cradled it between his. "I'm sorry."

"Don't fall for this imitation apology." Neil crowded between Jesse and me.

I wanted to jerk my hand back, but Jesse looked so sincere. And I liked the way his thumb tickled my palm.

"Give me another chance. I'm a different man." Jesse's voice purred in tones of rich velvet.

Neil raked his hands through his always well-groomed, brown hair. Ghostly strands stood on end. "I can't take this. The jerk dumped you for the class whore." A trail of Neil hung in the air for a split second and disappeared.

I scrutinized the man before me. The man I'd avoided most of my life, and ignored when I couldn't. Gone was the proud set of his chin and tilt of his head. Instead, he looked at me with an openness that drew me in. I forgot my anger. His puppy-dog eyes and his pouty lips revealed a vulnerability I'd never seen.

Jesse's lips spread into a grin. He took my hand and did his slow thumb-a-rhumba to my palm. "Let me make it up to you."

Like a snake charmer plying his trade, Jesse held me captive. Dinner passed in a blur. White coats and aprons shuffled appetizers, breads, salads, and entrées. I'm sure that everything tasted delicious, but even my taste buds were beguiled.

Jesse laid his napkin on the table. "It's only a little after nine. You have to be home early?"

"I don't have a curfew. "

"Want to check out the observation deck outside?"

"I need to stop by the ladies' room first."

When I came out of the restroom, Jesse's long, well-tended body leaned casually against the wall. He saw me, and his face lit up in a neon smile. A smile that a woman would do anything to get. He'd exposed a chink in his armor earlier, but this smile was pure Jesse.

He held out his hand. Long, slender fingers wove into mine and locked in a playful challenge. His eyes glinted in a feral, I-dare-you look.

My legs wobbled, threatening to fold in two like a worn pair of ballet slippers. Jesse tugged, and I glided after him along the wooden decking.

He stopped and sniffed. "Smell that?"

An earthy scent filled my nostrils. *My mission!* I clutched the handrail with both hands. Moonlight and nature's soft, sweet scents bushwhacked my Mission Impossible assignment. I relaxed my grip, leaned against the wooden railings, and breathed in long, slow breaths. I smoothed my little black dress and rolled back my shoulders.

Neil breezed by. "Let me recap the crimes of Jesse King: He made you a laughingstock more than once. He planted drugs on an opposing team's quarterback to win the State championship. And now he wants to ruin Eli."

"Stop. I can't do this." I closed my eyes and wished I'd never agreed to going out with Jesse or helping Neil.

Jesse reached for my hand. "What can't you do?"

I waved my arms. "This whole charade. You never missed an opportunity to harass or embarrass me. Growing up, I refused to be around you without your mom close by or at least in the vicinity."

"So that's why she got invited to all your birthday parties?" He laughed and nuzzled his nose to my cheek. "My mom loved you, Lib. And the smell of jasmine always reminds me of her."

No fair invoking the mom reference. She and Jesse had suffered at the hands of Mr. King. Like so many other women and children I'd met working with the Home Safe Foundation. Jesse might have been different if there had been a foundation in his day. Jesse was my Tommy Thornton.

The frightened face of Tommy Thornton blinked in my mind and wavered into a young, innocent Jesse King. Melancholy swept over me, and heaviness descended, but the sweet essence of jasmine enveloped me in a soothing balm. I lost track of my mission, my environment, my feet.

One second I'm walking upright, and the next, I'm falling face first. My hands shot out to meet the deck rushing up to greet me, leaving the skinny heel of my sassy sandal wedged in the crack between the wooden planks. Before making contact, Jesse scooped me up. He cinched me close and held on. I breathed in his expensive aftershave. Warning bells jangled, and I squirmed out of his grasp to retrieve my shoe. "These shoes are dangerous."

"Let me get that for you." Jesse dropped to one knee and carefully pried the heel from the crack. "Here you go."

I slid my foot into the shoe, and he ran his finger under the strap and secured it at the heel. "Nice shoes."

The trace of his finger singed my skin. "Thanks."

He stood. "Ready for the magic?"

I followed him to the edge of the cliff. Birmingham, the Magic City, winked below us. Jesse cupped my cheek and locked his eyes on mine. His mouth inched closer and closer and closer. I sloped toward him. My pocket vibrated.

Jesse chuckled. "That felt good. But not quite the tingle I was hoping for."

I pulled out my phone and looked down. "I'm sorry, but I have to take this." I answered. "Hi, Emily. Everything okay?"

"Now, Libby. I need you to stay calm."

Chapter 26
Meltdown

I need you to stay calm. Six words never to start a conversation with—especially to a parent.

Spikes of ice-cold fear gouged the muscles between my shoulder blades. I clutched my phone to my ear. Emily knew I was with Jesse. She wouldn't have called unless it was important. I clasped the phone tighter. "Emily, you're scaring me. What's wrong?"

"It's Trey." Emily choked out the words.

The walls of my chest collapsed. I pressed my fist to my sternum and pounded. Air wheezed through my windpipe. "What happened to my son?"

"We can't find him. He and Reagan had an argument and he stormed out."

A brother-sister argument? The vise in my chest backed off a tick. If Reagan and Trey were conscious, they were fighting. As long as no blood was involved, I could handle it. "He can't be far."

Emily sighed. "We've looked everywhere. Around the lake. In the boathouse. In the closets. Everywhere."

"Did you try his cell phone?" I asked.

"Reagan and I both tried. No answer," Emily said.

"It's probably on his dresser. His phone is not permanently attached like his sister's." My mom-panic turned into mom-practical. "He'll cool off and come home."

"Reagan's falling apart. I think you need to talk to her," Emily said.

What had Reagan done this time to bully her brother? "Oh, I plan on talking to that young lady."

"It's not what you think. You should let her explain," Emily said.

I grabbed Jesse's arm and directed him toward the parking lot. "I'll call her when we get to the car."

"Promise you'll listen to her side." Emily seemed overly concerned about Reagan's feelings.

"I promise." I hit end. "Sorry to cut this short. But Trey and Reagan had a fight and he ran off. Emily's in a tizzy, and Reagan's freaking out." I gave Jesse a Reaganesque eye roll. "I'm sure he's somewhere nearby, sulking."

"Yeah. You're probably right." He nodded to the valet. "We'll find him and get everybody settled down, and then you and I can enjoy some quiet time in your boathouse." He winked.

"I promised Emily I'd call Reagan and listen to her explanation. I'll put my phone on speaker and share the entertainment. Reagan has quite a flair for the dramatic." I tapped Reagan's number on my phone.

Reagan answered mid-ring and dove in. "Mom, I promise this time it's not my fault. We weren't even arguing. He's mad at you."

"Me? I wasn't home."

"For going out with Jesse. I was doing my nails, and he knocked all my stuff off the coffee table and kicked a throw pillow into the ceiling fan. The blades wobbled so bad I thought they might start flying. Then he started screaming that you dumped Eli for a kid-hating loser. Mom, he scared Sadie so bad she got her head stuck under the sofa trying to hide."

My fingers fumbled to disengage the speaker option. Embarrassment slammed me with lead boxing gloves. "So Sadie's okay?" My vocal chords stretched tight.

"Mom, Sadie's fine. Trey's gone! Marcus helped Andrea and me search around the lake. We kept calling and calling and calling. Then we ran to get Emily and Reggie. My throat hurts."

Her throat hurts. It's all about her. "We'll be home in half an hour. Ask Marcus to think hard. There's got to be some special place the two of them go." I disconnected the call and held my phone between my palms. "I'm so sorry you heard that. Trey didn't mean it."

Jesse shrugged and hit the accelerator. "Any idea where he might be?"

Neil crowded into the front seat. "The train tracks."

"The train tracks?" I asked.

Jesse looked at me. "Be my guess, too."

Neil scrunched between us above the console. "That's where the three of us went when we wanted to disappear."

I frowned at Neil. "The Three Musketeers."

"You guessed it," Jesse said. "Our hideout. Not so far outside our boundaries to get us into real trouble, but far enough from nosy parents."

Jesse didn't comment on Reagan's conversation, and I was too concerned about the events at home to engage in chitchat. He turned into my driveway, and his headlights illuminated the waiting search crew. Adding Jesse and me to Reagan, Reggie, Emily, and their two kids, bumped up our search party to seven.

Reagan bolted from the group. She jerked open my door and squatted beside the car. "I swear it's not my fault." She lay her head in my lap, clutching my legs. "Can we call Eli?"

Jesse's hand tightened on my shoulder. I patted Reagan's back and wished I could call Eli, too. "Your brother's had time to cool off; I'm sure he's fine. Let me out so we can go find him."

She lifted her head, and her eyes glistened. "It's really not my fault this time."

This time. I gave her a reassuring smile and abandoned any hope of gracefully removing myself from the low-slung bucket seat. Emily waited until I rolled out and handed me a sweatshirt and her once-white gardening shoes.

"Don't want you breaking an ankle traipsing through the woods in those." She pointed to my strappy heels.

I wriggled my feet into her comfy Keds. "Thanks. Still no word from him?"

Reagan wiped her nose with the heel of her hand. "I found his cell phone in his room."

Jesse walked around the rear of the car and gave Reagan a half-hearted, one-armed hug. "Don't worry. Big guns are here."

Reagan led us to the rest of the search party, and Reggie switched on his headband, demonstrating the one-eyed bulb glowing in the center of his forehead. He cycled through all three settings—low, medium, and blinding. Marcus held a long, black flashlight, and Andrea turned on the flashlight App on her cell phone.

Reggie eyed Jesse and placed an industrial-sized yellow and black portable spotlight into his hand. "Nice to meet you, Jesse. I'm Reggie."

The group whirred with energy. Checking batteries. Testing the light streams. *Trey Miller. When I find you I'm grounding you until you're twenty-one.* Right after I hugged and kissed him until I could breathe again.

Emily smiled at Jesse. "I'm Emily. We're glad you're here."

"I'm sorry. I should have introduced you guys," I said.

"Yes, by all means, let's be socially correct." Neil called from outside the arc of light. "I'm going after Trey."

"Don't you dare leave without us. We all want to find Trey," I shouted at the dark.

Emily pinched my arm and shook her head. She must have recognized my toxic Neil-tone and figured out he was close.

Emily held out a shirt, and I shared a weak smile before tugging the long, gray sweatshirt over my head. It smelled freshly laundered. "Has anyone seen Sadie?"

Reagan pulled and yanked to cover my dress with the sweatshirt. "She's not at home. She has to be with Trey."

"Okay, guys, when we call Trey, call Sadie too. She's minds better than he does," I announced to the search party. "If she hears us, she'll come and lead us to Trey."

Marcus led the convoy of lights snaking along the trail to the railroad tracks. We clomped the hard-packed dirt in single file. Neil flew in and out of our beams. At the tracks, the path widened, and the crew fanned out.

The air quivered over my head. "Of course his

dog's with him. Good girl."

I didn't acknowledge Neil's comment and fell in step with the group.

"Trey? Trey?" Reagan called out, her voice sharp and jumpy.

I whistled. "Sadie, come here, girl."

We stopped and listened. No response. Our party of four adults and three kids tromped through the forest with the stealth of a baby elephant stampede. I hoped Sadie heard us first.

"Trey!" Neil shouted.

I wanted to do a Reagan eye roll. "He can't hear you," I said.

Jesse took my arm. "Take it easy. If he's anywhere near, he'll hear us. And he might answer Reagan before one of us."

"I hear something." Neil zoomed out of the range of our lights.

I squeezed Jesse's arm and stopped. "Listen."

Sadie ran from the darkness and into our lights and dropped at my feet. I squatted and rubbed her head. "Good girl. Good girl." Reagan stumbled over and buried her head in Sadie's fur. I stood and clapped my hands. "Okay, girl, take us to Trey." I nudged her with my hands, and our entourage followed her down the trail.

"I see him!" Marcus ran, crunching small stones under his Nikes.

The group followed Marcus. He stopped abruptly, and seven bright beams zeroed in on one scrawny twelve-year-old and his dog. My eyes stung and then blurred. He was the most welcome vision I could imagine. Finally, a real breath inflated my lungs. Trey sat on the metal rail with his head sagging between his shoulders, hands between his knees. He was safe. He prodded Sadie with his shoe. "Traitor."

I handed Jesse my flashlight and knelt beside Trey. "You okay, son?"

Trey sniffed but said nothing. I touched his chin, and he turned away from me and wiped his cheeks on his sleeve. I stood and put my hand on his head. "We were worried about you."

Trey picked up a flashlight. "This thing is a piece of crap." He threw the light, and it crashed into the underbrush. "The light went out, and I was trapped here. I didn't know if you'd even come look for me."

I sat beside him on the narrow rail, sandwiched between the dense dark behind us and the bright lights in front of us. Like performers on stage, we sat in the spotlight. Characters acting in the play of life. "Of course I'd search for you. But what are you doing out here?"

"I got so mad. I didn't know where I was going."

"Why'd you run away?" I scratched his back.

Trey burrowed his face into his hands. "I need my dad."

An ache exploded behind my eyes. Hot tears boiled over and scalded my skin.

Neil wrapped trembling, opaque arms around his son's shoulders and cried. Desperation, despair, and hopelessness retched from deep inside his soul. A father mourning his loss. An iron fist struck my heart and broke it into tiny pieces.

I wanted to be in control, and now it was time to exercise my independence and console my son. I pushed my sadness aside and stroked the back of his head. "I know you miss your dad. But I feel him here with us."

Trey knocked my hand away and jumped up. "You don't care. You don't care about anybody but yourself." Spittle flew out with his words and hung in the aura of light around him.

His outburst confused me. "What are you talking about?"

Trey looked down at me. His face whirling in shades of anger and grief. "You messed up everything."

The look of misery in my twelve-year-old's eyes confused me. "Trey, I don't understand. What have I done? Why are you so angry at me?"

Trey gritted his teeth. "If I can't have my dad, I want Eli. Not Jesse." He sprinted into the dark.

The spotlights followed Trey's path, and I darted after him. "Trey, stop right there. Now!"

Trey stopped but kept his back to me. I reached for him and grabbed a handful of Neil.

Neil bent toward me. "He's upset."

I waved Neil out of my face. "I know he's upset. We're all upset. Now move."

Trey turned. "You dumped Eli. You ruined my only chance." His voice sounded cold. Distant.

"You've had lots to deal with. No kid should lose their dad, and I know you're sad. But this is adult business. And who I want in my adult life is my adult business."

Trey pounded his chest. "It is my business. And it's her business too." He squeezed his head between his hands. "We had a chance. We could'a had a family again."

Neil hovered overhead and waited for my reply.

I glared at Neil. "We are a family."

Trey's eyes closed, and his lips flat-lined across his face. "Doesn't feel like a family."

Trey's accusation knocked me backward. I wanted to argue, but I had no air to form my words.

"Lib, listen to Trey," Neil said.

I threw up my hands.

Jesse touched my elbow and I swung around. "I think our batteries are getting low. You guys ready to head back?"

Trey balled his fists. "Why'd you bring him?"

"Be polite," I said. "He was concerned about you."

Trey bunched his body into attack mode. "Mom, I don't think he likes kids. Not even his own."

"Sounds like he's got Jesse pegged," Neil said.

"You're not helping." I turned to Trey. "You're being rude and disrespectful." I rubbed my forehead. "Apologize right this minute."

"I apologize." Trey thrust his face at me. "If you die, who takes care of us?"

Reagan shoved Trey. "Don't say that. Mom can't die."

Trey shoved back. "Dad did." He looked at me. "What happens to us if you die?"

I had no good answer. My parents were gone, so legally Neil's folks and my two sisters were next of kin. "You have grandparents and two aunts."

"That's messed up. I want a dad. Eli's a dad." Trey crowded close to Reagan. "Tell Mom what we talked about."

Reagan coiled a long stand of hair around her finger. "Trey, let's just go home."

Trey kicked a grassy mound, and dirt balls

skittered across my feet. He stood on his toes to meet Reagan at her level. "I should'a known I couldn't count on you."

Reagan unwound her curl. "Fine." She shoved her brother out of the way. "I don't mean to hurt your feelings, Jesse. I think you're a really cool guy and all…but Eli makes Mom laugh." Reagan looked at me. "I really miss that."

"Train's coming." Emily walked into the middle of our awkward moment. I wanted to kiss her. "We're going home."

Reagan held out her phone. "My phone's dying. Can we go now?"

A single white light sliced through the darkness and behind it a metallic clatter. I hadn't been this close to an oncoming train in many years. We used to make the trek with the kids to put coins on the tracks but rarely saw an actual train. But I remembered how loud and overwhelming the engine and boxcars sounded rushing past. Being this close made me nervous. "Let's go, guys. Move it."

Trey sprawled in the dirt, scattering leaf debris. "I can't find it."

"What are you looking for?" I asked.

"I had it. Where'd it go?" Trey's hands sent rocks and dirt in all directions. "I lost it!"

I dropped down and grabbed his hand. "What are you looking for? We've got to get out of here."

Trey yanked his hand away and resumed his search. "It's Dad's watch. The one with the long gold chain."

An air horn blasted through the dark. Alarm shuddered through my body. I stood and tugged Trey's hand. "Come on. We'll look for it later."

"I'm not leaving it!"

Reagan joined him, raking her hands over the rough earthen floor. "We'll all look for it."

Marcus ditched his flashlight and dropped down on all fours. And then the grown-ups joined in.

Reggie swept his arms in wide arcs over the rough terrain. "It's not here, Trey."

Emily pulled at Marcus. "The train's too close."

Trey jumped up. "I must have dropped it on the tracks!" All flashlights merged on his face, giving him a ghostly mask.

Like a bull's-eye in the dark, the engine aimed a solid beam on the tracks. The ground trembled through the thin soles of my shoes. *Oh, God.* I knew that look. Fear galvanized by stubborn strength. I'd seen it the time he'd sliced open his hand, requiring six stitches. And I'd seen that look when I told him his father was dead. I took his hand in both of mine and smiled. "It has to be here, son. After the train, we'll—"

A cyclops made of iron and steel bore down. And then wheels locked and a metallic chaos drowned out my words.

Trey backed up. "Let me go! I can't lose it!"

I grasped tighter, and he pulled harder, digging his shoes into the dirt. An exposed root caught my heel, and I eased my grip. Trey propelled backward. Toward the tracks.

A discordant chorus of voices screamed.

I lunged for Trey, but strong arms held me in place. I kicked and fought, but Jesse's grip was vise-solid. "Trey! Trey! Trey!" I screamed his name over and over and over. My vocal chords shred to twisted threads.

Sound and time swirled to a zenith. A starburst of colorful sparks flew into the sky, and the train zipped past, leaving behind a whirlwind that froze the tears on my cheeks and the cries in my throat.

We were left with a vacuum of deafening silence. No rumbling box cars. No sleek passenger cars. No squeal of metal scraping metal. Only clouds of dust swirling, enveloping, choking its bystanders.

Jesse loosened his grip. I ducked under his arm and bolted. "Trey!" I stretched out his name, scraping the raw syllable over my icy lips.

I scrambled to where he lay. Face down on the hard-packed earth. I scrambled to him and fell to my knees. "Oh, dear God. Trey. Trey. Trey." No blood. Relief rushed out in a jagged breath. I grabbed handfuls of his t-shirt and yanked at his waistband.

Flashlights hit the ground, and Emily reached out and stilled my hands. "Hold it, Libby. We can't move him yet."

Trey sat upright and brushed our hands away like he was shooing gnats. "Bthaa. Bthaa." He sat up and spit. "Mom, did you see him?" He spat again.

I hugged him and rubbed my hands over his face and head and kissed his gritty cheeks.

His body tensed, and he pulled out of my reach. "Did you see him? Did you see who pushed me?"

My baby was safe. Tears filled my eyes and leaked down my face.

Trey grabbed my upper arms and shook hard. "Did you see him? Did you see him?"

I lifted the hem of Reggie's sweatshirt and dabbed my eyes and nose. A replay of Trey falling backward flashed in 3-D. I shuddered. "Who? I didn't see anyone."

"I'm okay, Mom. I'm okay. Listen." He moved close and whispered, "I felt hands on my back. They shoved me out of the way." His eyes flashed. "It was Dad."

Emily's hand went to her mouth, and the whites of her eyes shone in the dark. She took Reggie's hand and guided him and the others out of hearing range.

Reagan plopped down, landing cross-legged. She bowed her head. "I found this by the tracks." She extended her hand, dangling a gold chain between her fingers.

"Dad's watch!" Trey scrambled to his knees and crawled to his sister. "You found it." His voice a mixture of relief and joy.

Reagan prodded his arm. "Take it. It's yours."

Trey rubbed his hands on his jeans and reached into Reagan's hand. His unsteady fingers rattled the chain of the old pocket watch. "I thought I lost it for good." He pressed the clasp and the cover popped open. Light reflected off a crystal face.

I ran my finger over the glass. "Why did you bring your dad's watch out here?"

Trey snapped it shut. "I was mad." He wrapped the chain over his knuckles. "When I hold Dad's watch, kinda makes me feel close to him."

"But why'd you bring it here—to the train tracks?" I asked.

Trey's body trembled. "Dad said he used to come here as a kid." His tone skimmed the higher range of his voice, almost cracking. "Granddad gave this watch to Dad. Dad said he'd give it to me. But he didn't—" Trey's face warped like warm plastic, and he puffed quick shots of air through his wobbly lips, fighting not to cry.

My vision narrowed to where the lights captured my son's tortured face. Darkness closed in and pressed down. Neil was dead. I'd wanted my kids to forget their dad and let me start over. But I'd failed. How did I ever think I could raise my kids on my own? I reached out and put an arm around each of my children. I wanted to run home and hide. Hide until the kids were okay. Until I was okay.

Neil's shadowy form settled at our feet.

It's all your fault," I said to Neil.

Trey's chin hit his chest. "I'm sorry, Mom."

I hugged him tighter. "Oh, no, no, no, sweetheart. I was thinking out loud. It's all my fault. For not being there when you and your sister need me."

"I felt Dad," Trey whispered.

Reagan looked at me. "What's he talking about?"

"Dad pushed me off the tracks," Trey said.

Reagan slouched out of my hug. "Mom, is he crazy? Or in shock? He couldn't see Dad. Could he?"

Trey boosted his chin higher. I opened my mouth but clamped it shut. What do I say? Their dad is a ghost and saved me from a nasty fall, and he pushed Trey off the tracks? But how could I explain that? "What makes you think it was your dad?"

Trey held his hands in front of him. "The fingers. They were long and skinny and gripped hard as steel, like Dad did when I got in trouble."

"That's just wrong." Reagan wrapped her arms around her middle.

"I know Dad's dead. I'm not crazy," Trey said.

"So how could he knock you off the tracks?"

Reagan snuggled under my arm.

"It was Dad. I just know." Trey stood and tucked the watch into the front pocket of his jeans. "I don't care if you believe me or not. My dad saved me."

"Is he still here?" Her eyes searched the dark perimeter.

Trey shook his head. "Nope. He pushed me off the tracks, and then I saw fireworks."

Neil's distressed face floated to my eye level. "I didn't know if I could save him."

"I'm glad you did," I said.

Big, fat tears rolled down Reagan's cheeks. "But I didn't see him."

"Your dad is right here with us. You don't have to see him to know he's here."

Reagan sniffed and laid her head on my shoulder.

Jesse joined our tight group. He held the spotlight in one hand and finger-pressed his perfectly creased dress slacks. I was grateful for the privacy he'd given us, but it was obvious that his patience had reached its limits. "Little dude, talk about some scary shit. I didn't know if I was strong enough to hold your mom back. I guess it's true what they say about that adrenaline rush."

I picked up a broad-beamed flashlight and handed it to Trey. I clicked the flashlight function on my phone and gave it to Reagan. My hummingbird heartbeat had settled into an almost normal human rhythm, and I took a chance with my voice. "My phone has plenty of charge left. You two go on ahead. We'll be right behind you."

Jesse put his arm around me and nuzzled my ear. "Come on, tiger. I'm looking forward to letting you massage all the bruises you gave me."

I knocked his arm from my shoulder. "How dare to try to keep me from my child."

Jesse took a stutter-step back. "What are you talking about? You could have been killed."

Disgust left a grimy taste in my mouth, and I wanted to spit. I took a giant step and dug my index finger into his chest. "The whole parent thing. You just don't get it."

Jesse stared at me, his blank face held not a hint of understanding.

I leaned my face close to his. "I'd have gladly died for my son." I shoved his chest with both hands and propelled myself away. I walked toward the lights—toward my children.

"Too bad your hero wasn't here tonight." Jesse called after me.

The sarcasm in his voice flipped my switch. I stopped and made a slow circle, taking in a load of oxygen as I pranced back. His arrogant attitude oozed from the top of his perfectly groomed hair to the tip of his dusty leather loafers. "Knowing the kind of father you came from, I should cut you a break. But I won't. You've already had more than your share. I know you, Jesse King. And I know your dad, who was like all the other abusive fathers and husbands out there."

Jesse dismissed me with a smirk. "You don't know shit."

"I know about the night you buried Skipper, and I know what the Three Musketeers promised. I know you three boys signed a Valentine and shook on it."

He ducked like he'd dodge a blow.

"Your friends stood by you. And what'd you do in

return for their kindness? Scheme to ruin Eli's career and threaten Neil if he didn't go along. They were your brothers in every way but blood. They are the only ones who had your back. I asked myself how you could do something so hurtful. Jealousy? Greed? Then I realized the answer's simple. You're just like your dad. The drunken coward who beat your mother so badly she couldn't go out in public has created a son in his image. You're just plain mean. Thank God your wife had the courage to fight you and save her son."

Jesse's eyes registered pure hatred. "You done?"

"Not quite." I straightened up to all five feet and four inches and cocked my shoulders. "You're no father. Let me tell you what a real father would do. What Neil and Eli would do. They wouldn't have held me back. They'd have trampled me to save my son."

Jesse's body went rigid. I couldn't read his eyes, but the darkness in his soul oozed out, swelling around me. I stepped back. He moved toward me, and all I saw was a blur. And then Jesse flat on his back with Neil's foot pressing down on his chest.

Jesse tried to get up, and Neil pushed him back down. "What the hell?"

"It's my guardian angel." I turned to go and stopped. "I feel sorry for you."

I left Jesse behind, and as I got farther away, each step made me lighter and lighter. I could soar overhead with Neil or do cartwheels down the path. Ahead, the lights of the group bounced and swayed, and I ran to catch up. I wormed in between Reagan and Trey and wrapped my arms around each of them.

I clutched my kids to me and kissed each one. "I love you."

Reagan put her arm around my waist. "Love you too, Mom." Trey didn't pull out of my grasp, and smiled. A win-win.

Chapter 27
One Foot in Front of the Other

Jesse was gone. That bridge was ashes. Trey's train encounter put sibling rivalry on hold, and Reagan treated her brother like a living organism instead of a chewed piece of bubble gum. Their ceasefire made me melancholy. My children were growing up.

With only three more weeks left in the school year, the countdown had begun. My own children, as well as my seventh graders geared up for the downhill slide to the finish line. It was a challenge I relished. Neil and I fought for the good of our children, not each other. I began to heal.

The end of school meant the reunion loomed on the horizon. Three weeks until the end of school. Three weeks and six days until the reunion. I met the reunion committee on my front porch for our last meeting. Allison, Buddy, and Charlotte lined up in my driveway, and car doors slammed simultaneously. I blocked the sun with my hand. "You guys caravan over?"

Allison, always the line leader, jogged up the short flight of stairs and hugged me. She joined me as the welcoming committee. Charlotte held her phone to her ear and glided up to meet us. She raised her eyes skyward and held up one finger. Buddy slogged behind her.

Buddy got to the top step and paused. "Wish I had

a camera. You girls are pretty as a picture."

Charlotte tucked her phone into her pocket. "Forget the picture. I skipped lunch today, and I know Libby has something good to eat." She pecked Allison and me on the cheek and walked in.

I hooked my arm in Buddy's and ushered him inside. "I made some yummy rollup pin-wheels out of tortillas and low-fat cream cheese with bacon bits. I have all the stuff on trays for you and Charlotte to take to the boathouse."

"Your last chance to tempt me." Buddy shook his head side to side, disturbing not one hair.

"That's okay, Mr. President," Charlotte ushered Buddy toward the food, "I'll eat your share."

I loaded Buddy and Charlotte's arms with trays of snacks. "We'll be out there in five minutes." Allison stacked folders and papers on the island in the kitchen. I'd finagled to get her alone to ask about Eli. I pretended to be interested in a yellow folder. "I think this is Eli's folder. Is he coming tonight?" I struggled to make my voice sound nonchalant.

"Lover's spat?" she winked.

Her cozy comment twisted the knife. "If I knew, would I be asking?" I immediately felt bad. She was an innocent pawn in the crazy chess game in my head. "I'm sorry. I didn't mean to sound so hateful."

She leaned in close and placed her hand on my arm. "All I know is he texted me he wouldn't be here."

"He's coming to the reunion, isn't he?" It sounded like more of a plea than a question.

She rubbed my arm and smiled. "I'll find out."

"Thanks." I moved out of her contact and ran water over the spoon I'd used to make ranch dip for the raw vegetables. If I saw her sympathy, I wouldn't be able to hold back the tears that were already stinging my eyelids.

"It's serious between you guys, isn't it?"

I put the spoon into the dishwasher. "*Was.* I pretty much sabotaged my chances." I shut the dishwasher and tried to smile, but tears lingered on the periphery, waiting for me to break. "I don't want to think about it. And I don't want to talk about it."

Allison picked up the folders. "Have you found a dress yet?"

I flattened my shirt against my body and ran my hand down each button. "Not yet. You?"

"Of course. Black as always." Allison picked up her bag. "Let's get this last meeting started. It's been a lot of work, but I'll so miss seeing everyone every month when the reunion's over."

Allison updated the group and presented our final checklists for our June fifteenth reunion. Only one month away. Only one year since Neil's accident.

The door to the boathouse opened, and Jesse stuck his head inside. "Thought I'd find you guys up here."

I almost choked on the celery stick I was chewing. Jesse King was the last person I thought I'd ever see at my house again.

Jesse slipped through the doorway, glancing around the group, his eyes settling on me. "Hope you don't mind, Lib. I knocked and got no answer, so I came around back to see if you guys were up here." He looked on edge—even shy.

Buddy grasped Jesse's upper arm. "We're glad you're here. Allison may have some last minute details you can help us with."

Charlotte removed her glasses and swung them in a circle. "Promise you won't try to amuse us with any more grade school fairy tales."

"I promise I'm done with digging up the past." Jesse smiled. "Buried the shovel."

Allison offered Jesse the veggie platter. "Hungry?"

Jesse reached for a carrot, and Neil knocked the tray from Allison's hands. Carrots, broccoli, and celery hovered in mid-air and then plummeted to the floor.

Jesse squatted and began raking vegetables into a pile. "I'm so sorry."

Allison got on her knees and helped. "No, it's my fault."

Neil remained overhead, fists at his side. "The audacity of this guy."

Getting through our last meeting without incident was not to be. "You're a mind reader now?" I shouted at Neil. An involuntary groan escaped my lips, and my internal radar pinged in rapid succession detecting four pairs of eyes zeroed in on me like torpedoes pointing to their target. My stomach flipped and went bottom up. I smoothed the front of my shirt and clasped my hands over my belly button, quieting the commotion within. "Jesse's here for a reason; and since none of us are mind readers, I'd like to hear what he has to say."

"Libby doesn't need my help on Neil's memorial. But I want to do something." Jesse's eyes landed on each one of us like punctuation.

"You have something in mind?" Buddy asked.

Jesse scrubbed his palms on his jeans. "It seems Libby's work with abused children has gone unnoticed. Eli got a medal from the mayor, but Libby got zilch." He sounded sincere, but Jesse had a talent of sucking people in before stabbing them in the back.

Neil sulked and waited in the corner. "Sounds like some sort of backdoor apology to me."

"Good idea." Buddy bobbed his head at Jesse and asked Charlotte, "What about the other thing?"

"I like his suggestion. Perhaps we can incorporate it into—" Charlotte began.

"Hold it. Hold it. Hold it." I waved my hands. "Don't I have a say in this?"

"You don't want an award?" Buddy asked.

"Doing Neil's thing is all I'm up for. If you want to honor someone, honor Eli."

Allison made eye contact with Charlotte and Buddy, and then she smiled at Jesse. "Thank you for your suggestion. It was so sweet." She shrugged. "But you heard the lady. And to be honest, our program is already pretty full." Allison rapped a stack of folders on the top of the coffee table. "Well, folks, less than a month until showtime. Any hitches, give me a call."

"I'm still not convinced about Jesse's motive." Neil droned around my head. "However, should you need assistance in writing my memorial, I'm happy to help."

"One more thing." Jesse handed a check to Allison. "I know it's late, but this is for my guest."

"Bringing anyone we know?" Charlotte asked.

Jesse's hand dropped to his side. "Let's just say it'll be a surprise."

Jesse chatted with Buddy and Charlotte while I walked behind them, herding them to their cars. Allison's car was still in the driveway, and I realized she didn't come down with the rest. She usually left first—always places to go and things to do. Instead, I found her in the boathouse picking up empty bottles and paper plates.

I couldn't hide my amazement. "What are you still doing here? No guitar lessons or soccer practice or jujitsu?"

Allison packed the trash down, pulled the plastic bag out of the garbage can, and tied the red plastic strings. "Can we sit and talk a while?"

There was a time when we were like Trey and Marcus. Wherever you saw one, you saw the other. Tonight, a cozy quilt of familiarity warmed me to the core, and I remembered why she had been my friend for so long.

Allison sat on the sofa and motioned for me to join her. "I know something's wrong. I can see it in your eyes."

"It hasn't been one of my best days." I rubbed my temple. "It hasn't been one of my best years." I exhaled an artificial laugh.

Allison drew up her legs and got comfortable. "Do you remember what we used to say when things got bad?"

I leaned my head back and closed my eyes. "Of course."

"I've still got your back, Lib," Allison whispered.

"I threw Eli away. I was scared and ran. Now it's too late." There was no way for me to stem the tide this time. Like a river overflowing its banks, tears coursed down my cheeks. Words rolled and tumbled from my mouth sharing the terror of Trey's close encounter with death, my fear of my leaving the kids parentless, the loneliness of flying solo.

Allison held my hand and let words bounce off the

walls and blow away in the breeze. I grabbed a napkin from the table, dried my eyes, and then blew my nose. "Until Trey's encounter, I had no idea the kids worried about me dying, too. And then the mammogram re-do scared the hell out of me. I just knew I had breast cancer, and all I could think about was fighting it alone and leaving my kids to face life without me."

"In a single year you lost your husband, almost lost your son, and then dealt with a scary mammogram." Allison rested her head against mine. "I thought Eli made things easier."

"He was wonderful. The kids love him. But he got jealous and decided we needed to get married. I wasn't ready. He boxed me into a corner, and I came out swinging some pretty harsh words." I put my face in my hands. "I don't know if I'll ever be ready. Or if I'll even have the opportunity again."

"You need to talk to him. My guess is he's suffering as badly as you," Allison said.

I looked at black blobs of mascara that had smudged under Allison's eyes and laughed. "You have raccoon eyes."

Allison rubbed her eyes, smearing it worse. "You ought to see yours."

We sat quietly for a while, shoulder to shoulder. I walked to the window. "I don't even want to go to the reunion. It's bad enough that I have to get up in front of two hundred people and eulogize Neil, but I have to worry about seeing Eli. What if he has a date? I can't handle it."

Allison joined me. "Quit tormenting yourself. Talk to him."

"It's too late." Heaviness squeezed my heart. "I

said terrible things."

Allison took my hand. "Right now his ego's injured. If he knew you've changed your mind—" Allison snapped her fingers.

"Don't you dare tell him." I grabbed her shoulders. "Allison, promise me you won't call Eli. He has to be the one to want me."

Neil sailed by and occupied the space I'd vacated on the sofa. "I hate to change the subject from such a critical issue, but the committee's planning something behind your back."

"Behind my back?" I asked.

Allison gave me a leery look. "What's behind your back?"

I rubbed my chin. *How do I cover this?* "I was just wondering out loud why Charlotte and Buddy were looking at each other so weird tonight."

"You mean about recognizing Eli?" Allison asked.

Neil shifted to a prone position. "I distinctly heard Buddy whisper to Charlotte tonight about *the other thing*."

"What is the *other thing* Buddy mentioned to Charlotte?" I asked.

"You caught that, huh?" Allison chuckled. "Buddy never learned to use his inside voice."

I got in Allison's face. "So, what is the *other* thing?"

Allison held up her hands. "Okay, okay. But if I tell you, you have to act surprised. Okay?"

"I get it." I wanted to pull out my hair. "So just tell me."

Allison licked her napkin and swiped under her eyes. "I'm presenting you a special community service

311

award."

"Allison's not presenting the award. But she may not know it yet. That's the big surprise." Neil soared through the window.

"What's the big surprise?" I asked.

Allison opened her mouth—

"Knock, knock." Emily's lilting voice interrupted Allison before she got started. "I saw the lights on out here."

Allison ran to her. "Emily! How in the world are you doing?"

Emily smiled. "All good here. And you? Your kids?"

"Not kids anymore. My Gracie's a junior this year; and, of course you know, Mark's in sixth grade with Marcus and Trey."

I gave Emily a neighborly hug. "Something to drink?"

"Thanks. Saw your lights and wanted to stop by." She bounced her hands at her sides and looked everywhere except at me.

Allison's phone rang. "Excuse me, girls. It's Jackson." She stepped outside.

I took a soda from the bar fridge and handed it to Emily. "What's wrong?"

Emily popped the top. "Nothing that can't wait." She took a sip.

Allison charged in and grabbed her bag. "Sorry. Jackson's battery died and Gracie's waiting for him at cheerleading practice. Next year she'll be driving herself. But tonight, I have to run. Great seeing you, Emily." She pecked Emily's cheek. She hugged me and whispered, "Love you, girl."

I ran to the door and caught her before she hit the bottom step. "Do me a favor? Close the gate when you leave?"

Allison gave me a thumbs up. "Consider it done."

"Thanks," I yelled down the stairs.

Emily set her drink on the coffee table and took a deep breath. "I need to tell you something before you see the sign in my front yard."

"What kind of sign?" And then it hit me square in the gut. Comprehension rippled through my body. "No. Don't tell me." I dropped to the sofa beside her.

Emily held my hand. "The agent's putting the sign in the yard tomorrow." She wiped her eyes with her sleeve. "She says she already has someone interested."

"Why? Where? Now?" Coherent words were lost to me.

"A week ago my parents offered Reggie and me ten acres of their farm. With the equity in our house, we can build a smaller house and not have a mortgage." Her eyes begged me to understand. "I wanted to tell you, but it was all so fast."

I rolled the words over in my head. This was real. My best friend was leaving me. "I'm in shock. I thought Reggie was doing well at his new job."

"He is. But in two years, Andrea goes to college. This is a break we've been needing. We have to do this." Emily's voice grew stronger with each word.

I had no worries about the financial side of college thanks to Neil's attention to detail. "You two have a plan, and it makes perfect sense. But I so hate losing you." I bottled up my sadness and put the top on really tight. I had to be happy for my friend.

Emily hugged me. "I'll only be an hour away. And

the kids know how to get there."

She could be a light-year away. I was losing my best friend, my confidante, my rock. It was the right move for Emily and Reggie.

Emily stood. "We're both starting over."

"Starting over? Then I'm at the right place."

Our heads spun in unison to find Jesse King standing in the doorway, knuckles knocking on air. He shifted from one foot to the other and attempted a feeble smile. "The door was open."

"What the—Who's next? The Pope?" Neil's body-less voice filled the boathouse.

I felt like someone had hit me in the back with a two by four. "What are you doing here?"

"I rang the bell at the house. Kids were glad to see me till they realized I wasn't the pizza guy." He gurgled a nervous chuckle. "Sorry to interrupt. Just need to talk to you for a minute."

Neil broke in. "Don't trust that self-deprecating disguise. Remember the *Invasion of the Body Snatchers*?"

Emily touched Jesse's arm. "Nice seeing you again, but my kids are waiting for pizza, too." She turned to me. "I'll talk to you tomorrow."

Panic crawled up my throat. "Don't go."

She winked. "I'm just across the driveway." She waved goodbye, and I was left with Jesse.

"I'm still here." Neil's ghostly presence brought comfort.

I remained standing, hoping Jesse'd say what he needed to say and be gone. "Allison must have forgotten to close the gate."

"The gate was closed. I parked outside the gate and

walked." Jesse swiped his forehead and rubbed his hand on his jeans. His shoulders drooped and he was reluctant to make eye contact. He looked like one of my seventh graders who'd gotten caught cheating.

Neil launched his body like a projectile at Jesse and formed a transparent barrier. "Hope he didn't scuff his pretty shoes." Neil's lips stretched over his teeth into a snarl.

Neil. An attack ghost. The image was so ludicrous, I almost laughed out loud. I walked to the fridge and dipped my head inside to hide my grin. "How about a water?"

He twisted off the top and guzzled half the bottle. "Thanks."

"Guess walking made you thirsty?" I said.

Neil moved to the other side of Jesse. "Don't be so nice."

"I want to hear." I looked at Neil and gulped. "Uh…hear what you walked all this way to tell me."

Jesse finished his water and sat on the sofa. He crushed the plastic bottle in one hand. "You were right. About everything."

Neil settled on his perch in the corner. "This ought to be good."

Jesse's head fell forward, and he studied his hands. "I don't want to be like him."

His voice was so faint I wasn't sure I heard correctly. "I don't think I heard—"

"When my dad died, I felt…" Jesse's voice choked out. "I felt relief. I don't want my son to feel relief when I die." He dropped his face into his hands.

I looked to Neil for help, but he had nothing. Instinct superseded rational thought, and I went to Jesse and put my arms around him.

He looked up at me, and real tears filled his red-rimmed eyes and flowed out the corners and down. "I promised my mom I wouldn't be like him. I promised." He stared at his fists clenched in his lap; and his voice, thick with emotion, contained power and conviction and something else rare in Jesse King—humility.

"Jesse, I don't know what to say."

"I've let everybody down. Especially my kid." Jesse jerked his head up and wiped his eyes with his palms. "But I never hit Rebecca. Never once crossed my mind. Tell me that's something." His eyes begged for my affirmation.

My heart went out to the Jesse, who, like most abused kids, suffered at the hands of the ones supposed to love him most. And his dad probably did love him and Jesse's mom, in his own sick, bizarre way. "I wish I had a time machine."

"An interesting thought." He walked to the window and stared into the dark.

I tapped my hands against my knees. "Okay, you've identified the problem. What are you going to do about it?"

"I'm luckier than I deserve to be." Jesse's voice came from a genuine place deep inside.

"We all know that." Neil said. "But how do you fix stupid?"

I gave Neil a charitable look. "Let's be kind."

Jesse turned to me. "I want to be kind. The kind of man who jumps in front of a train to save his son."

Gone was Jesse's bloated arrogance and air of intimidation. Happiness bathed me with joy and love. I kissed his cheek. "I think I could get to like the new

Jesse."

Neil's form wilted. "As far as I'm concerned, the verdict's still out."

The dim, muted lighting couldn't hide the little-boy glow on Jesse's face. "I'm just getting started. Already called Ryan's coach and volunteered to help coach his soccer team, and I'm bringing Rebecca to the reunion."

Hope curled around my heart, and I breathed out a warm sigh. "It's been a night of surprises."

The lines in Jesse's face shifted into happy, and he glowed with promise. "Had our first counseling session today. I know I don't deserve it, but she's giving me another chance."

"I'm so happy." My eyes burned, and I fanned away the tears.

Jesse took both my hands. "The counselor suggested I thank you."

"Me?"

"She said you cared enough to stand up to me." Jesse kissed my hands. "Thank you."

Neil rested his shadow on the coffee table. "Okay, he's convinced me he wants to be a better man, so ask him if he still plans to assassinate Eli's character."

I hated to tarnish Jesse's moment, but I needed to know. "Jesse, what about your plan to disgrace Neil and Eli?"

Jesse freed my hands. "I can't believe Neil told you."

"Yeah, well, I was surprised too." I swept crumbs from the table into my palm.

Jesse got the trash can by the bar and held it for me to dump the crumbs. "I'm embarrassed that I ever said anything."

Neil crossed his arms. "He didn't answer the question."

"That was our last conversation," Jesse said.

Rapid footsteps pounded up the stairs, and the boathouse swayed. The door blasted open so hard the doorknob hit the wall and bounced back into Trey's face. Panting and then shrieks filled the room. Trey ran inside and Reagan followed close behind. Trey hid behind me and peeked over my shoulder. Reagan dodged Jesse and charged Trey. I stiff-armed her. They'd broken their truce.

Reagan's eyes narrowed to dark slits, and if her laser-focus could fry her brother, he'd be crispy. "You better hide behind Mom, you, you, ahhhhh!" She reached around me and tried to swat Trey.

"Hold it!" I used my body as a shield between them. "Tell me what he did this time."

She attempted another punch. "I caught the little brat in my room reading my emails!"

"Ask him if he found information we need to know." Neil had left his coffee table position and joined Trey behind me.

Jesse coughed. "You have a crisis to handle. I'll let myself out."

I tried for a smile but made do with an almost grin and choreographed a wave while blocking blows. "Your time's coming. Ryan will be a teenager before you know it."

"Looking forward to it." Jesse winked and jogged away. His whistling faded into the night.

Reagan kicked at her brother and missed. I doubled over and caressed my shin bone, grateful it was summer and she wasn't wearing boots.

I cracked my hands together. "Enough!"

Reagan backed off. She crossed her arms and locked her mouth shut. A white line outlined her lips.

I twisted my head around to look at Trey. "Why would you read your sister's emails?"

A sickly pink colored his cheeks. "'Cause I don't get any."

"Because you're an idiot." Reagan groaned and rolled her eyes until her eyelids hit the back of her head. "Please tell me I'm adopted."

"No one's stupid and no one's—" The recognizable rumble of an engine and faulty muffler disturbed my thoughts.

Trey ran for the door. "It's that car again."

"Come on, Mom," Reagan said, "Call him."

Chapter 28
For Auld Lang Syne

Reagan held out her phone. "Please call Eli. We need him."

"Yeah, Mom. He said call if we saw the car again." Trey inclined his head at Reagan's phone.

I was tempted. Just to hear his voice. How long had it been? Three weeks? A month? I waited until I heard the car pass us by. "See, he's already through the gate. No harm. No foul." I tried to put on a relieved face, but refusing her phone had taken all my energy. My muscles wouldn't make a smile.

Reagan's lips shriveled into a mocking smile-sneer, and her eyes communicated with her brother in a way only kids in collusion can. My mom rating fell into the negative category.

That stupid car. Why did it have to show up again? I hadn't heard its rotten muffler in weeks, long enough to lull me into forgetting about it. Not anymore. Its grumbling delivered an ominous reminder I had no Eli. Only me.

****

June is the most treasured month on a teacher's calendar. I'd hoped this one would be better than the last. This June marked the one-year anniversary of Neil's death. Which also marked the one-year anniversary of my catching him cheating. In some ways it seemed longer than a year. Much longer.

June also brought the class reunion. For the most part, planning it had been a healing distraction. Until the distraction and I parted ways. Allison allowed me no wimpy whining time for Eli. She structured our days around her to-do list and my free time. On the second week of summer vacation, Neil's folks took the kids to Disney World; and on the first day of my seven-day-reprieve, I helped Allison stuff one hundred ninety-seven gift bags. The reunion countdown had begun. Three. Two. One day until the culmination of all our planning.

Allison had negotiated room discounts from the hotel where the reunion was staged, and we committee members got an early check-in. Before we had time to check out the mini-bar, Allison began knocking on doors and barking out orders. She kept me busy. So busy I didn't have time to fret over whether Eli would show. Or how I'd face him if he did. Neil was otherwise engaged, skulking on the sidelines.

Across the hall from our meeting room, the ballroom sat ready for music and dancing. We'd decorated the walls in the main hall with old yearbook photos blown up to life size. Classmates congregated, laughing and pointing at candid shots of the band, the sports teams, and the clubs. Even the senior prom. Our senior yearbook photo adorned our name tags.

Clipboard snugged in the crook of her left elbow, Allison climbed on a chair and cupped her mouth with her right hand. "Okay, people. Program starts in fifteen minutes." She held her right hand aloft and twirled her finger overhead. The masses shuffled toward the door. Pure Allison.

I pushed through the masses to check Allison's clipboard for placement of chairs at the podium. Buddy and Charlotte blocked my path. It wasn't the presence of bodies, but Charlotte's silk, jade green suit that stopped me cold. The fabric hung and clung to all the right places and her eyes looked dyed to match. Adding heels to the ensemble made her tower over Buddy, who was duded-up in his dark suit and plain white shirt. He flashed his signature smile, and every hair lay in place.

Neil butted in between us. "That's a mismatched pair—Buddy in his Sunday best, and Ms. Crocker-Crane straight from *Vogue*."

I waggled jazz hands in Neil's face. "It's showtime. Move it!"

"You running on caffeine?" Charlotte ran her hand over her lapel. "You've been a busy girl. But we have one more job for you."

Buddy smiled and gave a thumbs up to someone checking in, and then gave me his earnest attention. "Libby, it's a small job. Charlotte has to help me, and I need you to run get the trophies."

I turned to see the recipient of Buddy's interest, and a woman I'm sure I was supposed to recognize waved at me. I waved back. "Where are they?"

Neil poked me with an air finger and did a wolf whistle. "It's Jane Fullenwider. They can't kid her about her name anymore."

"You saw Jane?" I scanned the crowd for her, but the guests had already formed a line. All I saw were backsides.

Buddy tapped my shoulder. "Jane looks good, huh? Never know she and Lorraine started Weight Watchers together, would you? Now if you'd run get those trophies for us, I'd sure appreciate it. The box is in the storeroom next to the elevator."

I strode down the main hallway and opened the door. I ran my hand over the wall and couldn't find the light switch, so I engaged my phone's flashlight function. Metal shelving stacked with boxes lined the walls farther than my light penetrated. The elevator dinged and the storeroom door closed with a swoosh. I shuffled my feet over the carpet. Was this a scavenger hunt? If anyone but Charlotte had sent me, I would think I was being pranked. My big toe rammed the corner of a box. "Crap!" I aimed my light at my feet. It was a wonder I hadn't tripped over the darn box sitting in the middle of the floor. I laid my phone on top of the cardboard box and found the hand holes on the side. I turned carefully, keeping my phone balanced on top. A man stood at the door. He startled me, and I jumped. "Oh!" My phone—and my source of light—hit the floor. "Who are you?" I plunked the box down hard, and the trophies clanked. I collected my phone from the floor. "This is the Grayson Valley High School Reunion. You must be in the wrong place." I picked up my box and replaced the phone on top.

He leaned against the door and crossed his arms. "Oh, I'm in the right place." He reached behind him, and the lights came on.

I squinted and looked down and blinked a few times. "Thanks. I couldn't find the switch when I came in." He took two steps and got within a few feet. My initial shock evaporated. He was a kid. College age probably. "We reserved the ballroom for our class reunion, and I don't think you graduated from high school twenty years ago." I chuckled at my statement of the obvious. His dark hair hid most of his forehead. He flipped his head sideways and revealed deep-set brown eyes. I walked another step closer. He didn't look mysterious or threatening. He looked sad.

"How do you sleep at night?"

My hands tightened on the box. "I beg your pardon?"

"Where do you get off messing with people's lives?" His strained voice held no menace, only an aching resignation.

His misery got to me, but I had a part on the program and needed to hurry. "I'm sorry, but you've mistaken me for someone else. And I really have to get back. Excuse me." I sidestepped him and aimed for the door. Reinforcements waited across the hall.

He moved in front of me and placed his hands on the box. He tossed his hair to the side again. "You meddle with families and don't care whose life you destroy. But it doesn't touch you in your fancy lake house with all your friends and pretty flowers."

My fingernails dug into the cardboard. "How do you know where I live?"

"Bet those flowers at your mailbox don't look so pretty anymore, do they?" He lifted his chin.

A sliver of fear lodged in my ribcage. Four hands gripped the box, and it was all that separated us. "Why are you stalking me?" The words chilled my lips.

He tried for a half grin. "You don't recognize me, do you? Everybody says we look alike."

I couldn't show fear. I calmed my breathing. Eli'd gotten his tag number, and Jesse admitted he worked for him. I straightened my back and assumed my teacher persona. "Does Jesse King know you spend your time on the job tailing me?"

He brushed his hair to the side. "Don't blame Jesse. I saw you on TV."

I eyed my phone on top of the box, wondering if I should try to dial 911. "Okay, you found out where I work on The Morning Show. But how do you know where I live? And how did you know to come here?"

He let out a fake laugh and ran his hand through his bangs. "Jesse talks and I listen. And what I didn't get from him, a few keystrokes on Google and I was golden. Took a little legwork to find your parking spot at school."

I stomped my foot. "You're the one who keyed my car!"

He ducked like I'd charged him, and he looked at me through a curtain of hair. "It was right after I saw you on TV." He tossed his hair out of his eye. "I was mad." He words tumbled out.

"Explain how my TV debut turned you into a stalker."

He let go of the box and held his arms rigid at his sides. His shoulders lifted up and down as he breathed. He raised his head slowly and trained his eyes on me. "Tom Thornton." He spit Tom's name at me like the words tasted bitter.

During the interview I never mentioned Tom Thornton. Only his son Tommy. I searched the young man's face.

"Do you know what happens to families after you get involved?" He batted his arms against his sides.

"Of course I do." But I doubted he'd believed me if I told him of the numerous hours I spent following up with families. Hours taken away from my own family.

He flung his hair back. "It wasn't enough to just ruin Tom's *family*. No, you kept on punching and digging till you destroyed everything. Till you destroyed him." His voice grew louder and angrier with each syllable. "They're giving you an award for killing my brother." His eyes were wild and wide and lost. The resemblance slapped me in the face.

"Oh. Dear. God." I set down the box. "You're Tom's brother."

His body sagged. Dark hair fell over his eyes, but he made no effort to sweep it away. "Technically his half-brother." He looked at me. "But he never felt like anything but my whole brother." His eyes glistened behind a veil of bangs. "Because of you, they arrested him. And because of you, his wife and kid left him. And because of you, he's dead."

Pain shone in his eyes, and I reached out. "What do you want from me?"

He lurched away. "The newspaper printed your lies. And your lies killed him." His chest heaved with every breath. "What do I want? I want you to tell the truth."

"The truth." I sat on the box. "I wanted to keep your nephew and his mom safe."

His eyes met mine. "Did you have to call the police? Why didn't you talk to Tom?" His voice caught on *police,* and his gaze slithered downhill and then dissolved into the carpet pattern.

I rubbed my hands over my meticulously applied makeup. "First of all, the details in the paper didn't come from me, they came from the police. You didn't live with Tommy. You didn't see the bruises. Or live with the terror of waiting for his father to attack again.

When you were born, Tom was in college. You saw the Tom *he* wanted you to see. Ask your mom."

His head jerked up, spreading long, dark bangs over his eyes and forehead. "You know my mom?"

"I've met your mom several times. I'd forgotten her last name or would've put it together when I found out Ben Purvis owned the car driving around my lake."

He bent forward and lowered his voice. "You were going to send him to prison."

"The truth was going to send him to prison."

The young man crumbled and sat at my feet. "There must have been another way." He didn't hide the tears on his cheeks. "My brother blew his brains out because he couldn't deal with what you'd done."

"Maybe he couldn't deal with what he'd done."

"He was sick. Why didn't you try to save him?"

"Because I had to save your nephew." I took pictures of the bruises I found on Tommy that awful day, and I saved them on my phone. Not to share. But as a reminder. No child should ever have to suffer like Tommy did, and when I need a little kick to keep going, I look at it. "Maybe it's time to share something with you that wasn't in the news."

Chapter 29
Showtime

We walked into the auditorium and applause erupted. I set my box on the floor and squeezed Ben's arm, and he took his seat next to Mrs. Thornton. Her eyes opened wide and her back pressed back in her chair. I smiled and nodded to let her know all was well.

Allison motioned for me to come up to the stage, and when Buddy and Charlotte stepped to the side, I saw my surprise. Standing on stage dressed in a stylish gray suit was Tommy Thornton. At fifteen, he stood head to head with Buddy. A football-sized lump lodged in my throat. Tommy swung his bangs to the side and flashed me a grin to let me know he was in cahoots with the others. My eyes burned like fire. I ran up the stairs and hugged him.

"My mom and Uncle Ben are here." Tommy spoke softly so only I could hear.

I held his shoulders at an arm's length to look at him. "I talked to your Uncle Ben."

Tommy's eyes searched my face. "He didn't say anything stupid, did he?"

"Nothing can ruin this night." I hugged him.

Neil stood behind Tommy. Shoulders squared, hands crossed in front like a security guard. He gave me a thumbs up.

Allison spoke into the microphone. "We have a

special guest to present a special award to a special person. This is Tommy Thornton. The young man who was the motivation for the creation of the Home Safe Foundation. She turned and spoke to Tommy. "Thank you for coming, Tommy. And for bringing your family." Allison yielded the podium to a grinning young man. The audience welcomed Tommy loudly.

He cleared his throat a couple of times and looked down. The certificate shook in his hands. I joined him at the podium and put my hand on his back. He stood up straight and spoke into the microphone. "Guess you can tell I'm kinda nervous." His words slid out hitting the highest pitch with a chuckle.

I patted Tommy's back and strained to see my classmates. Speaking in front of a group took guts, and I willed courage for my Tommy.

"Mrs. Miller was my seventh grade teacher," Tommy read from his note card. "My mom and I wouldn't be here if she hadn't noticed my bruises and taken action."

The hall went silent. Mrs. Thornton sat stoically. Ben's shoulders collapsed, and he looked at his lap. Without taking her eyes from Tommy, she laid her hand over Ben's.

"My dad wasn't a bad man. He was sick. But that didn't make the beatings not hurt." Tommy looked up from his prepared speech. "He was mean when he was drunk. Wasn't he, Mom? I was scared to go to sleep at night worrying he'd come home drunk and beat up my mom or me. Mom and I tried running away, but he always found us. One time when he passed out, I tried to hit him with a baseball bat. I raised the bat up and held it over his head, but I couldn't hit him." Tommy fidgeted with his cards until he found his place. "I never missed school because I was safe there. But in seventh grade my life changed, thanks to Mrs. Miller. She stood up to my dad, and she wasn't scared one bit. She came to our house and helped us move. I was the first, but there were lots of other kids she helped after me."

Tommy looked into the faces of my friends. "I don't know if you know about this, but my dad committed suicide a few months ago." Tommy took in a breath, and the hitch echoed over the attentive crowd. Tears welled up in his eyes. The note card crumpled in his hand, but he squared his shoulders and continued. "It was real sad." His voice broke, and he swiped at his eyes roughly. He bent close to the microphone. "But I don't worry about my dad hurting my mom or me anymore."

He held the certificate high. "I'm here to give this to Mrs. Miller. It says it's for outstanding community service. I think it should say for being brave enough to face the bullies." He handed the certificate to me. Applause erupted and Tommy held up his hands and spoke into the microphone. "Hold on. Hold on. One more thing." The clapping diminished and then stopped. "And for being the world's greatest teacher, I have something for you. From me."

Tommy's mom walked up and handed him a fabric bag. The audience was so silent I heard my stomach growl. Tommy pulled out a sculpture of a hand. He lifted it high so all could see the bronzed colored hand, palm up and fingers reaching. "I made this in art class. When I showed it to my mom she asked me why I made a hand. Simple. Mrs. M. took my hand and made me feel safe enough to go home."

The audience pounded their hands together and then stood as one. But I didn't see them stand. My heart got so full, it spilled over into my eyes.

I didn't know if my voice would work, but I tried anyway. "I'm overwhelmed." I talked over their applause. "There are no words to tell you how much I love this kid." I pointed to Mrs. Thornton. "And his brave mother." Applause broke out again. "They and all the women and children who suffer silently deserve this." I clutched the hand to my heart. "Thank you, Tommy."

Tommy leaned over my shoulder. "Mrs. Andrews just handed me this check to give you."

I blinked, trying to clear the haze so I could read. The payee was the Home Safe Foundation. When I saw the amount of fifty thousand dollars, I rubbed my eyes to read that it was from the graduates of Grayson Valley High School.

My heart fluttered and flapped inside my chest. I blew out three short bursts of air. "Did you know that you guys raised fifty thousand dollars for the Foundation?" Applause answered. "Thank you, so very much. It will go to good use. Buddy? Come save me before I cry all over everything."

I retrieved my yellow legal pad from my seat and sat down before my knees gave way.

Tommy trotted down the stairs and sat by his mom. Buddy thanked our guests, and he thanked the crowd. Tommy took his mom's hand, Mrs. Thornton linked her hand through Ben's elbow, and they walked toward the exit. Tommy stopped at the door and waved.

Charlotte and Buddy stood at the podium. I still had to do Neil's memorial. My feelings were wrung dry. I stared at my legal pad, and I tuned out Buddy and Charlotte's voices as they presented entertaining awards for un-accomplishments like living farthest away or having the most hair. The black ink formed symbols on the yellow paper in my hands but made no sense. Neil deserved this memorial. But I couldn't read the words.

Thundering applause brought me to the present. Buddy was beating his hands together and looking at me.

Neil pushed me. "Buddy's waiting for you." And then he swooped down and sat in the first row, crossed his legs, and tapped his foot. Waiting for all the good things I should say.

I walked to the microphone and spread out my speech. "Like many of you, Neil and I got married right out of high school. And like you, we spent our years building a life. Neil was proud of his success as a businessman and community servant. But if he could tell you himself, he'd share my opinion that our children are our greatest accomplishment." I looked up to make eye contact.

A solitary figure leaned against the back wall under the green exit sign. Massive arms folded over a massive chest. Eli. My pulse rate doubled. Our eyes locked. I wanted to fling my yellow-lined papers into the air and run to him. He looked away. Connection lost. Sadness pierced my heart like a poison dart. I pressed my prepared speech to my chest and watched him walk away again. But this time he turned, and a whisper of a smile touched his lips. My breath caught in my throat. And then he was gone. I couldn't think about Eli. I had a job to do.

I wadded up the yellow pages and leaned toward

the microphone. "Do you guys believe in ghosts?" Neil sat straight up, and horror flickered across his face. "I didn't used to. But since Neil died a year ago, I see him everywhere. And I talk to him all the time.

"Getting up here in front of all of you is a little nerve-wracking. I tried imagining you guys in your underwear, but it didn't paint a pretty picture." I waited for laughter to mute. "I want you to know something. Neil is still with us."

Neil grasped the arms of the chair. "Please, Libby. Don't."

"Look at the front row. Neil is sitting there with Arnold Meeker." I waved at Arnold. "You and Neil were on the football team, weren't you?"

"We rode the pine four straight years." Arnold held up four fingers.

Jesse yelled from the middle of the crowd. "Hey, Arnie, I'll bet that bench still has yours and Neil's cheek marks." Jesse's ex-wife swatted his arm, and the crowd bellowed. Jesse pulled Rebecca in tight and kissed her forehead.

Neil rushed the stage. "Stop this nonsense. Now."

I held out my hands. "Neil's with me right now."

Neil whizzed over the heads of the committee.

I turned to Buddy sitting on the stage behind me. "How about you, Buddy? Can you feel Neil beside you?"

Buddy smoothed his bangs and gave me a nervous look. "Metaphorically speaking, I guess so."

Neil's eyes bugged out and his cheeks swelled like a puffer fish. "Stop this. Think of the kids."

I turned my back to Neil and looked at my classmates. "In the metaphorical words of our president, Neil is with us. And for many of you, probably around April 15th, you wished he'd been with you more than metaphorically." The crowd chuckled. "We all miss him. Especially my kids. I need all of you to help me keep Neil's memories alive." I pointed to Jesse. "Can I count on the Musketeers?"

Jesse nodded. Emotion welled up in his eyes.

"Another way I plan to keep Neil's memory alive is through the beautiful office building he loved so much. It will become The Miller House. A safe haven for abused women and children." The audience clapped and clapped. And so did Neil, his face vibrant. Happy.

"We all share a past. And even though it doesn't define who we are, it will always be a part of who we've become. Whether a bench warmer or valedictorian, we influenced each other. We are a part of each other. Even Neil. He left us way too soon. And we miss him." Neil lowered his head and drifted upward. I followed him with my eyes. "Neil, the world was a better place for having you here. Wish everyone could see you like I do." I threw him a kiss.

The group clapped as one, and the applause lasted until well after Buddy replaced me at the podium. I dropped into my chair beside Allison. Limp as a dish cloth.

"Well done, my friend." She put her hand over mine. "You know I've got your back, right?"

I turned to the sound of her voice. "Of course. Why would you ask?"

Allison's eyes were intense and she bent to my ear. "I want you to do something and not ask any questions. Trust me?"

Neil swooped in behind Allison. "Do you trust

me?"

I gave her a confident nod but spoke to Neil. "Yes, I do."

"Get up right now and go to the ballroom." Her voice was abrupt and final.

I opened my mouth to ask why, but the tender look Neil gave me withered the words on my lips. I glanced at the podium where Buddy held it in both hands, talking to his constituents. Charlotte winked. Allison nudged me. I took a deep breath and slithered down the stairs in the middle of laughter as Buddy presented himself with a trophy for best hair.

I slipped into the corridor. Silence. The double doors looming across the carpet reminded me of the story "The Lady or the Tiger." But I promised Allison.

"Go, go, go." Neil shooed me toward the door.

"You know what this is about?"

Neil placed his spectral hands on his missing hips. "No questions. You promised Allison."

"Great. I need another surprise." I stomped across the hall, my annoyance soaking into the deep pile. Grabbing the knob in both hands, I twisted and shoved both doors open.

Disco balls sparkled overhead, and Van Morrison sang "Someone Like You" through multiple speakers. I threw my hands up. "What now?"

"I think this is our song."

I whirled around. A dark shape hid in the shadows, but the voice I knew like my own. "Eli."

"I was afraid you wouldn't come." He walked toward me. The disco ball spun, showering his face with diamonds. Closer. Closer. Closer.

Butterflies tip-toed around my heart. "Allison's

hard to refuse."

He reached for me, and then let his hand fall to his side. "Libby—"

I put my fingers to his lips. "You were right. About everything."

He took my hand and kissed each finger. "No. I pushed you too hard, too soon." He pressed my hand to his chest.

His warm hand covered mine, soothing my ache and binding my heart.

He pulled me close. "I get why you need to be independent, and I get why you're pissed off at the past." He stroked my hair. "The last year's been tough, and I know you've hurt like hell. But if changing the past took away this moment right now, I wouldn't change a thing, even if I could." He wound his hand into my hair and pulled us within a breath apart. "I love you, Libby Carlisle."

I inhaled his words and kissed him. "And I love you, Elijah Anderson."

He kissed the top of my head. "You don't have to marry me. But I'm not leaving."

I wrapped my arms around his neck. "Does that mean you're going to quit asking?"

He pulled back to look at me. "No way. I figure I'll eventually wear you down."

Neil's head appeared on Eli's shoulder. "Just say yes and quit dragging this out."

"He's here, isn't he?" He scrubbed his head.

I laughed. "This time he's working for your side."

Eli looked around the room. "Thanks, dude. I'll take all the help I can get."

Neil saluted and vanished.

"Neil's gone." I leaned in. "My kids are in Disney World. Want to sneak out and go to my house?"

Eli jumped back. "And let Allison blame me for ruining her reunion? Not a chance."

I crossed my arms and gave him a look. "A big man like you afraid of little ol' Allison?"

"Damn straight." Eli was serious.

I tucked his tie inside his coat. "We should get back to the program before they come looking for us."

He waggled his eyebrows. "I have to play one more song. Wait right here. Our buddy Mike set this up for me."

"Good ol' Mike. Let me guess. The Commodores and their golden oldie…"

He took off his jacket and tossed it aside and spun around on one foot, amazingly agile for a grizzly bear. Eli hummed along to "Brick House," rocking and gyrating.

Eli's long arms snagged my hand, and in a single motion twirled me into his body and then walled me into a snug cocoon. "Marry me?" His words warmed my skin, and a shimmering kaleidoscope of light danced on me and my partner.

Partner. I liked the sound of that.

Chapter 30
Nervous Nellie

Eli opened the back door and a blast of summer heat and bright sunlight came in with him. "Man, it smells good in here."

I rinsed my hands and reached for a towel. "You know I cook and clean when I get nervous." I offered my cheek for a perfunctory kiss. But he was having none of that.

He picked me up in a bear hug, pinning my arms between us, and planted wet kisses all over my face. "Why're you being such a nervous Nellie? The kids love me."

I wriggled and he loosened his grip, letting me slide down the front of his body. I pressed my hands to his chest and locked my elbows. "It's not just the kids. There are other issues."

He took my hands in his. "Crazy dude no longer stalking. Mammogram A-OK." Eli looked toward the ceiling. "That problem, we have no control over."

"You're right." I melted into his embrace and breathed in his confidence.

He reached behind me and lifted the lid on a large stock pot simmering on the stove. "What's in here?"

"Vegetable soup."

He opened the oven and smiled. "Fresh bread, too? Mmmm. I like it when you're nervous."

I stirred the soup. "I know I shouldn't be afraid to tell the kids. But it feels like I'm asking my dad permission to go to the prom." I shook my spoon at him. "With someone he warned me about."

"You should be nervous." Neil's voice grazed past my ear and I jumped.

The wooden spoon leapt from my grasp like it had sprouted wings, clanking on the vent fan and back down on the ceramic cooktop. The air shimmered and a light blue shirt and khakis came into focus and balanced on the range hood.

Eli grabbed the dishcloth and cleaned the mess sizzling on the cooktop. "Don't know why you're so jumpy. We're way past prom night." Eli raised an eyebrow. "Uh-oh. My head's tingling."

Trey and Lee sprinted into the kitchen. Trey peeled off to the refrigerator. "What's tingling?" Trey yanked open the door and stuck his head inside. "There's nothing to eat in here. We're starving."

Reagan breezed past us and opened the pantry door. "You're always starving."

"What's up, dudes and dudette?" Eli swatted at Reagan with the dish towel, and she laughed and dodged out of his range.

"Close the refrigerator and get out of the pantry." I said. "I have vegetable soup on the stove and bread in the oven."

Trey raised the lid and sniffed. "I hate vegetable soup."

"Bread smells great, but vegetable soup in summer doesn't do it for me," Reagan said.

Lee looked at his dad and then at me. "I like vegetable soup."

Neil eased into the crowd at the stove. "Your vegetable soup was never my favorite either. Too many vegetables. Now your chili. When you made it extra spicy." Neil sighed. "Wish I could get a good case of heartburn again."

My nerves were already strung tight as my last year's jeans. "Wish I could give you a good case of heartburn!" I threw the dishcloth into the sink and stormed out. Attempted to storm out. Eli linked my elbow in his and spun me around in an impromptu do-si-do.

"How about I take us all out to dinner?" Eli nuzzled my cheek. "That is if your mom's okay with saving the soup for me."

Five faces aimed at me. I waved my hands in surrender. "I don't care. But the bread still has about eight minutes to cook. Think you can last that long?"

"Don't let Trey and Lee pick the restaurant. They always choose Japanese." Reagan leaned against the island, and Neil maneuvered until his faint blue sleeves corralled her in a hug. She tilted her head sideways and rested her head against her dad's. I gasped, and tears sprang to my eyes. The pose was one I'd seen them in so many times. It was like she knew he was there. "You okay, Mom?"

Cheek to cheek. She had her father's chocolaty brown eyes. His long straight nose. His full lips that were quick to pout. I put my hand under her chin and stroked her cheek with my thumb. "I'm fine, sweetie. You remind me so much of your dad."

Neil closed his eyes and deep furrows puckered his ethereal brow. Sadness rolled down his face. Sympathy filled the chambers of my heart.

Reagan's skin was warm and alive under my hand. She blinked hard and gulped. "Does it make you sad that I look like Dad?"

Trey poked Reagan. "You look like Dad, and I look like Mom. Nothing sad about that." He popped an entire cookie into his mouth.

Neil pulled him into their circle. The three of them—like a framed family portrait. Warm and tender. My throat tightened. Guilt plunged me into a pit of what could-have-beens. *No!* I can't change things. This is my chance to start over. I promised Eli we'd tell the kids, and I won't let Neil ruin my chance at happiness.

Eli clapped his hands once. "Okay, guys, move in close. Your mom and I have something to tell you." A smile started at his lips and wrapped around his face. His eyebrows danced on his forehead, and his body pulsed with excitement.

Neil lurched to face me. He knew. My body tensed. And then he smiled. "Good choice."

I wanted to cry. Laugh. High five the Universe. "Eli's going to be your stepdad."

"Y'all getting married?" Trey asked.

Reagan did a half-hearted eye roll. "How else could he be our stepdad?"

Eli slipped one arm around my shoulder and pulled Lee in with the other. "You guys cool with Lee and me joining your team?"

Reagan bolted to Eli and hugged him. "I'm cool with a stepdad."

Trey didn't move.

Eli embraced Reagan in the huddle and looked at Trey. "How about you, big guy? Need a little more time?"

Trey studied the toes of his shoes. "I'm glad you'll be my new dad." He looked up and studied Eli's arm around my shoulder. "You think Dad would be sad if we loved you, too?"

Eli paused and his arm tightened around me. "I loved your father. We didn't have the same mom and dad, but he was my brother." Eli's shoulders rolled forward and his body tensed. A mountain of a man held back an avalanche of emotion. His macho façade stayed intact—except for the moisture shining in his eyes and the thick tone of his voice. "And I couldn't love you guys more if you were my own flesh and blood."

I rested my head on Eli's shoulder. He was more than a source of strength. Eli had grown into an honorable man with a reservoir of love. We shared a past—a direct link to Neil that he'd share with our children. Best of all, he knew how to love and showed it.

With Reagan anchored next to Lee, Eli thrust out his fist. Trey bumped fists and crowded between Eli and me, lassoing us into a tight circle. Our new team. Huddled for the game ahead. Eli ruffled Trey's hair. "You realize it'll be us three guys against only two girls."

Neil sat on the counter with his chin resting on his chest and long, lanky legs hanging over the side, crossed at the ankles. His muffled voice surprised me. I expected him to be sad or worse. But he looked content.

"You loved him like a brother, too." I cringed and looked around to see if anyone noticed I'd spoken.

Eli winked at me and tightened our circle. "No one can love you as much as your dad. But I can love you like a dad."

Reagan's body trembled. Tears glistened in her eyes and made shining trails on her cheeks. Her mouth curved down, reminding me of the vulnerable little girl I'd held close and kissed her boo-boos. My throat ached and my saliva dried up. I couldn't fix this. My child had to grieve.

Reagan sniffed. "Sometimes I can't remember what his face looks like." She grabbed a handful of Trey's shirt. "Aren't you afraid you'll forget him?"

Tears pooled in Trey's eyes but didn't fall. He touched his sister's hand. "Eli knows all kinds of stuff about Dad. He won't let us forget him. Will you, Eli?"

Eli shook his head. "Your dad will always be your dad. I'm not trying to take his place. No one can do that. And I do know lots of good stories."

The corner of Trey's mouth ticked up, reminding me so much of his dad's crooked grin.

Trey nudged Reagan. "Eli's not trying to take Dad's place. He's kind of like a pinch hitter."

The young man beside me showed wisdom beyond his years. His blind faith in the future and his open heart crowded out any stubborn traces of animosity hiding in my heart. A child's innocence had bridged the divide. Trey's simple words promised a place to store his father's memories but gave all of us permission to move on.

The air crackled with loss, acceptance, and love. Neil absorbed the emotions like a lightning rod. "Are you okay?" I asked.

"I am. Really," Neil said. "In fact, I've been meaning to tell you I plan on staying a while."

I let go of Eli and Trey. "What about the door? Aren't you looking for the door and the light?" Oh, no.

I rubbed my hands over my face.

"What door, Mom?" Reagan asked.

"I don't see a door," Lee said.

Eli scratched his head and covered for me. "We're thinking of replacing the front door. One with clear glass to let in more light."

An impish grin played on Neil's thin lips. "Nice recovery." Neil stuffed his hands into his pockets. "There's something I've been meaning to tell you about the door. Now don't get mad and spoil this perfect moment." Neil raised his hands. "But it seems that the door is always open."

"You mean that you've always seen the door and the light?" I clenched my teeth.

Eli gripped my shoulder. "Yes, a new door will give lots of light." Eli's voice strained an octave higher.

Neil fluttered over Reagan. "The good thing is that I can leave anytime. I needed to hang around until I knew everything was good."

He could have left and didn't tell me. I was past caring who heard. "We're okay. We're fine. We're great. Find the door."

Eli scrubbed both hands over the top of his head. "Yeah, we're gonna go find that door. Real soon, right, babe?" Eli tilted his head upward and twitched his eyebrows up and down.

Neil spread his arms outward. "Might hang around until say, Reagan gets her driver's license or Trey goes to college."

I rapped the side of my head. "How can this be?"

"Did what I do best. I found a loophole." Neil placed his hands behind his head and reclined in mid-air.

I shut my eyes. "A loophole? What kind of loophole?"

"Simple, actually. I stay out of the light, I stay here with you. But one toe touch, and pfft. I'm history." Neil stretched.

I snapped my fingers. "Just like that?"

Reagan pressed my arm. "Who are you talking to?"

"Dad." Trey said, peeling a banana.

I looked at Eli. Eli looked at me. And then we all stared at Trey.

Trey shrugged. "You do it all the time." Words squeezed out around his mouth full of banana.

I tried to speak, but the words tripped over my tongue.

Reagan snatched the half of banana heading to Trey's mouth. "What are you talking about?"

"I figure it's like when Grandad's driving. He knows the other drivers can't hear him, but he still tells them how to drive." Trey stuck out his hand to Reagan and waited for his banana.

Neil skimmed the air near my ear. "This entire arrangement is doomed unless you stay focused."

My dead husband was a ghost. My future husband and I would live with a ghost. A ghost who shared our past, present, and now our future. I started giggling. I put my hand over my mouth, but the giggles escaped between my fingers.

Reagan looked at Trey. "Why's she laughing? Did I miss something?"

Trey scrunched his shoulders. "Must be one of those grown-up things."

"Glad you're taking this all so well." Eli leaned over and kissed my forehead. "Top of my head's on fire."

I caressed Eli's head. "Maybe you'll build up a tolerance. Or try a tin-foil hat." I broke out in giggles again.

"You're taking the news much better than I hoped." Neil soared overhead and flipped backward. "You won't even know I'm here. I promise."

A word about the author...

Sandra Tilley grew up in a small town near Birmingham, Alabama, where friends always entered through the back door and where everyone spoke the same language—Southern. After a successful teaching career, she packed up her pearls and headed toward her inspiration: the sugar-white beaches of Orange Beach, Alabama, on the blue-green waters of the Gulf of Mexico.

http://SandraTilley.com

www.ingramcontent.com/pod-product-compliance
Lightning Source LLC
Chambersburg PA
CBHW071516260626
47170CB00002B/397